HORIZON

VOLUME 02 REMNANT

HORIZON CREATED BY
BRANDON THOMAS AND JUAN GEDEON

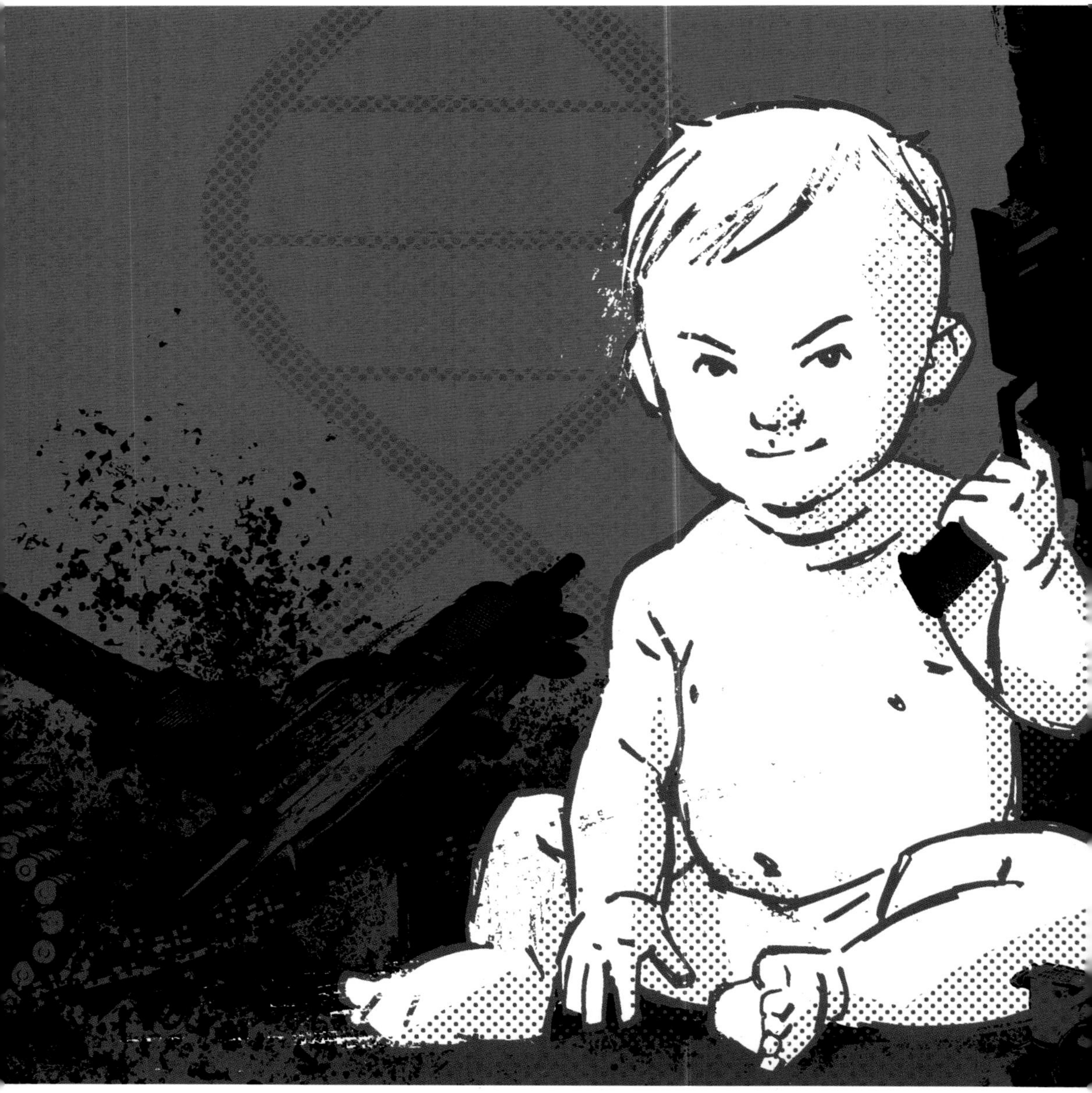

FOR SKYBOUND ENTERTAINMENT

ROBERT KIRKMAN *CHAIRMAN* // DAVID ALPERT *CEO* // SEAN MACKIEWICZ *SVP, EDITOR-IN-CHIEF* // SHAWN KIRKHAM *SVP, BUSINESS DEVELOPMENT* // BRIAN HUNTINGTON *ONLINE EDITORIAL DIRECTOR* // JUNE ALIAN *PUBLICITY DIRECTOR* // ANDRES JUAREZ *ART DIRECTOR* // JON MOISAN *EDITOR* // ARIELLE BASICH *ASSISTANT EDITOR* // PAUL SHIN *BUSINESS DEVELOPMENT ASSISTANT* // JOHNNY O'DELL *ONLINE EDITORIAL ASSISTANT* // SALLY JACKA *ONLINE EDITORIAL ASSISTANT* // DAN PETERSEN *DIRECTOR OF OPERATIONS & EVENTS* // NICK PALMER *OPERATIONS COORDINATOR*

INTERNATIONAL INQUIRIES: AG@SEQUENTIALRIGHTS.COM
LICENSING INQUIRIES: CONTACT@SKYBOUND.COM

WWW.SKYBOUND.COM

® IMAGE COMICS, INC.

ROBERT KIRKMAN *CHIEF OPERATING OFFICER* // ERIK LARSEN *CHIEF FINANCIAL OFFICER* // TODD MCFARLANE *PRESIDENT* // MARC SILVESTRI *CHIEF EXECUTIVE OFFICER* // JIM VALENTINO *VICE-PRESIDENT* // ERIC STEPHENSON *PUBLISHER* // COREY MURPHY *DIRECTOR OF SALES* // JEFF BOISON *DIRECTOR OF PUBLISHING PLANNING & BOOK TRADE SALES* // CHRIS ROSS *DIRECTOR OF DIGITAL SALES* // JEFF STANG *DIRECTOR OF SPECIALTY SALES* // KAT SALAZAR *DIRECTOR OF PR & MARKETING* // BRANWYN BIGGLESTONE *CONTROLLER* // SUE KORPELA *ACCOUNTS MANAGER* // DREW GILL *ART DIRECTOR* // BRETT WARNOCK *PRODUCTION MANAGER* // LEIGH THOMAS *PRINT MANAGER* // TRICIA RAMOS *TRAFFIC MANAGER* // BRIAH SKELLY *PUBLICIST* // ALY HOFFMAN *EVENTS & CONVENTIONS COORDINATOR* // SASHA HEAD *SALES & MARKETING PRODUCTION DESIGNER* // DAVID BROTHERS *BRANDING MANAGER* // MELISSA GIFFORD *CONTENT MANAGER* // DREW FITZGERALD *PUBLICITY ASSISTANT* // VINCENT KUKUA *PRODUCTION ARTIST* // ERIKA SCHNATZ *PRODUCTION ARTIST* // RYAN BREWER *PRODUCTION ARTIST* // SHANNA MATUSZAK *PRODUCTION ARTIST* // CAREY HALL *PRODUCTION ARTIST* // ESTHER KIM *DIRECT MARKET SALES REPRESENTATIVE* // EMILIO BAUTISTA *DIGITAL SALES REPRESENTATIVE* // LEANNA CAUNTER *ACCOUNTING ASSISTANT* // CHLOE RAMOS-PETERSON *LIBRARY MARKET SALES REPRESENTATIVE* // MARLA EIZIK *ADMINISTRATIVE ASSISTANT*

WWW.IMAGECOMICS.COM

BRANDON THOMAS
WRITER

JUAN GEDEON
ARTIST

MIKE SPICER
COLORIST

RUS WOOTON
LETTERER

SEAN MACKIEWICZ
EDITOR

ARIELLE BASICH
ASSISTANT EDITOR

JASON HOWARD
COVER

HORIZON VOLUME 2: REMNANT. FIRST PRINTING. ISBN: 978-1-5343-0227-3. PUBLISHED BY IMAGE COMICS, INC. OFFICE OF PUBLICATION: 2701 NW VAUGHN ST., STE. 780, PORTLAND, OR 97210. COPYRIGHT © 2017 SKYBOUND, LLC. ALL RIGHTS RESERVED. ORIGINALLY PUBLISHED IN SINGLE MAGAZINE FORM AS HORIZON #7-12. HORIZON™ (INCLUDING ALL PROMINENT CHARACTERS FEATURED HEREIN), ITS LOGO AND ALL CHARACTER LIKENESSES ARE TRADEMARKS OF SKYBOUND, LLC, UNLESS OTHERWISE NOTED. IMAGE COMICS® AND ITS LOGOS ARE REGISTERED TRADEMARKS AND COPYRIGHTS OF IMAGE COMICS, INC. ALL RIGHTS RESERVED. NO PART OF THIS PUBLICATION MAY BE REPRODUCED OR TRANSMITTED IN ANY FORM OR BY ANY MEANS (EXCEPT FOR SHORT EXCERPTS FOR REVIEW PURPOSES) WITHOUT THE EXPRESS WRITTEN PERMISSION OF IMAGE COMICS, INC. ALL NAMES, CHARACTERS, EVENTS AND LOCALES IN THIS PUBLICATION ARE ENTIRELY FICTIONAL. ANY RESEMBLANCE TO ACTUAL PERSONS (LIVING OR DEAD), EVENTS OR PLACES, WITHOUT SATIRIC INTENT, IS COINCIDENTAL. PRINTED IN THE U.S.A. FOR INFORMATION REGARDING THE CPSIA ON THIS PRINTED MATERIAL CALL: 203-595-3636 AND PROVIDE REFERENCE # RICH - 748124.

LANGUAGE KEY

NATIVE
VALIAN

EARTH
ENGLISH

MALEN
CODE

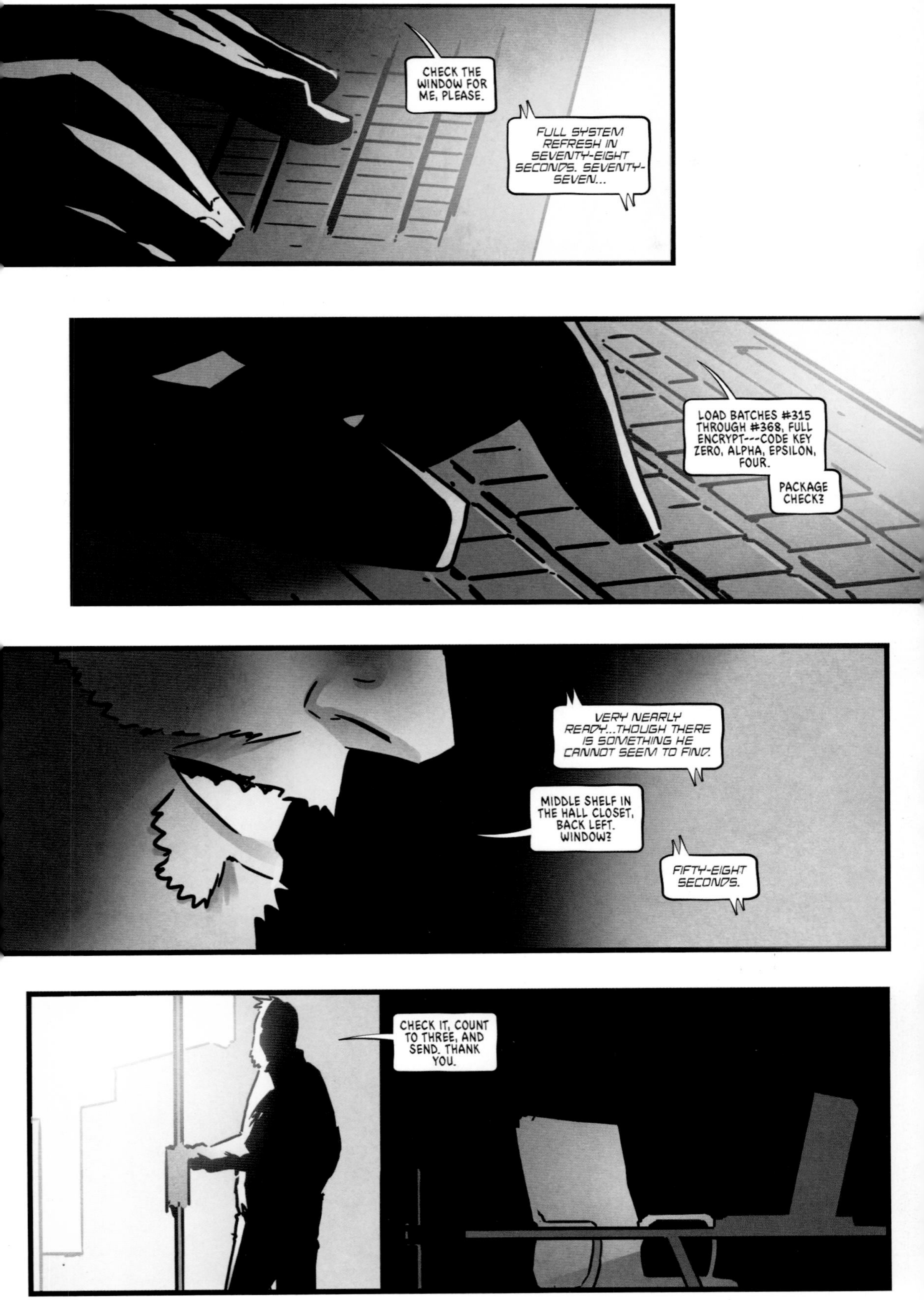
CHECK THE WINDOW FOR ME, PLEASE.
FULL SYSTEM REFRESH IN SEVENTY-EIGHT SECONDS. SEVENTY-SEVEN...
LOAD BATCHES #315 THROUGH #368, FULL ENCRYPT---CODE KEY ZERO, ALPHA, EPSILON, FOUR.
PACKAGE CHECK?
VERY NEARLY READY...THOUGH THERE IS SOMETHING HE CANNOT SEEM TO FIND.
MIDDLE SHELF IN THE HALL CLOSET, BACK LEFT. WINDOW?
FIFTY-EIGHT SECONDS.
CHECK IT, COUNT TO THREE, AND SEND. THANK YOU.

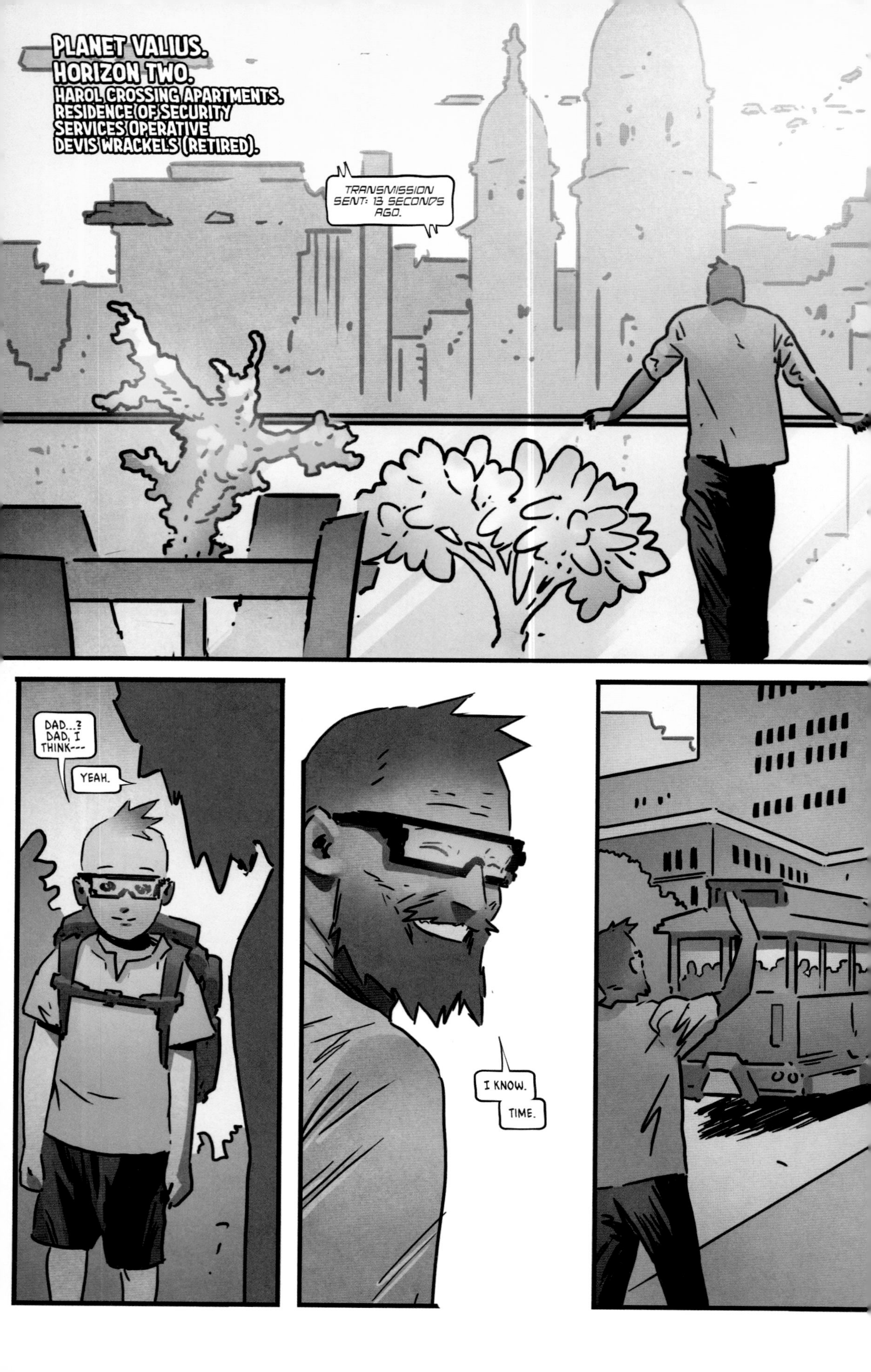

PLANET VALIUS.
HORIZON TWO.
HAROL CROSSING APARTMENTS. RESIDENCE OF SECURITY SERVICES OPERATIVE DEVIS WRACKELS (RETIRED).
TRANSMISSION SENT: 13 SECONDS AGO.
DAD...? DAD, I THINK---
YEAH.
I KNOW.
TIME.

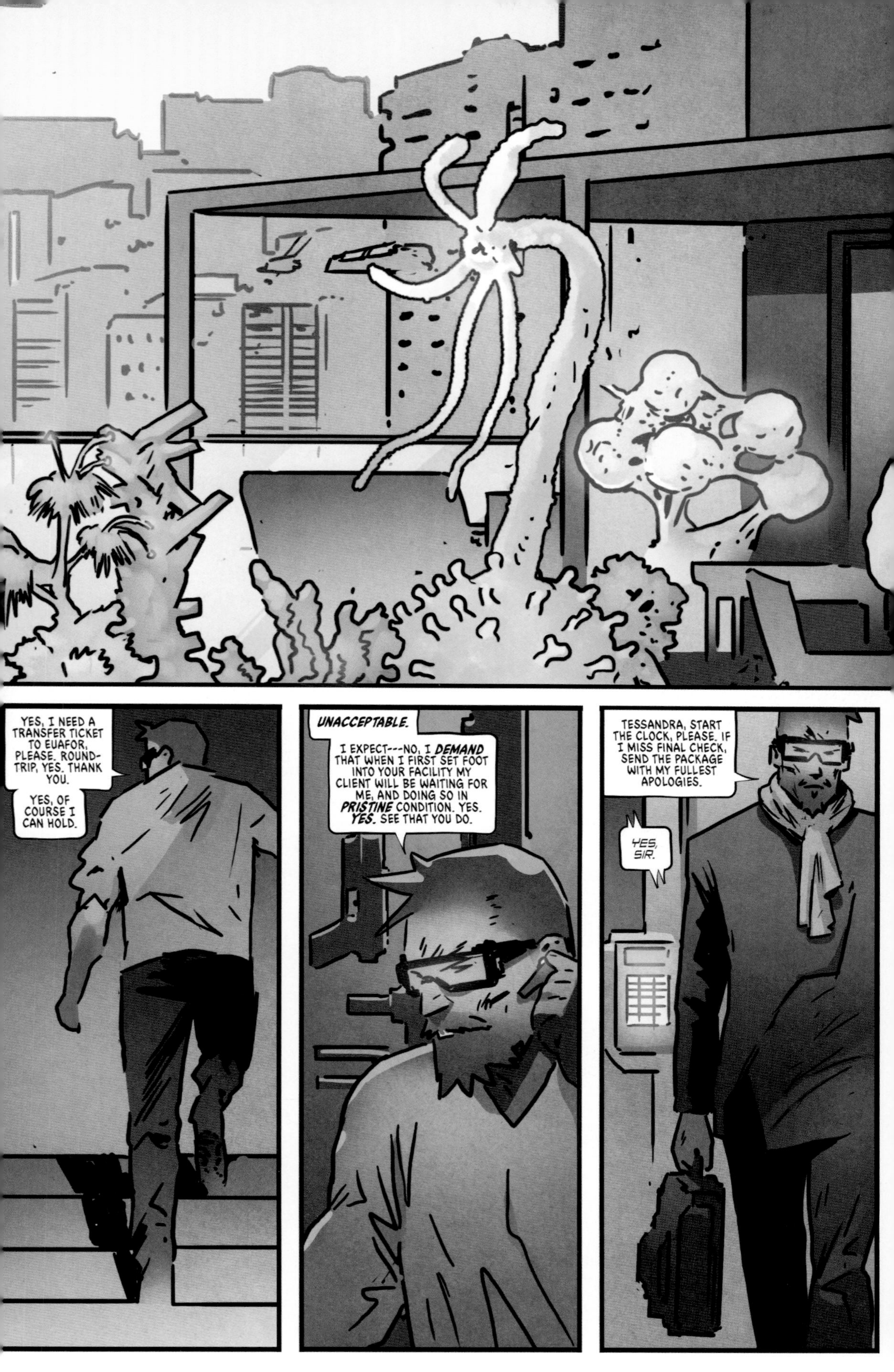
YES, I NEED A TRANSFER TICKET TO EUAFOR, PLEASE. ROUND-TRIP, YES. THANK YOU.
YES, OF COURSE I CAN HOLD.
UNACCEPTABLE.
I EXPECT---NO, I DEMAND THAT WHEN I FIRST SET FOOT INTO YOUR FACILITY MY CLIENT WILL BE WAITING FOR ME, AND DOING SO IN PRISTINE CONDITION. YES. YES. SEE THAT YOU DO.
TESSANDRA, START THE CLOCK, PLEASE. IF I MISS FINAL CHECK, SEND THE PACKAGE WITH MY FULLEST APOLOGIES.
YES, SIR.

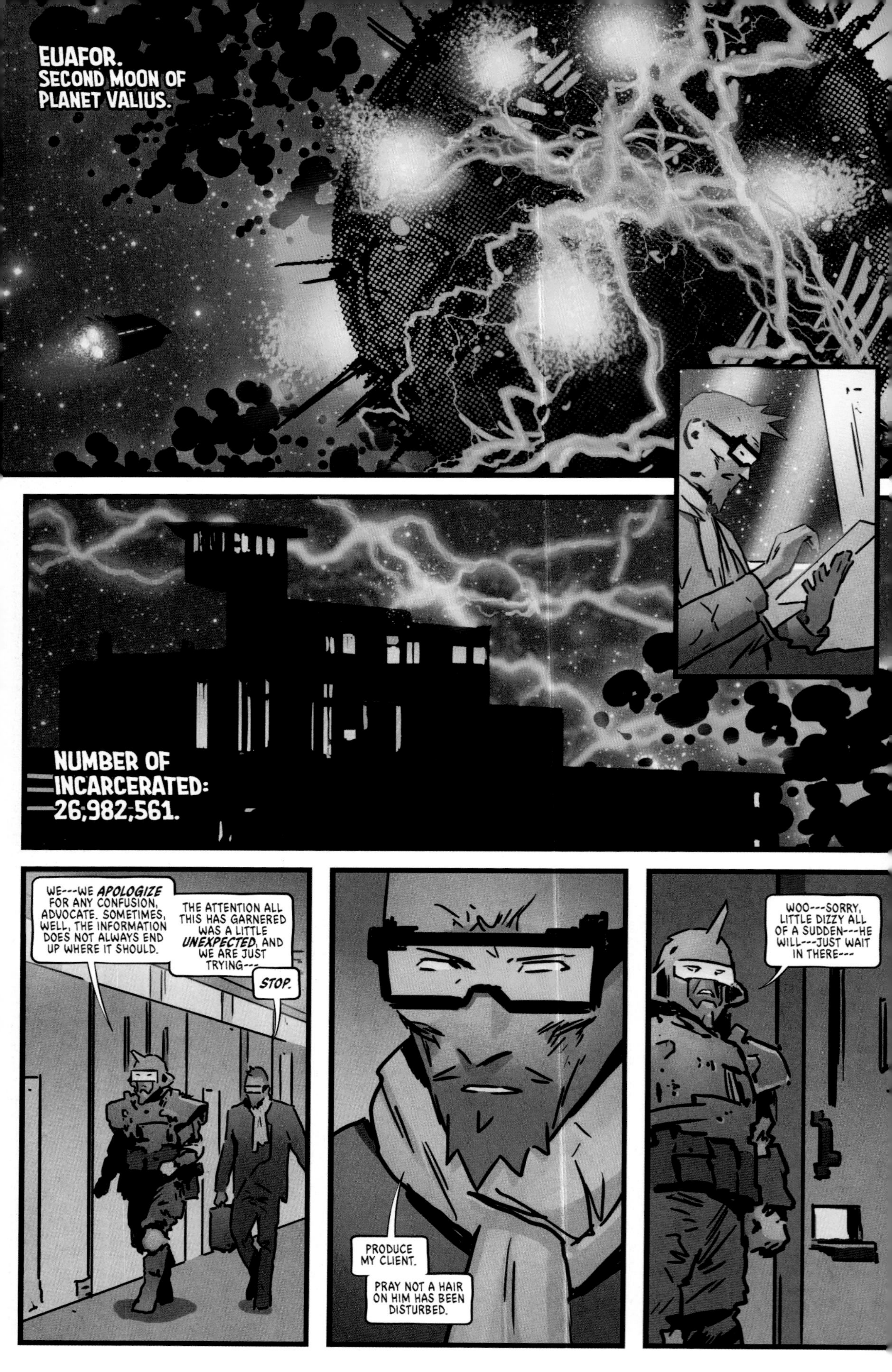
EUAFOR. SECOND MOON OF PLANET VALIUS.
NUMBER OF INCARCERATED: 26,982,561.
WE---WE APOLOGIZE FOR ANY CONFUSION, ADVOCATE. SOMETIMES, WELL, THE INFORMATION DOES NOT ALWAYS END UP WHERE IT SHOULD.
THE ATTENTION ALL THIS HAS GARNERED WAS A LITTLE UNEXPECTED, AND WE ARE JUST TRYING---
STOP.
PRODUCE MY CLIENT.
PRAY NOT A HAIR ON HIM HAS BEEN DISTURBED.
WOO---SORRY, LITTLE DIZZY ALL OF A SUDDEN---HE WILL---JUST WAIT IN THERE---

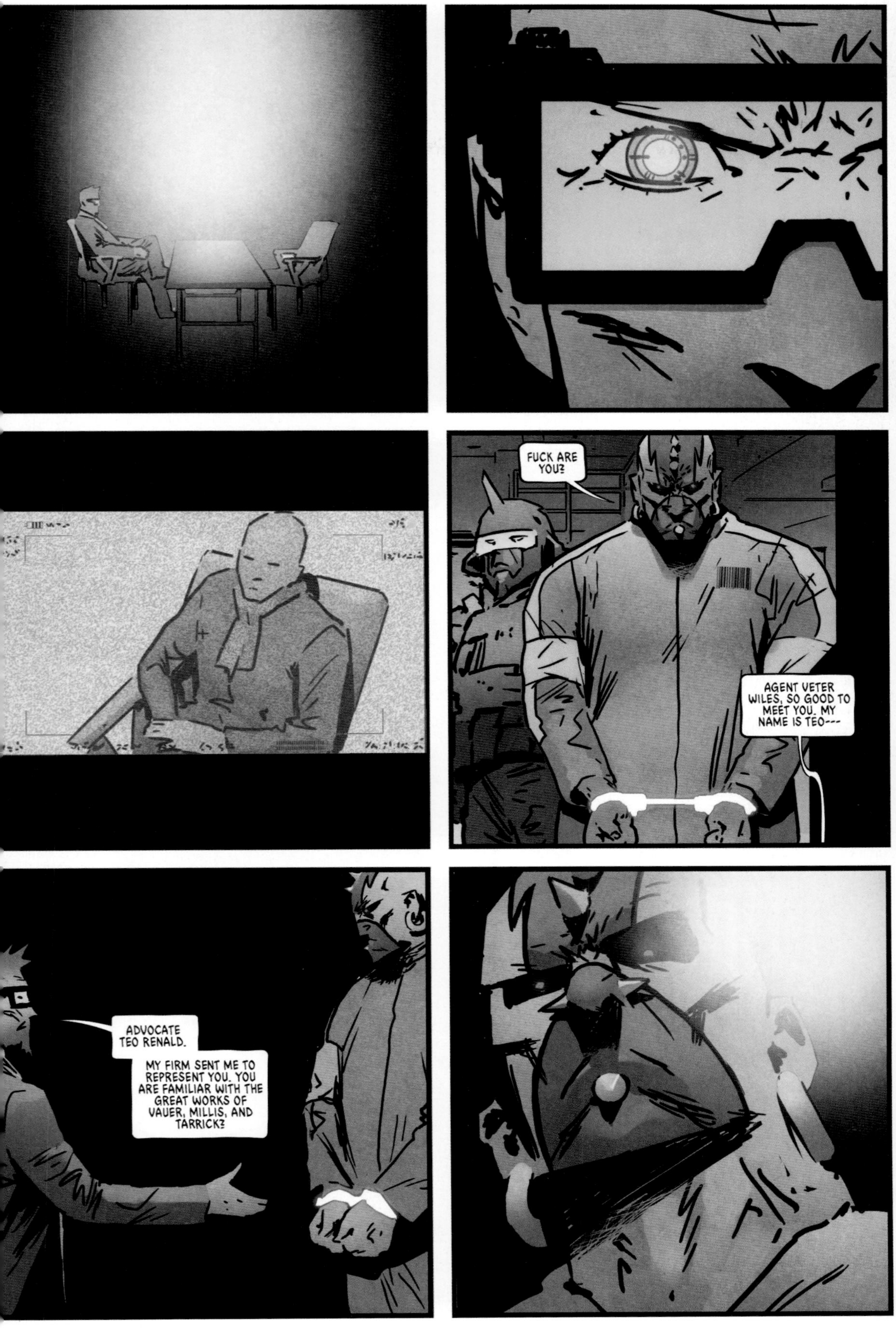
FUCK ARE YOU?
AGENT VETER WILES, SO GOOD TO MEET YOU. MY NAME IS TEO---
ADVOCATE TEO RENALD.
MY FIRM SENT ME TO REPRESENT YOU. YOU ARE FAMILIAR WITH THE GREAT WORKS OF VAUER, MILLIS, AND TARRICK?

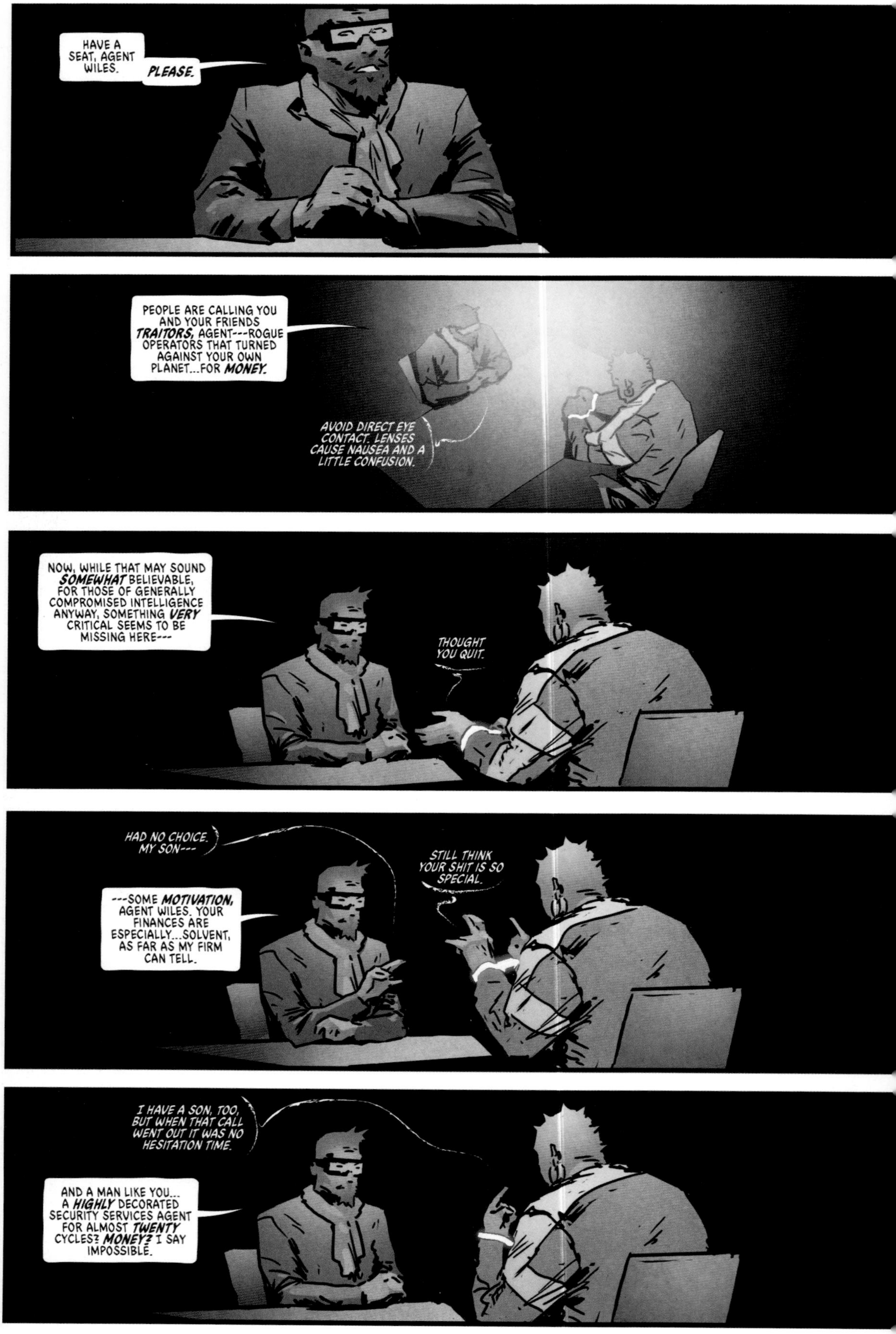
HAVE A SEAT, AGENT WILES.
PLEASE.
PEOPLE ARE CALLING YOU AND YOUR FRIENDS TRAITORS, AGENT---ROGUE OPERATORS THAT TURNED AGAINST YOUR OWN PLANET...FOR MONEY.
AVOID DIRECT EYE CONTACT. LENSES CAUSE NAUSEA AND A LITTLE CONFUSION.
NOW, WHILE THAT MAY SOUND SOMEWHAT BELIEVABLE, FOR THOSE OF GENERALLY COMPROMISED INTELLIGENCE ANYWAY, SOMETHING VERY CRITICAL SEEMS TO BE MISSING HERE---
THOUGHT YOU QUIT.
HAD NO CHOICE. MY SON---
---SOME MOTIVATION, AGENT WILES. YOUR FINANCES ARE ESPECIALLY...SOLVENT, AS FAR AS MY FIRM CAN TELL.
STILL THINK YOUR SHIT IS SO SPECIAL.
I HAVE A SON, TOO, BUT WHEN THAT CALL WENT OUT IT WAS NO HESITATION TIME.
AND A MAN LIKE YOU... A HIGHLY DECORATED SECURITY SERVICES AGENT FOR ALMOST TWENTY CYCLES? MONEY? I SAY IMPOSSIBLE.

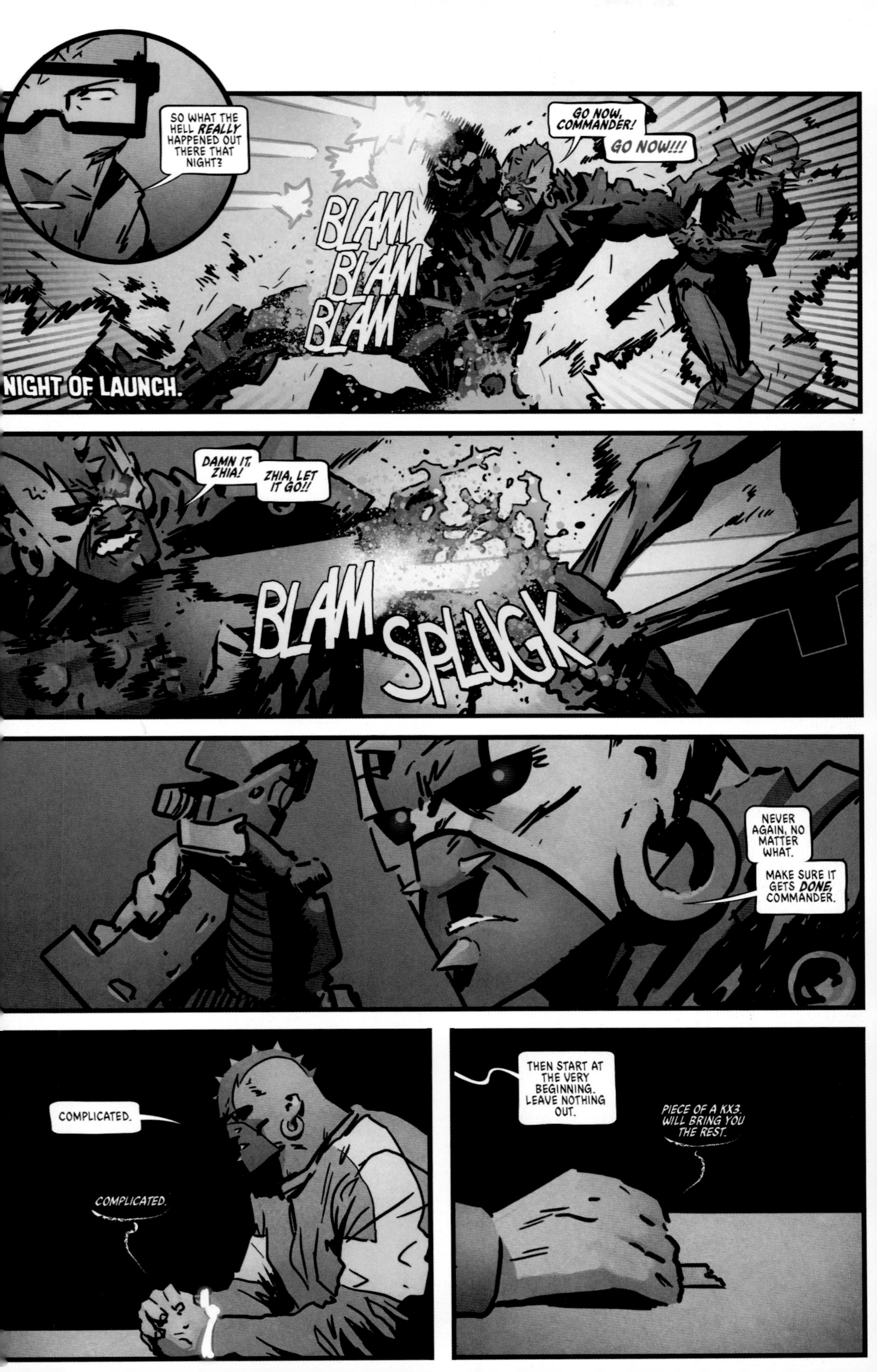

SO WHAT THE HELL *REALLY* HAPPENED OUT THERE THAT NIGHT?
NIGHT OF LAUNCH.
GO NOW, COMMANDER!
GO NOW!!!
BLAM BLAM BLAM
DAMN IT, ZHIA!
ZHIA, LET IT GO!!
BLAM
SPLUGK
NEVER AGAIN, NO MATTER WHAT.
MAKE SURE IT GETS *DONE,* COMMANDER.
COMPLICATED.
COMPLICATED.
THEN START AT THE VERY BEGINNING. LEAVE NOTHING OUT.
PIECE OF A KX3. WILL BRING YOU THE REST.

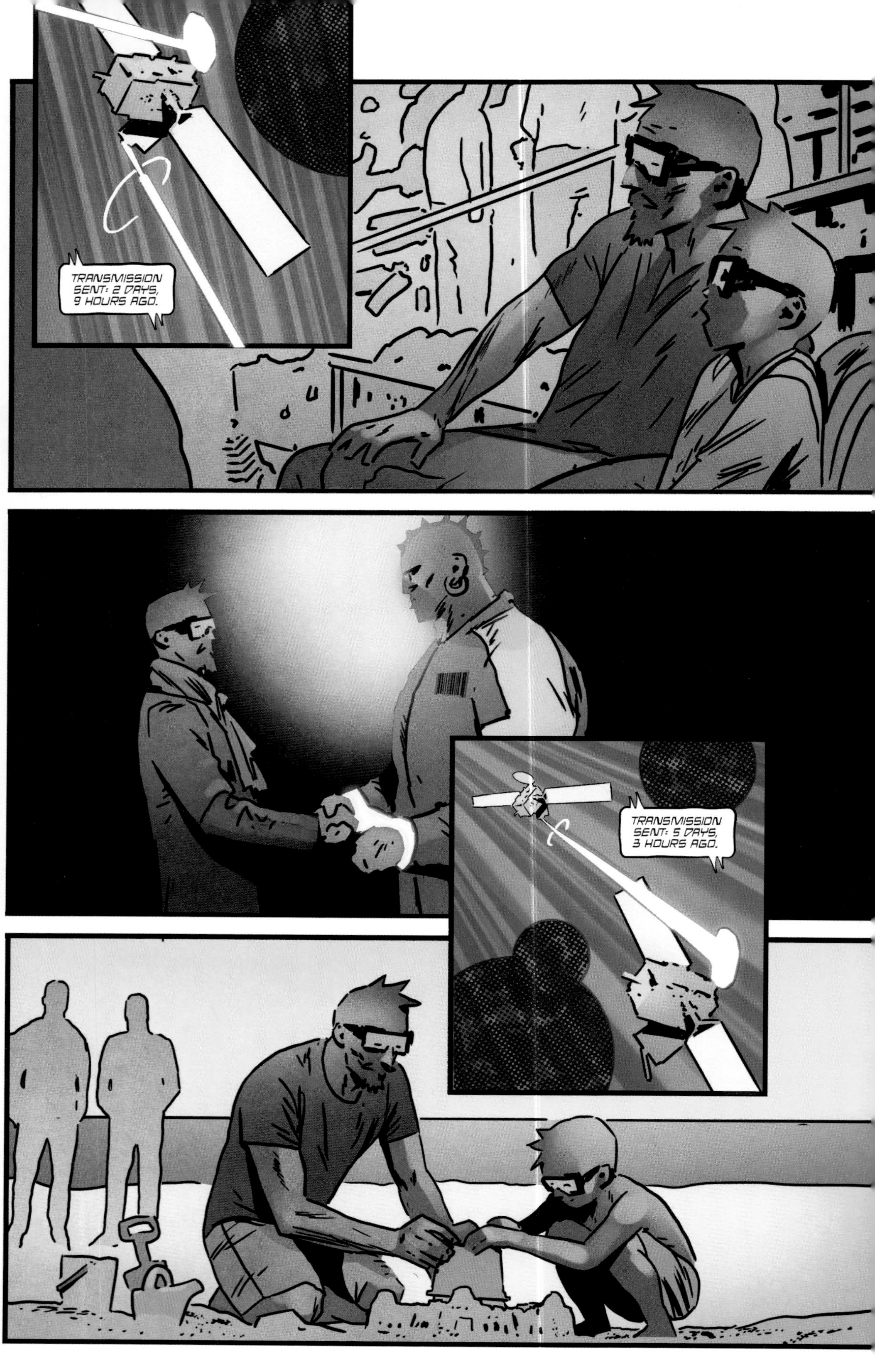
TRANSMISSION SENT: 2 DAYS, 9 HOURS AGO.
TRANSMISSION SENT: 5 DAYS, 3 HOURS AGO.

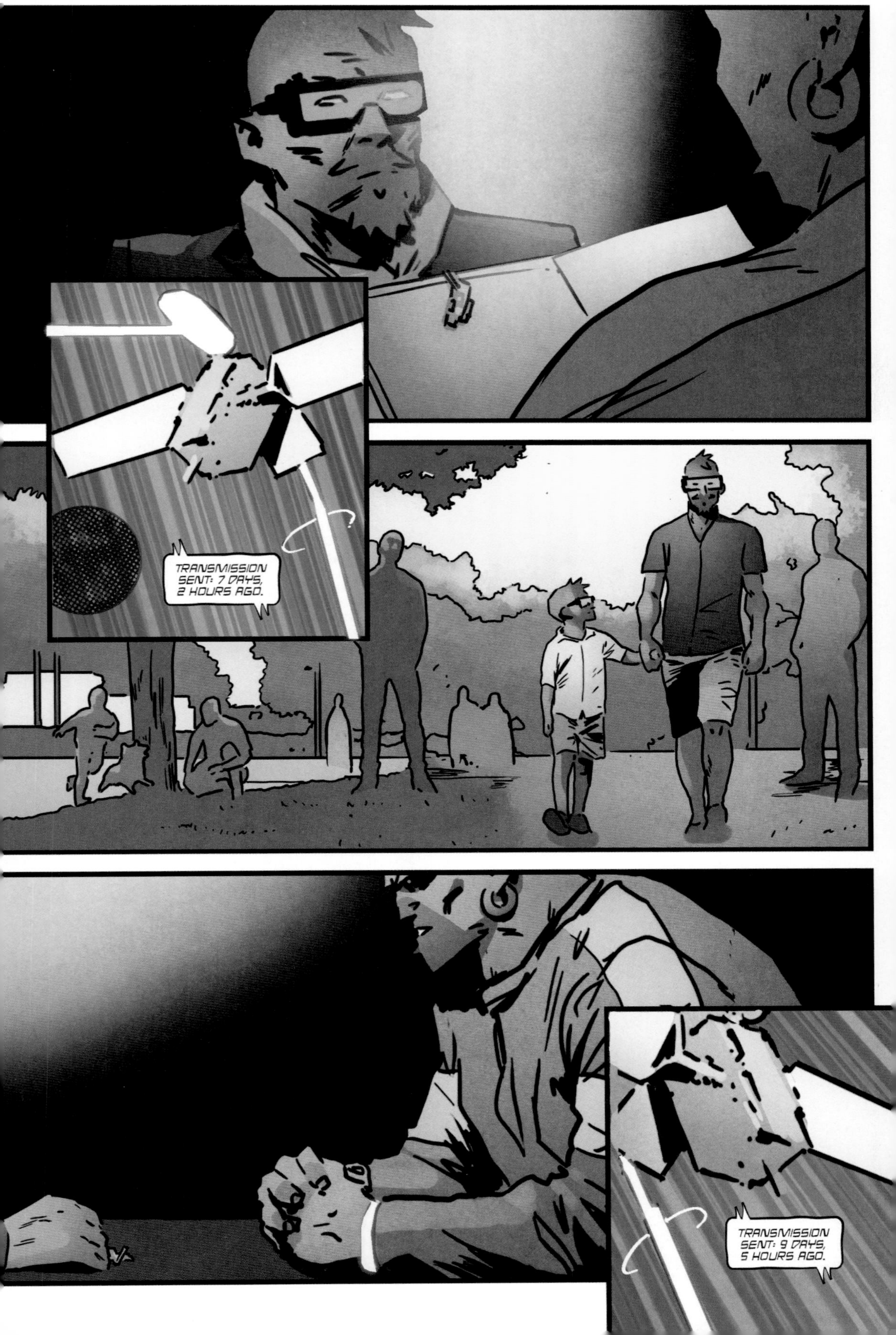
TRANSMISSION SENT: 7 DAYS, 2 HOURS AGO.
TRANSMISSION SENT: 9 DAYS, 5 HOURS AGO.

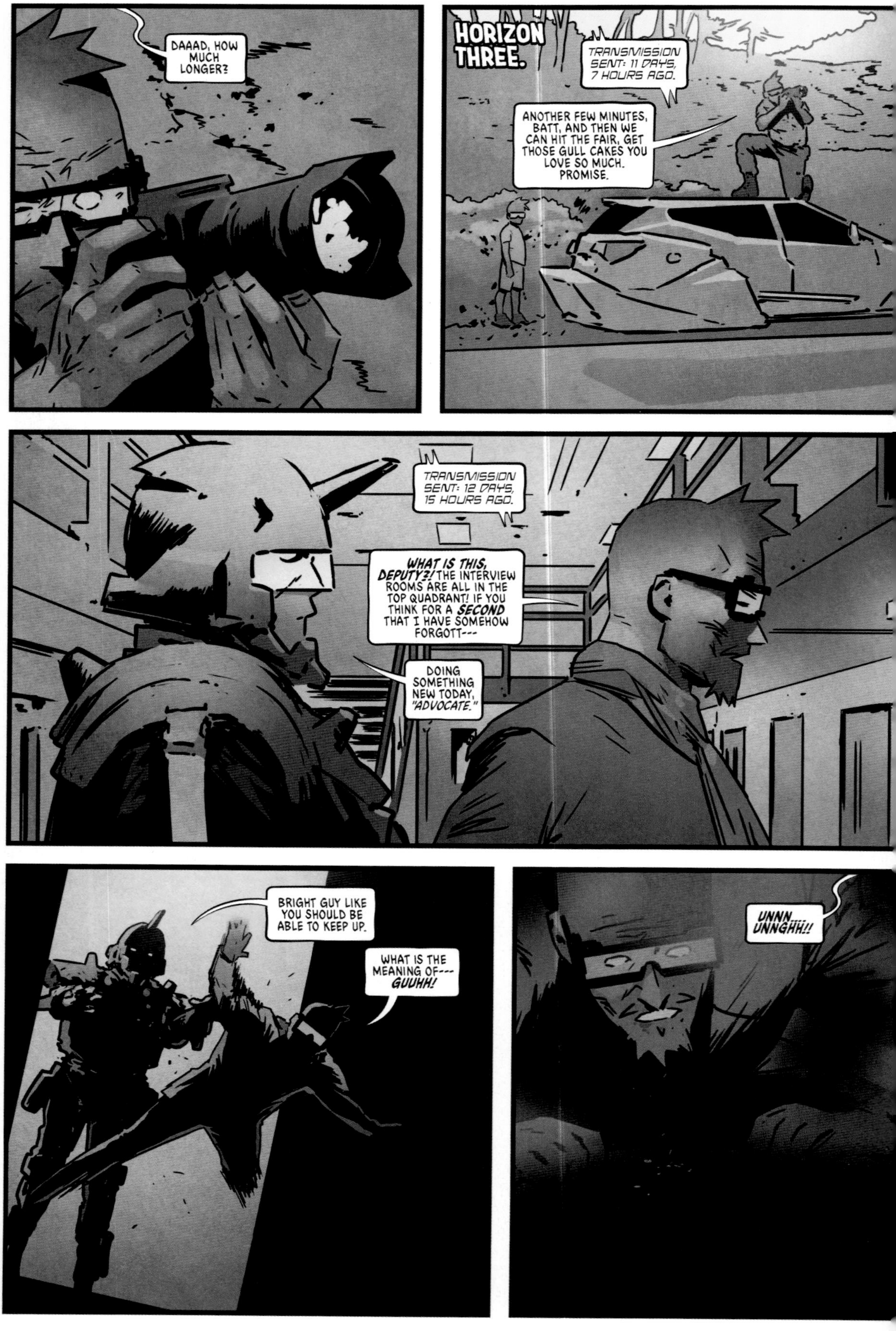
DAAAD, HOW MUCH LONGER?
HORIZON THREE.
TRANSMISSION SENT: 11 DAYS, 7 HOURS AGO.
ANOTHER FEW MINUTES, BATT, AND THEN WE CAN HIT THE FAIR, GET THOSE GULL CAKES YOU LOVE SO MUCH. PROMISE.
TRANSMISSION SENT: 12 DAYS, 15 HOURS AGO.
WHAT IS THIS, DEPUTY?! THE INTERVIEW ROOMS ARE ALL IN THE TOP QUADRANT! IF YOU THINK FOR A SECOND THAT I HAVE SOMEHOW FORGOTT---
DOING SOMETHING NEW TODAY, "ADVOCATE."
BRIGHT GUY LIKE YOU SHOULD BE ABLE TO KEEP UP.
WHAT IS THE MEANING OF--- GUUHH!
UNNN.... UNNGHH!!

RAARRRR!

ALWAYS THE THING ABOUT YOU, WRACKELS---YOU AND EVERY OTHER SORRY EXCUSE FOR AN OPERATOR THAT MALEN EVER RAN WITH---

SOMEBODY TOLD YOU ONCE THAT YOU WERE *SO* MUCH FUCKING SMARTER THAN *EVERYBODY* ELSE, AND YOU *BELIEVED* THEM.

THAT WOMAN WAS A *TRAITOR*, WILES IS A TRAITOR, AND THAT COULD HAVE BEEN THAT. BUT *NOW---* THIS RENALD NONSENSE MAKES ME WONDER ABOUT YOUR LITTLE "RESIGNATION."

BRAGO...

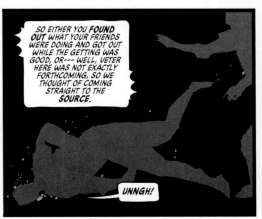

SO EITHER YOU *FOUND OUT* WHAT YOUR FRIENDS WERE DOING AND GOT OUT WHILE THE GETTING WAS GOOD, OR--- WELL, VETER HERE WAS NOT EXACTLY FORTHCOMING, SO WE THOUGHT OF COMING STRAIGHT TO THE *SOURCE.*

UNNGH!

YOU TELL US THE *TRUTH* ABOUT COMMANDER MALEN. YOU TELL US THAT RIGHT NOW, AND YOU BOTH CAN LIVE.

YOU DO YOUR JOB, DEVIS. *DO YOUR JOB!*

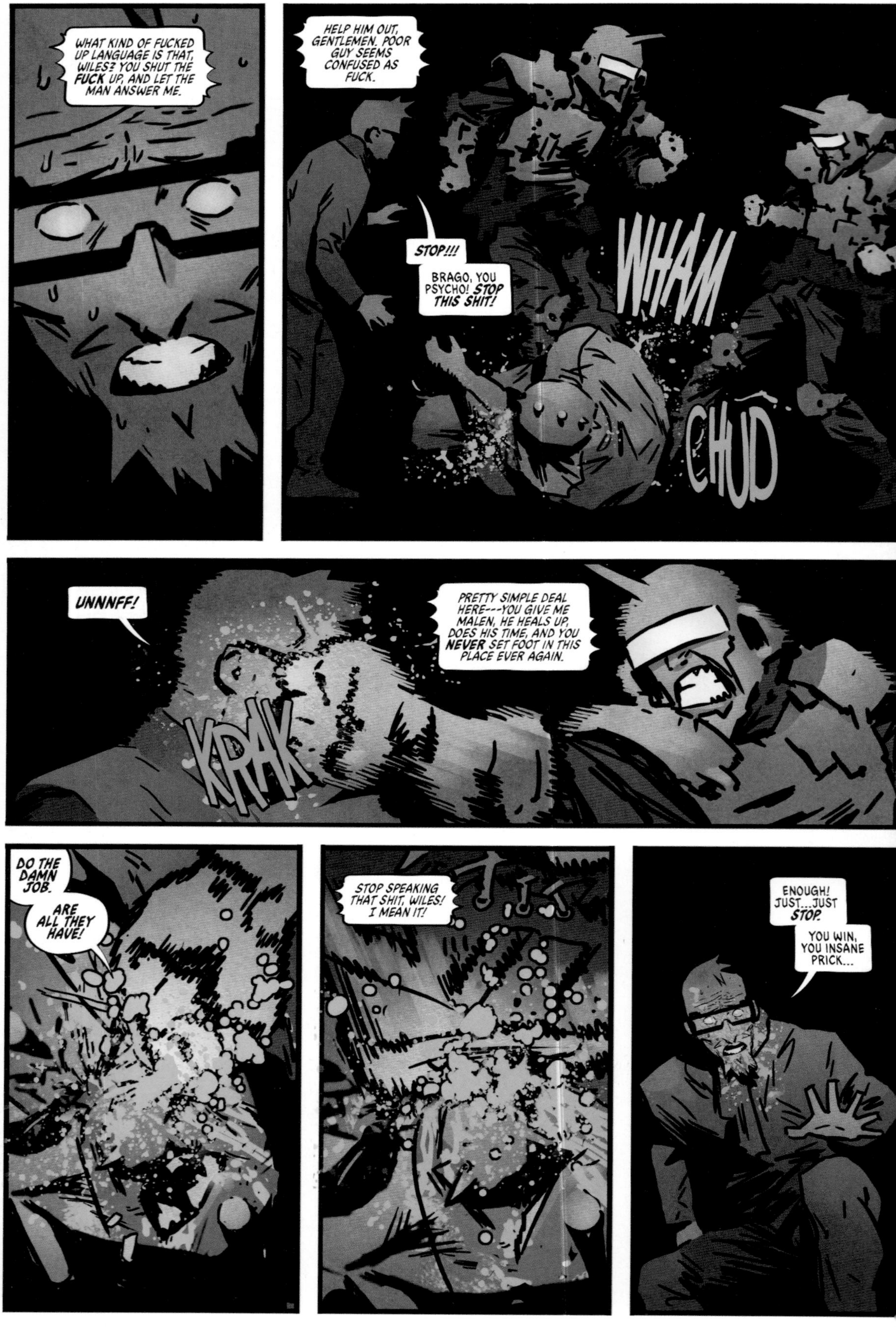
WHAT KIND OF FUCKED UP LANGUAGE IS THAT, WILES? YOU SHUT THE **FUCK** UP, AND LET THE MAN ANSWER ME.
HELP HIM OUT, GENTLEMEN. POOR GUY SEEMS CONFUSED AS FUCK.
STOP!!!
BRAGO, YOU PSYCHO! **STOP THIS SHIT!**
WHAM
CHUD
UNNNFF!
PRETTY SIMPLE DEAL HERE---YOU GIVE ME MALEN, HE HEALS UP, DOES HIS TIME, AND YOU **NEVER** SET FOOT IN THIS PLACE EVER AGAIN.
KRAK
DO THE DAMN JOB.
ARE ALL THEY HAVE!
STOP SPEAKING THAT SHIT, WILES! I MEAN IT!
ENOUGH! JUST...JUST **STOP.**
YOU WIN, YOU INSANE PRICK...

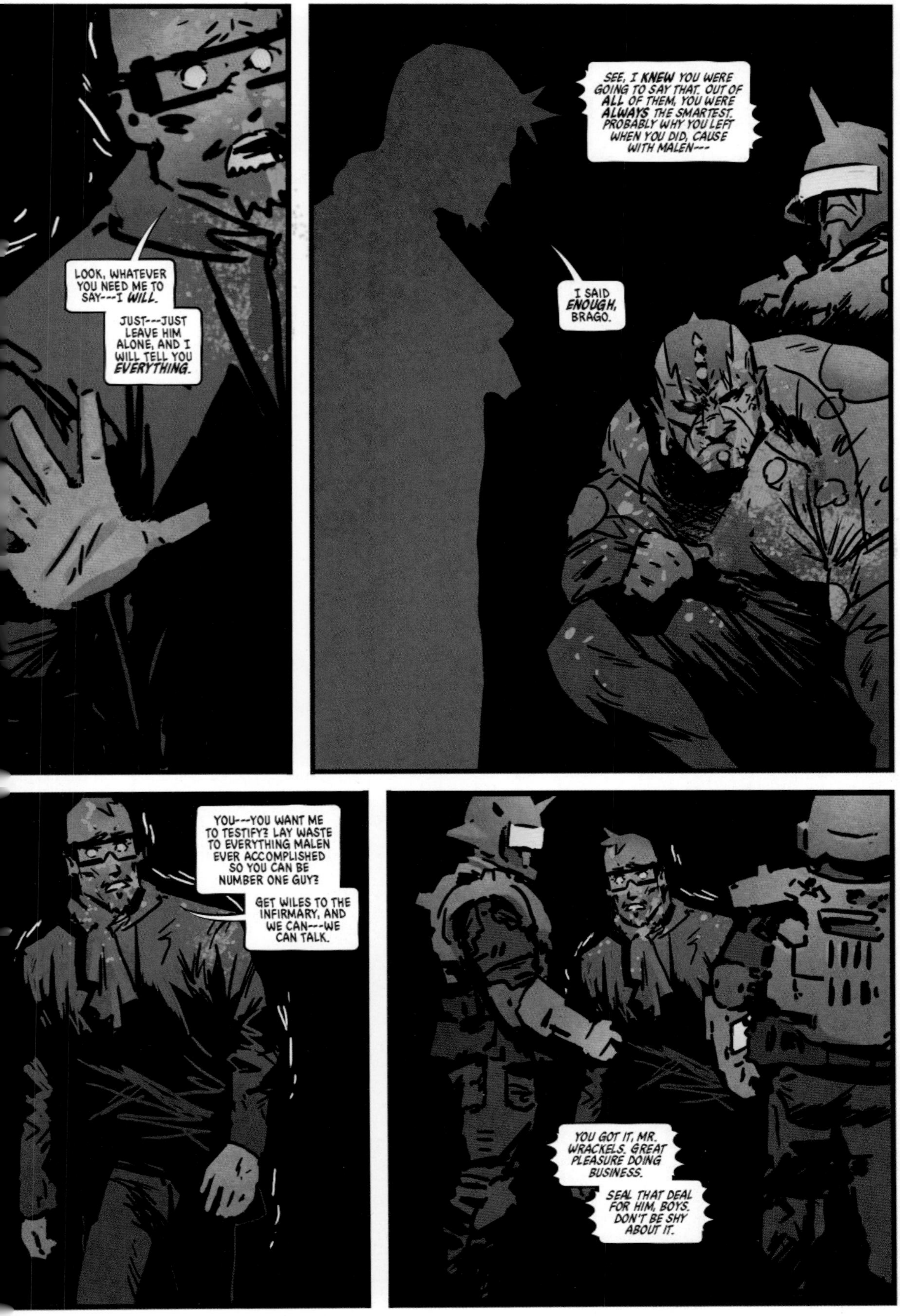
LOOK, WHATEVER YOU NEED ME TO SAY---I *WILL*.
JUST---JUST LEAVE HIM ALONE, AND I WILL TELL YOU *EVERYTHING*.
SEE, I **KNEW** YOU WERE GOING TO SAY THAT. OUT OF **ALL** OF THEM, YOU WERE **ALWAYS** THE SMARTEST. PROBABLY WHY YOU LEFT WHEN YOU DID, CAUSE WITH MALEN---
I SAID *ENOUGH*, BRAGO.
YOU---YOU WANT ME TO TESTIFY? LAY WASTE TO EVERYTHING MALEN EVER ACCOMPLISHED SO YOU CAN BE NUMBER ONE GUY?
GET WILES TO THE INFIRMARY, AND WE CAN---WE CAN TALK.
YOU GOT IT, MR. WRACKELS. GREAT PLEASURE DOING BUSINESS.
SEAL THAT DEAL FOR HIM, BOYS. DON'T BE SHY ABOUT IT.

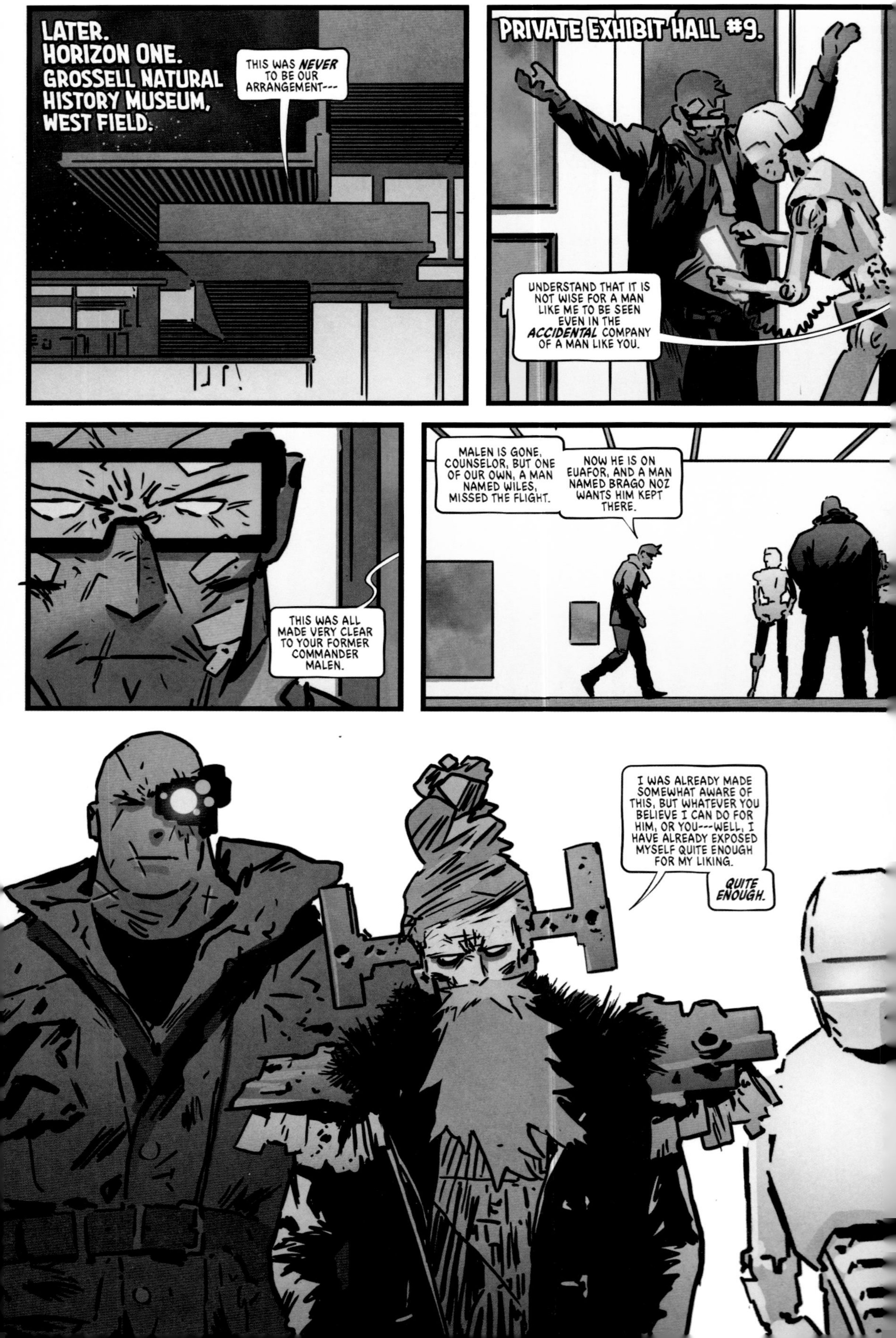
LATER. HORIZON ONE. GROSSELL NATURAL HISTORY MUSEUM, WEST FIELD.
THIS WAS NEVER TO BE OUR ARRANGEMENT---
PRIVATE EXHIBIT HALL #9.
UNDERSTAND THAT IT IS NOT WISE FOR A MAN LIKE ME TO BE SEEN EVEN IN THE ACCIDENTAL COMPANY OF A MAN LIKE YOU.
THIS WAS ALL MADE VERY CLEAR TO YOUR FORMER COMMANDER MALEN.
MALEN IS GONE, COUNSELOR, BUT ONE OF OUR OWN, A MAN NAMED WILES, MISSED THE FLIGHT.
NOW HE IS ON EUAFOR, AND A MAN NAMED BRAGO NOZ WANTS HIM KEPT THERE.
I WAS ALREADY MADE SOMEWHAT AWARE OF THIS, BUT WHATEVER YOU BELIEVE I CAN DO FOR HIM, OR YOU---WELL, I HAVE ALREADY EXPOSED MYSELF QUITE ENOUGH FOR MY LIKING.
QUITE ENOUGH.

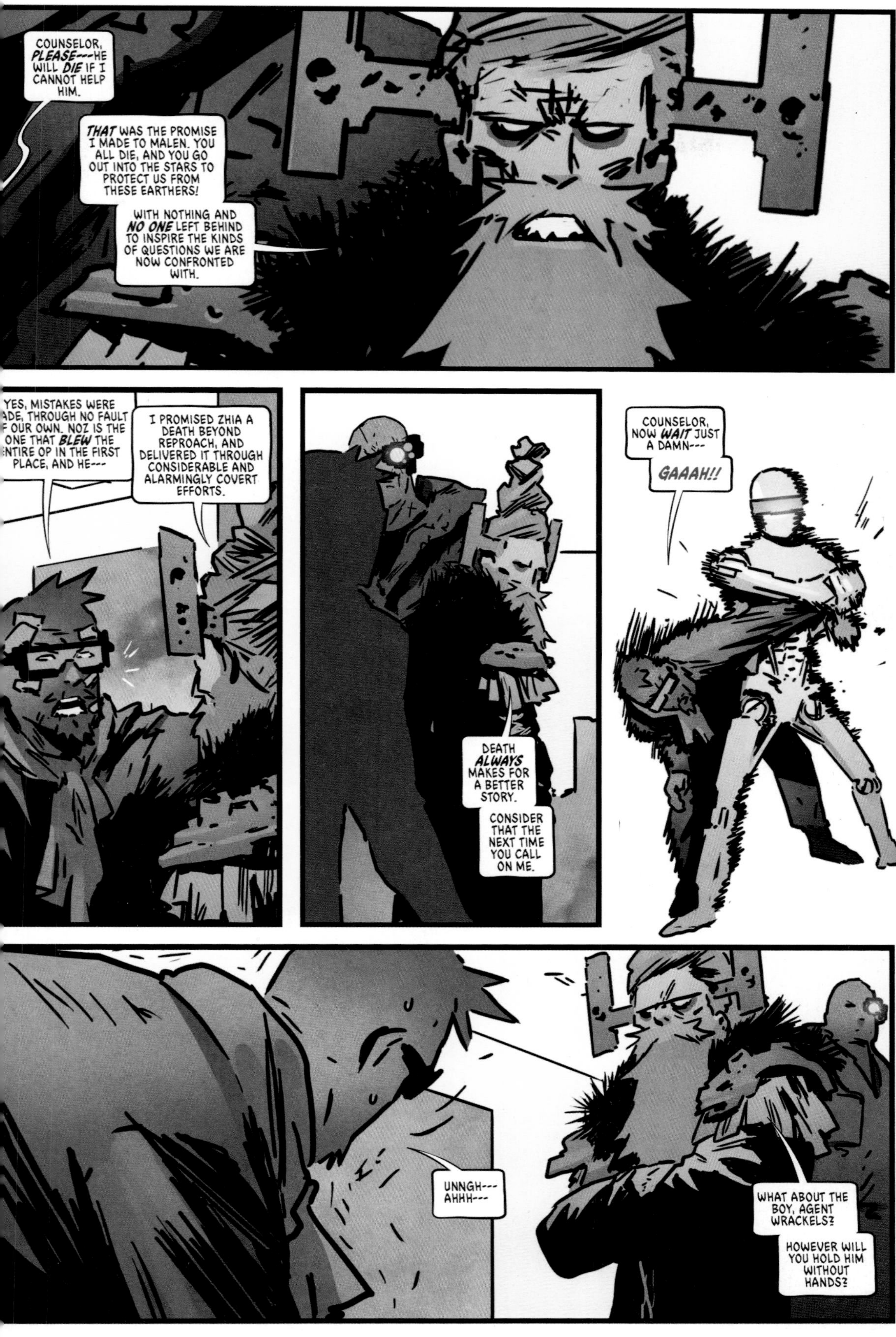
COUNSELOR, PLEASE---HE WILL DIE IF I CANNOT HELP HIM.
THAT WAS THE PROMISE I MADE TO MALEN. YOU ALL DIE, AND YOU GO OUT INTO THE STARS TO PROTECT US FROM THESE EARTHERS!
WITH NOTHING AND NO ONE LEFT BEHIND TO INSPIRE THE KINDS OF QUESTIONS WE ARE NOW CONFRONTED WITH.
YES, MISTAKES WERE ADE, THROUGH NO FAULT F OUR OWN. NOZ IS THE ONE THAT BLEW THE NTIRE OP IN THE FIRST PLACE, AND HE---
I PROMISED ZHIA A DEATH BEYOND REPROACH, AND DELIVERED IT THROUGH CONSIDERABLE AND ALARMINGLY COVERT EFFORTS.
DEATH ALWAYS MAKES FOR A BETTER STORY.
CONSIDER THAT THE NEXT TIME YOU CALL ON ME.
COUNSELOR, NOW WAIT JUST A DAMN---
GAAAH!!
UNNGH--- AHHH---
WHAT ABOUT THE BOY, AGENT WRACKELS?
HOWEVER WILL YOU HOLD HIM WITHOUT HANDS?

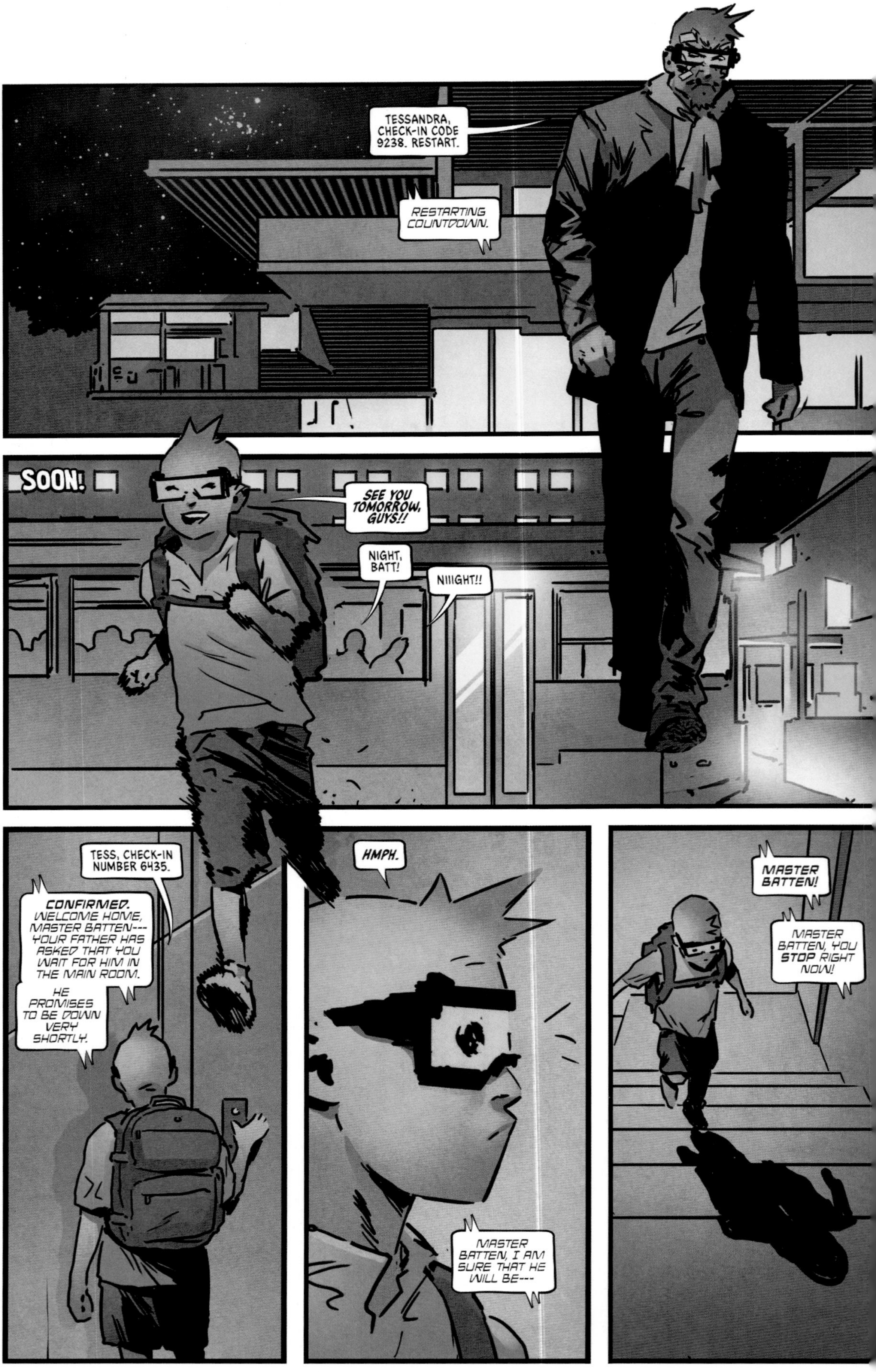
TESSANDRA, CHECK-IN CODE 9238. RESTART.
RESTARTING COUNTDOWN.
SOON!
SEE YOU TOMORROW, GUYS!!
NIGHT, BATT!
NIIIGHT!!
TESS, CHECK-IN NUMBER 6435.
CONFIRMED. WELCOME HOME, MASTER BATTEN--- YOUR FATHER HAS ASKED THAT YOU WAIT FOR HIM IN THE MAIN ROOM.
HE PROMISES TO BE DOWN VERY SHORTLY.
HMPH.
MASTER BATTEN, I AM SURE THAT HE WILL BE---
MASTER BATTEN!
MASTER BATTEN, YOU STOP RIGHT NOW!

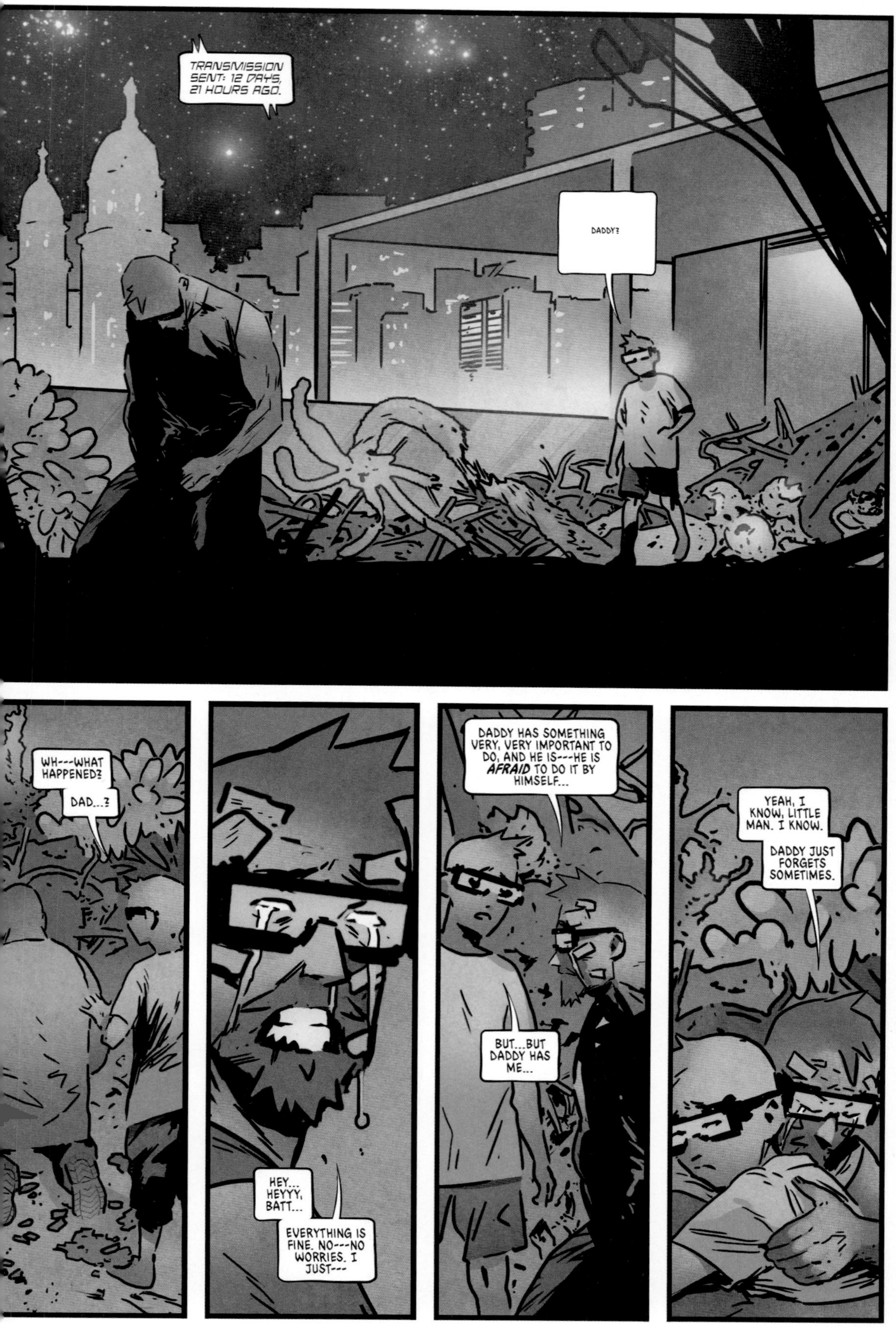
TRANSMISSION SENT: 12 DAYS, 21 HOURS AGO.
DADDY?
WH---WHAT HAPPENED?
DAD...?
HEY... HEYYY, BATT...
EVERYTHING IS FINE. NO---NO WORRIES. I JUST---
DADDY HAS SOMETHING VERY, VERY IMPORTANT TO DO, AND HE IS---HE IS *AFRAID* TO DO IT BY HIMSELF...
BUT...BUT DADDY HAS ME...
YEAH, I KNOW, LITTLE MAN. I KNOW.
DADDY JUST FORGETS SOMETIMES.

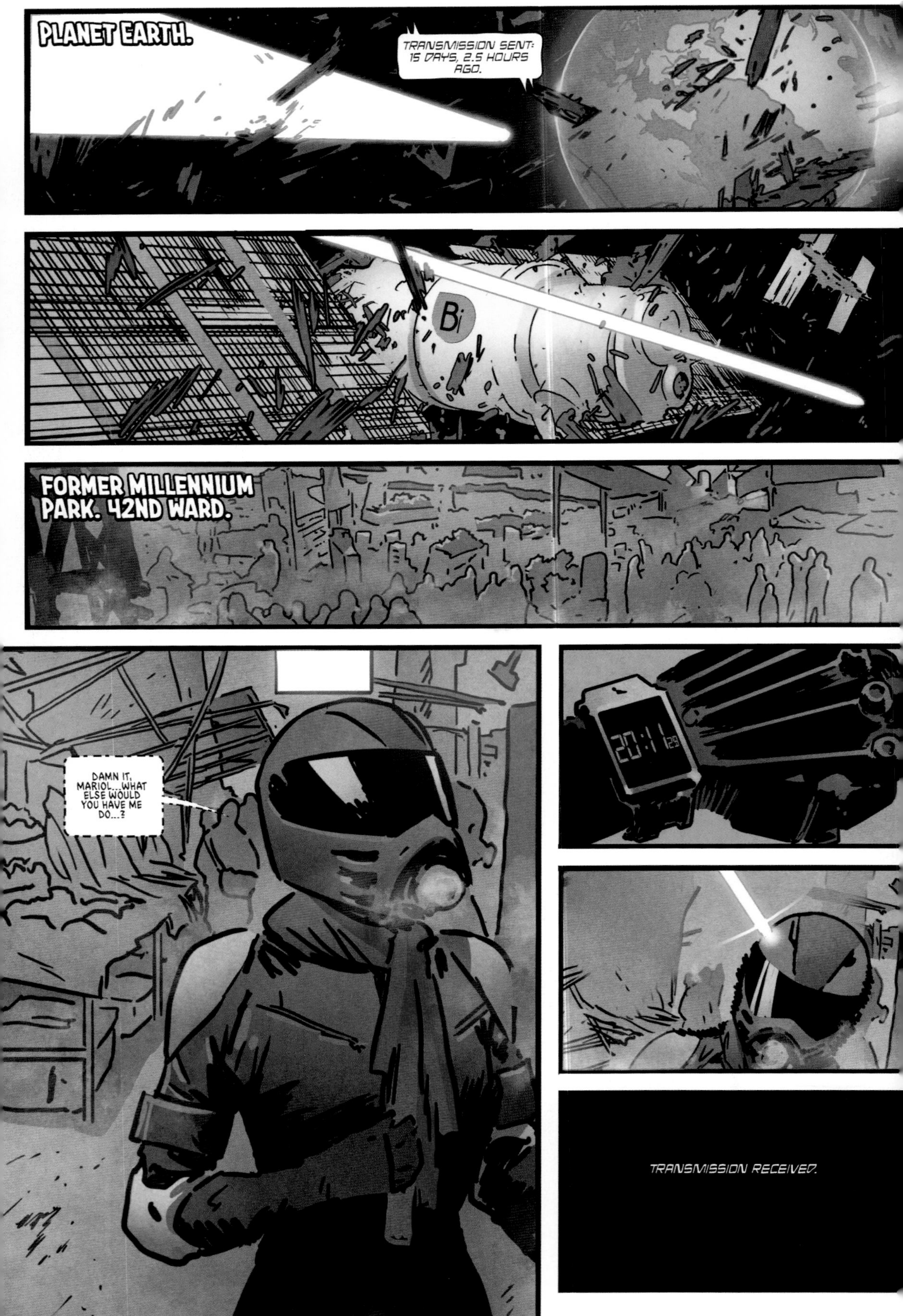
PLANET EARTH.
TRANSMISSION SENT: 15 DAYS, 2.5 HOURS AGO.
Bi
FORMER MILLENNIUM PARK. 42ND WARD.
DAMN IT, MARIOL...WHAT ELSE WOULD YOU HAVE ME DO...?
TRANSMISSION RECEIVED.

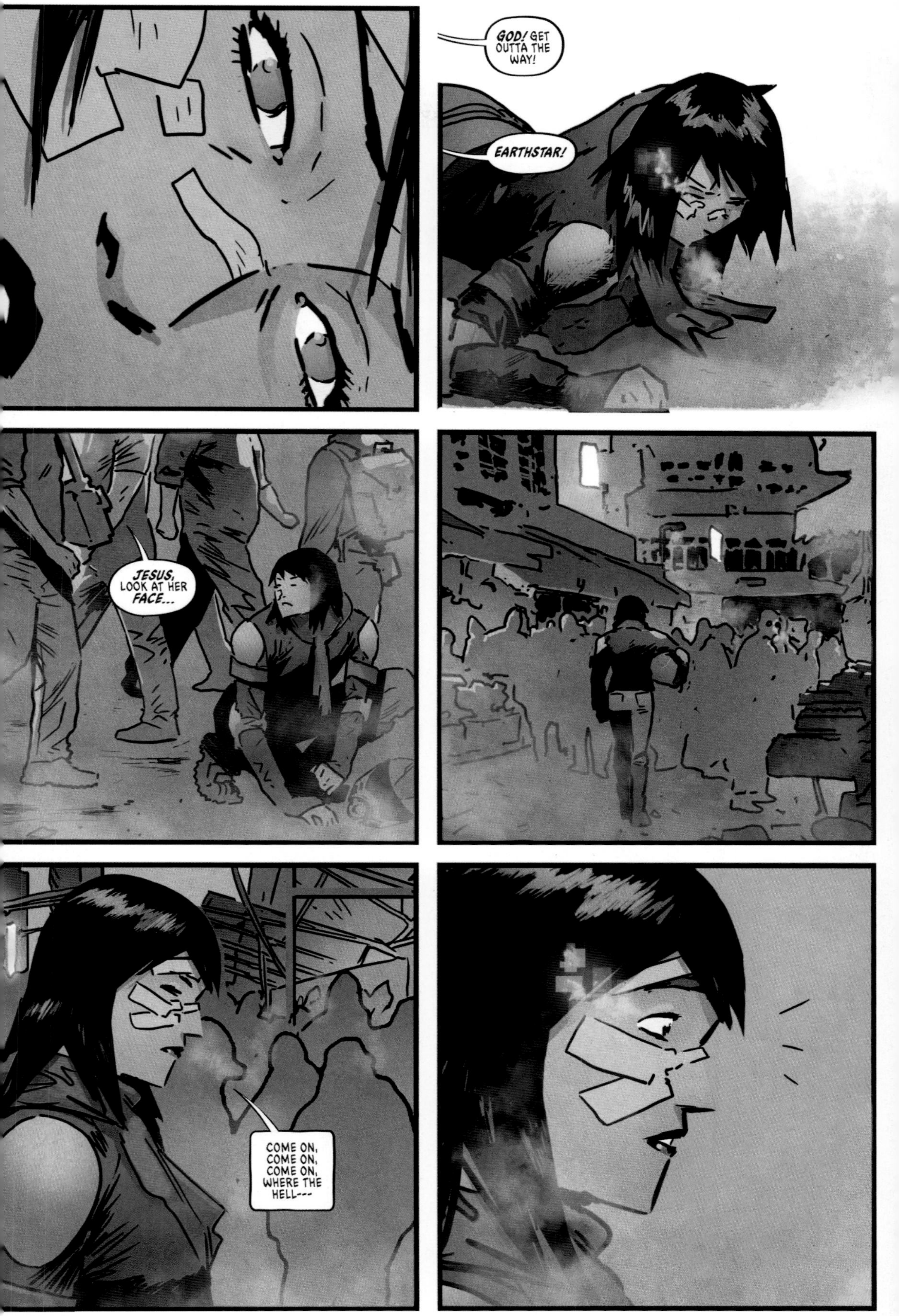
GOD! GET OUTTA THE WAY!
EARTHSTAR!
JESUS, LOOK AT HER FACE...
COME ON, COME ON, COME ON, WHERE THE HELL---

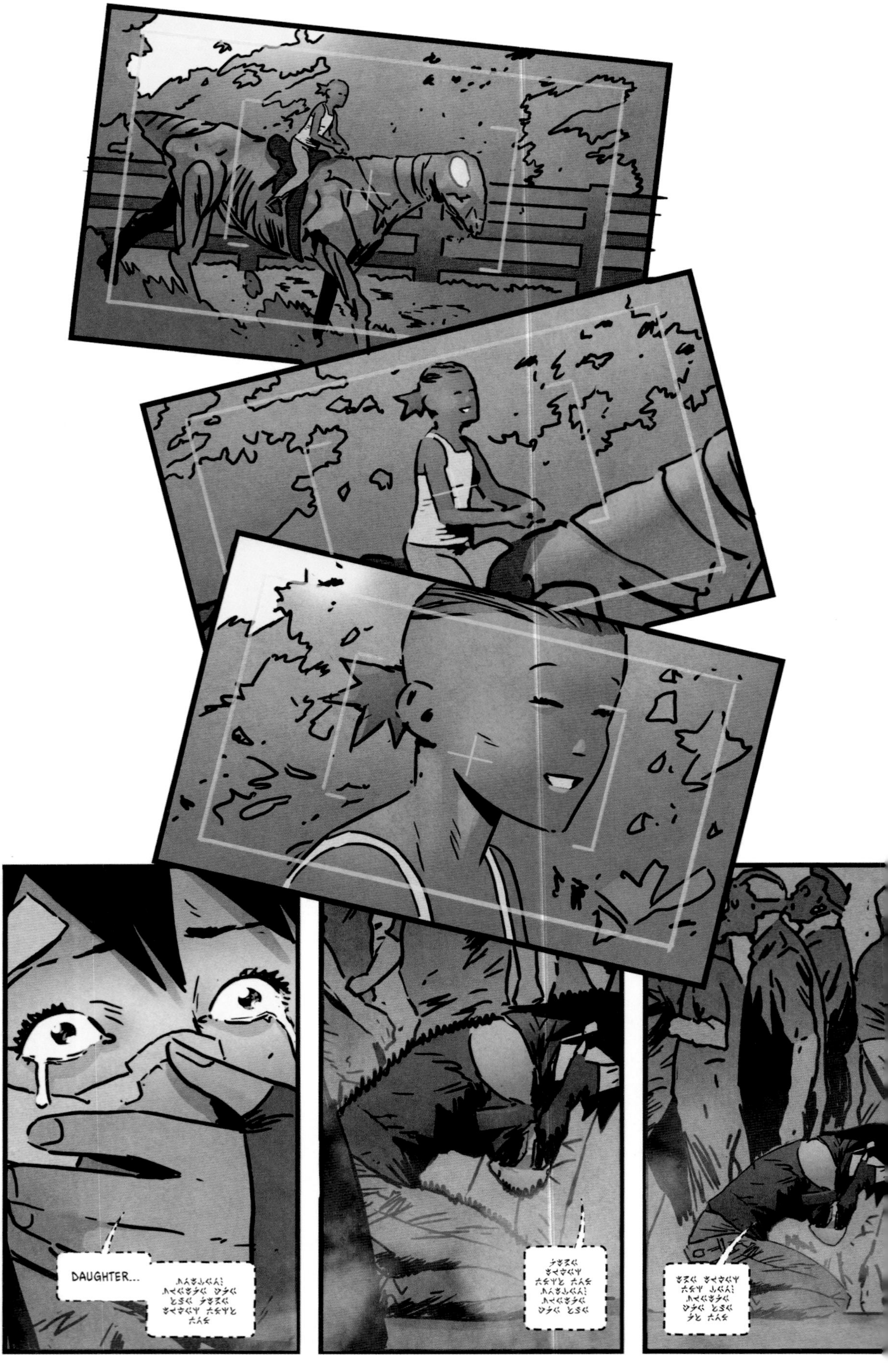
DAUGHTER...

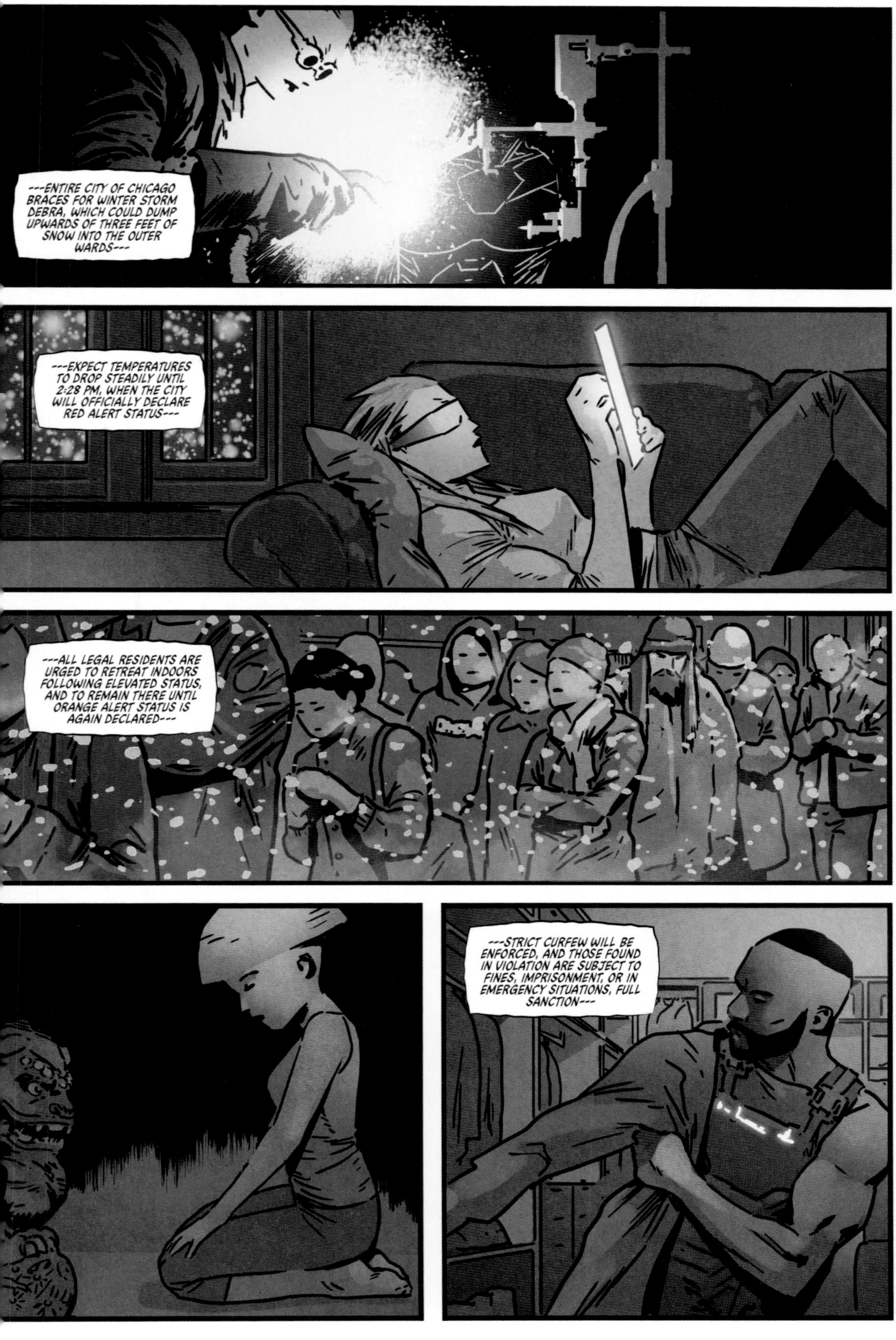
---ENTIRE CITY OF CHICAGO BRACES FOR WINTER STORM DEBRA, WHICH COULD DUMP UPWARDS OF THREE FEET OF SNOW INTO THE OUTER WARDS---
---EXPECT TEMPERATURES TO DROP STEADILY UNTIL 2:28 PM, WHEN THE CITY WILL OFFICIALLY DECLARE RED ALERT STATUS---
---ALL LEGAL RESIDENTS ARE URGED TO RETREAT INDOORS FOLLOWING ELEVATED STATUS, AND TO REMAIN THERE UNTIL ORANGE ALERT STATUS IS AGAIN DECLARED---
---STRICT CURFEW WILL BE ENFORCED, AND THOSE FOUND IN VIOLATION ARE SUBJECT TO FINES, IMPRISONMENT, OR IN EMERGENCY SITUATIONS, FULL SANCTION---

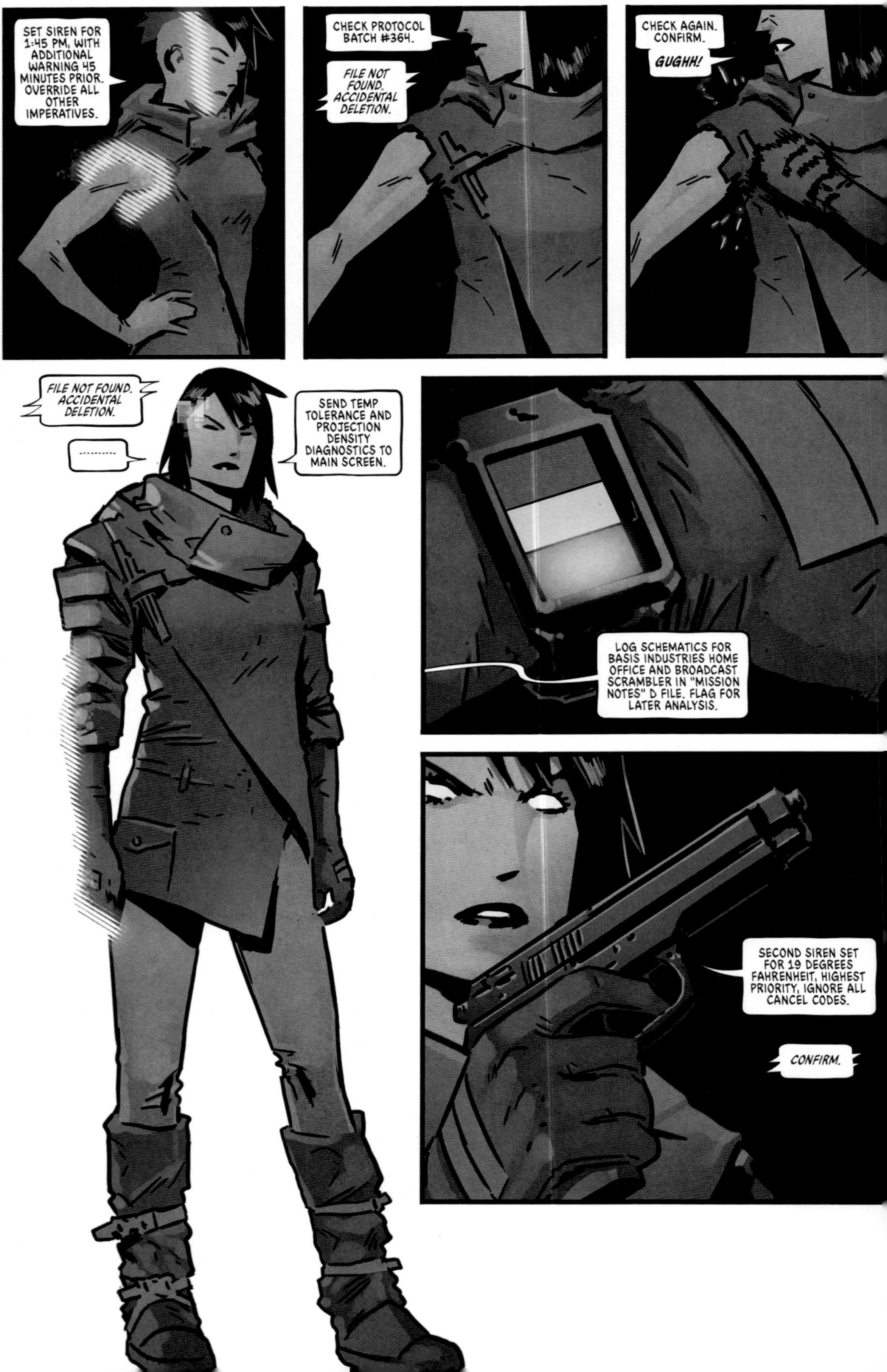
SET SIREN FOR 1:45 PM, WITH ADDITIONAL WARNING 45 MINUTES PRIOR. OVERRIDE ALL OTHER IMPERATIVES.
CHECK PROTOCOL BATCH #364.
FILE NOT FOUND. ACCIDENTAL DELETION.
CHECK AGAIN. CONFIRM.
GUGHH!
FILE NOT FOUND. ACCIDENTAL DELETION.
....
SEND TEMP TOLERANCE AND PROJECTION DENSITY DIAGNOSTICS TO MAIN SCREEN.
LOG SCHEMATICS FOR BASIS INDUSTRIES HOME OFFICE AND BROADCAST SCRAMBLER IN "MISSION NOTES" D FILE. FLAG FOR LATER ANALYSIS.
SECOND SIREN SET FOR 19 DEGREES FAHRENHEIT, HIGHEST PRIORITY, IGNORE ALL CANCEL CODES.
CONFIRM.

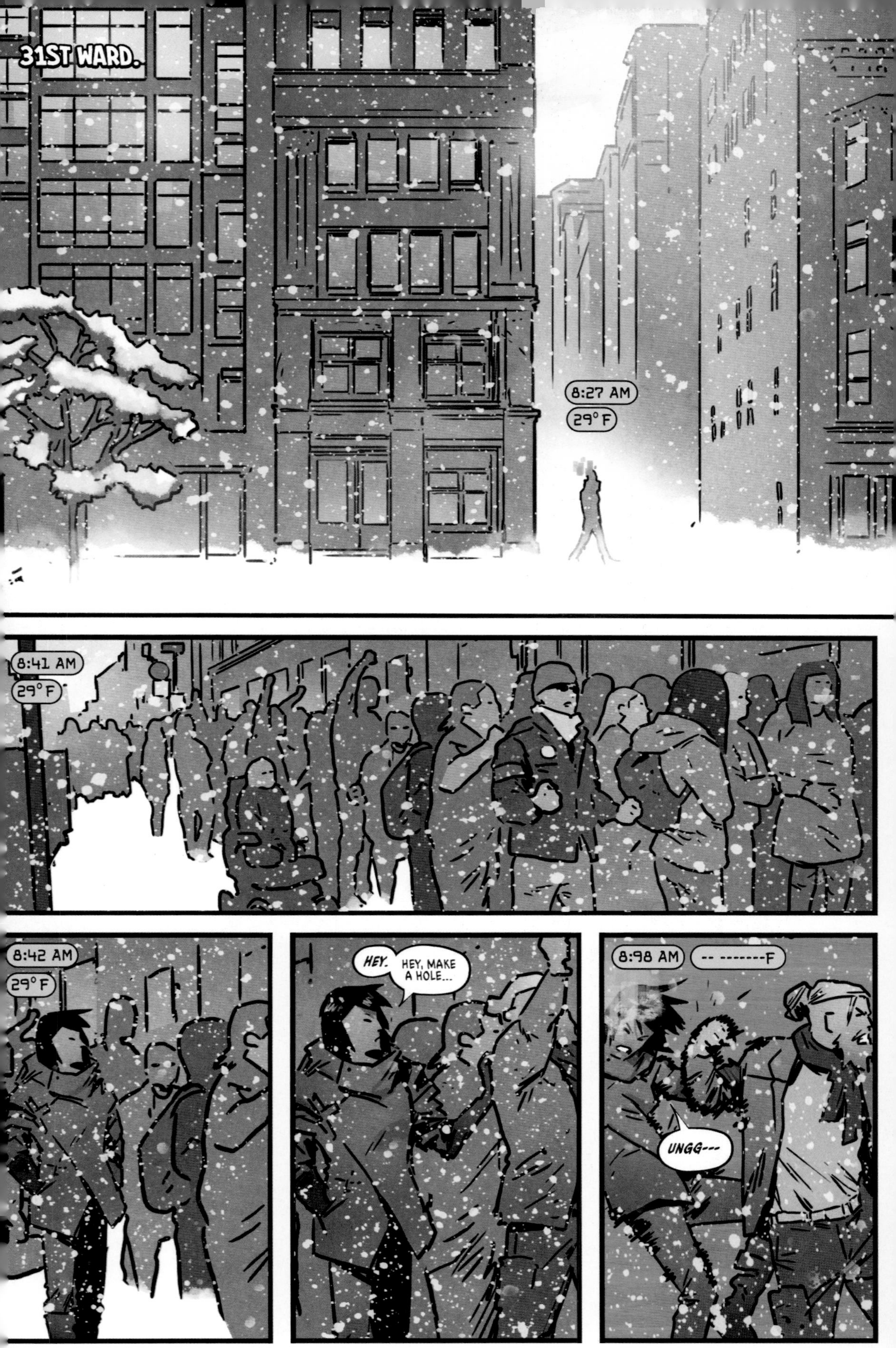
31ST WARD.
8:27 AM
29° F
8:41 AM
29° F
8:42 AM
29° F
HEY.
HEY, MAKE A HOLE...
8:98 AM
-- -------F
UNGG---

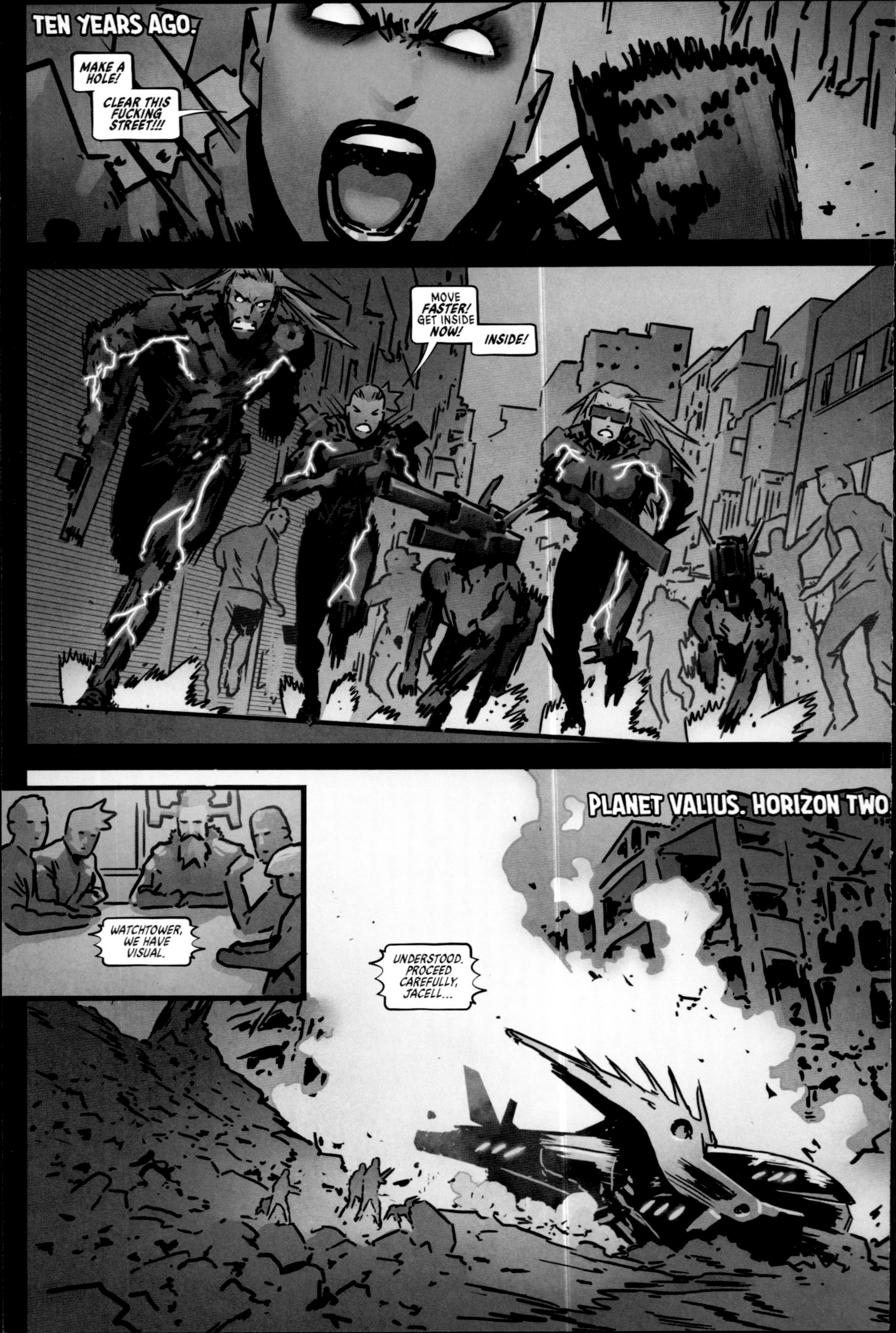

TEN YEARS AGO.
MAKE A HOLE!
CLEAR THIS FUCKING STREET!!!
MOVE FASTER! GET INSIDE NOW!
INSIDE!
PLANET VALIUS. HORIZON TWO.
WATCHTOWER, WE HAVE VISUAL.
UNDERSTOOD. PROCEED CAREFULLY, JACELL...

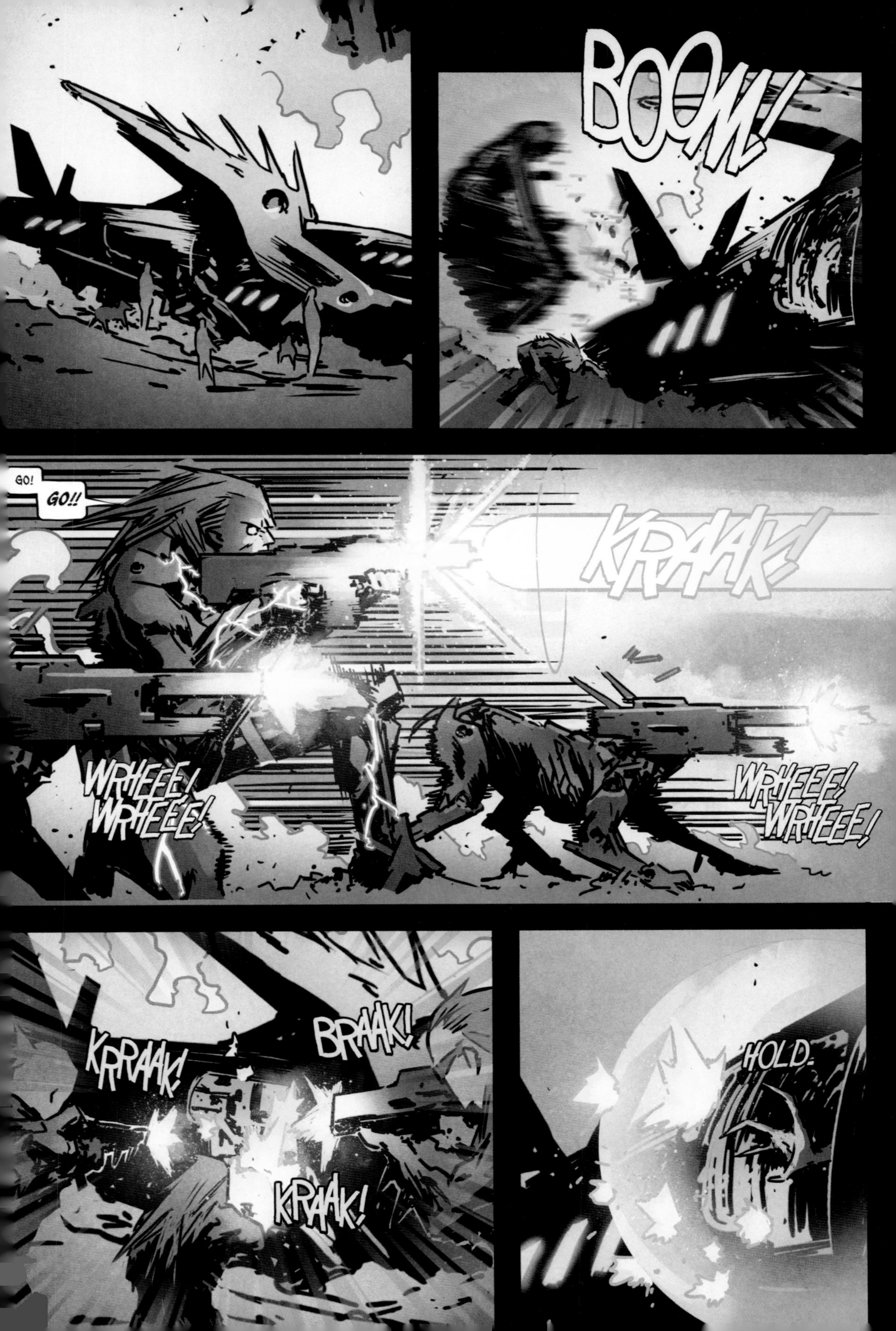
BOOM!
GO! GO!!
KRAAK!
WRHEEE! WRHEEE!
WRHEEE! WRHEEE!
KRRAAK!
BRAAK!
KRAAK!
HOLD

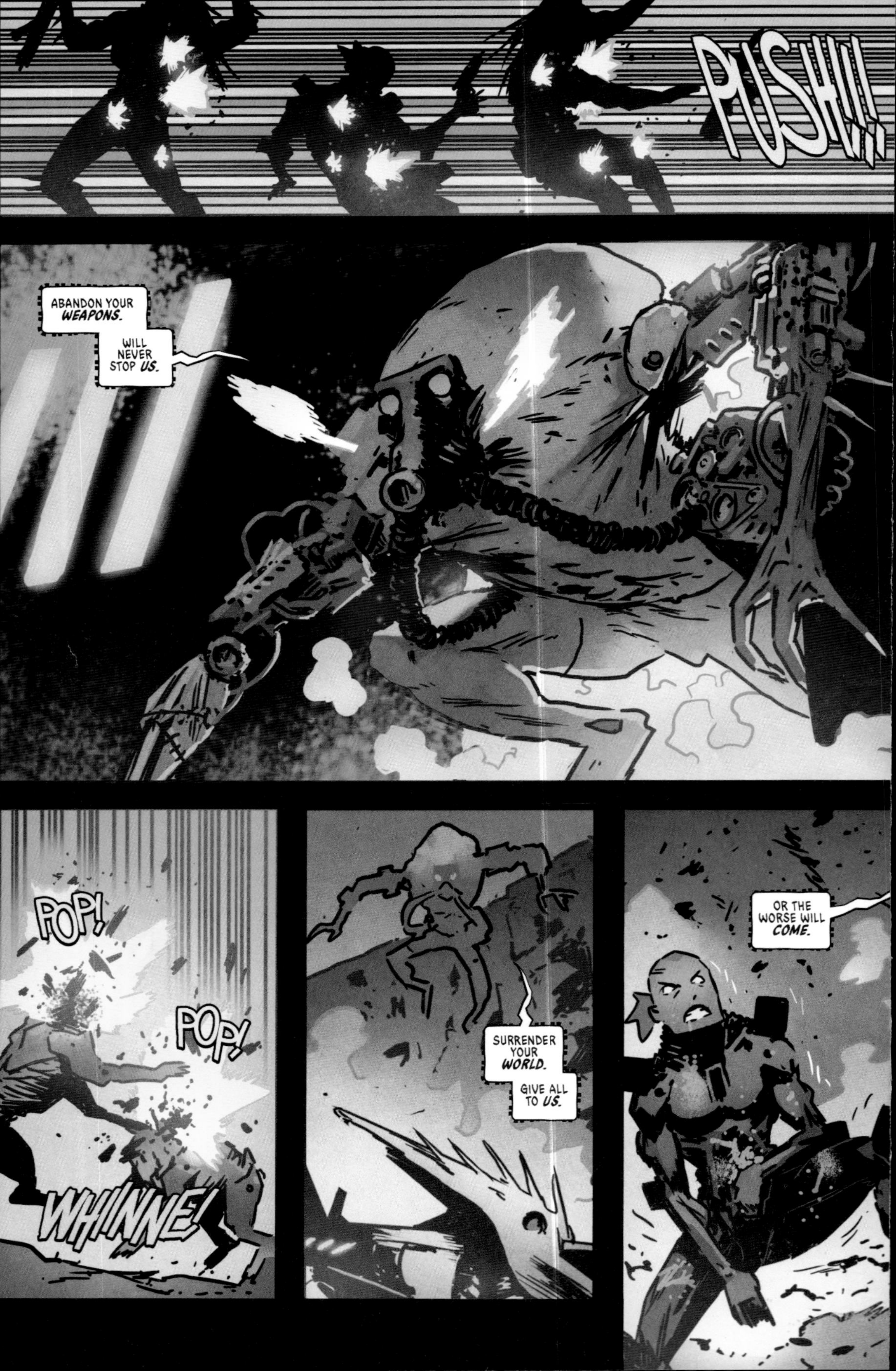
PUSH!!!
ABANDON YOUR WEAPONS.
WILL NEVER STOP US.
POP!
POP!
WHINNE!
SURRENDER YOUR WORLD.
GIVE ALL TO US.
OR THE WORSE WILL COME.

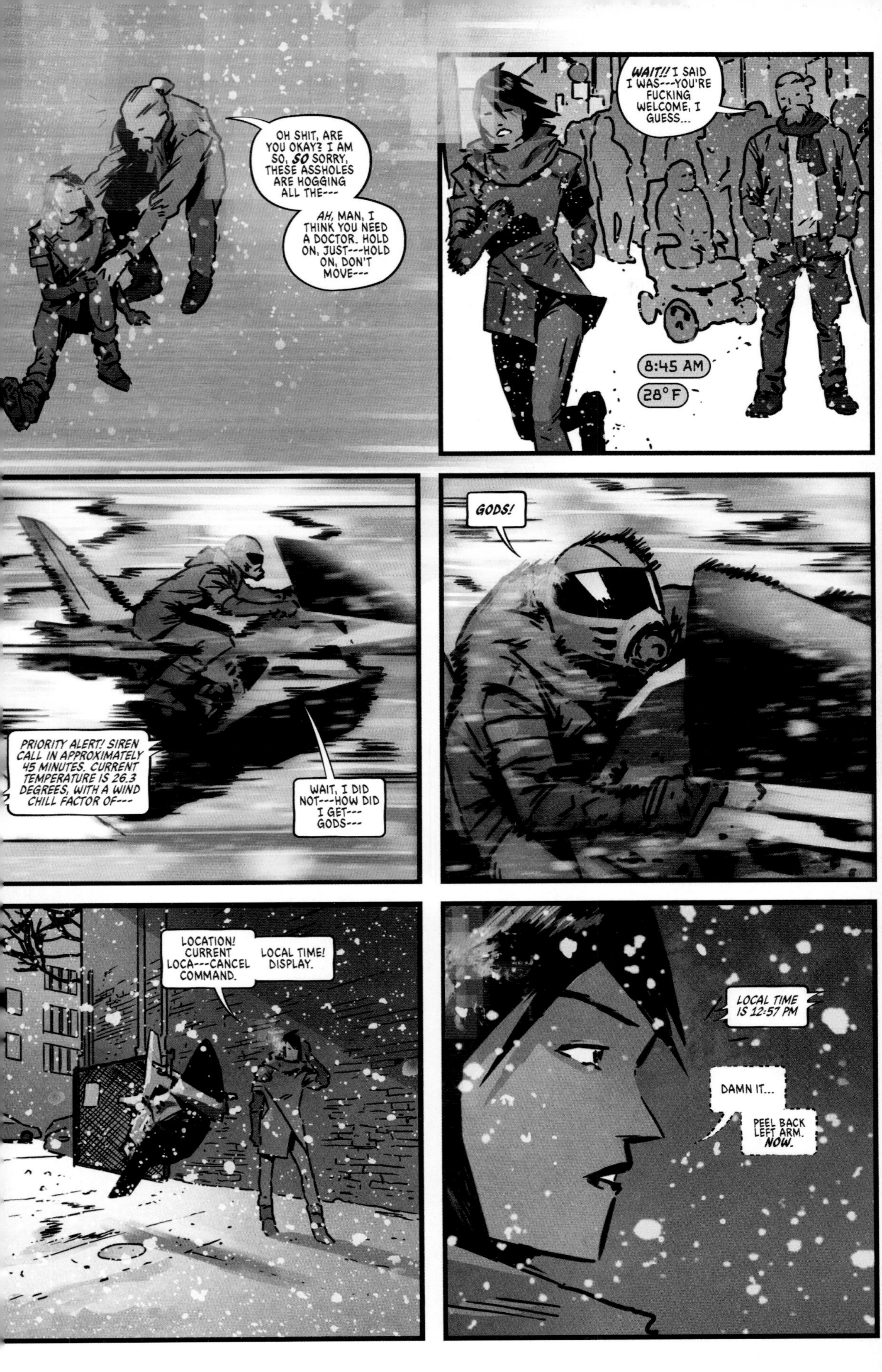
OH SHIT, ARE YOU OKAY? I AM SO, SO SORRY, THESE ASSHOLES ARE HOGGING ALL THE---
AH, MAN, I THINK YOU NEED A DOCTOR. HOLD ON, JUST---HOLD ON, DON'T MOVE---
WAIT!! I SAID I WAS---YOU'RE FUCKING WELCOME, I GUESS...
8:45 AM
28°F
PRIORITY ALERT! SIREN CALL IN APPROXIMATELY 45 MINUTES. CURRENT TEMPERATURE IS 26.3 DEGREES, WITH A WIND CHILL FACTOR OF---
WAIT, I DID NOT---HOW DID I GET--- GODS---
GODS!
LOCATION! CURRENT LOCA---CANCEL COMMAND.
LOCAL TIME! DISPLAY.
LOCAL TIME IS 12:57 PM
DAMN IT...
PEEL BACK LEFT ARM. NOW.

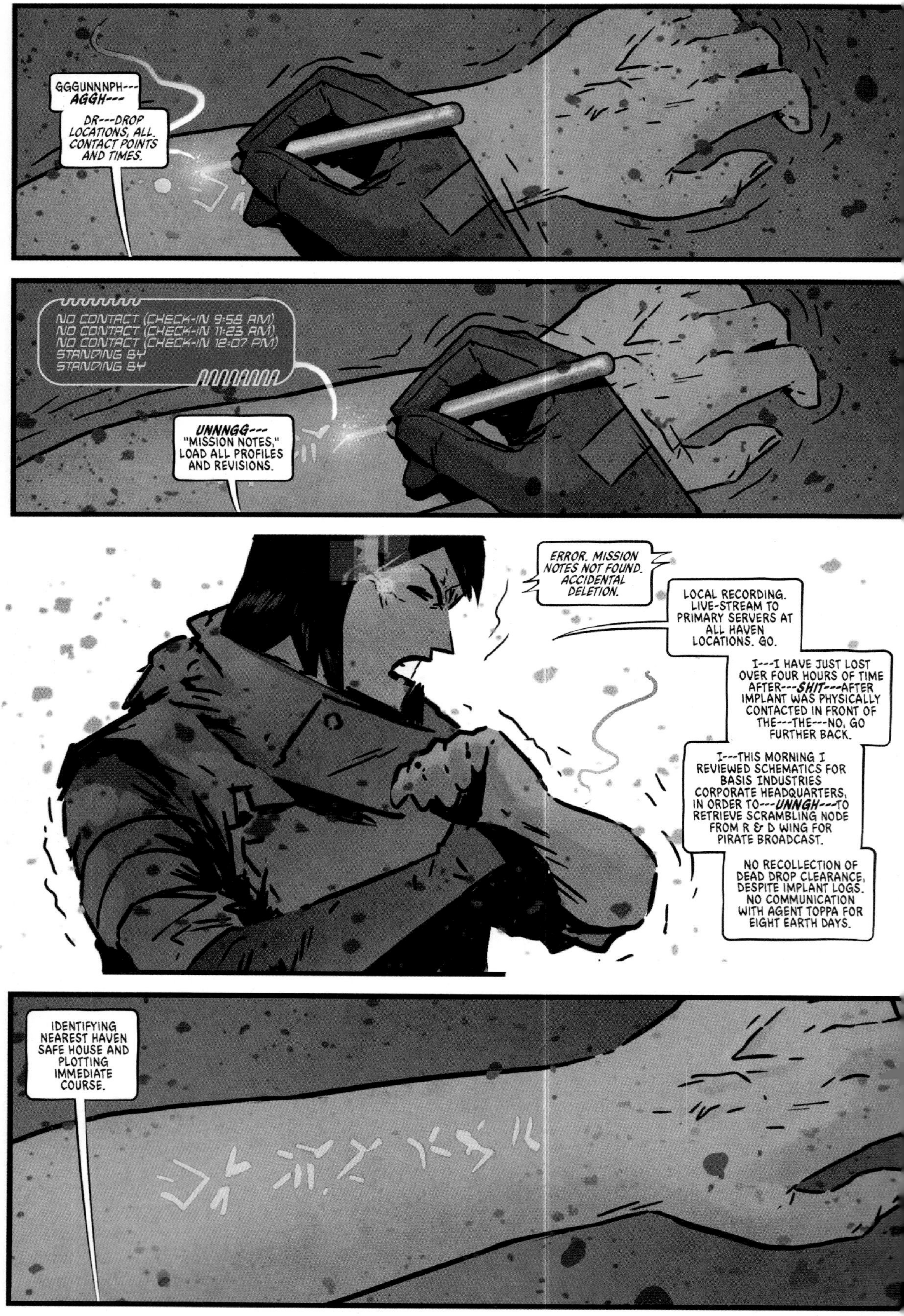
GGGUNNNPH---
AGGH---
DR---DROP LOCATIONS, ALL. CONTACT POINTS AND TIMES.
NO CONTACT (CHECK-IN 9:58 AM)
NO CONTACT (CHECK-IN 11:23 AM)
NO CONTACT (CHECK-IN 12:07 PM)
STANDING BY
STANDING BY
UNNNGG---
"MISSION NOTES," LOAD ALL PROFILES AND REVISIONS.
ERROR. MISSION NOTES NOT FOUND. ACCIDENTAL DELETION.
LOCAL RECORDING. LIVE-STREAM TO PRIMARY SERVERS AT ALL HAVEN LOCATIONS. GO.
I---I HAVE JUST LOST OVER FOUR HOURS OF TIME AFTER---SHIT---AFTER IMPLANT WAS PHYSICALLY CONTACTED IN FRONT OF THE---THE---NO, GO FURTHER BACK.
I---THIS MORNING I REVIEWED SCHEMATICS FOR BASIS INDUSTRIES CORPORATE HEADQUARTERS, IN ORDER TO---UNNGH---TO RETRIEVE SCRAMBLING NODE FROM R & D WING FOR PIRATE BROADCAST.
NO RECOLLECTION OF DEAD DROP CLEARANCE, DESPITE IMPLANT LOGS. NO COMMUNICATION WITH AGENT TOPPA FOR EIGHT EARTH DAYS.
IDENTIFYING NEAREST HAVEN SAFE HOUSE AND PLOTTING IMMEDIATE COURSE.

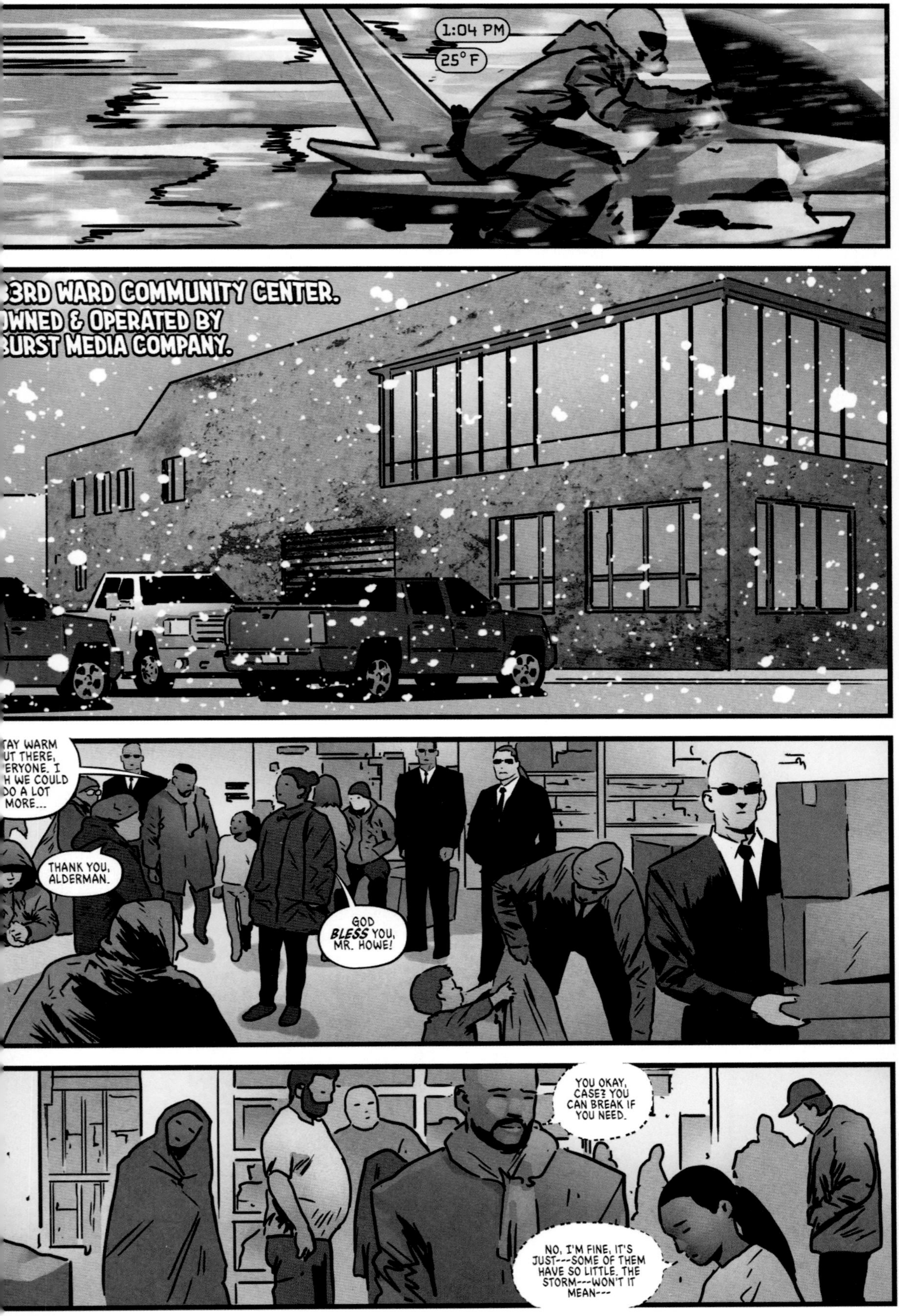
1:04 PM
25° F
3RD WARD COMMUNITY CENTER. OWNED & OPERATED BY BURST MEDIA COMPANY.
TAY WARM UT THERE, ERYONE. I H WE COULD DO A LOT MORE...
THANK YOU, ALDERMAN.
GOD BLESS YOU, MR. HOWE!
YOU OKAY, CASE? YOU CAN BREAK IF YOU NEED.
NO, I'M FINE, IT'S JUST---SOME OF THEM HAVE SO LITTLE. THE STORM---WON'T IT MEAN---

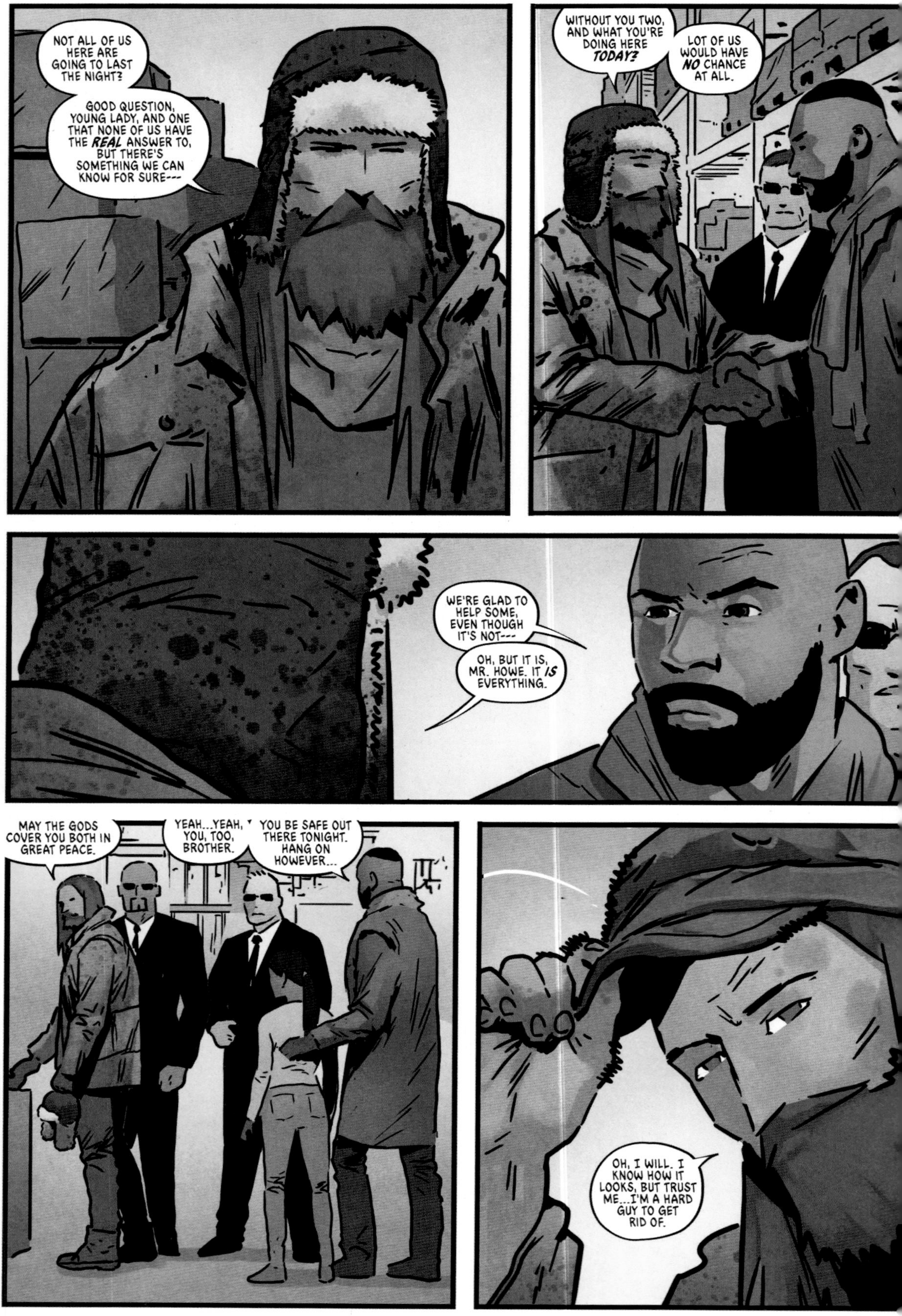
NOT ALL OF US HERE ARE GOING TO LAST THE NIGHT?
GOOD QUESTION, YOUNG LADY, AND ONE THAT NONE OF US HAVE THE REAL ANSWER TO, BUT THERE'S SOMETHING WE CAN KNOW FOR SURE---
WITHOUT YOU TWO, AND WHAT YOU'RE DOING HERE TODAY?
LOT OF US WOULD HAVE NO CHANCE AT ALL.
WE'RE GLAD TO HELP SOME, EVEN THOUGH IT'S NOT---
OH, BUT IT IS, MR. HOWE. IT IS EVERYTHING.
MAY THE GODS COVER YOU BOTH IN GREAT PEACE.
YEAH...YEAH, YOU, TOO, BROTHER.
YOU BE SAFE OUT THERE TONIGHT. HANG ON HOWEVER...
OH, I WILL. I KNOW HOW IT LOOKS, BUT TRUST ME...I'M A HARD GUY TO GET RID OF.

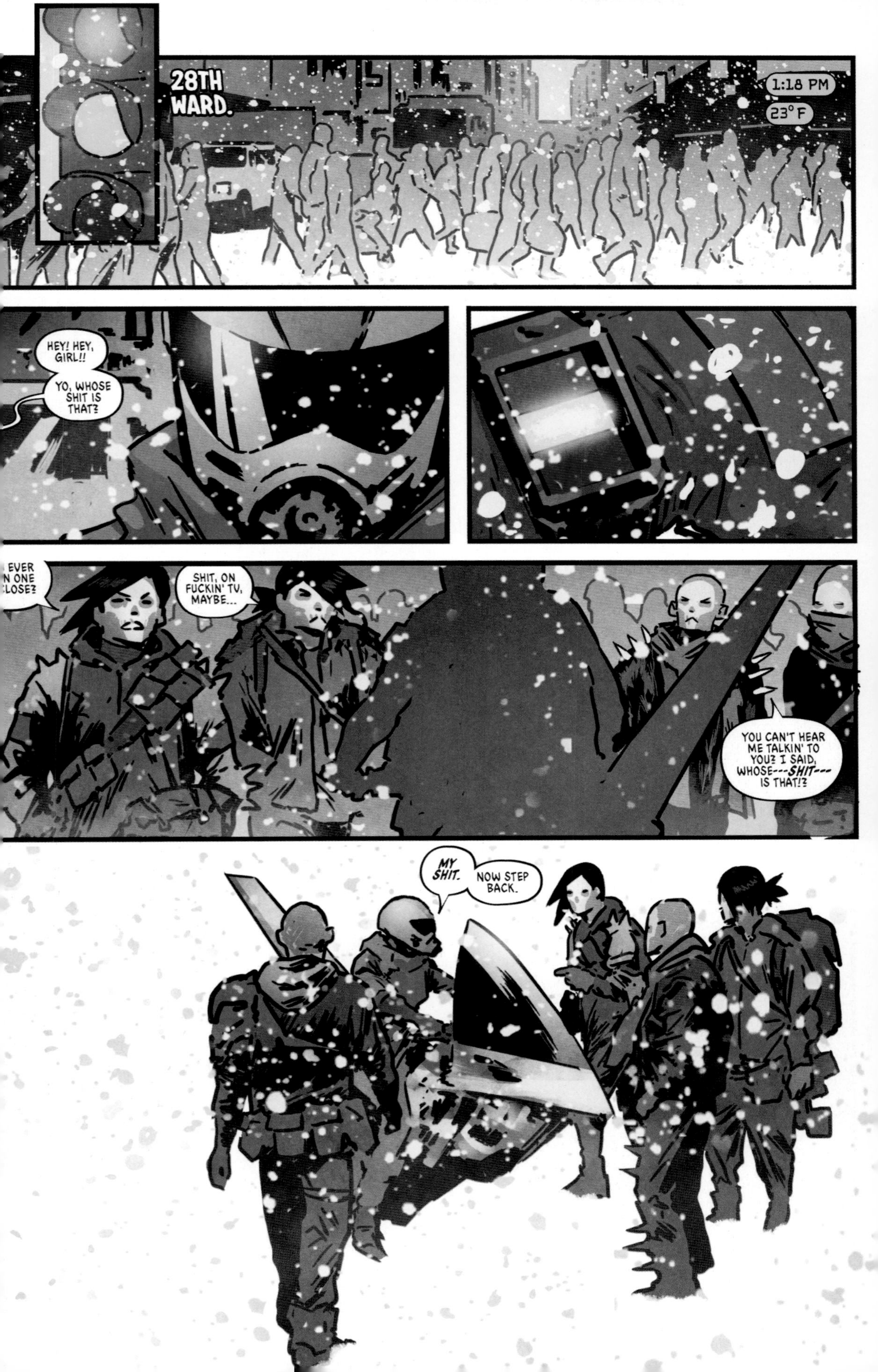
28TH WARD.
1:18 PM
23° F
HEY! HEY, GIRL!!
YO, WHOSE SHIT IS THAT?
SHIT, ON FUCKIN' TV, MAYBE...
YOU CAN'T HEAR ME TALKIN' TO YOU? I SAID, WHOSE---SHIT--- IS THAT!?
MY SHIT.
NOW STEP BACK.

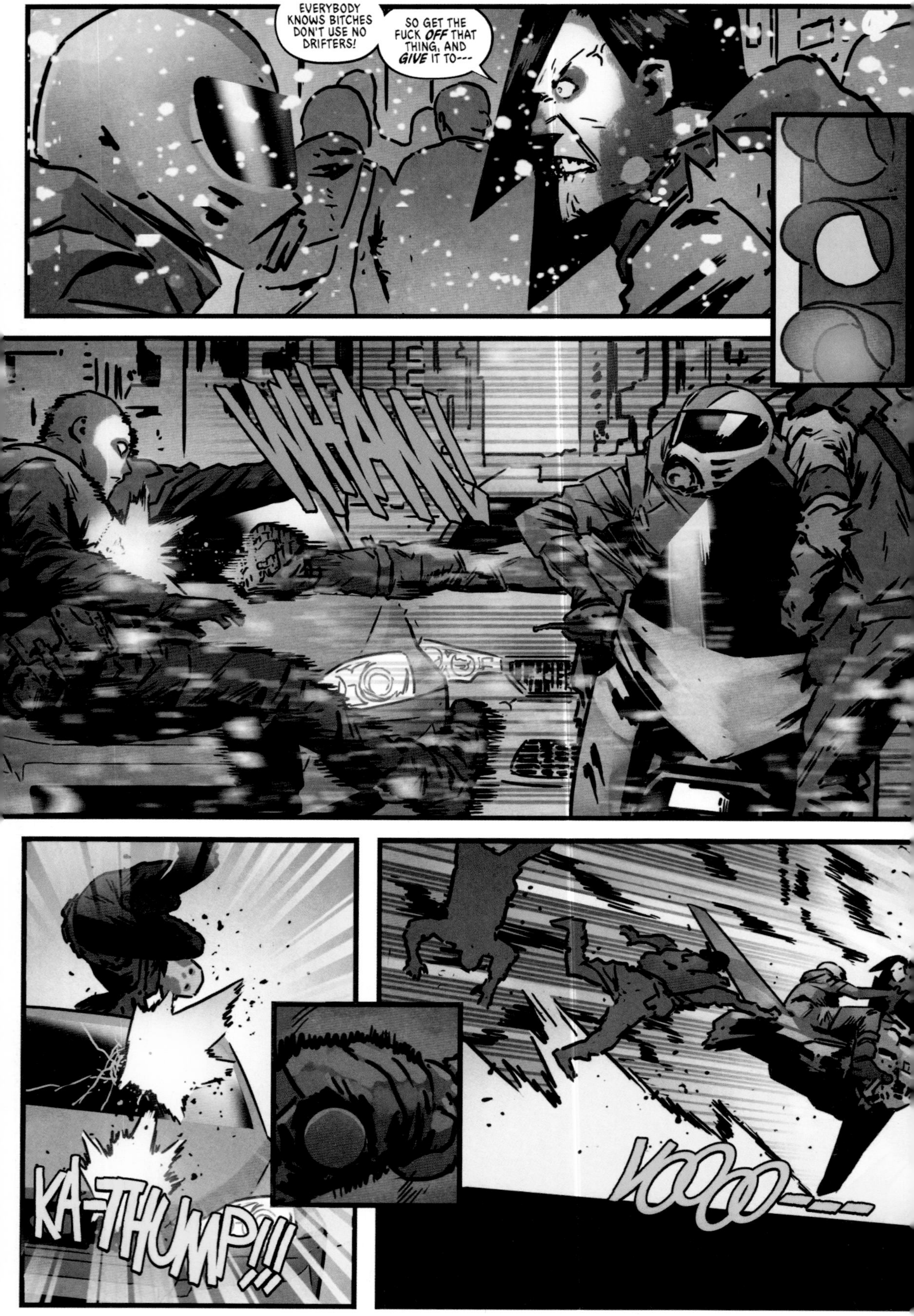
EVERYBODY KNOWS BITCHES DON'T USE NO DRIFTERS!
SO GET THE FUCK *OFF* THAT THING, AND *GIVE* IT TO---
WHAM
KA-THUMP!!!
VOOOOO----

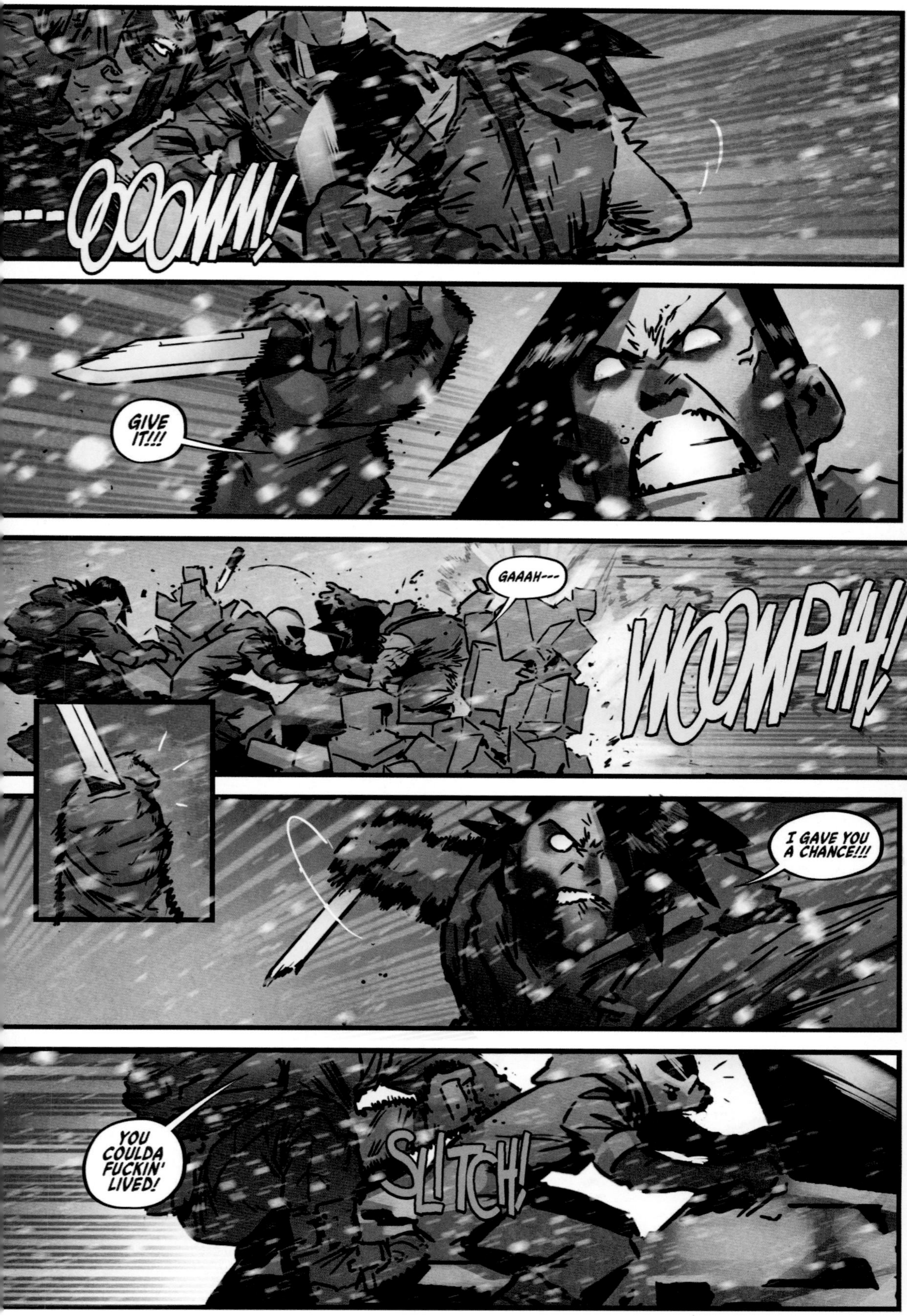
---OOOMM!
GIVE IT!!!
GAAAH---
WOOMPHH!
I GAVE YOU A CHANCE!!!
YOU COULDA FUCKIN' LIVED!
SLITCH!

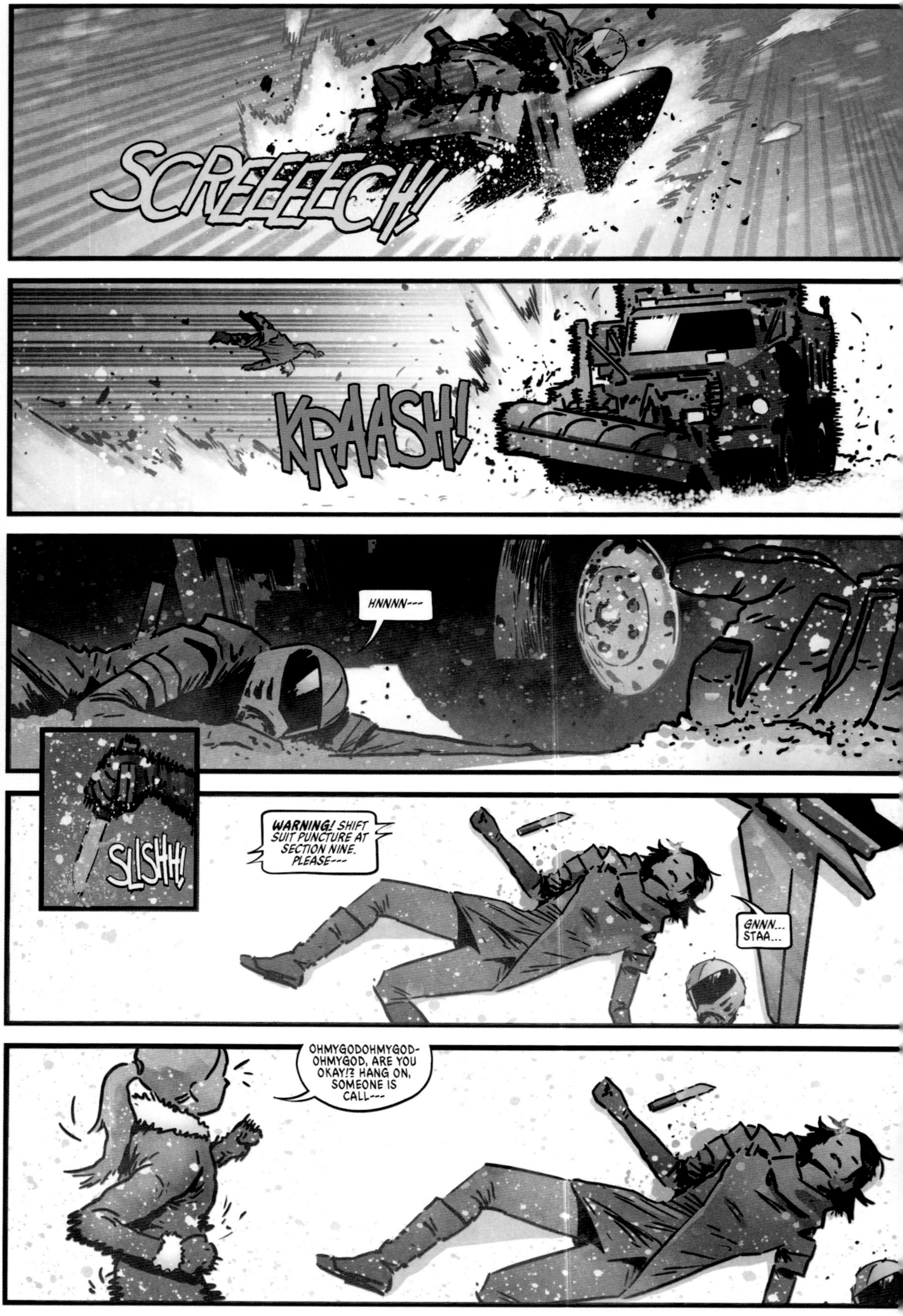
SCREEEEECH!
KRAASH!
HNNNN---
SLISHH!
WARNING! SHIFT SUIT PUNCTURE AT SECTION NINE. PLEASE---
GNNN... STAA...
OHMYGODOHMYGOD-OHMYGOD, ARE YOU OKAY!? HANG ON, SOMEONE IS CALL---

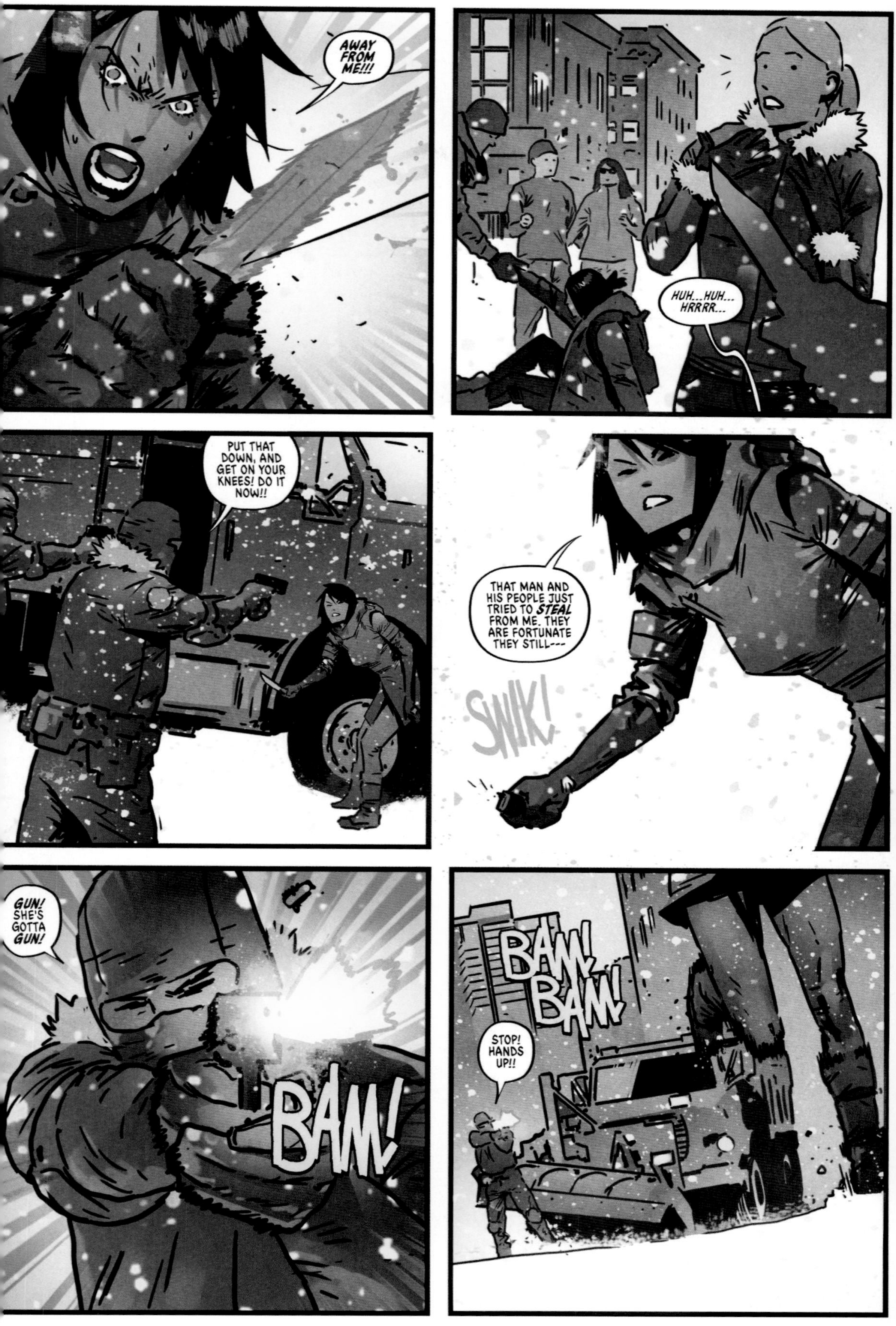
AWAY FROM ME!!!
HUH...HUH... HRRRR...
PUT THAT DOWN, AND GET ON YOUR KNEES! DO IT NOW!!
THAT MAN AND HIS PEOPLE JUST TRIED TO STEAL FROM ME. THEY ARE FORTUNATE THEY STILL---
SWIK!
GUN! SHE'S GOTTA GUN!
BAM!
BAM! BAM!
STOP! HANDS UP!!

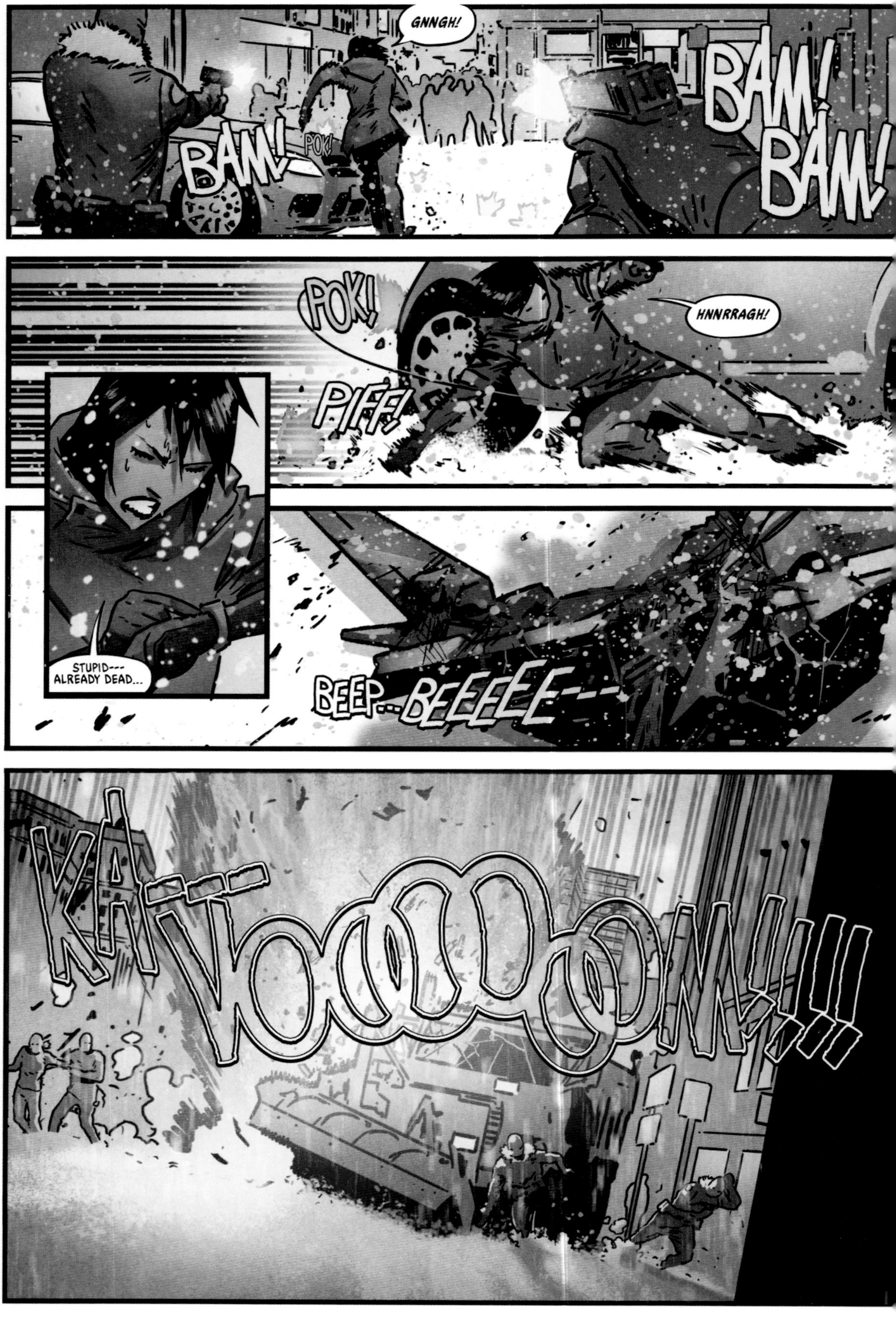

GNNGH!
BAM!
POK!
BAM!
BAM!
POK!
HNNRRAGH!
PIFF!
STUPID--- ALREADY DEAD...
BEEP...BEEEEE---
KA-VOOOOOOM!!!!

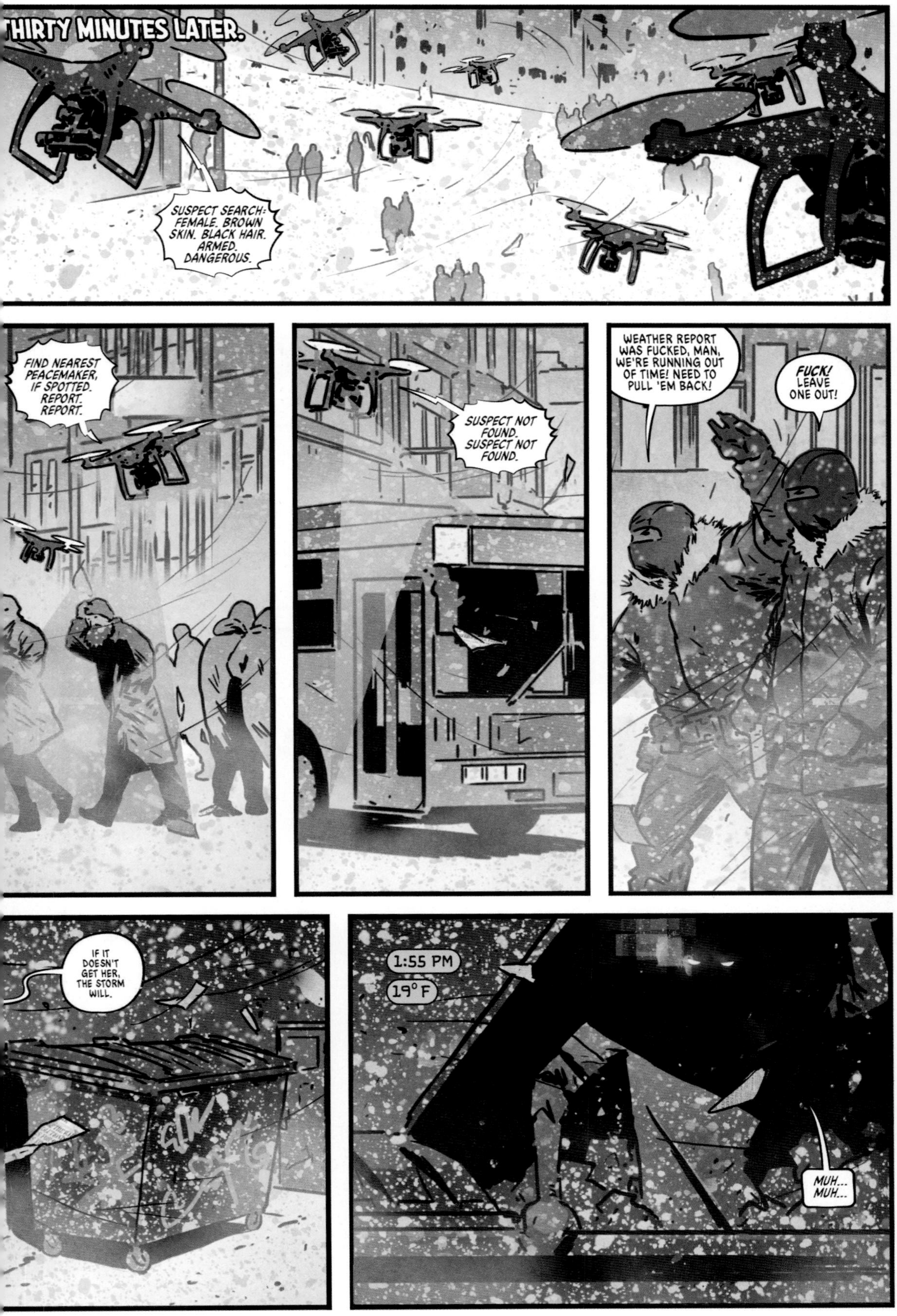
THIRTY MINUTES LATER.
SUSPECT SEARCH: FEMALE. BROWN SKIN. BLACK HAIR. ARMED. DANGEROUS.
FIND NEAREST PEACEMAKER, IF SPOTTED. REPORT. REPORT.
SUSPECT NOT FOUND. SUSPECT NOT FOUND.
WEATHER REPORT WAS FUCKED, MAN, WE'RE RUNNING OUT OF TIME! NEED TO PULL 'EM BACK!
FUCK! LEAVE ONE OUT!
IF IT DOESN'T GET HER, THE STORM WILL.
1:55 PM
19° F
MUH... MUH...

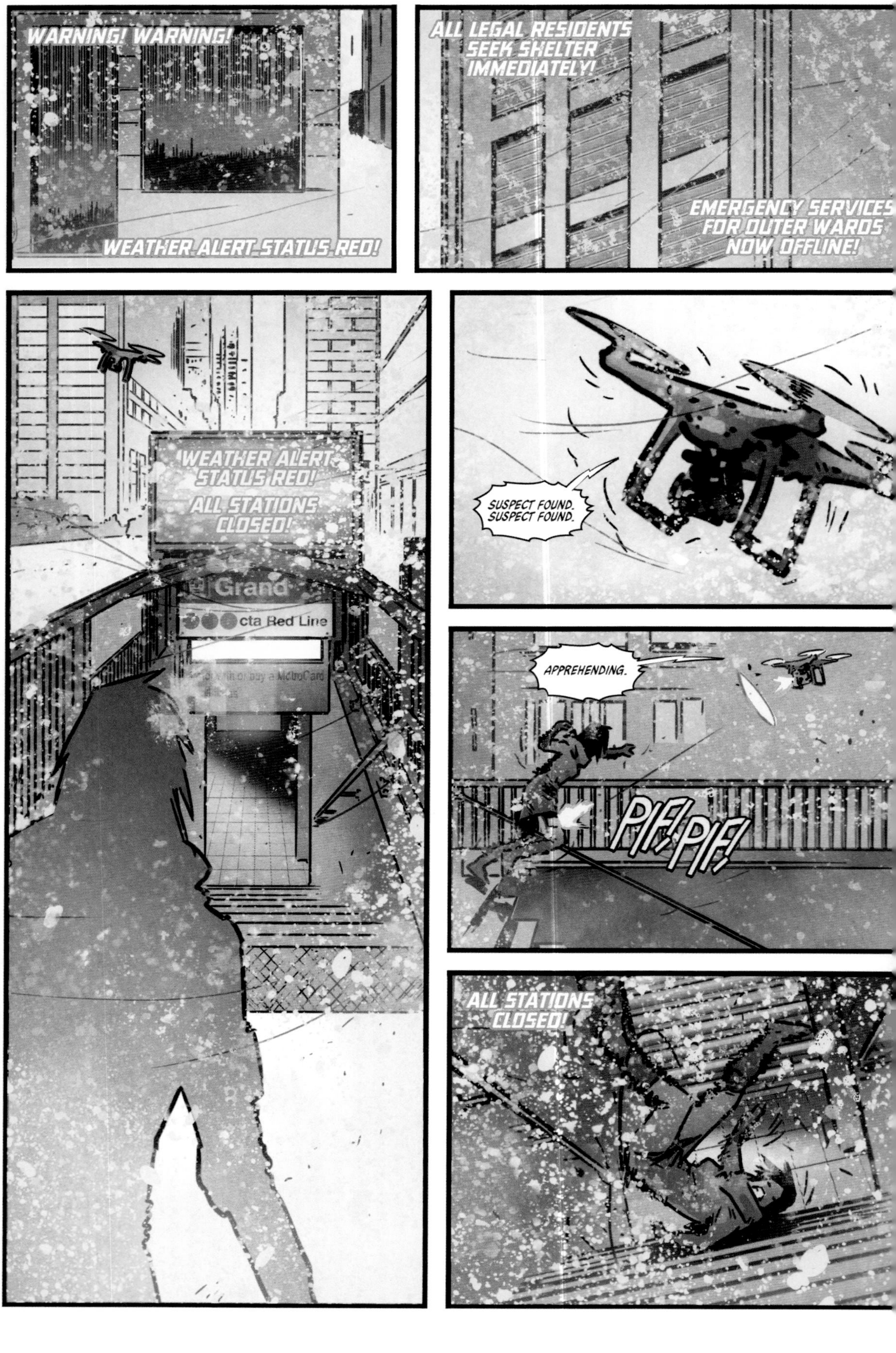
WARNING! WARNING!
WEATHER ALERT STATUS RED!
ALL LEGAL RESIDENTS SEEK SHELTER IMMEDIATELY!
EMERGENCY SERVICES FOR OUTER WARDS NOW OFFLINE!
WEATHER ALERT STATUS RED!
ALL STATIONS CLOSED!
Grand
cta Red Line
SUSPECT FOUND. SUSPECT FOUND.
APPREHENDING.
PIF! PIF!
ALL STATIONS CLOSED!

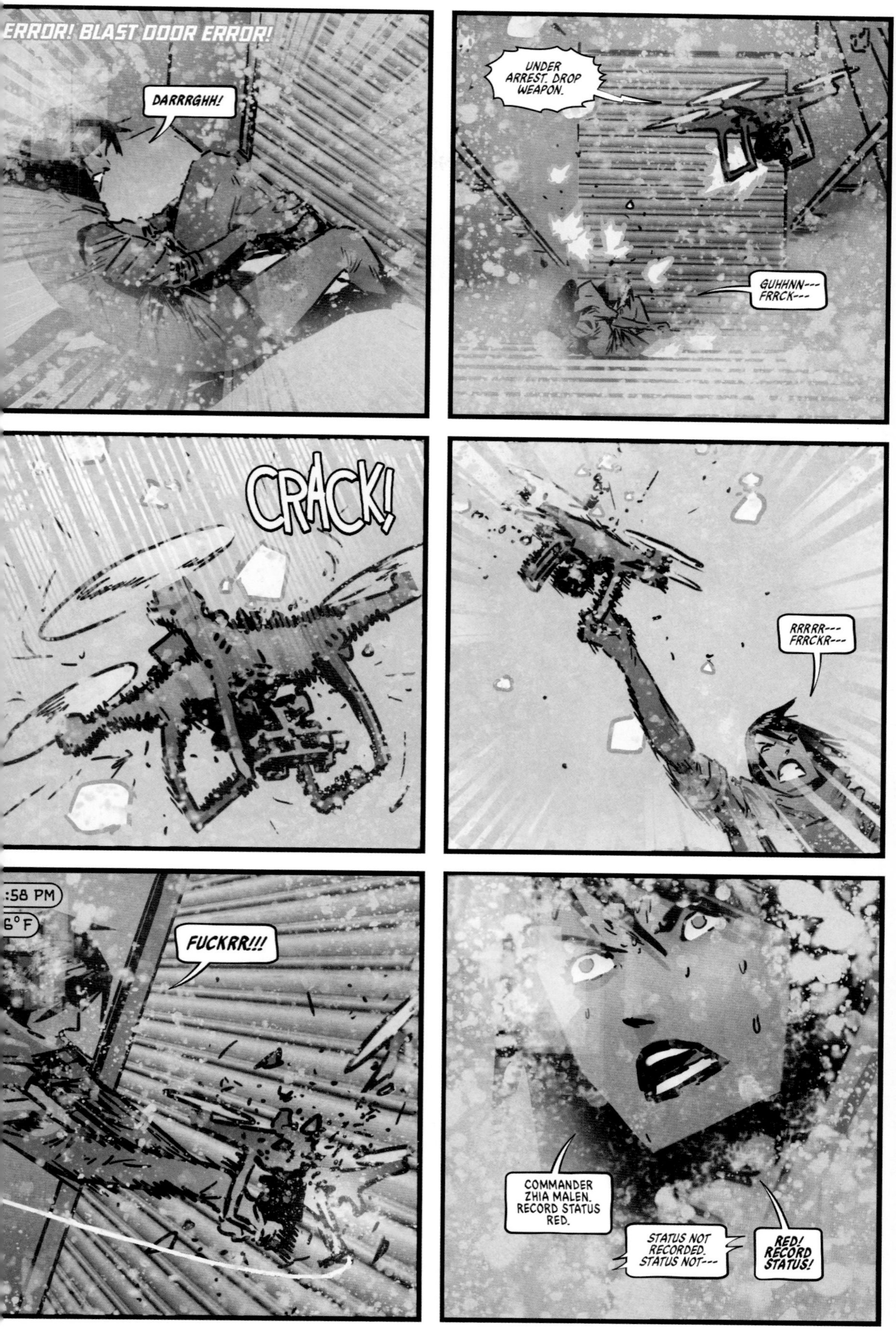

ERROR! BLAST DOOR ERROR!
DARRRGHH!
UNDER ARREST. DROP WEAPON.
GUHHNN--- FRRCK---
CRACK!
RRRRR--- FRRCKR---
:58 PM
6°F
FUCKRR!!!
COMMANDER ZHIA MALEN. RECORD STATUS RED.
STATUS NOT RECORDED. STATUS NOT---
RED! RECORD STATUS!

Grand

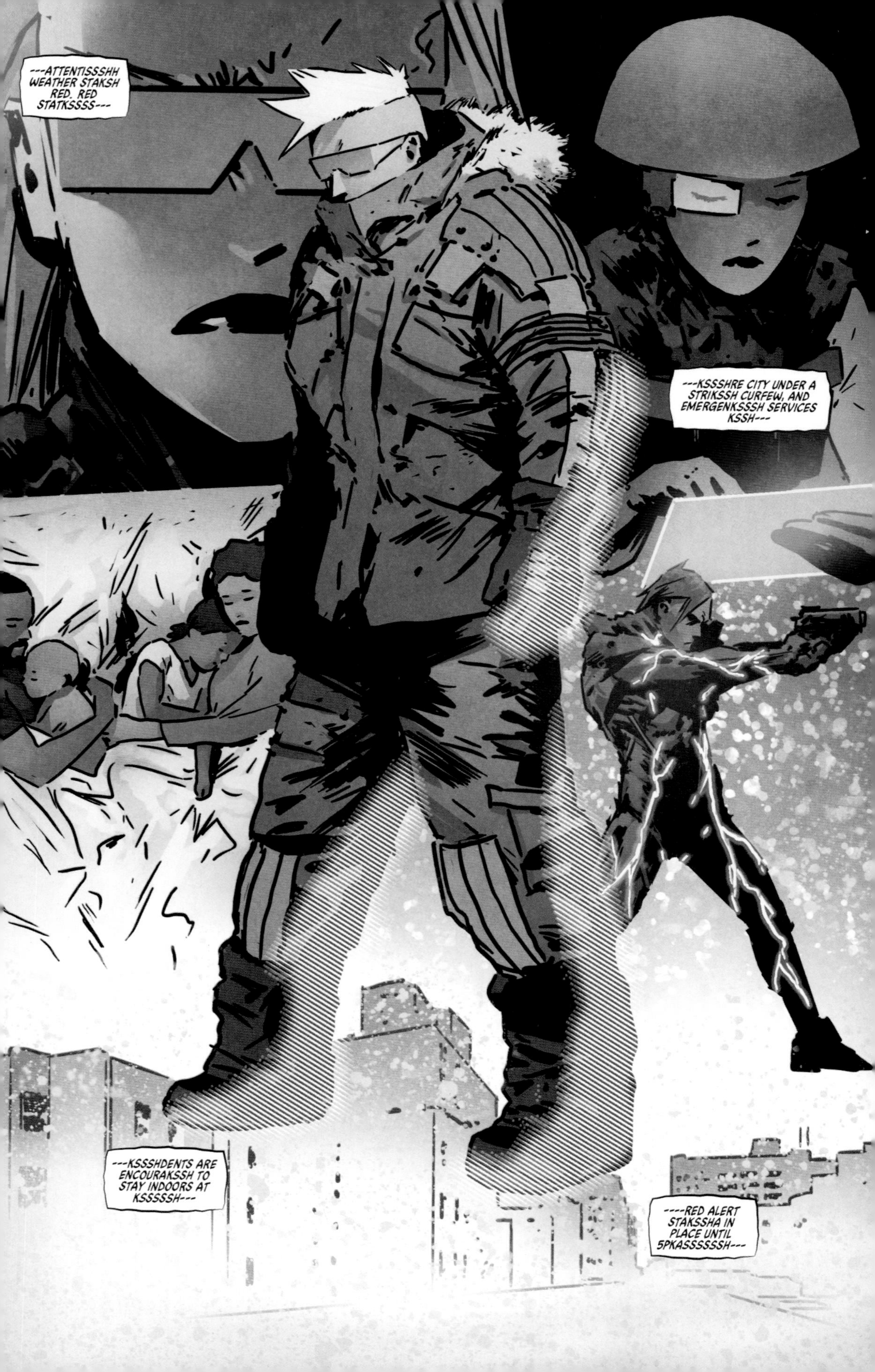
---ATTENTISSSHH WEATHER STAKSH RED. RED STATKSSSS---
---KSSSHRE CITY UNDER A STRIKSSH CURFEW, AND EMERGENKSSSH SERVICES KSSH---
---KSSSHDENTS ARE ENCOURAKSSH TO STAY INDOORS AT KSSSSSH---
----RED ALERT STAKSSHA IN PLACE UNTIL 5PKASSSSSSH---

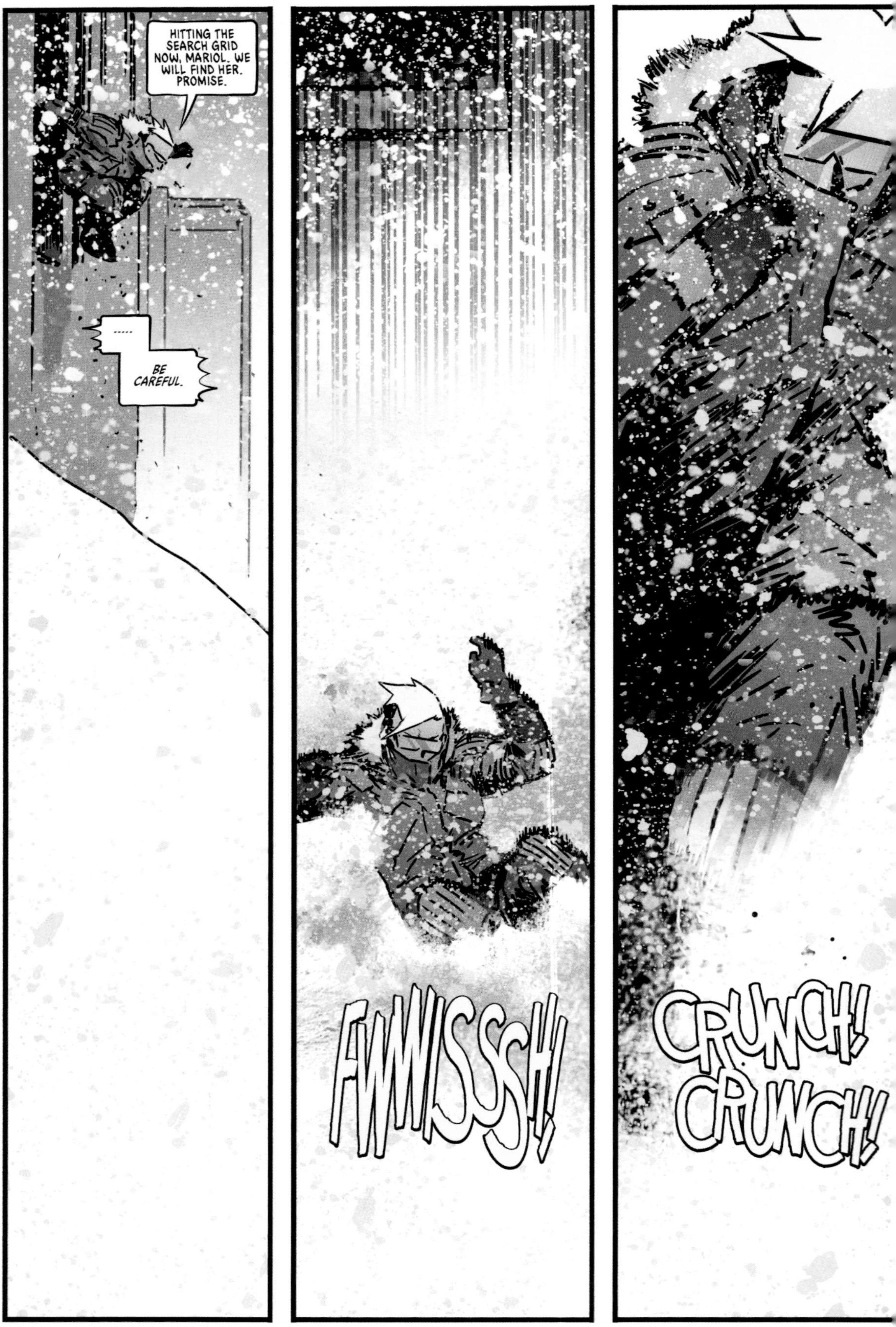
HITTING THE SEARCH GRID NOW, MARIOL. WE WILL FIND HER. PROMISE.

BE CAREFUL.
FWWISSSH!
CRUNCH! CRUNCH!

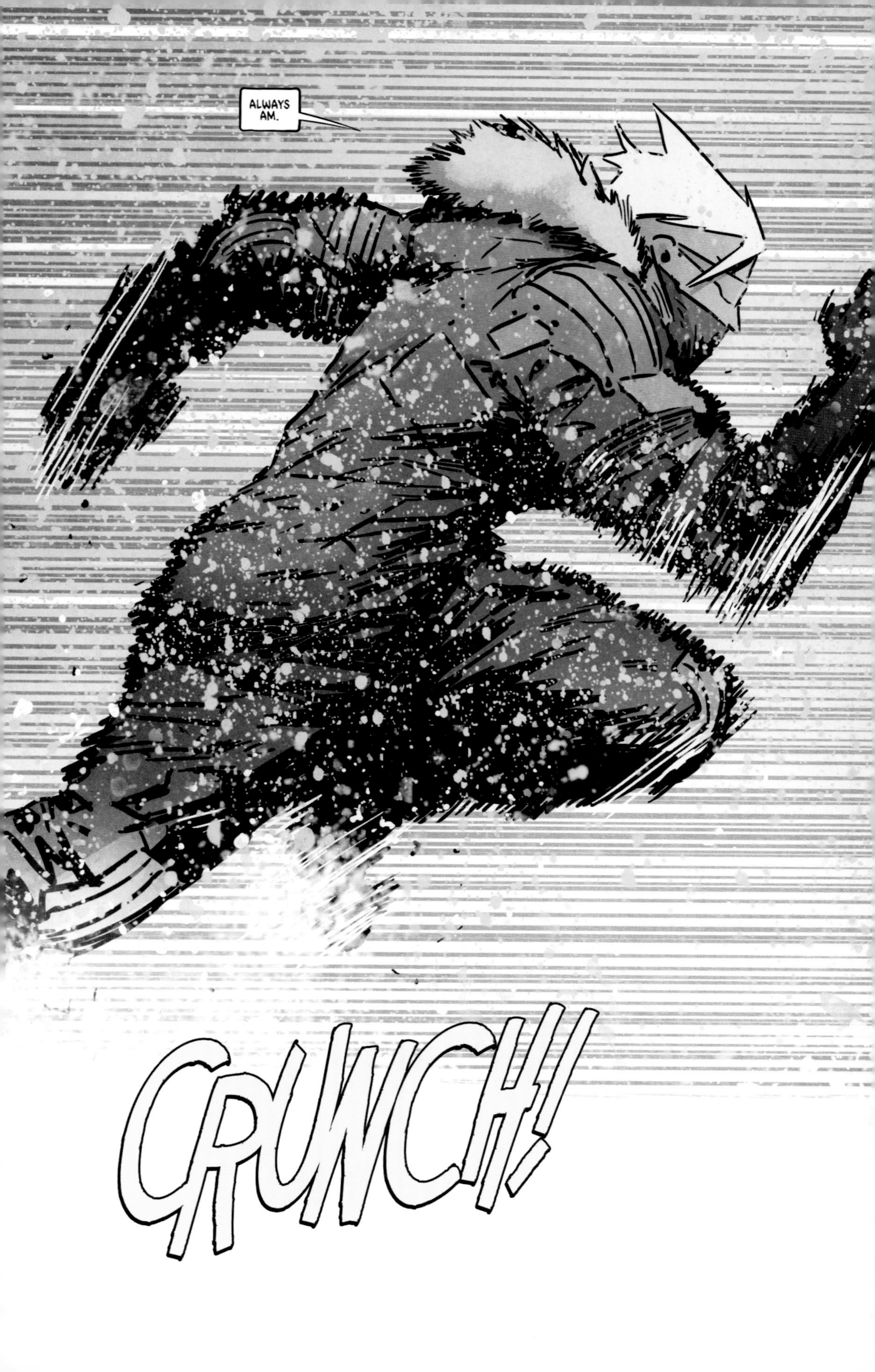
ALWAYS AM.
CRUNCH!

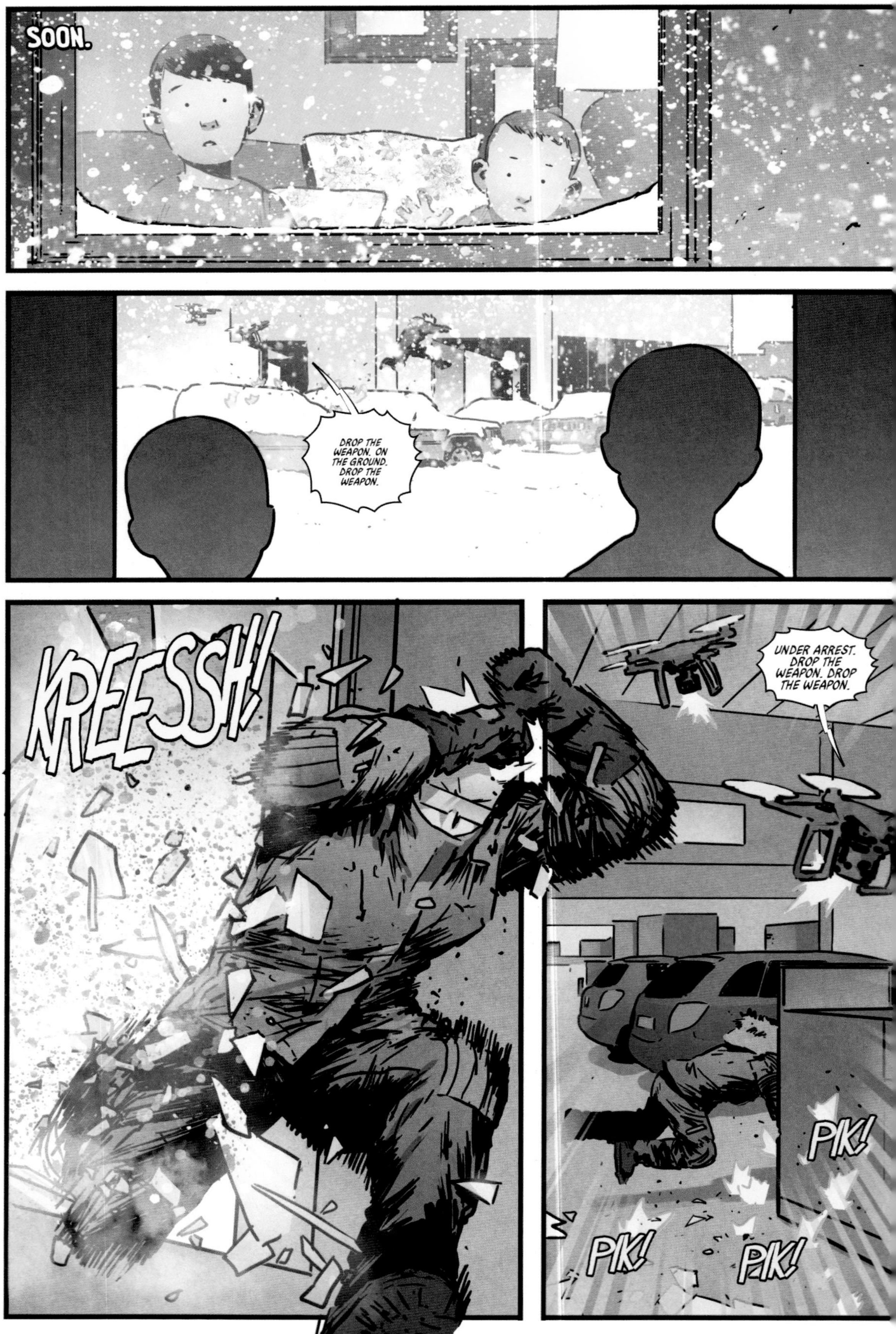
SOON.
DROP THE WEAPON. ON THE GROUND. DROP THE WEAPON.
KREESSH!
UNDER ARREST. DROP THE WEAPON. DROP THE WEAPON.
PIK!
PIK!
PIK!

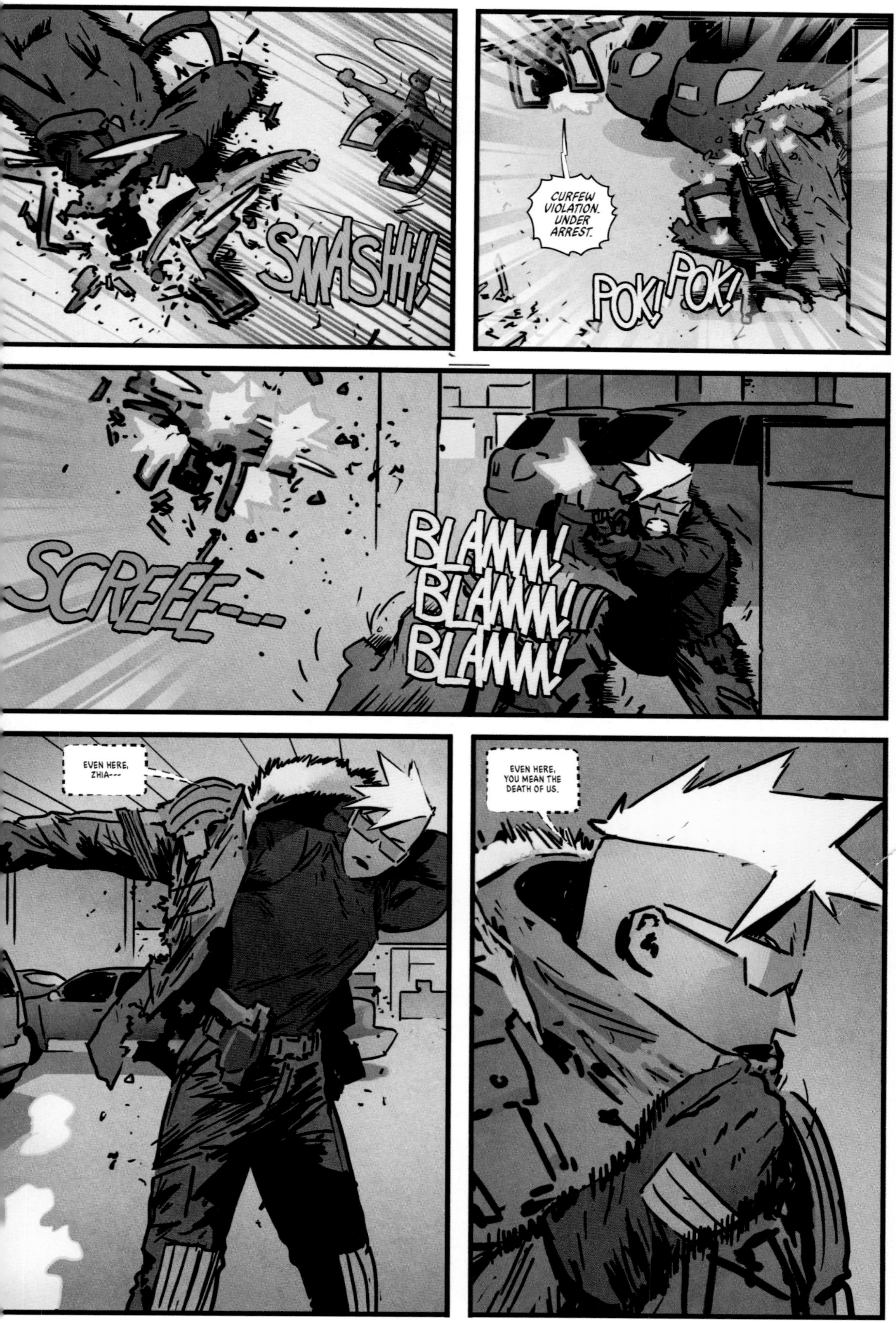
SWASHH!
CURFEW VIOLATION. UNDER ARREST.
POK! POK!
SCREEE---
BLAMM! BLAMM! BLAMM!
EVEN HERE, ZHIA---
EVEN HERE, YOU MEAN THE DEATH OF US.

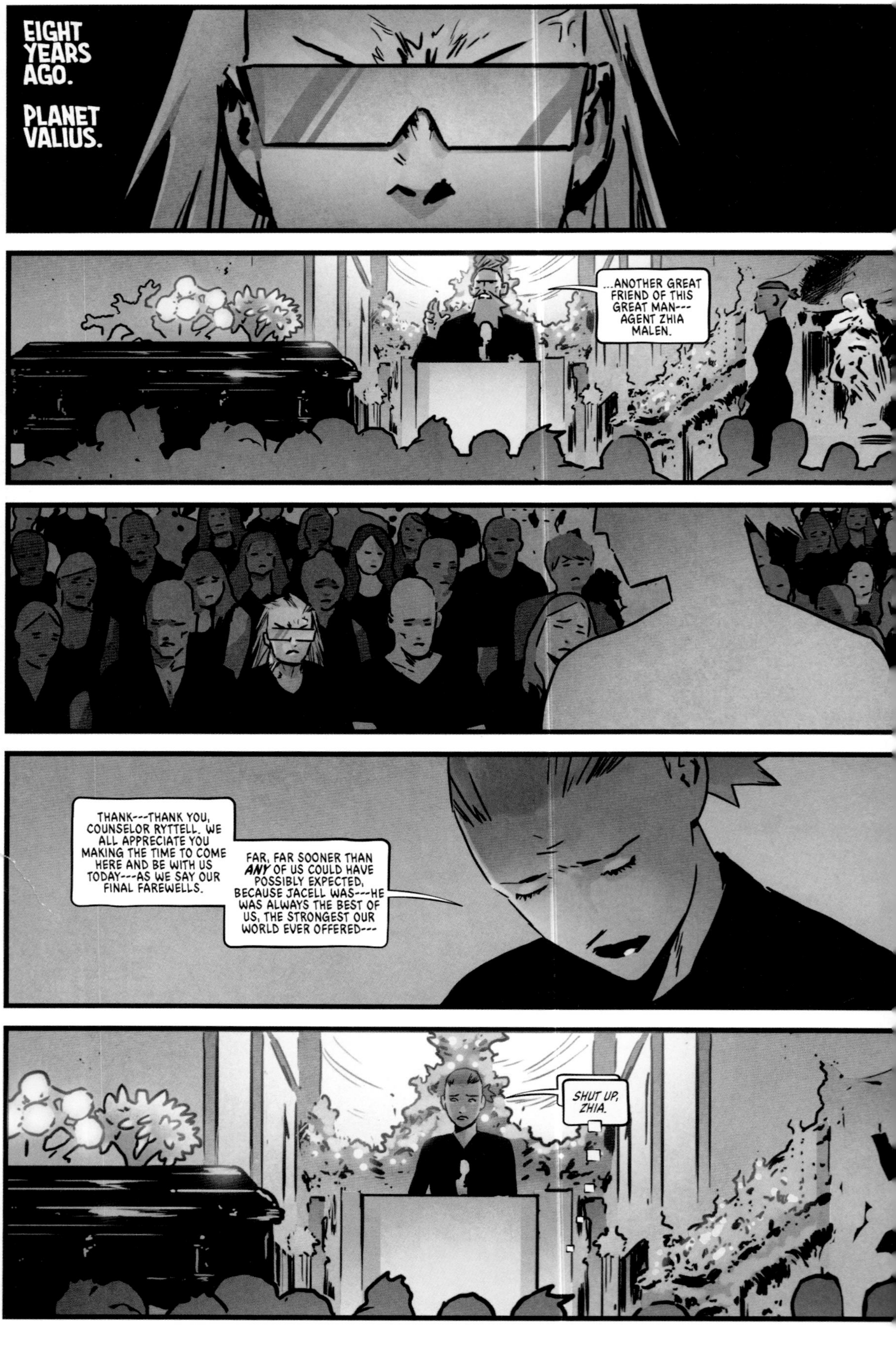
EIGHT YEARS AGO.
PLANET VALIUS.
...ANOTHER GREAT FRIEND OF THIS GREAT MAN---AGENT ZHIA MALEN.
THANK---THANK YOU, COUNSELOR RYTTELL. WE ALL APPRECIATE YOU MAKING THE TIME TO COME HERE AND BE WITH US TODAY---AS WE SAY OUR FINAL FAREWELLS.
FAR, FAR SOONER THAN ANY OF US COULD HAVE POSSIBLY EXPECTED, BECAUSE JACELL WAS---HE WAS ALWAYS THE BEST OF US, THE STRONGEST OUR WORLD EVER OFFERED---
SHUT UP, ZHIA.

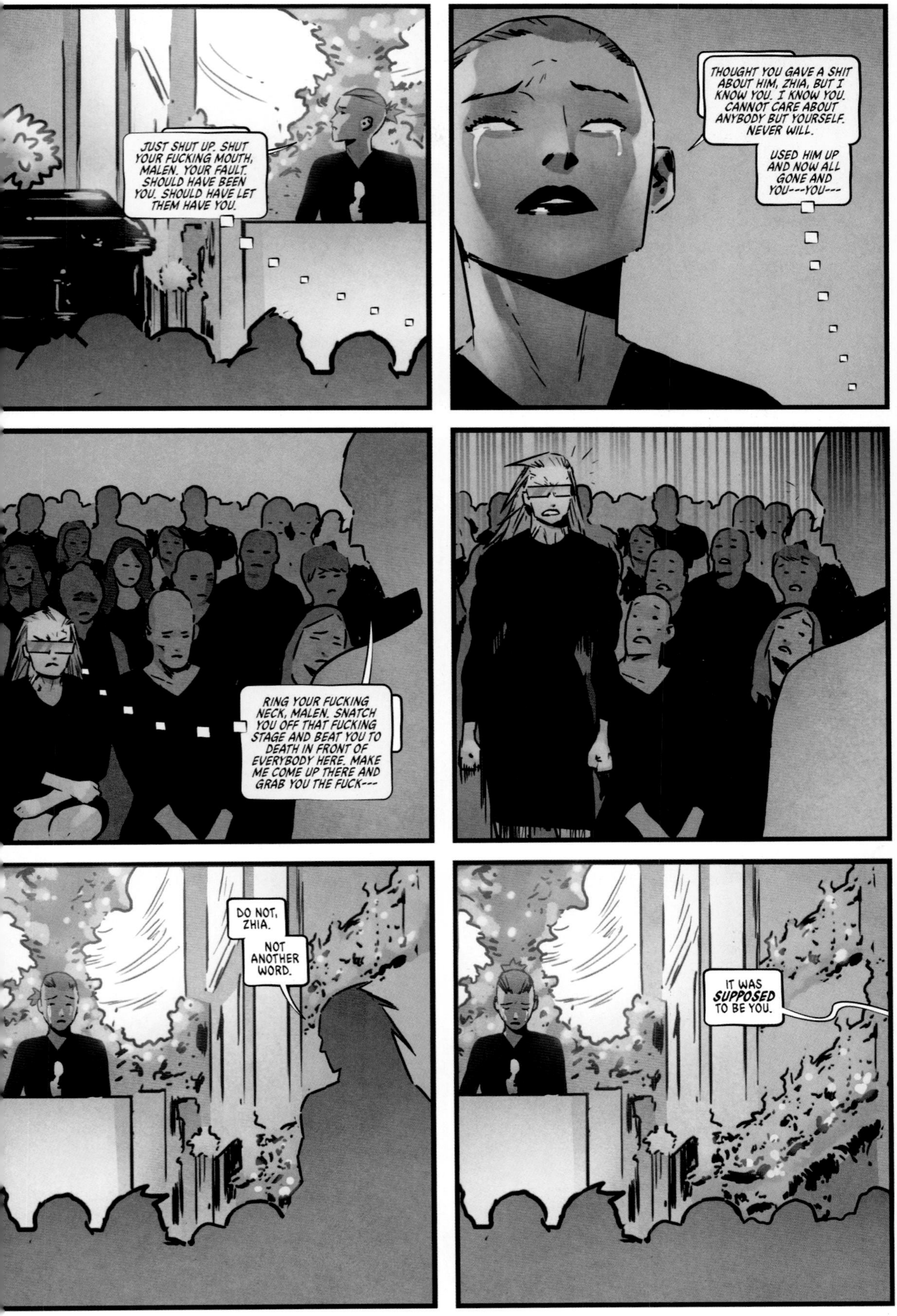
JUST SHUT UP. SHUT YOUR FUCKING MOUTH, MALEN. YOUR FAULT. SHOULD HAVE BEEN YOU. SHOULD HAVE LET THEM HAVE YOU.
THOUGHT YOU GAVE A SHIT ABOUT HIM, ZHIA, BUT I KNOW YOU. I KNOW YOU. CANNOT CARE ABOUT ANYBODY BUT YOURSELF. NEVER WILL.
USED HIM UP AND NOW ALL GONE AND YOU---YOU---
RING YOUR FUCKING NECK, MALEN. SNATCH YOU OFF THAT FUCKING STAGE AND BEAT YOU TO DEATH IN FRONT OF EVERYBODY HERE. MAKE ME COME UP THERE AND GRAB YOU THE FUCK---
DO NOT, ZHIA.
NOT ANOTHER WORD.
IT WAS SUPPOSED TO BE YOU.

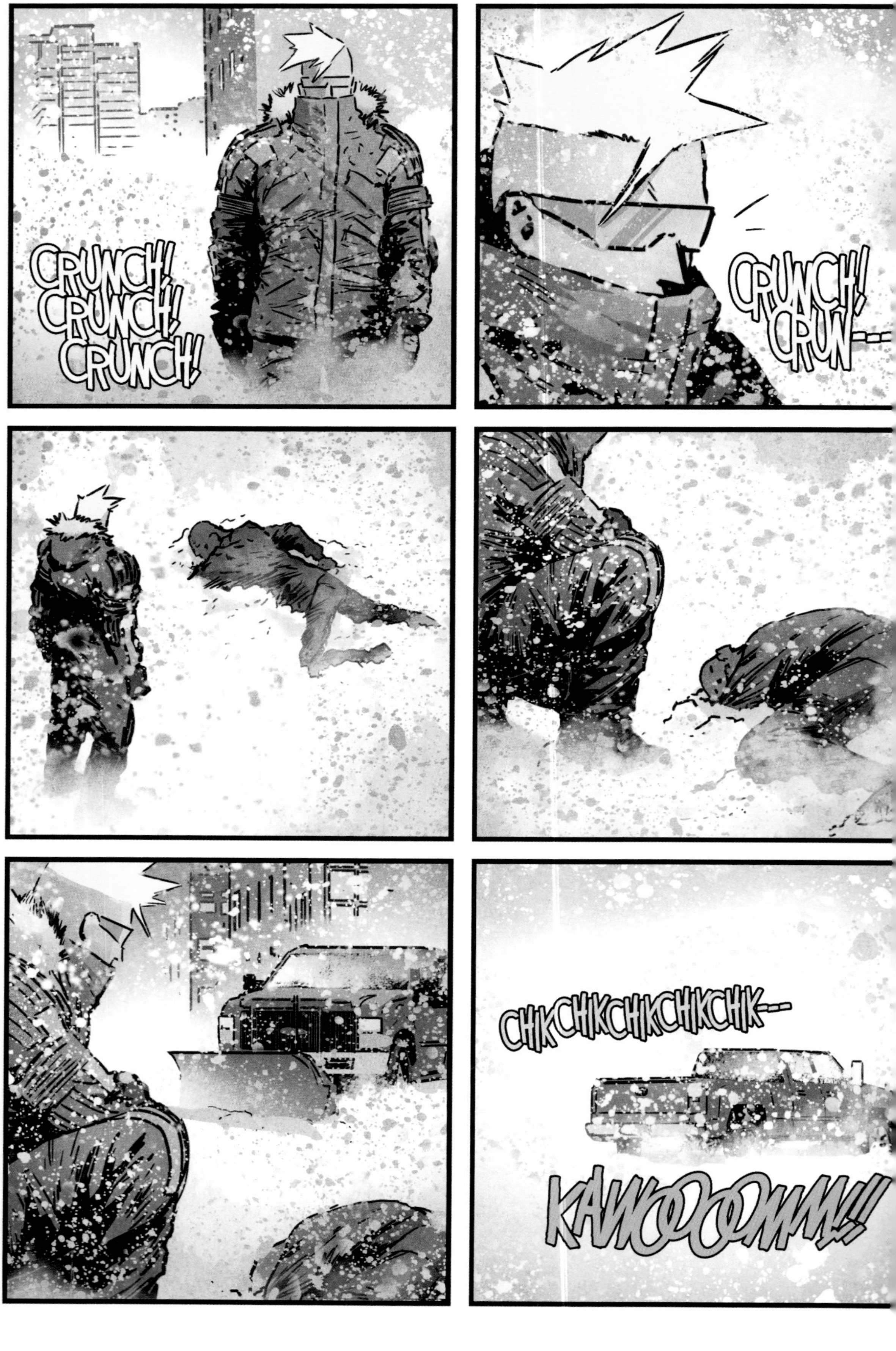
CRUNCH!
CRUNCH!
CRUNCH!
CRUNCH!
CRUN---
CHIKCHIKCHIKCHIKCHIK---
KAWOOOOMM!!

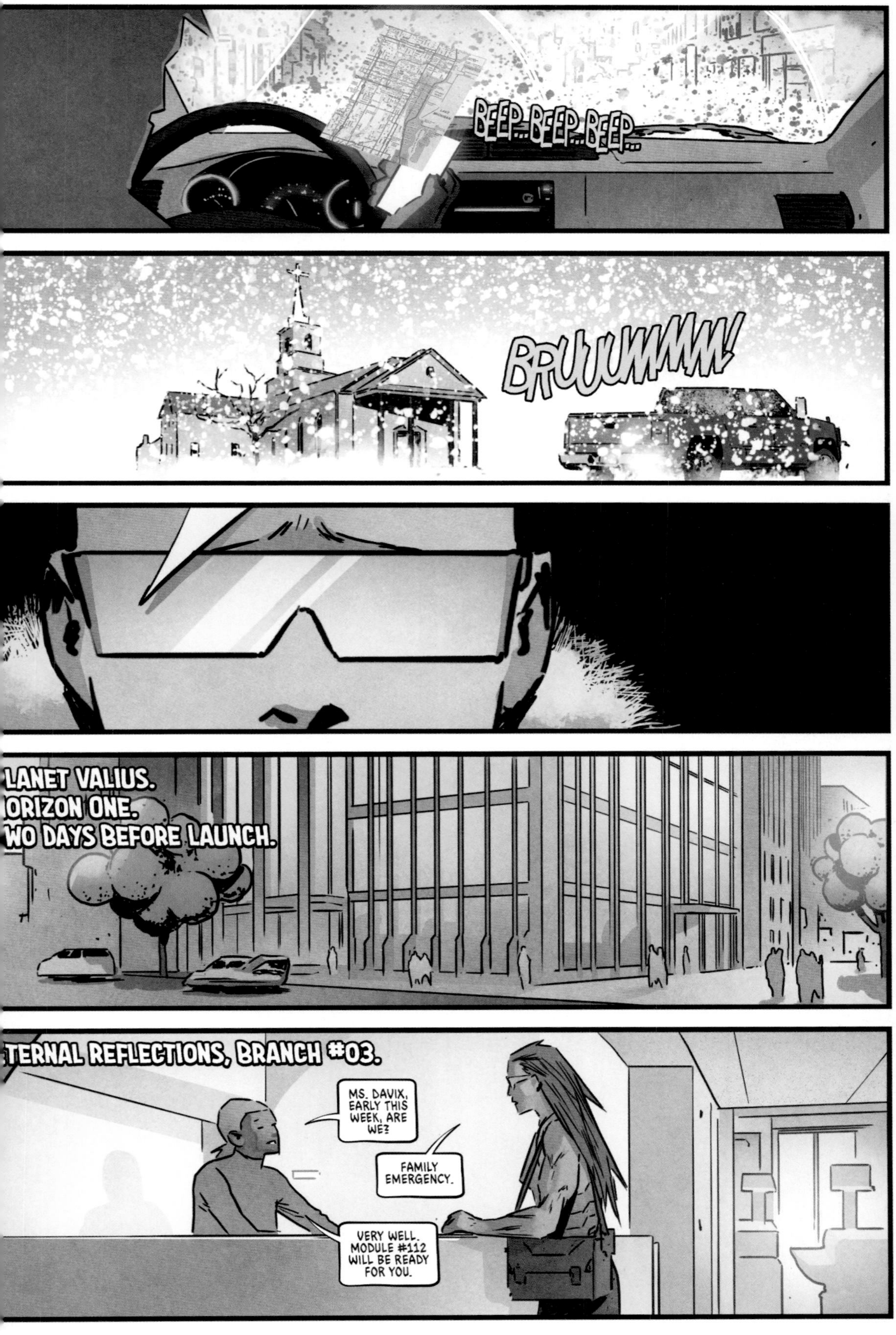
BEEP...BEEP...BEEP...
BRUUUMMM!
LANET VALIUS.
ORIZON ONE.
WO DAYS BEFORE LAUNCH.
TERNAL REFLECTIONS, BRANCH #03.
MS. DAVIX, EARLY THIS WEEK, ARE WE?
FAMILY EMERGENCY.
VERY WELL. MODULE #112 WILL BE READY FOR YOU.

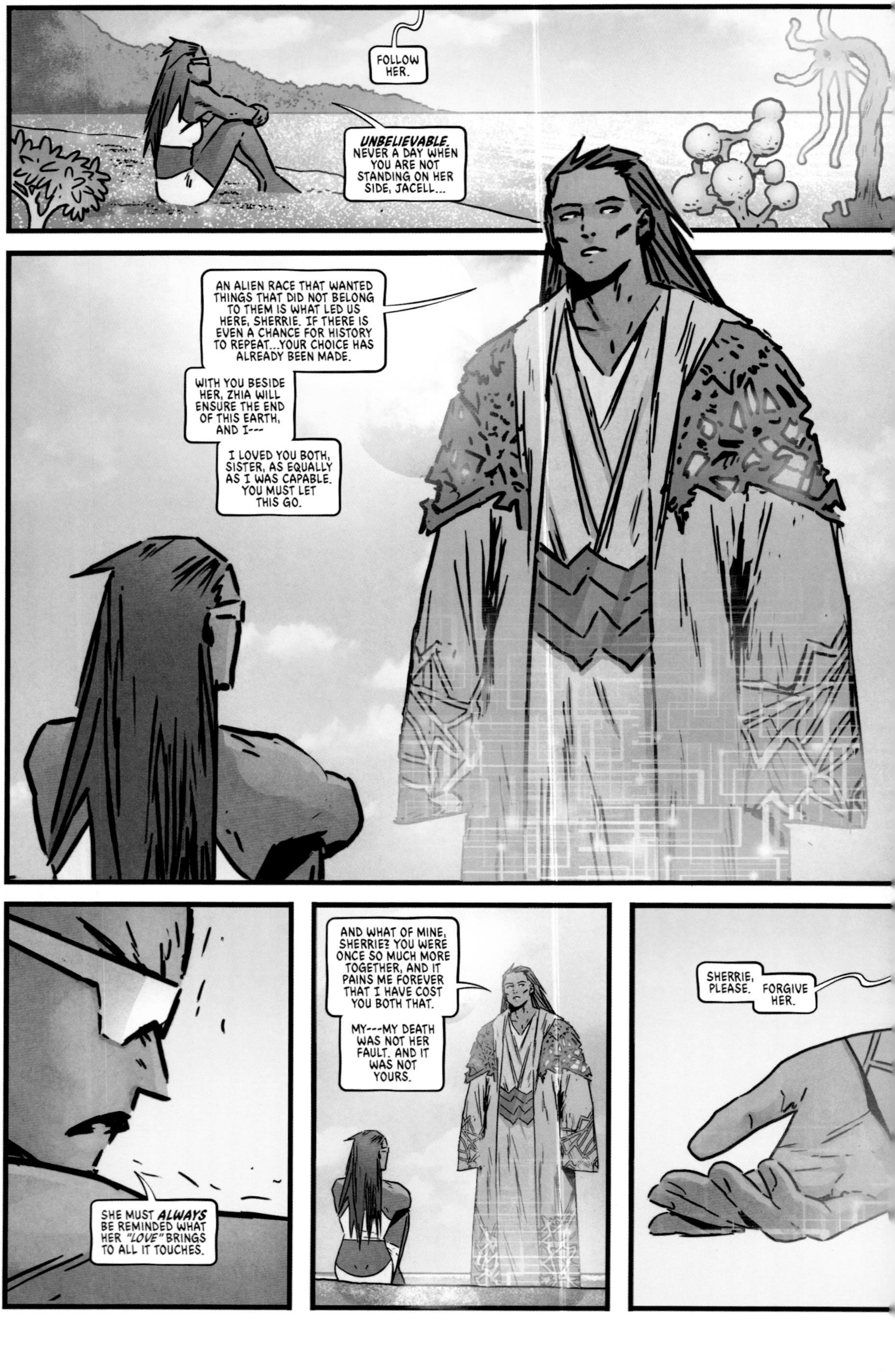

FOLLOW HER.
UNBELIEVABLE. NEVER A DAY WHEN YOU ARE NOT STANDING ON HER SIDE, JACELL...
AN ALIEN RACE THAT WANTED THINGS THAT DID NOT BELONG TO THEM IS WHAT LED US HERE, SHERRIE. IF THERE IS EVEN A CHANCE FOR HISTORY TO REPEAT...YOUR CHOICE HAS ALREADY BEEN MADE.
WITH YOU BESIDE HER, ZHIA WILL ENSURE THE END OF THIS EARTH, AND I---
I LOVED YOU BOTH, SISTER, AS EQUALLY AS I WAS CAPABLE. YOU MUST LET THIS GO.
SHE MUST ALWAYS BE REMINDED WHAT HER "LOVE" BRINGS TO ALL IT TOUCHES.
AND WHAT OF MINE, SHERRIE? YOU WERE ONCE SO MUCH MORE TOGETHER, AND IT PAINS ME FOREVER THAT I HAVE COST YOU BOTH THAT.
MY---MY DEATH WAS NOT HER FAULT. AND IT WAS NOT YOURS.
SHERRIE, PLEASE.
FORGIVE HER.

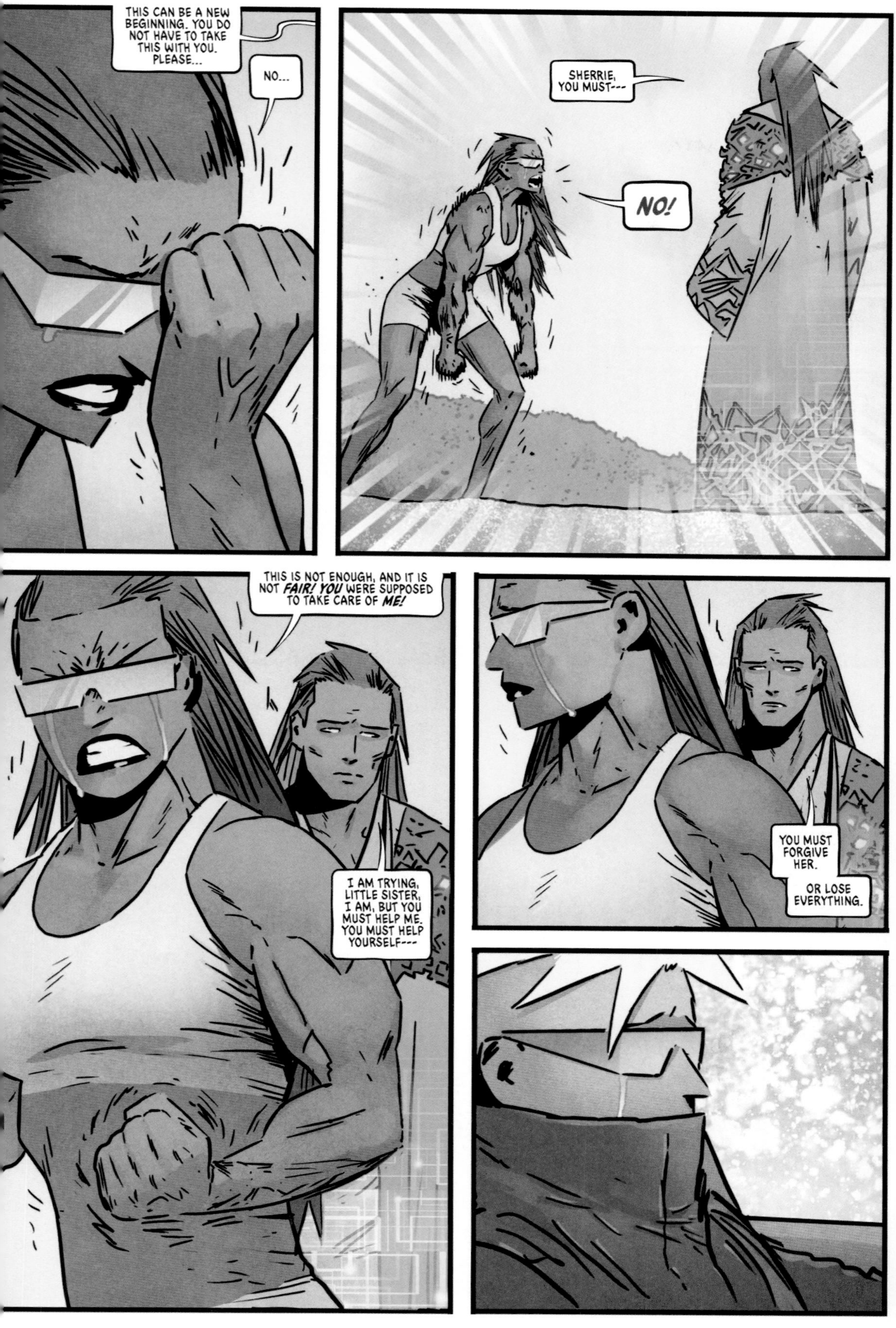
THIS CAN BE A NEW BEGINNING. YOU DO NOT HAVE TO TAKE THIS WITH YOU. PLEASE...
NO...
SHERRIE, YOU MUST---
NO!
THIS IS NOT ENOUGH, AND IT IS NOT FAIR! YOU WERE SUPPOSED TO TAKE CARE OF ME!
I AM TRYING, LITTLE SISTER, I AM, BUT YOU MUST HELP ME. YOU MUST HELP YOURSELF---
YOU MUST FORGIVE HER.
OR LOSE EVERYTHING.

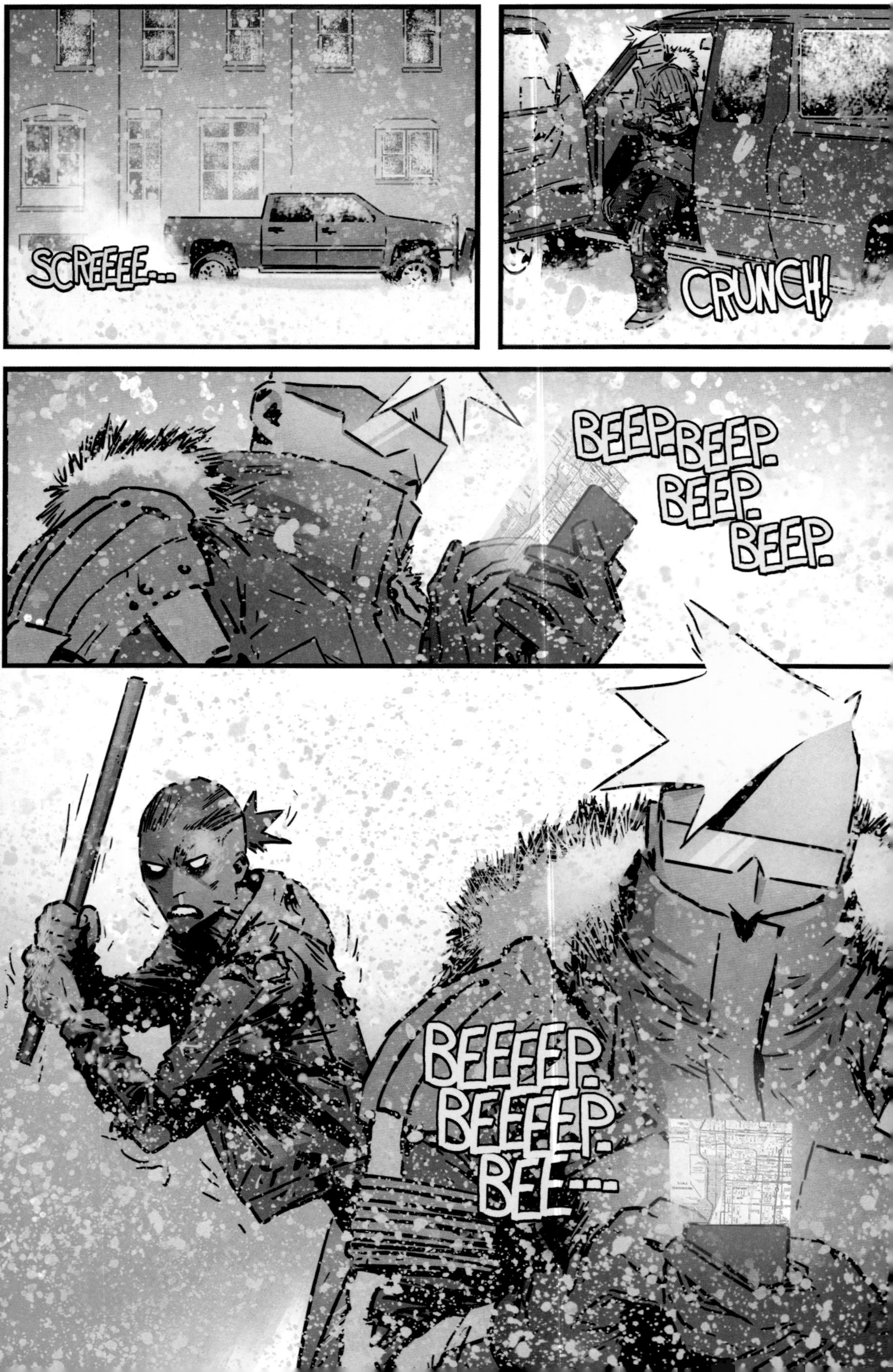
SCREEEE...
CRUNCH!
BEEP-BEEP.
BEEP.
BEEP.
BEEEEP.
BEEEEP.
BEE...

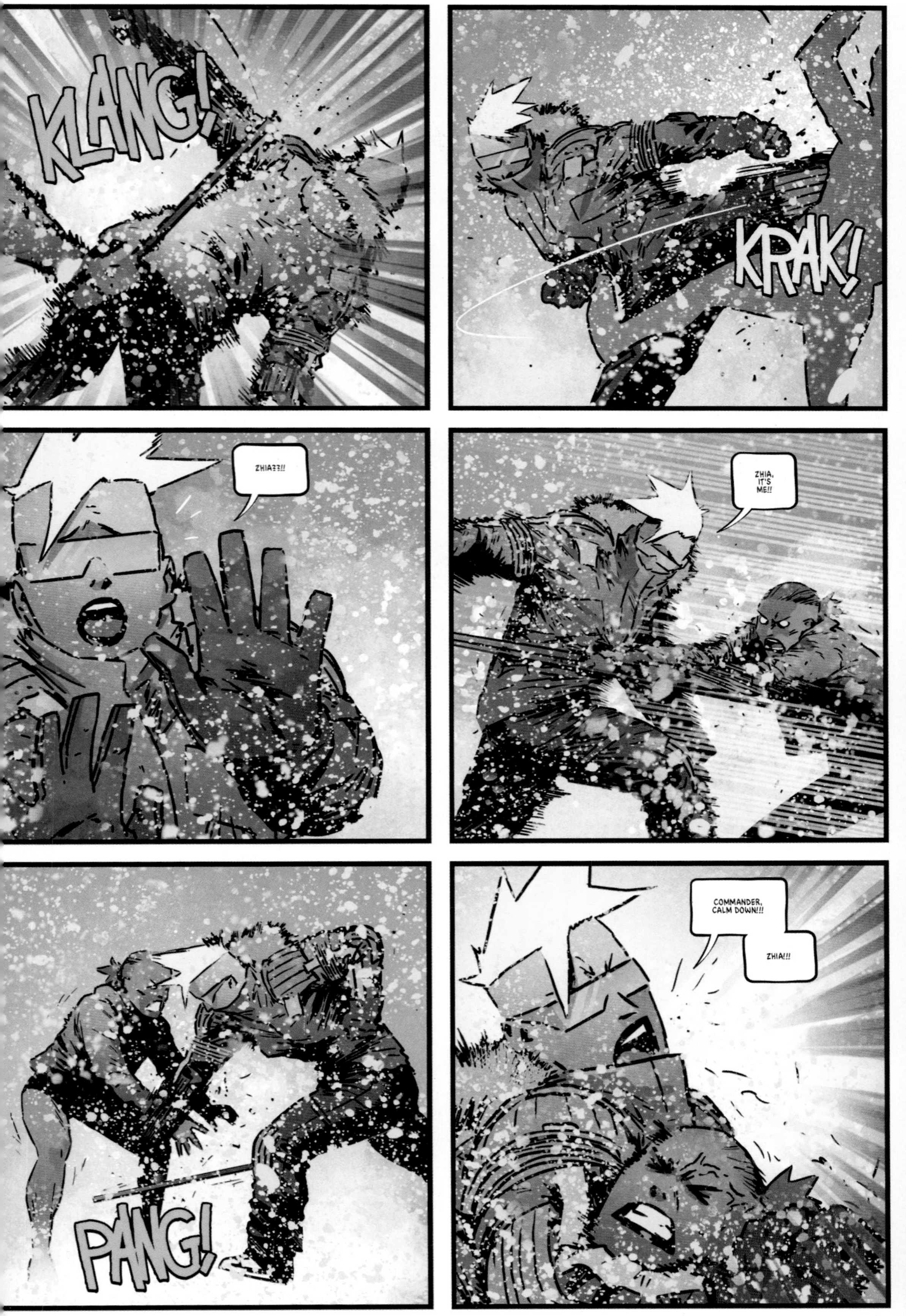
KLANG!
KRAK!
ZHIAƐƐ!!
ZHIA, IT'S ME!!
PANG!
COMMANDER, CALM DOWN!!!
ZHIA!!!

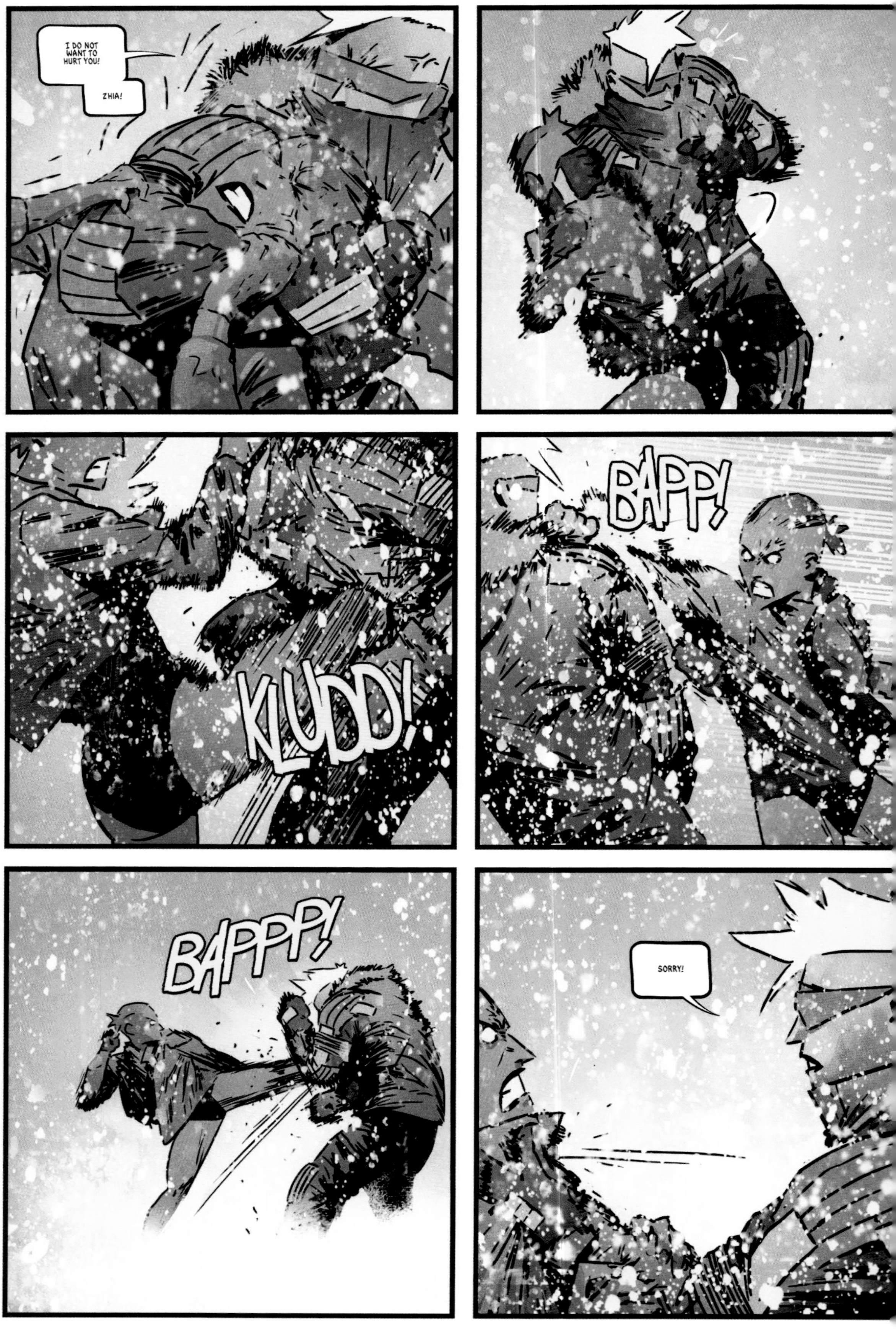
I DO NOT WANT TO HURT YOU!
ZHIA!
KLUDD!
BAPP!
BAPPP!
SORRY!

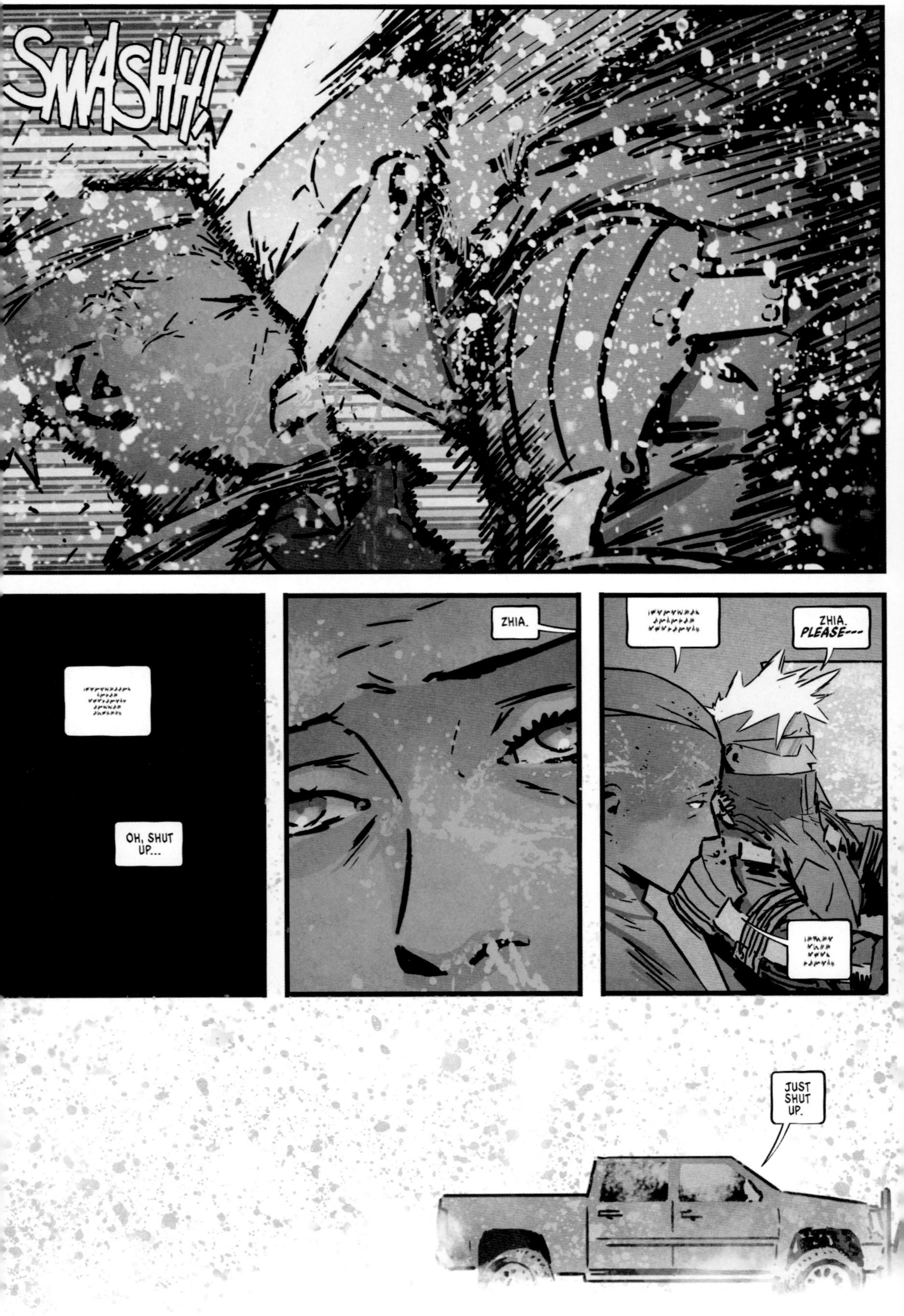
SWASHH!
OH, SHUT UP...
ZHIA.
ZHIA. PLEASE---
JUST SHUT UP.

53RD WARD.

UUUHHH... *PLEASE*... PLEASE DON'T KILL MY---

GUNNGHH!

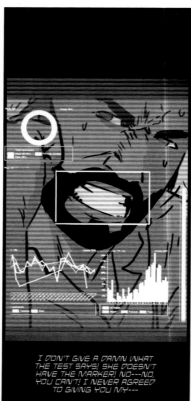

I DON'T GIVE A DAMN WHAT THE TEST SAYS! SHE DOESN'T HAVE THE MARKER! NO---NO, YOU CAN'T! I NEVER AGREED TO GIVING YOU MY---

NOT EVEN HERE FOR YOU. YOUR NEIGHBOR HAS SOMETHING I NEED, SO WE CAN *END* YOU.

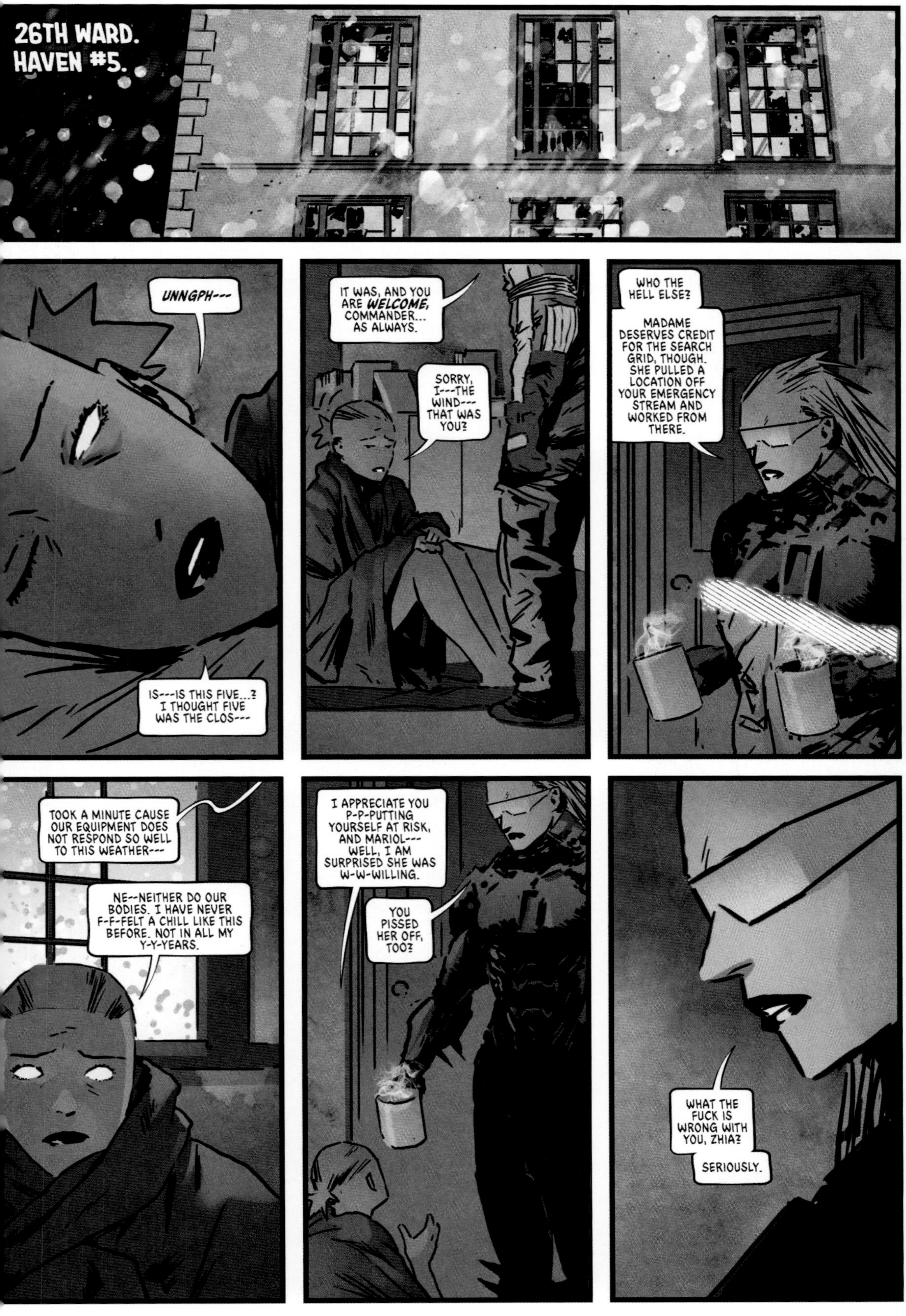
26TH WARD.
HAVEN #5.
UNNGPH---
IS---IS THIS FIVE...? I THOUGHT FIVE WAS THE CLOS---
IT WAS, AND YOU ARE WELCOME, COMMANDER... AS ALWAYS.
SORRY, I---THE WIND---THAT WAS YOU?
WHO THE HELL ELSE?
MADAME DESERVES CREDIT FOR THE SEARCH GRID, THOUGH. SHE PULLED A LOCATION OFF YOUR EMERGENCY STREAM AND WORKED FROM THERE.
TOOK A MINUTE CAUSE OUR EQUIPMENT DOES NOT RESPOND SO WELL TO THIS WEATHER---
NE--NEITHER DO OUR BODIES. I HAVE NEVER F-F-FELT A CHILL LIKE THIS BEFORE. NOT IN ALL MY Y-Y-YEARS.
I APPRECIATE YOU P-P-PUTTING YOURSELF AT RISK, AND MARIOL---WELL, I AM SURPRISED SHE WAS W-W-WILLING.
YOU PISSED HER OFF, TOO?
WHAT THE FUCK IS WRONG WITH YOU, ZHIA?
SERIOUSLY.

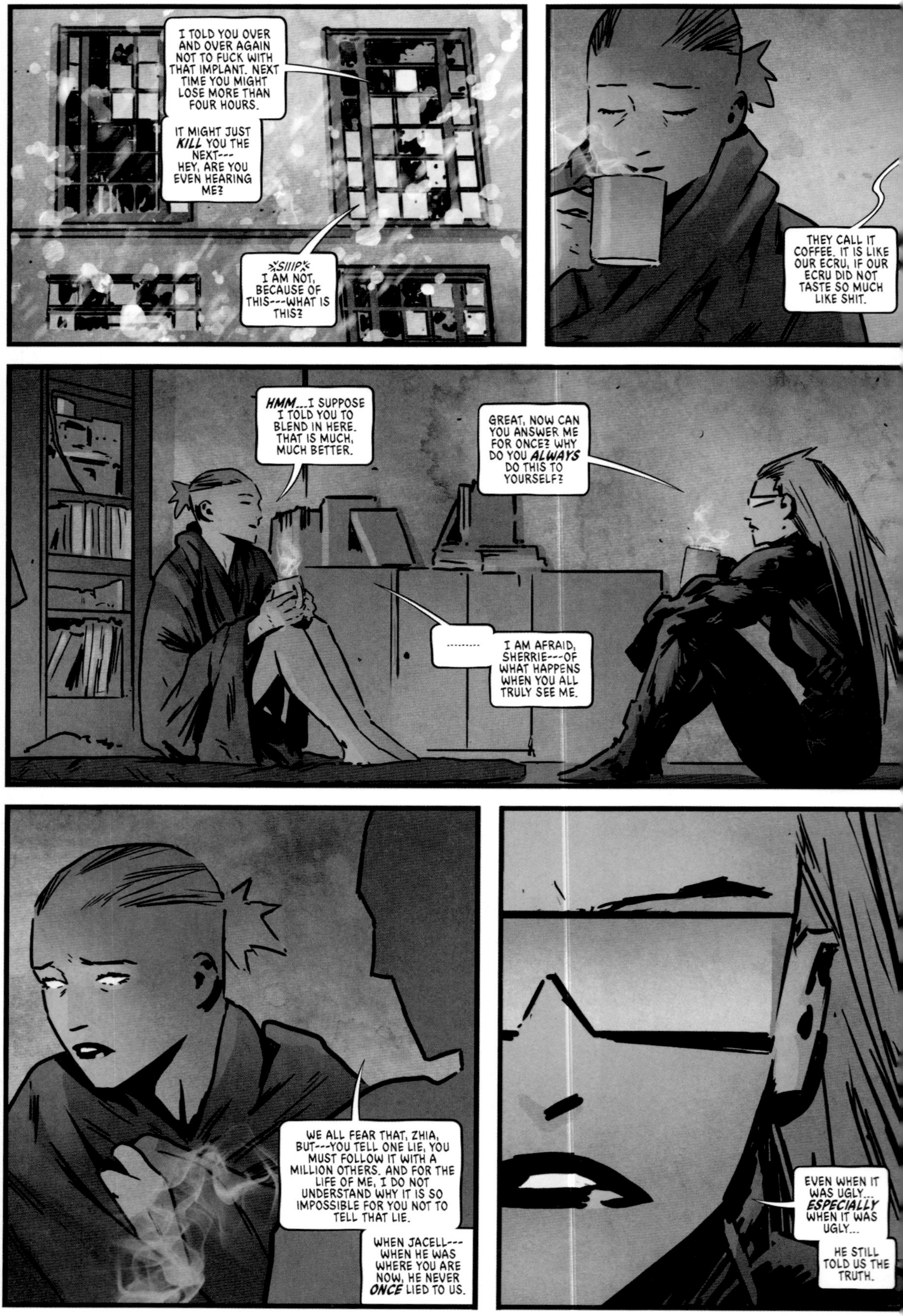
I TOLD YOU OVER AND OVER AGAIN NOT TO FUCK WITH THAT IMPLANT. NEXT TIME YOU MIGHT LOSE MORE THAN FOUR HOURS.
IT MIGHT JUST KILL YOU THE NEXT--- HEY, ARE YOU EVEN HEARING ME?
SIIIP
I AM NOT, BECAUSE OF THIS---WHAT IS THIS?
THEY CALL IT COFFEE. IT IS LIKE OUR ECRU, IF OUR ECRU DID NOT TASTE SO MUCH LIKE SHIT.
HMM...I SUPPOSE I TOLD YOU TO BLEND IN HERE. THAT IS MUCH, MUCH BETTER.
GREAT, NOW CAN YOU ANSWER ME FOR ONCE? WHY DO YOU ALWAYS DO THIS TO YOURSELF?
....
I AM AFRAID, SHERRIE---OF WHAT HAPPENS WHEN YOU ALL TRULY SEE ME.
WE ALL FEAR THAT, ZHIA, BUT---YOU TELL ONE LIE, YOU MUST FOLLOW IT WITH A MILLION OTHERS. AND FOR THE LIFE OF ME, I DO NOT UNDERSTAND WHY IT IS SO IMPOSSIBLE FOR YOU NOT TO TELL THAT LIE.
WHEN JACELL--- WHEN HE WAS WHERE YOU ARE NOW, HE NEVER ONCE LIED TO US.
EVEN WHEN IT WAS UGLY... ESPECIALLY WHEN IT WAS UGLY...
HE STILL TOLD US THE TRUTH.

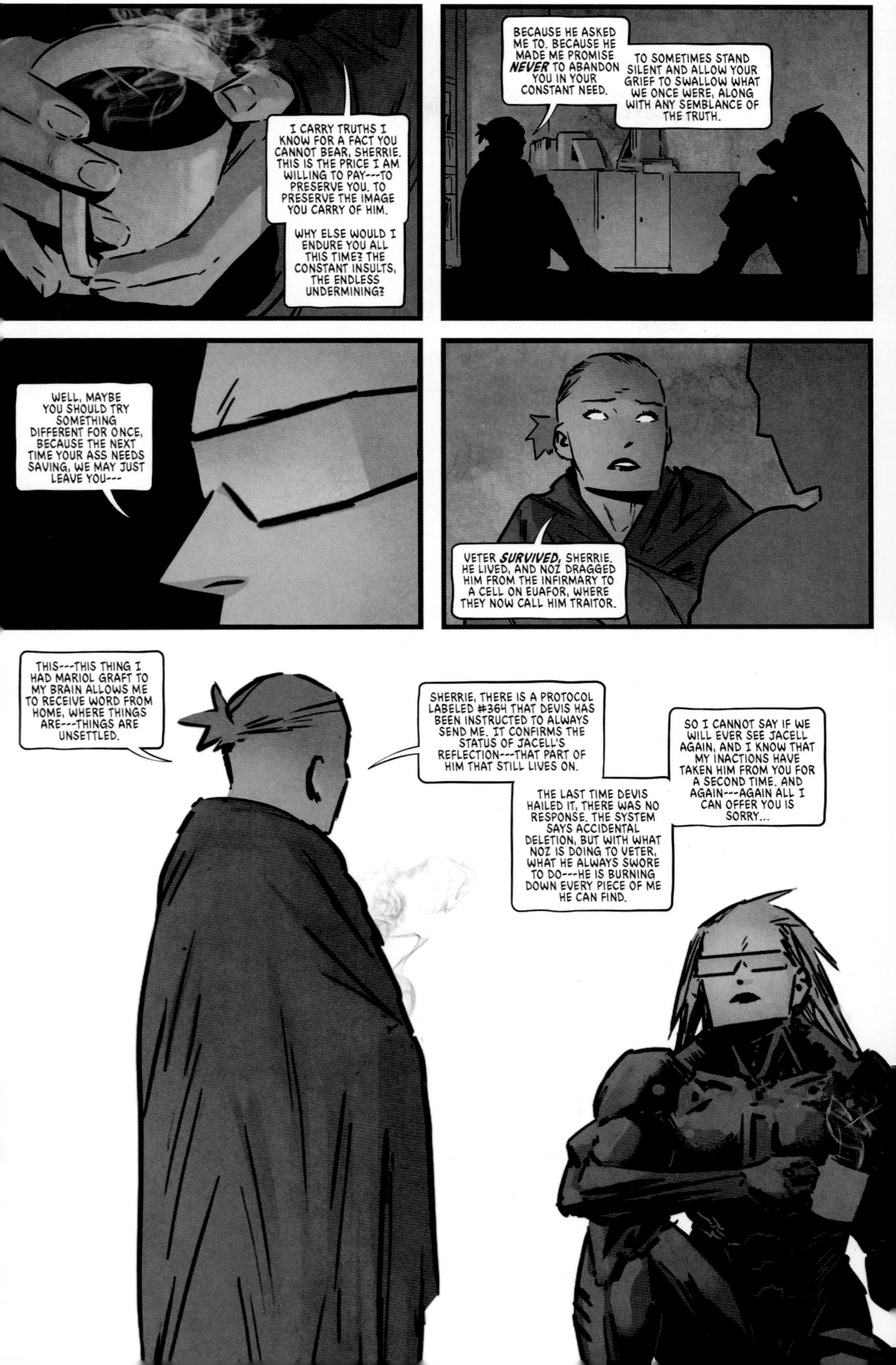
I CARRY TRUTHS I KNOW FOR A FACT YOU CANNOT BEAR, SHERRIE. THIS IS THE PRICE I AM WILLING TO PAY---TO PRESERVE YOU. TO PRESERVE THE IMAGE YOU CARRY OF HIM.
WHY ELSE WOULD I ENDURE YOU ALL THIS TIME? THE CONSTANT INSULTS, THE ENDLESS UNDERMINING?
BECAUSE HE ASKED ME TO. BECAUSE HE MADE ME PROMISE NEVER TO ABANDON YOU IN YOUR CONSTANT NEED.
TO SOMETIMES STAND SILENT AND ALLOW YOUR GRIEF TO SWALLOW WHAT WE ONCE WERE, ALONG WITH ANY SEMBLANCE OF THE TRUTH.
WELL, MAYBE YOU SHOULD TRY SOMETHING DIFFERENT FOR ONCE, BECAUSE THE NEXT TIME YOUR ASS NEEDS SAVING, WE MAY JUST LEAVE YOU---
VETER SURVIVED, SHERRIE. HE LIVED, AND NOZ DRAGGED HIM FROM THE INFIRMARY TO A CELL ON EUAFOR, WHERE THEY NOW CALL HIM TRAITOR.
THIS---THIS THING I HAD MARIOL GRAFT TO MY BRAIN ALLOWS ME TO RECEIVE WORD FROM HOME, WHERE THINGS ARE---THINGS ARE UNSETTLED.
SHERRIE, THERE IS A PROTOCOL LABELED #364 THAT DEVIS HAS BEEN INSTRUCTED TO ALWAYS SEND ME. IT CONFIRMS THE STATUS OF JACELL'S REFLECTION---THAT PART OF HIM THAT STILL LIVES ON.
THE LAST TIME DEVIS HAILED IT, THERE WAS NO RESPONSE. THE SYSTEM SAYS ACCIDENTAL DELETION, BUT WITH WHAT NOZ IS DOING TO VETER, WHAT HE ALWAYS SWORE TO DO---HE IS BURNING DOWN EVERY PIECE OF ME HE CAN FIND.
SO I CANNOT SAY IF WE WILL EVER SEE JACELL AGAIN, AND I KNOW THAT MY INACTIONS HAVE TAKEN HIM FROM YOU FOR A SECOND TIME. AND AGAIN---AGAIN ALL I CAN OFFER YOU IS SORRY...

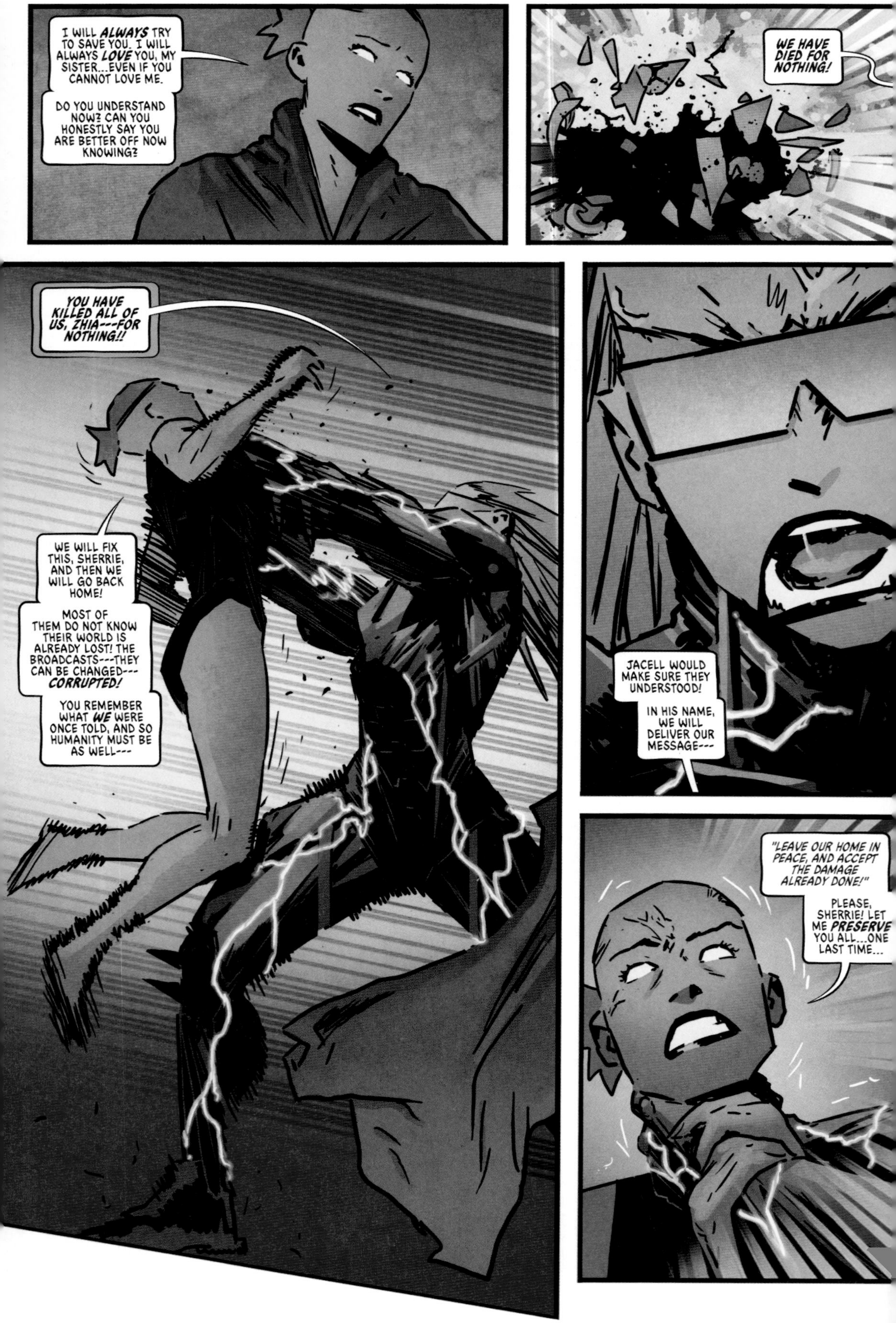
I WILL ALWAYS TRY TO SAVE YOU. I WILL ALWAYS LOVE YOU, MY SISTER...EVEN IF YOU CANNOT LOVE ME.
DO YOU UNDERSTAND NOW? CAN YOU HONESTLY SAY YOU ARE BETTER OFF NOW KNOWING?
WE HAVE DIED FOR NOTHING!
YOU HAVE KILLED ALL OF US, ZHIA---FOR NOTHING!!
WE WILL FIX THIS, SHERRIE, AND THEN WE WILL GO BACK HOME!
MOST OF THEM DO NOT KNOW THEIR WORLD IS ALREADY LOST! THE BROADCASTS---THEY CAN BE CHANGED---CORRUPTED!
YOU REMEMBER WHAT WE WERE ONCE TOLD, AND SO HUMANITY MUST BE AS WELL---
JACELL WOULD MAKE SURE THEY UNDERSTOOD!
IN HIS NAME, WE WILL DELIVER OUR MESSAGE---
"LEAVE OUR HOME IN PEACE, AND ACCEPT THE DAMAGE ALREADY DONE!"
PLEASE, SHERRIE! LET ME PRESERVE YOU ALL...ONE LAST TIME...

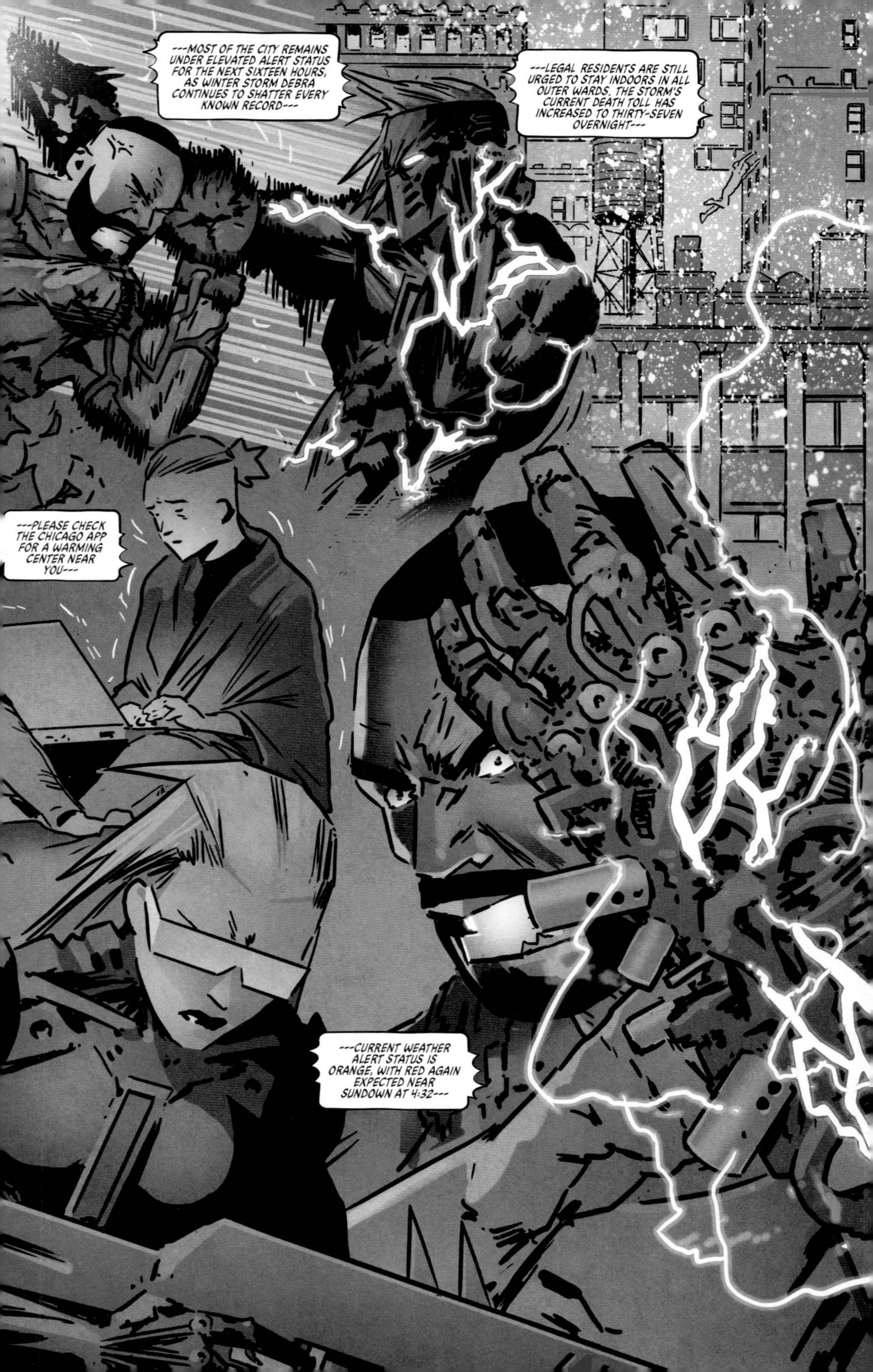
---MOST OF THE CITY REMAINS UNDER ELEVATED ALERT STATUS FOR THE NEXT SIXTEEN HOURS, AS WINTER STORM DEBRA CONTINUES TO SHATTER EVERY KNOWN RECORD---
---LEGAL RESIDENTS ARE STILL URGED TO STAY INDOORS IN ALL OUTER WARDS. THE STORM'S CURRENT DEATH TOLL HAS INCREASED TO THIRTY-SEVEN OVERNIGHT---
---PLEASE CHECK THE CHICAGO APP FOR A WARMING CENTER NEAR YOU---
---CURRENT WEATHER ALERT STATUS IS ORANGE, WITH RED AGAIN EXPECTED NEAR SUNDOWN AT 4:32---

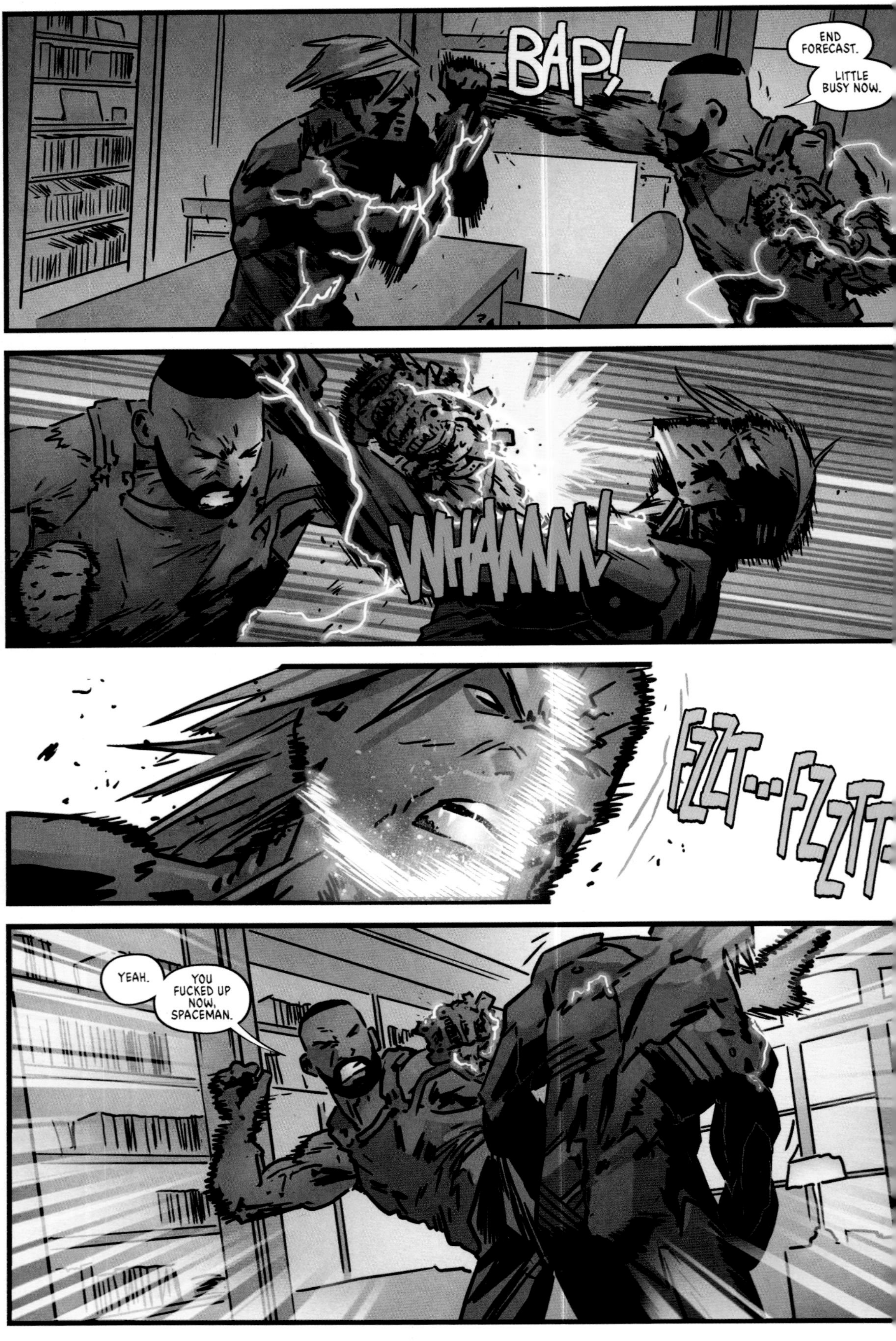
BAP!
END FORECAST.
LITTLE BUSY NOW.
WHAMM!
FZZT--FZZTT-
YEAH.
YOU FUCKED UP NOW, SPACEMAN.

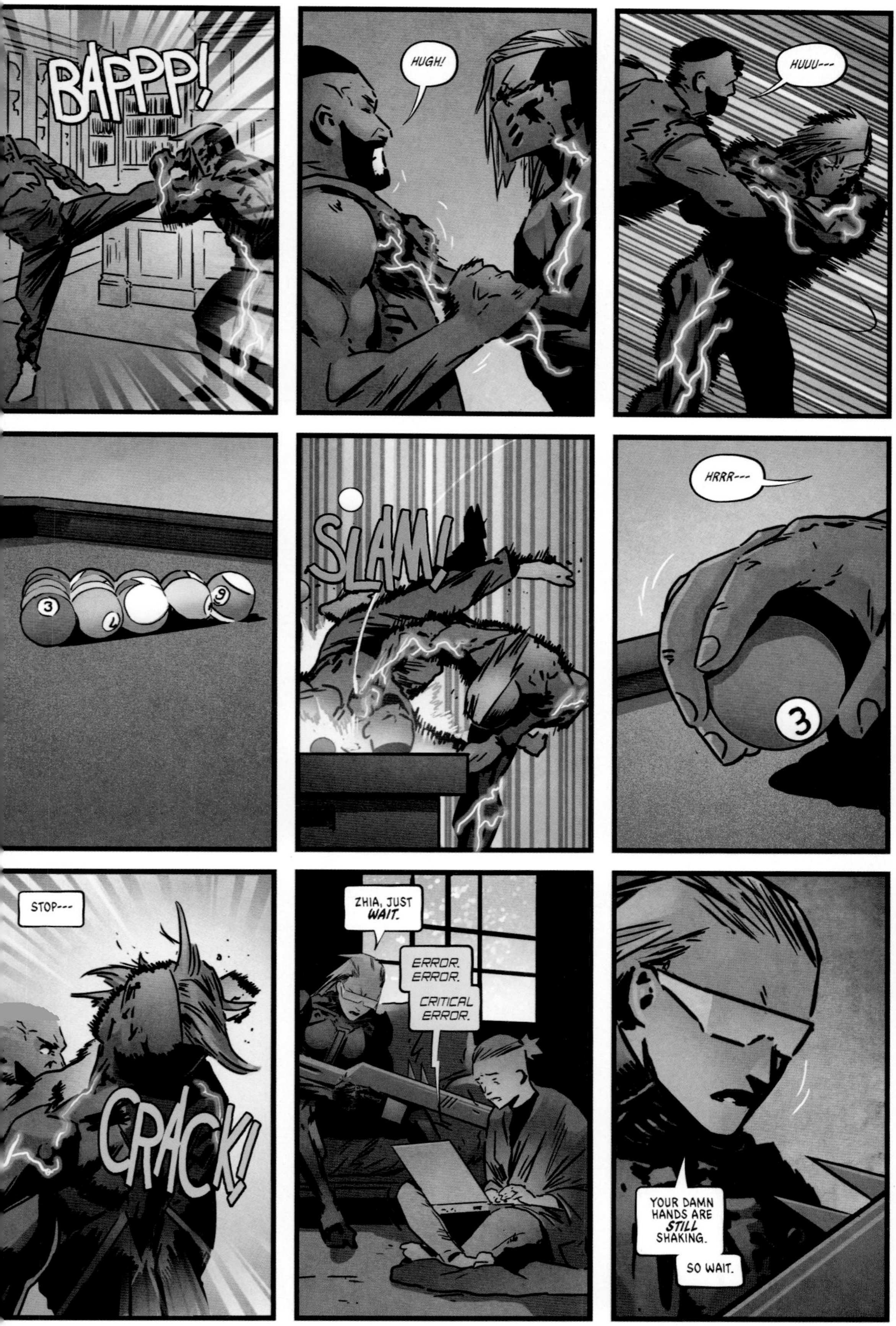
BAPPP!
HUGH!
HUUU---
SLAM!
HRRR---
STOP---
CRACK!
ZHIA, JUST WAIT.
ERROR. ERROR.
CRITICAL ERROR.
YOUR DAMN HANDS ARE STILL SHAKING.
SO WAIT.

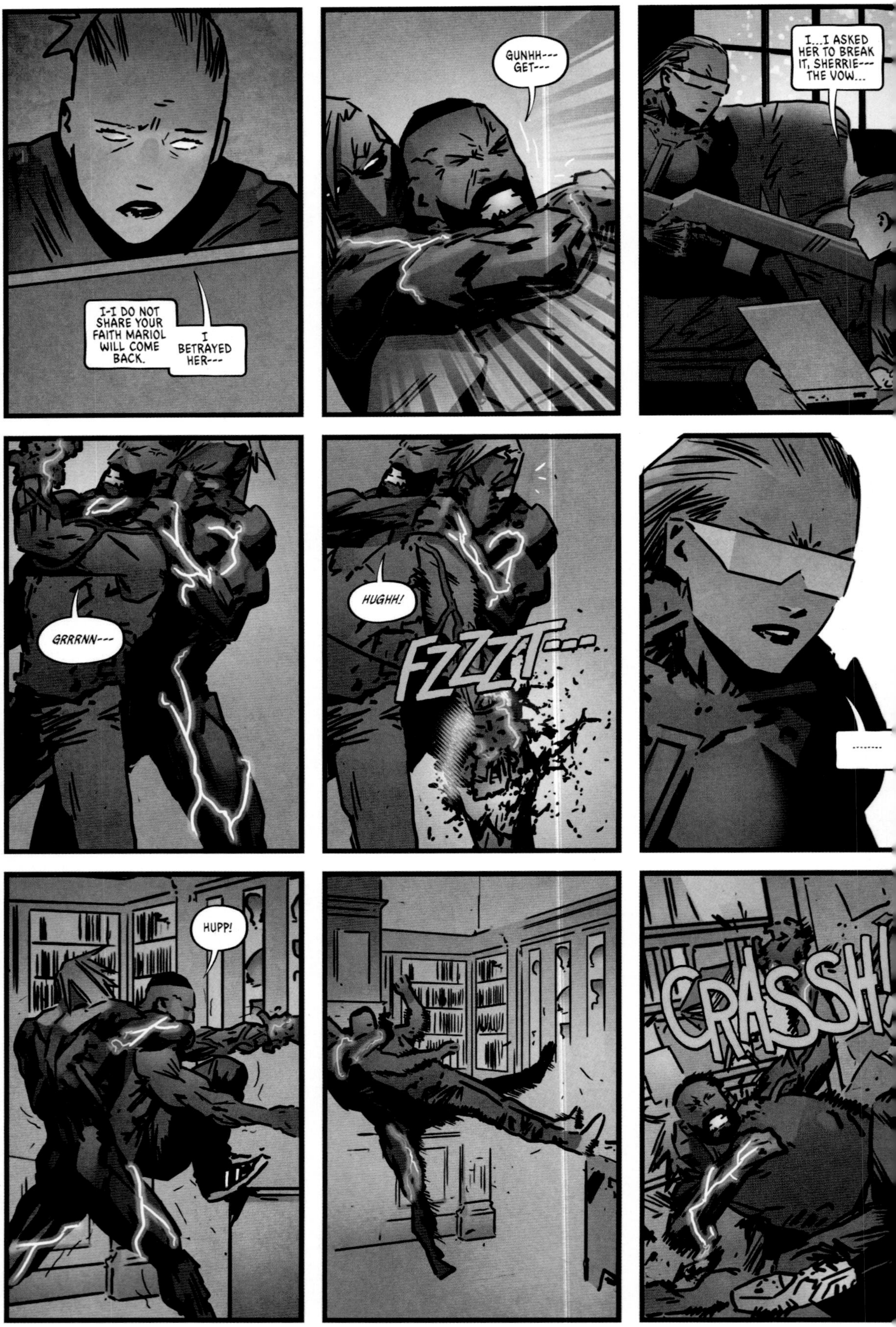
I-I DO NOT SHARE YOUR FAITH MARIOL WILL COME BACK.
I BETRAYED HER---
GUNHH--- GET---
I...I ASKED HER TO BREAK IT, SHERRIE--- THE VOW...
GRRRNN---
HUGHH!
FZZZT---

HUPP!
CRASSH!

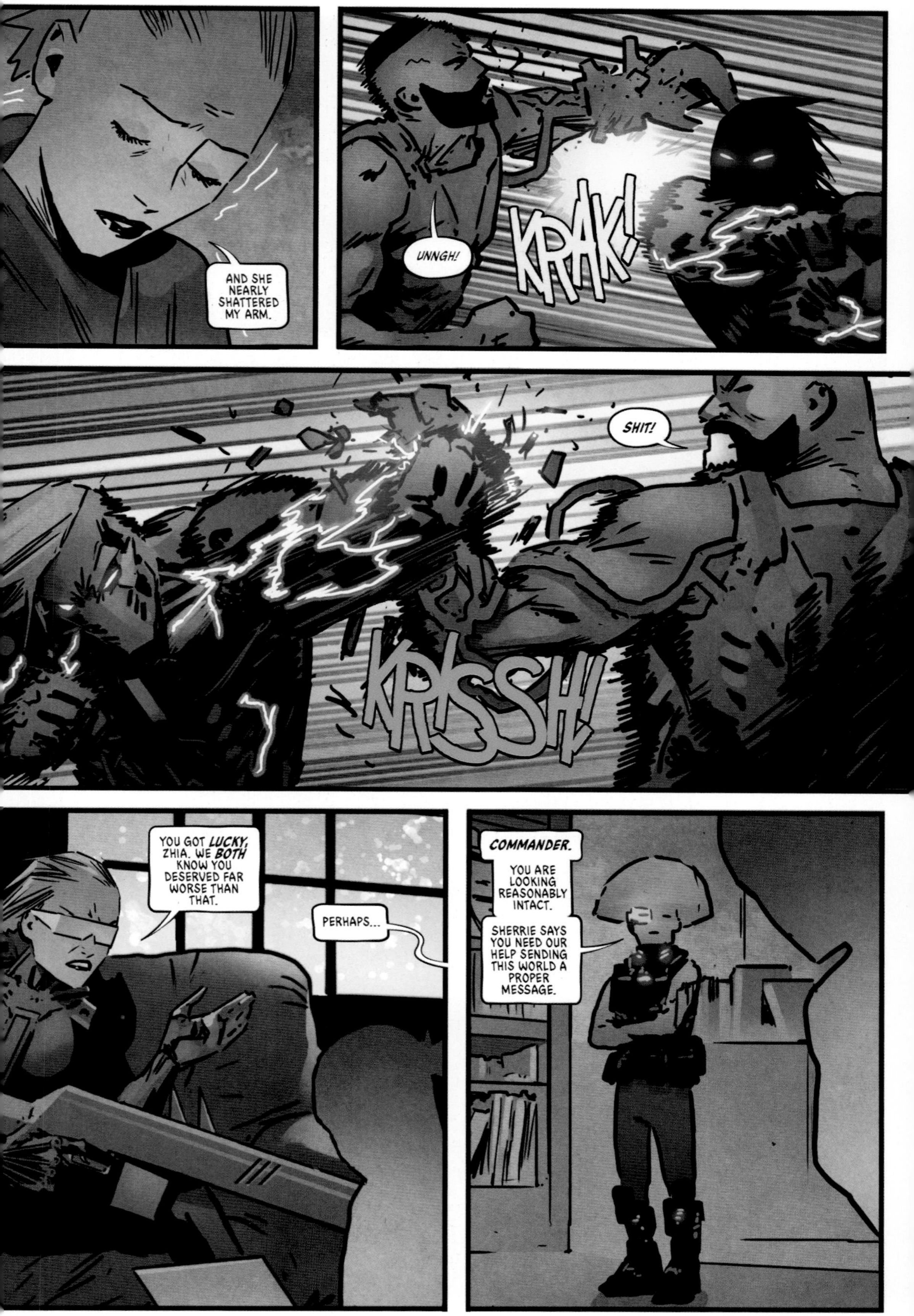
AND SHE NEARLY SHATTERED MY ARM.
UNNGH!
KRAK!
SHIT!
KRISSH!
YOU GOT LUCKY, ZHIA. WE BOTH KNOW YOU DESERVED FAR WORSE THAN THAT.
PERHAPS...
COMMANDER.
YOU ARE LOOKING REASONABLY INTACT.
SHERRIE SAYS YOU NEED OUR HELP SENDING THIS WORLD A PROPER MESSAGE.

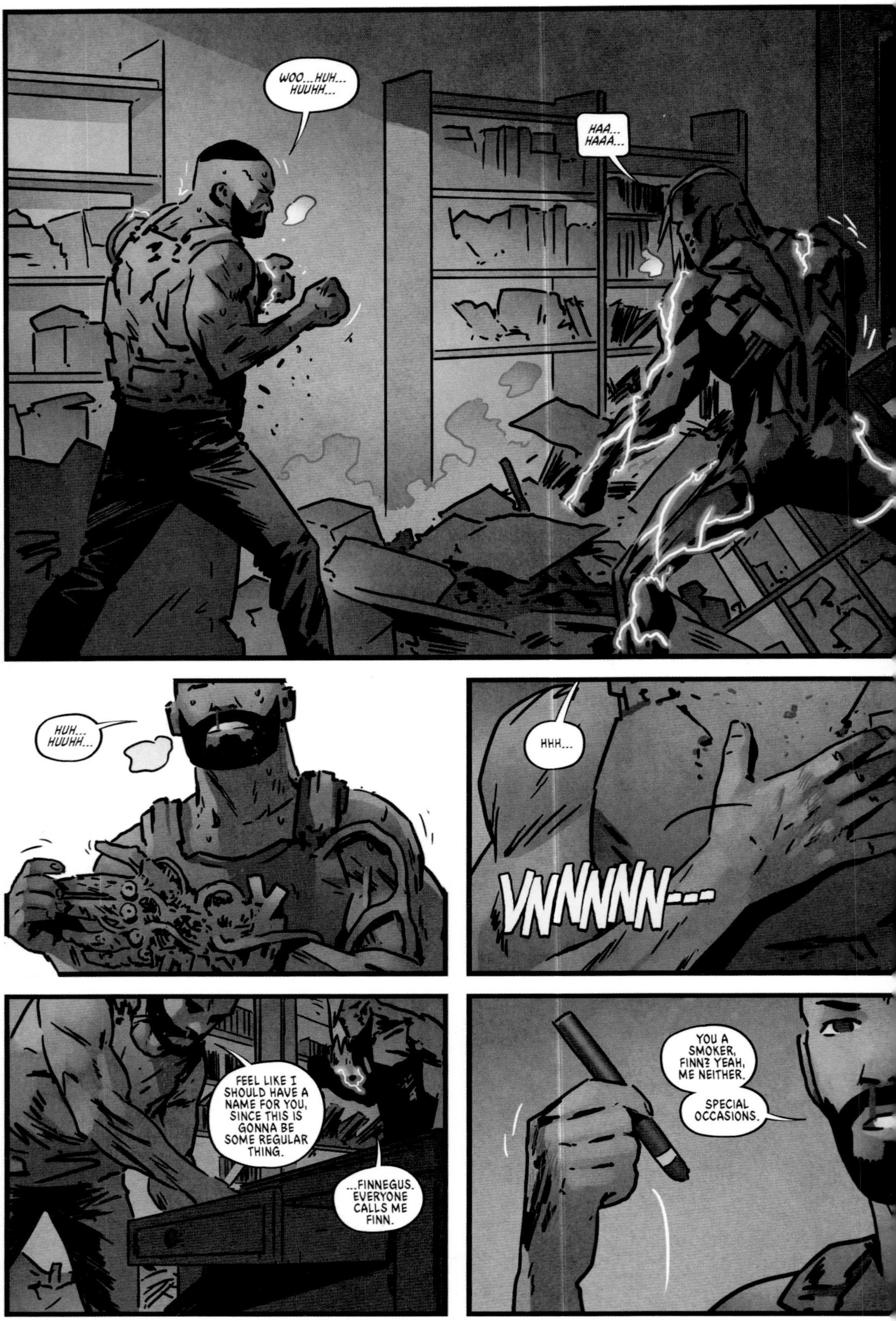
WOO...HUH... HUUHH...
HAA... HAAA...
HUH... HUUHH...
HHH...
VNNNNN---
FEEL LIKE I SHOULD HAVE A NAME FOR YOU, SINCE THIS IS GONNA BE SOME REGULAR THING.
...FINNEGUS. EVERYONE CALLS ME FINN.
YOU A SMOKER, FINN? YEAH, ME NEITHER.
SPECIAL OCCASIONS.

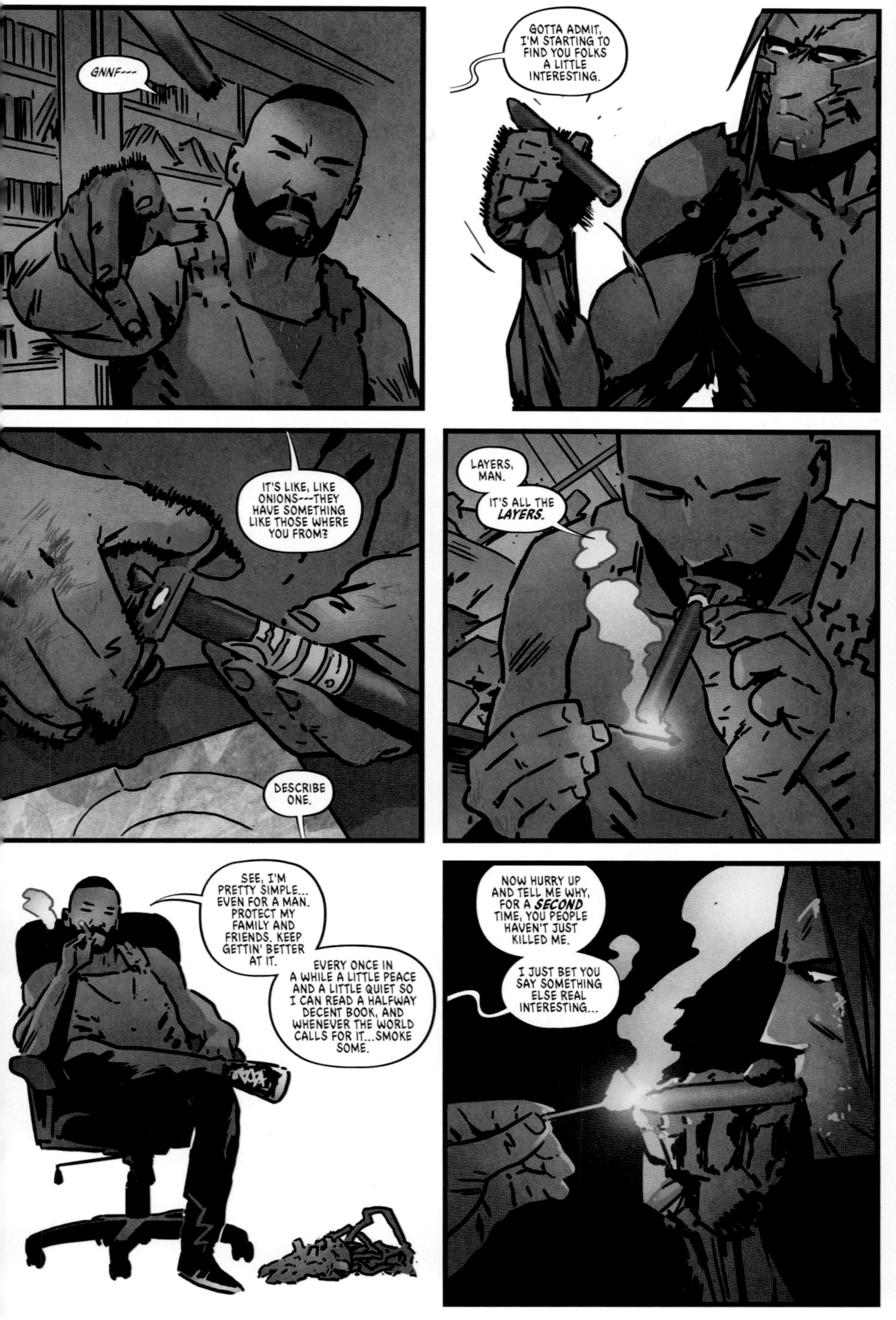
GNNF---
GOTTA ADMIT, I'M STARTING TO FIND YOU FOLKS A LITTLE INTERESTING.
IT'S LIKE, LIKE ONIONS---THEY HAVE SOMETHING LIKE THOSE WHERE YOU FROM?
DESCRIBE ONE.
LAYERS, MAN.
IT'S ALL THE LAYERS.
SEE, I'M PRETTY SIMPLE... EVEN FOR A MAN. PROTECT MY FAMILY AND FRIENDS. KEEP GETTIN' BETTER AT IT.
EVERY ONCE IN A WHILE A LITTLE PEACE AND A LITTLE QUIET SO I CAN READ A HALFWAY DECENT BOOK, AND WHENEVER THE WORLD CALLS FOR IT...SMOKE SOME.
NOW HURRY UP AND TELL ME WHY, FOR A SECOND TIME, YOU PEOPLE HAVEN'T JUST KILLED ME.
I JUST BET YOU SAY SOMETHING ELSE REAL INTERESTING...

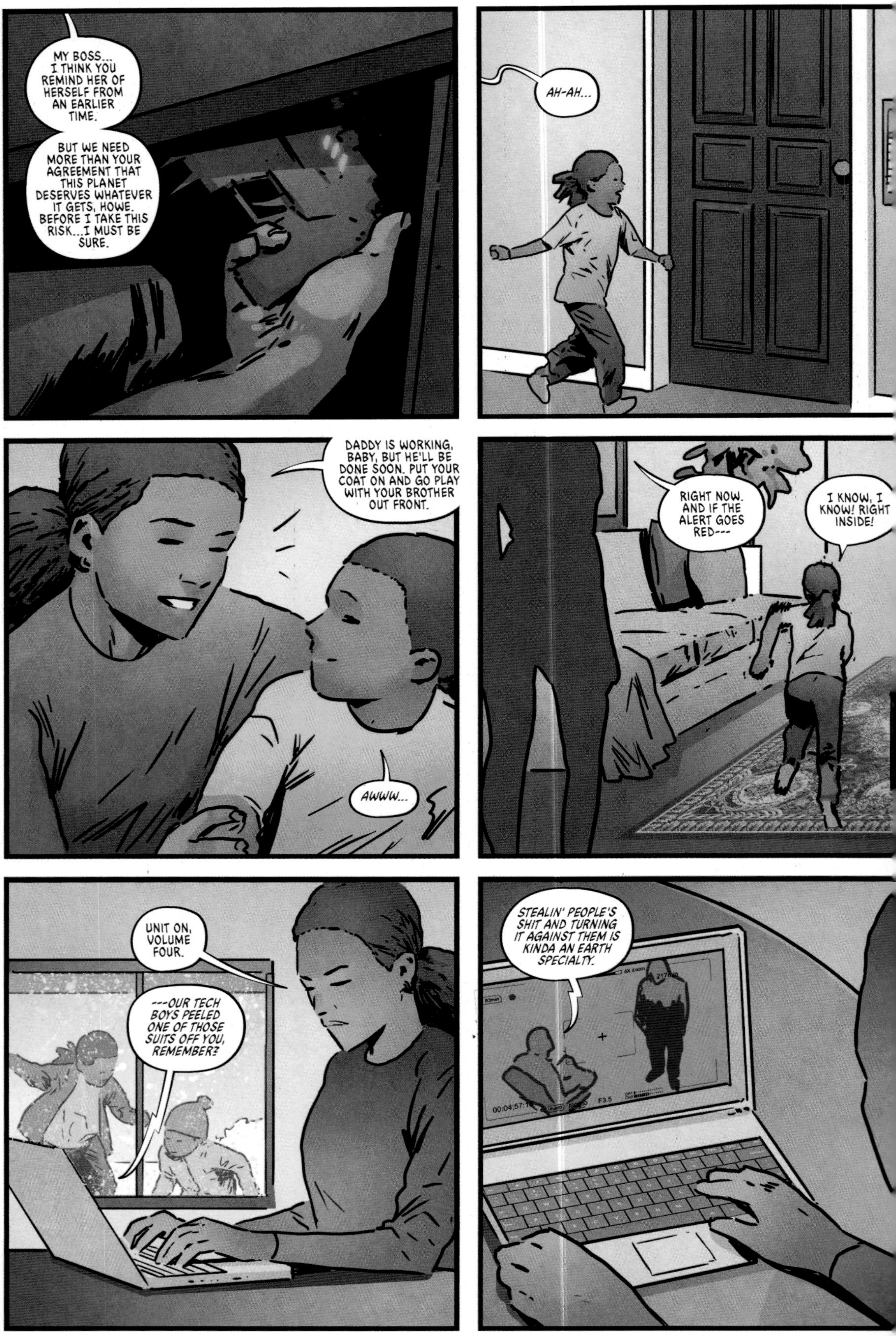
MY BOSS... I THINK YOU REMIND HER OF HERSELF FROM AN EARLIER TIME.
BUT WE NEED MORE THAN YOUR AGREEMENT THAT THIS PLANET DESERVES WHATEVER IT GETS, HOWE. BEFORE I TAKE THIS RISK...I MUST BE SURE.
AH-AH...
DADDY IS WORKING, BABY, BUT HE'LL BE DONE SOON. PUT YOUR COAT ON AND GO PLAY WITH YOUR BROTHER OUT FRONT.
AWWW...
RIGHT NOW. AND IF THE ALERT GOES RED---
I KNOW, I KNOW! RIGHT INSIDE!
UNIT ON, VOLUME FOUR.
---OUR TECH BOYS PEELED ONE OF THOSE SUITS OFF YOU, REMEMBER?
STEALIN' PEOPLE'S SHIT AND TURNING IT AGAINST THEM IS KINDA AN EARTH SPECIALTY.

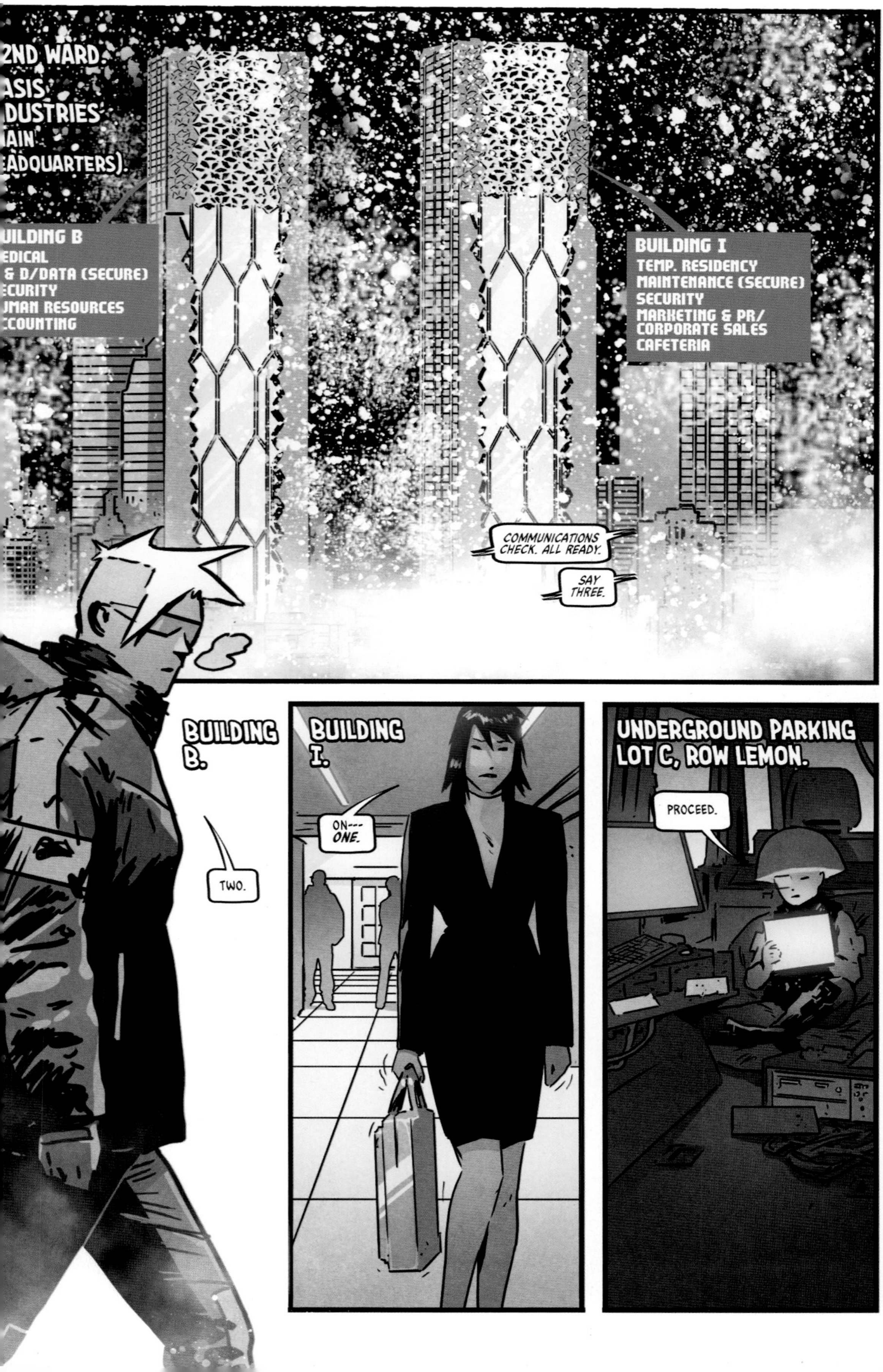

2ND WARD
ASIS
DUSTRIES
AIN
EADQUARTERS).
UILDING B
EDICAL
& D/DATA (SECURE)
ECURITY
UMAN RESOURCES
CCOUNTING
BUILDING I
TEMP. RESIDENCY
MAINTENANCE (SECURE)
SECURITY
MARKETING & PR/
CORPORATE SALES
CAFETERIA
COMMUNICATIONS CHECK. ALL READY.
SAY THREE.
BUILDING B.
TWO.
BUILDING I.
ON--- ONE.
UNDERGROUND PARKING LOT C, ROW LEMON.
PROCEED.

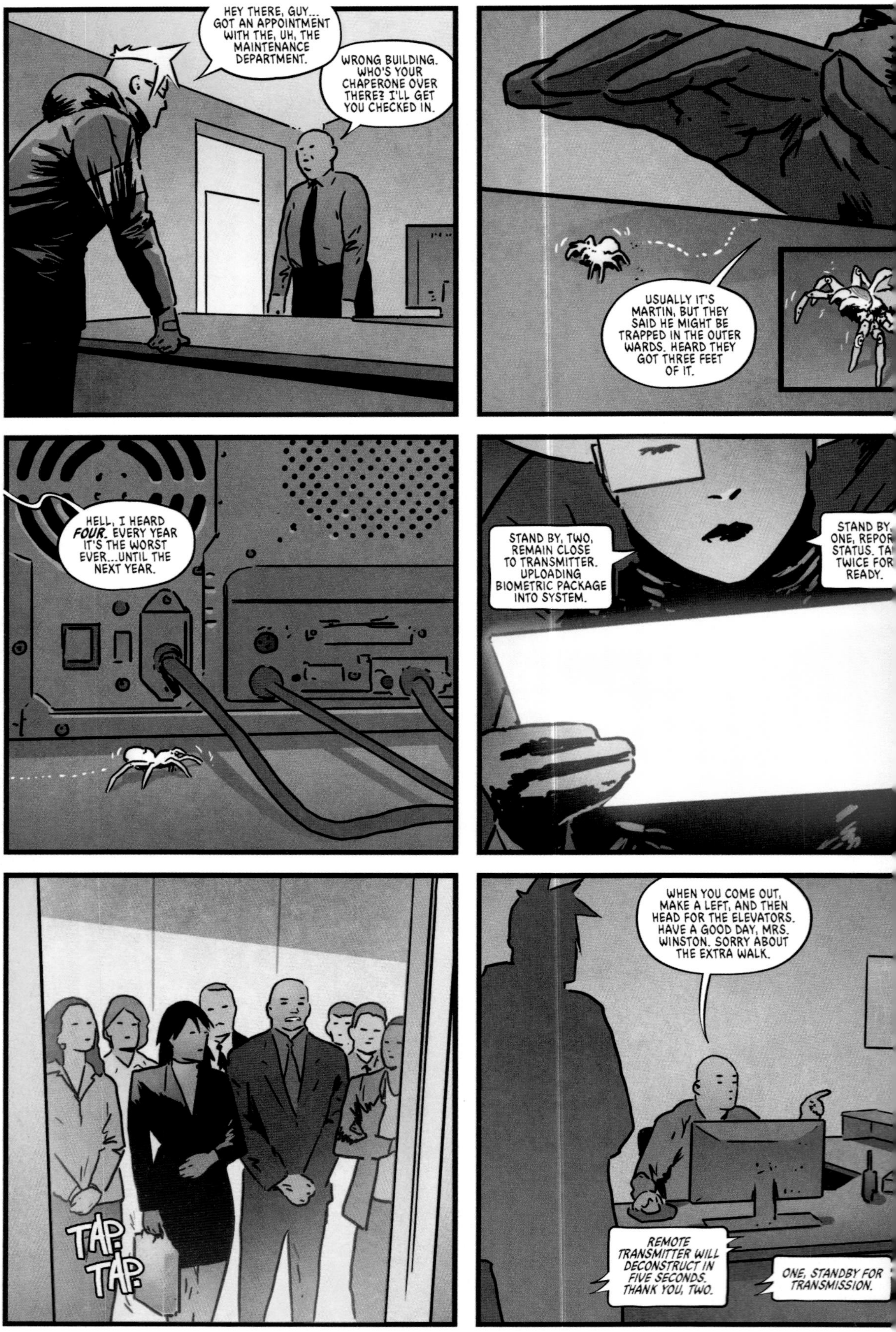
HEY THERE, GUY... GOT AN APPOINTMENT WITH THE, UH, THE MAINTENANCE DEPARTMENT.
WRONG BUILDING. WHO'S YOUR CHAPERONE OVER THERE? I'LL GET YOU CHECKED IN.
USUALLY IT'S MARTIN, BUT THEY SAID HE MIGHT BE TRAPPED IN THE OUTER WARDS. HEARD THEY GOT THREE FEET OF IT.
HELL, I HEARD FOUR. EVERY YEAR IT'S THE WORST EVER...UNTIL THE NEXT YEAR.
STAND BY, TWO, REMAIN CLOSE TO TRANSMITTER. UPLOADING BIOMETRIC PACKAGE INTO SYSTEM.
STAND BY, ONE, REPOR STATUS. TA TWICE FOR READY.
TAP. TAP.
WHEN YOU COME OUT, MAKE A LEFT, AND THEN HEAD FOR THE ELEVATORS. HAVE A GOOD DAY, MRS. WINSTON. SORRY ABOUT THE EXTRA WALK.
REMOTE TRANSMITTER WILL DECONSTRUCT IN FIVE SECONDS. THANK YOU, TWO.
ONE, STANDBY FOR TRANSMISSION.

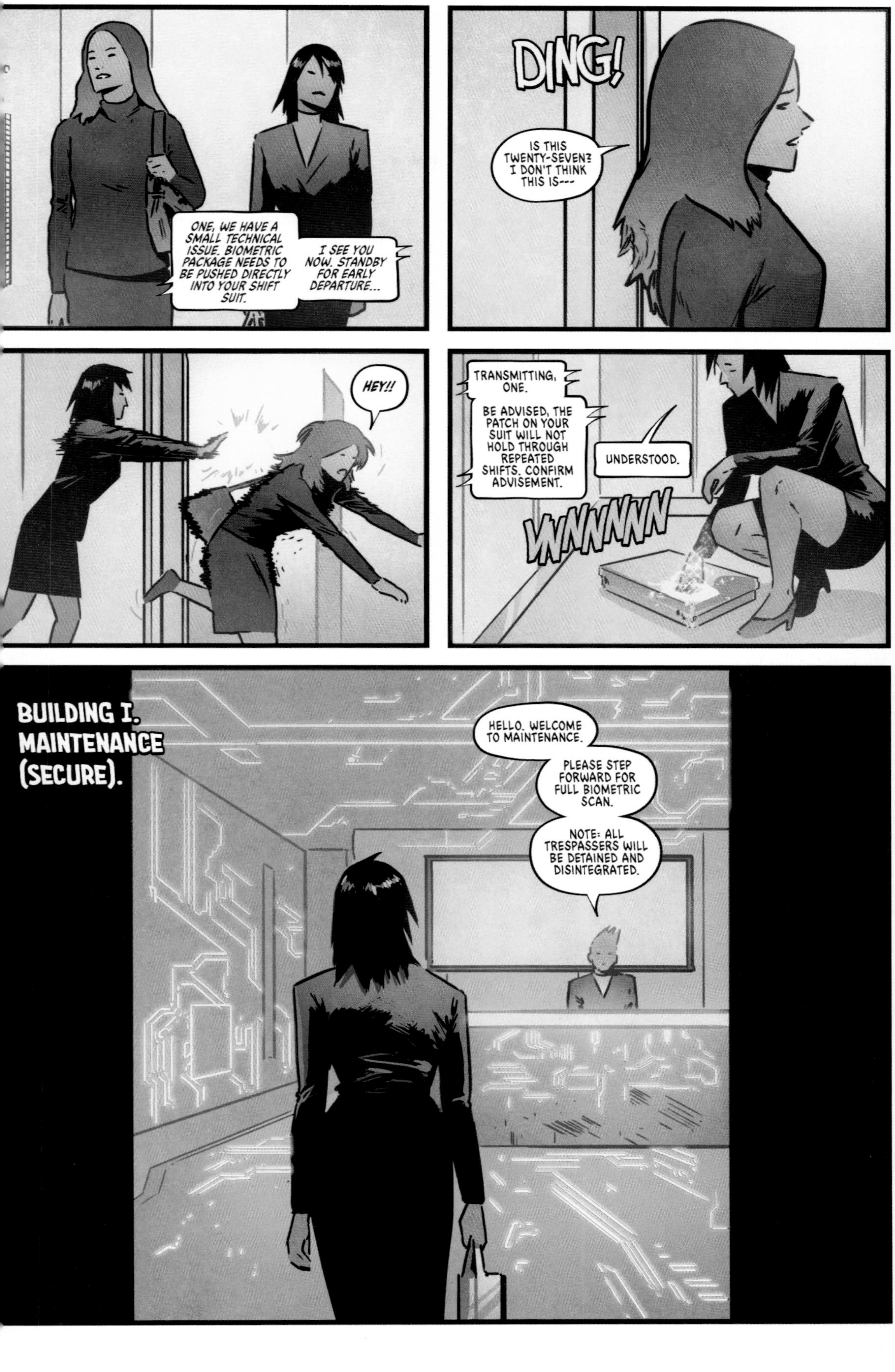
ONE, WE HAVE A SMALL TECHNICAL ISSUE. BIOMETRIC PACKAGE NEEDS TO BE PUSHED DIRECTLY INTO YOUR SHIFT SUIT.
I SEE YOU NOW. STANDBY FOR EARLY DEPARTURE...
DING!
IS THIS TWENTY-SEVEN? I DON'T THINK THIS IS---
HEY!!
TRANSMITTING, ONE.
BE ADVISED, THE PATCH ON YOUR SUIT WILL NOT HOLD THROUGH REPEATED SHIFTS. CONFIRM ADVISEMENT.
UNDERSTOOD.
VNNNNNN
BUILDING I. MAINTENANCE (SECURE).
HELLO. WELCOME TO MAINTENANCE.
PLEASE STEP FORWARD FOR FULL BIOMETRIC SCAN.
NOTE: ALL TRESPASSERS WILL BE DETAINED AND DISINTEGRATED.

TWO, WE HAVE SPLASHDOWN. REPEAT, FABRICATED BIOMETRIC KEY ACCEPTED.

NO DISINTEGRATIONS.

YEAH--- OKAY...

TWO?

THOUGHT I RECOGNIZED SOMEONE. LET ME KNOW IF SHE NEEDS ME LATER, THREE.

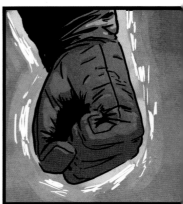

I REMEMBER YOU, MOTHER FUCKER..

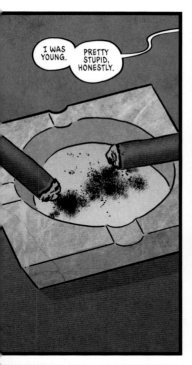

I WAS YOUNG.

PRETTY STUPID, HONESTLY.

SEVEN YEARS AGO.

"VIOLENT."

"CRIME IS NOT TOLERATED ON MY WORLD, BUT WE WERE AT WAR.

"A HOSTILE ALIEN RACE WITH ABILITIES WE DID NOT UNDERSTAND WANTED OUR PLANET, AND WE WERE DESPERATE TO SURVIVE THEM.

SO EITHER I ENLISTED... OR I TRIED MY LUCK AS A JUNIOR BADASS INSIDE EUAFOR, A PRISON SO VIOLENT AND DANGEROUS, WE PUT IT ON ONE OF OUR NEARBY MOONS.

WE DO THE SAME SHIT HERE, REALLY. TURNED LOCKIN' FOLKS UP INTO AN ART FORM, AND WHAT DO YOU KNOW...NOW WE NEED EVERY FREE HAND.

YOU LEAVE ANY KIDS BEHIND? LITTLE FINNS?

HEY, DON'T SWEAT IT, MAN. I UNDERSTAND THAT FEAR.

"SHIT, USED TO THINK I KNEW WHAT FEAR WAS. BUT IT'S DIFFERENT, RIGHT---SO MUCH WORSE THAN I EVER COULD'VE IMAGINED, SPECIALLY IN *THIS* FUCKED UP WORLD---"

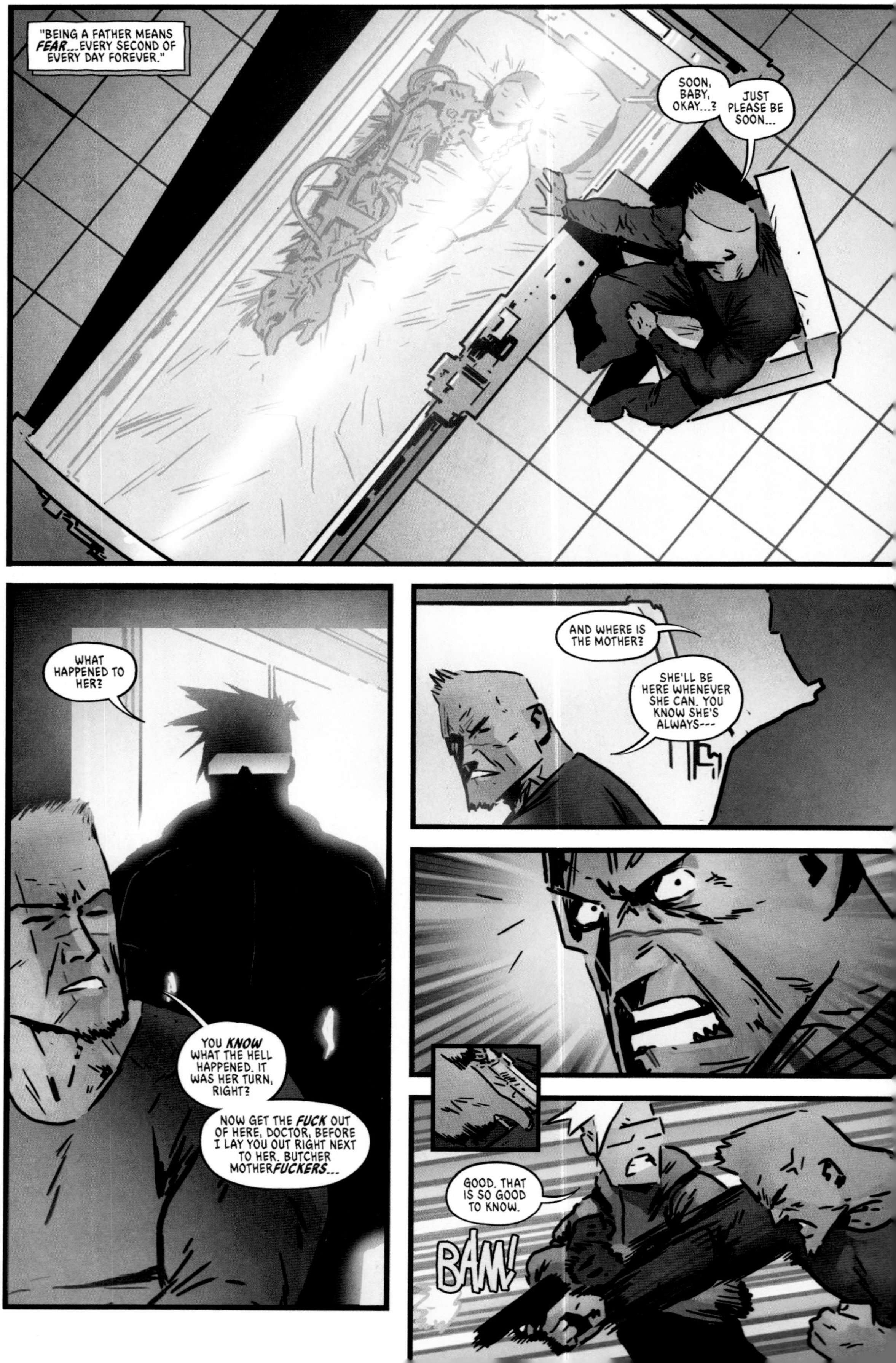
"BEING A FATHER MEANS FEAR... EVERY SECOND OF EVERY DAY FOREVER."
SOON, BABY, OKAY...?
JUST PLEASE BE SOON...
WHAT HAPPENED TO HER?
YOU KNOW WHAT THE HELL HAPPENED. IT WAS HER TURN, RIGHT?
NOW GET THE FUCK OUT OF HERE, DOCTOR, BEFORE I LAY YOU OUT RIGHT NEXT TO HER. BUTCHER MOTHERFUCKERS...
AND WHERE IS THE MOTHER?
SHE'LL BE HERE WHENEVER SHE CAN. YOU KNOW SHE'S ALWAYS---
GOOD. THAT IS SO GOOD TO KNOW.
BAM!

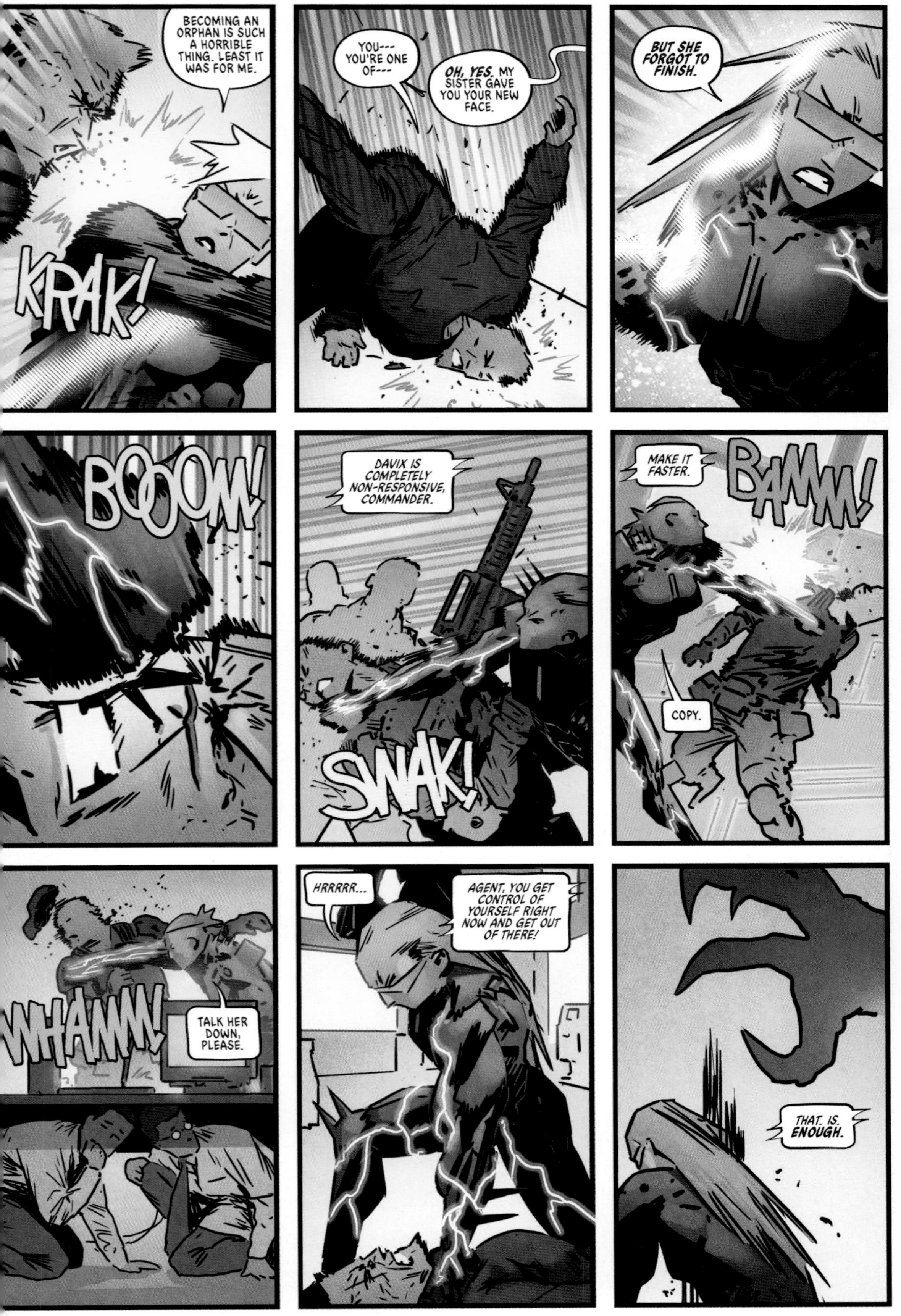

BECOMING AN ORPHAN IS SUCH A HORRIBLE THING. LEAST IT WAS FOR ME.
KRAK!
YOU--- YOU'RE ONE OF---
OH, YES. MY SISTER GAVE YOU YOUR NEW FACE.
BUT SHE FORGOT TO FINISH.
BOOOM!
DAVIX IS COMPLETELY NON-RESPONSIVE, COMMANDER.
SWAK!
MAKE IT FASTER.
BAMM!
COPY.
WHAMM!
TALK HER DOWN, PLEASE.
HRRRRR...
AGENT, YOU GET CONTROL OF YOURSELF RIGHT NOW AND GET OUT OF THERE!
THAT. IS. ENOUGH.

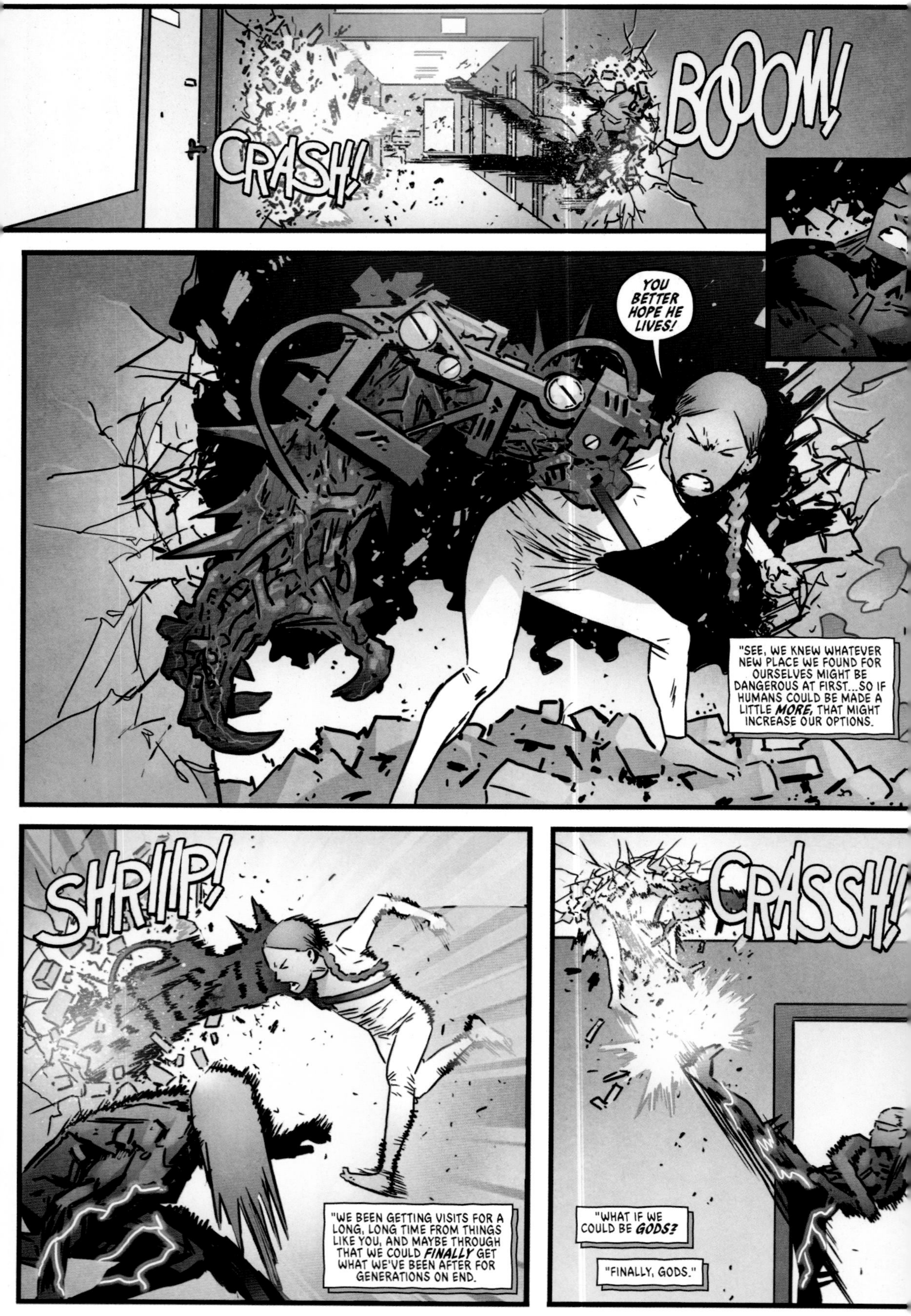
CRASH!
BOOM!
YOU BETTER HOPE HE LIVES!
"SEE, WE KNEW WHATEVER NEW PLACE WE FOUND FOR OURSELVES MIGHT BE DANGEROUS AT FIRST...SO IF HUMANS COULD BE MADE A LITTLE MORE, THAT MIGHT INCREASE OUR OPTIONS.
SHRIIIP!
"WE BEEN GETTING VISITS FOR A LONG, LONG TIME FROM THINGS LIKE YOU, AND MAYBE THROUGH THAT WE COULD FINALLY GET WHAT WE'VE BEEN AFTER FOR GENERATIONS ON END.
CRASSH!
"WHAT IF WE COULD BE GODS?
"FINALLY, GODS."

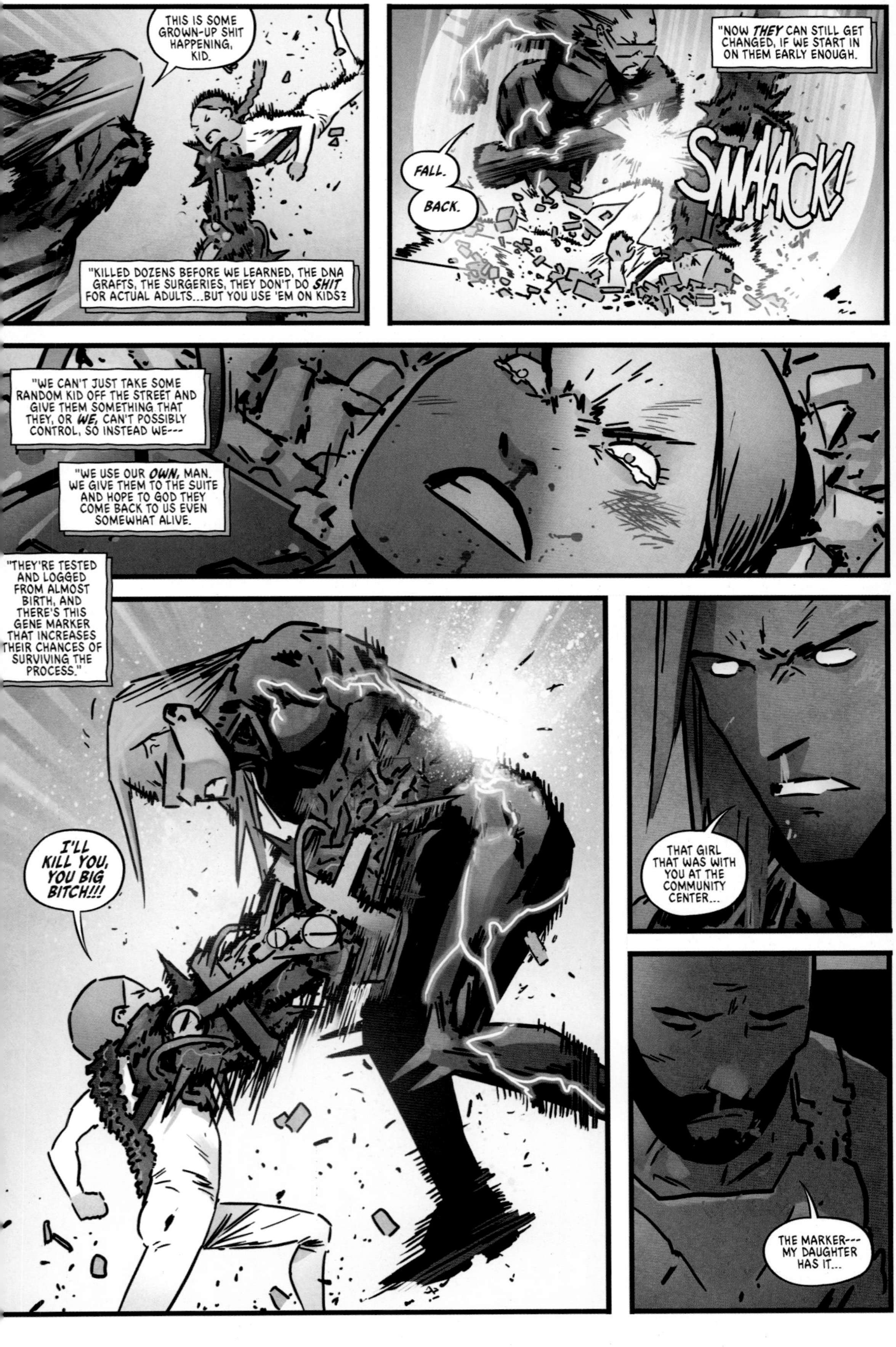
THIS IS SOME GROWN-UP SHIT HAPPENING, KID.
"KILLED DOZENS BEFORE WE LEARNED, THE DNA GRAFTS, THE SURGERIES, THEY DON'T DO SHIT FOR ACTUAL ADULTS...BUT YOU USE 'EM ON KIDS?
"NOW THEY CAN STILL GET CHANGED, IF WE START IN ON THEM EARLY ENOUGH.
FALL.
BACK.
SWAACK!
"WE CAN'T JUST TAKE SOME RANDOM KID OFF THE STREET AND GIVE THEM SOMETHING THAT THEY, OR WE, CAN'T POSSIBLY CONTROL, SO INSTEAD WE---
"WE USE OUR OWN, MAN. WE GIVE THEM TO THE SUITE AND HOPE TO GOD THEY COME BACK TO US EVEN SOMEWHAT ALIVE.
"THEY'RE TESTED AND LOGGED FROM ALMOST BIRTH, AND THERE'S THIS GENE MARKER THAT INCREASES THEIR CHANCES OF SURVIVING THE PROCESS."
I'LL KILL YOU, YOU BIG BITCH!!!
THAT GIRL THAT WAS WITH YOU AT THE COMMUNITY CENTER...
THE MARKER--- MY DAUGHTER HAS IT...

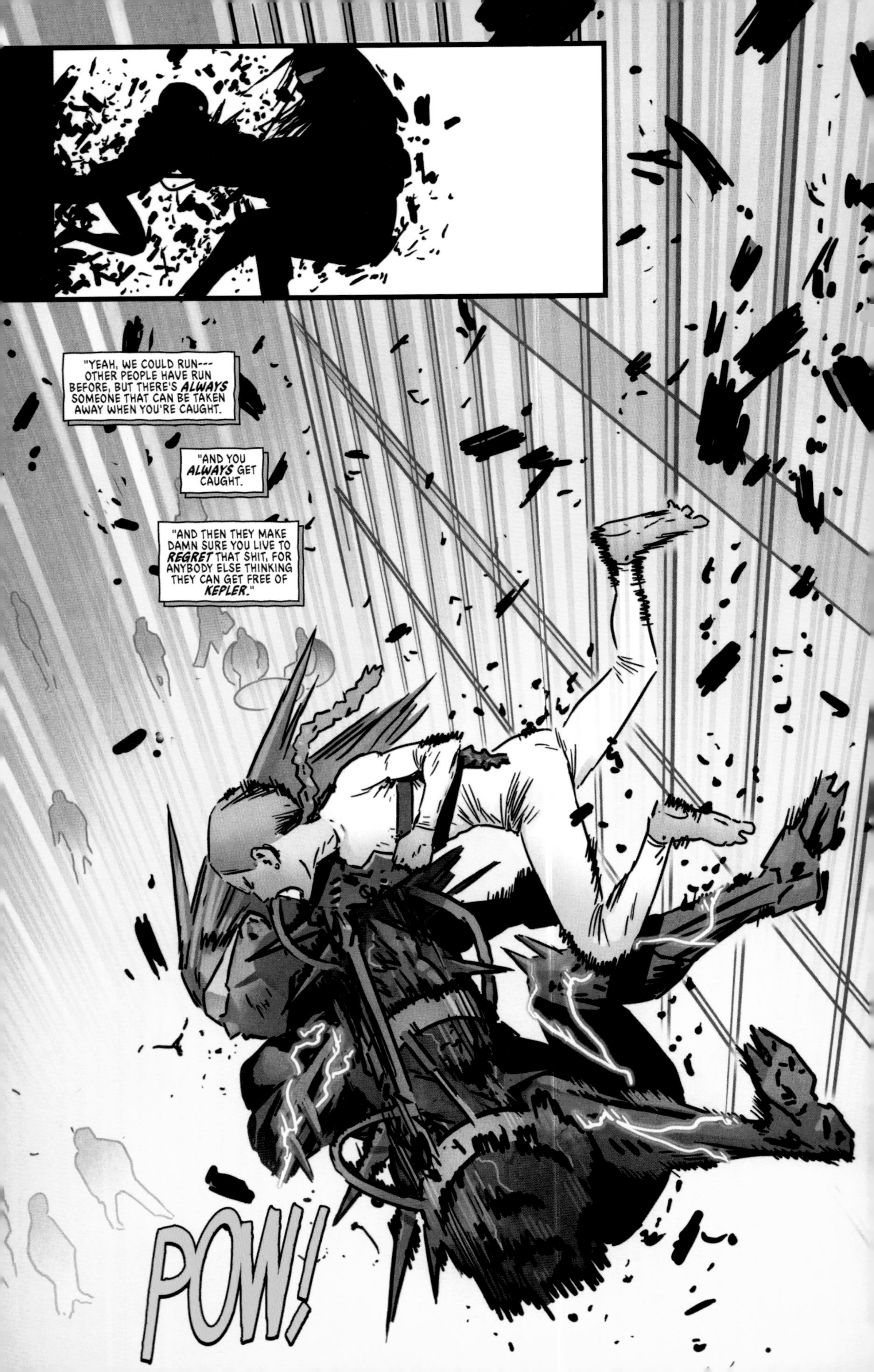
"YEAH, WE COULD RUN---OTHER PEOPLE HAVE RUN BEFORE, BUT THERE'S ALWAYS SOMEONE THAT CAN BE TAKEN AWAY WHEN YOU'RE CAUGHT.
"AND YOU ALWAYS GET CAUGHT.
"AND THEN THEY MAKE DAMN SURE YOU LIVE TO REGRET THAT SHIT, FOR ANYBODY ELSE THINKING THEY CAN GET FREE OF KEPLER."
POW!

SMAAASSSH!

ZH---ZHIA--- DO NOT COME AFTER---FINISH--- *FINISH* THESE STUPID FUCKS---

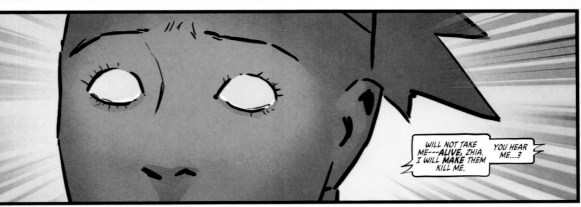

WILL NOT TAKE ME---*ALIVE,* ZHIA. I WILL *MAKE* THEM KILL ME.

YOU HEAR ME...?

YOU BETTER KILL ME, YOU DUMB-FUCK BUGS! LIKE YOU DID THIS PLANET!

YOU---YOU TELL FINN, ZHIA---

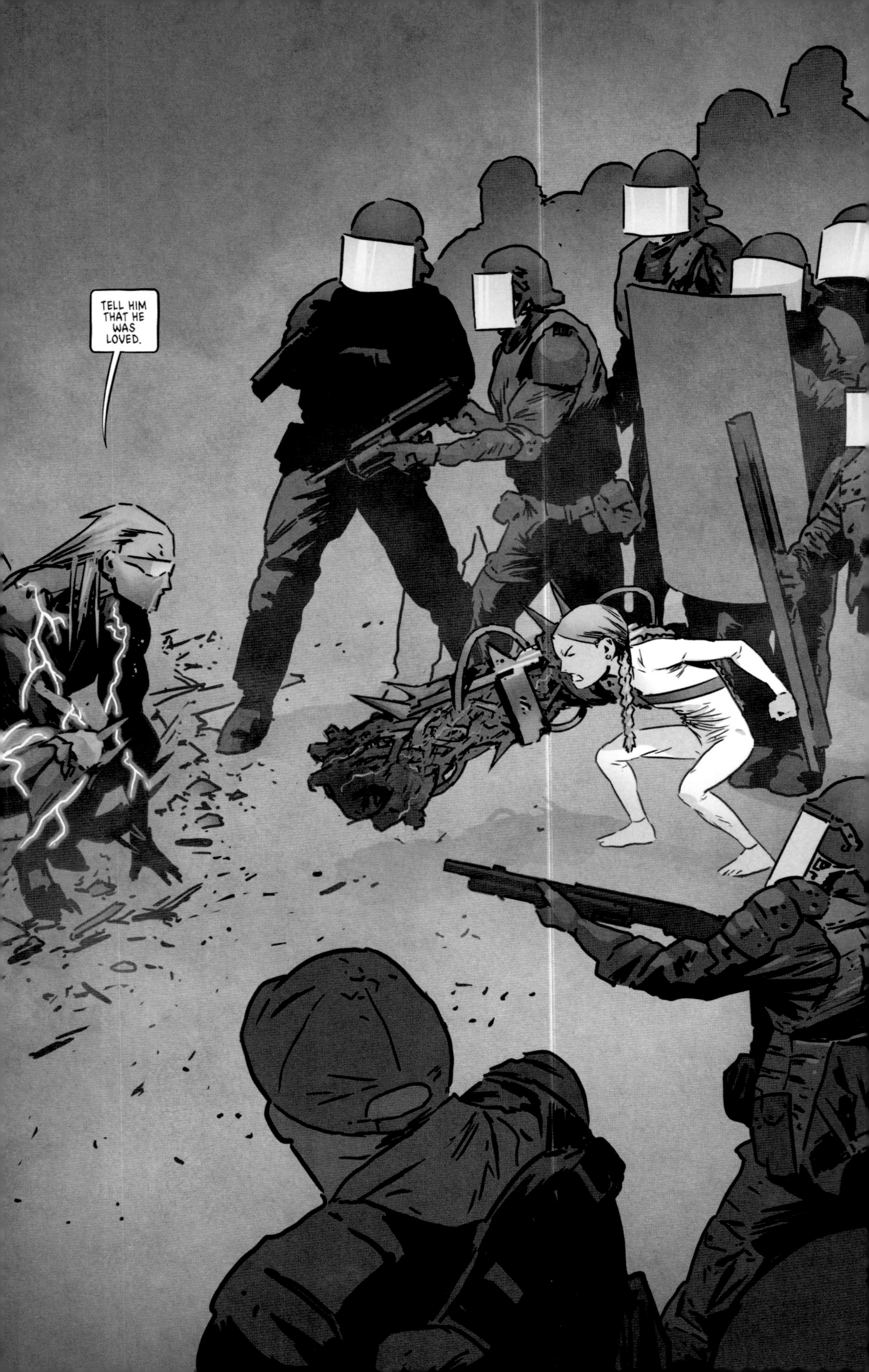
TELL HIM THAT HE WAS LOVED.

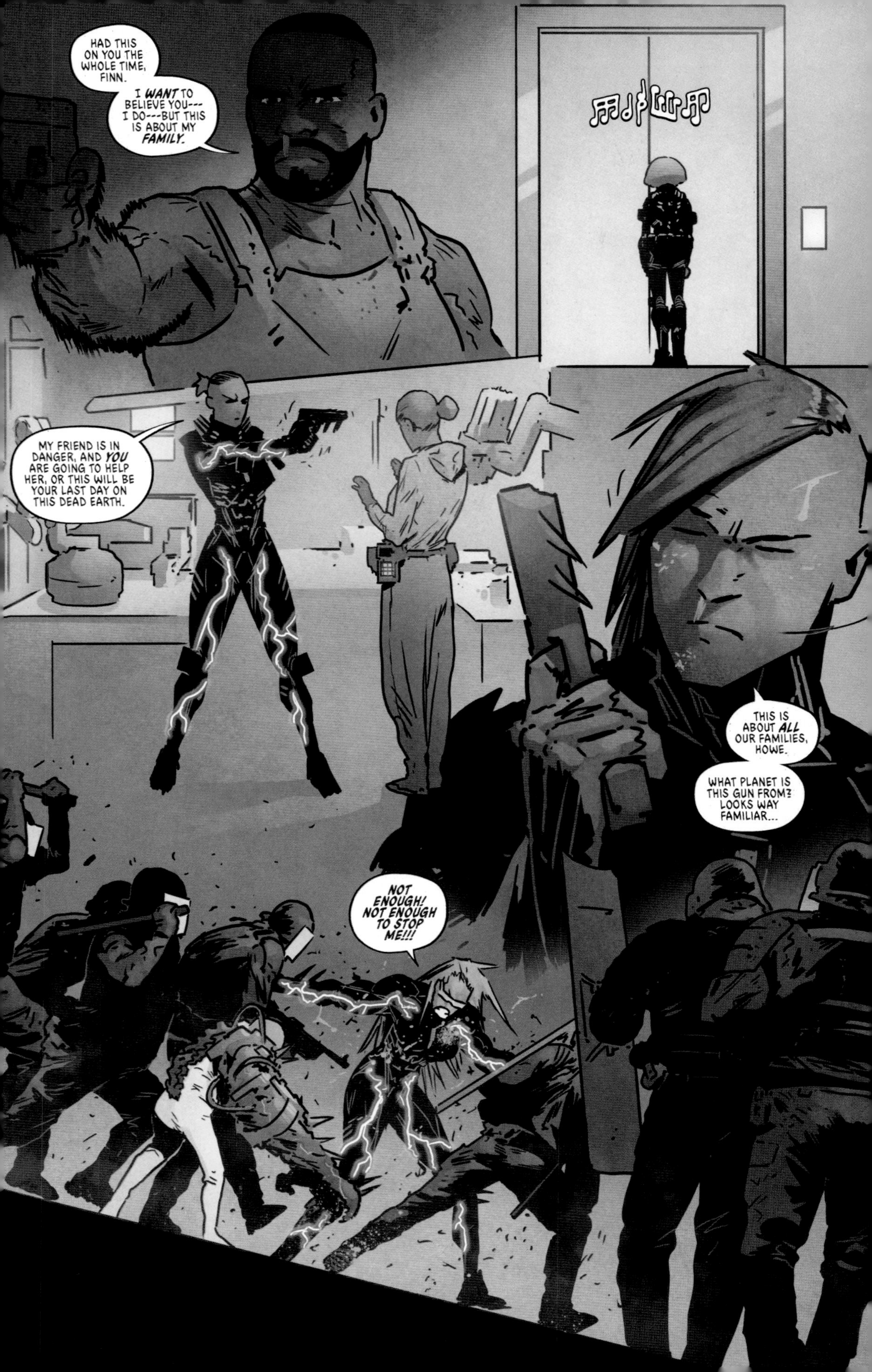
HAD THIS ON YOU THE WHOLE TIME, FINN.
I WANT TO BELIEVE YOU--- I DO---BUT THIS IS ABOUT MY FAMILY.
MY FRIEND IS IN DANGER, AND YOU ARE GOING TO HELP HER, OR THIS WILL BE YOUR LAST DAY ON THIS DEAD EARTH.
THIS IS ABOUT ALL OUR FAMILIES, HOWE.
WHAT PLANET IS THIS GUN FROM? LOOKS WAY FAMILIAR...
NOT ENOUGH! NOT ENOUGH TO STOP ME!!!

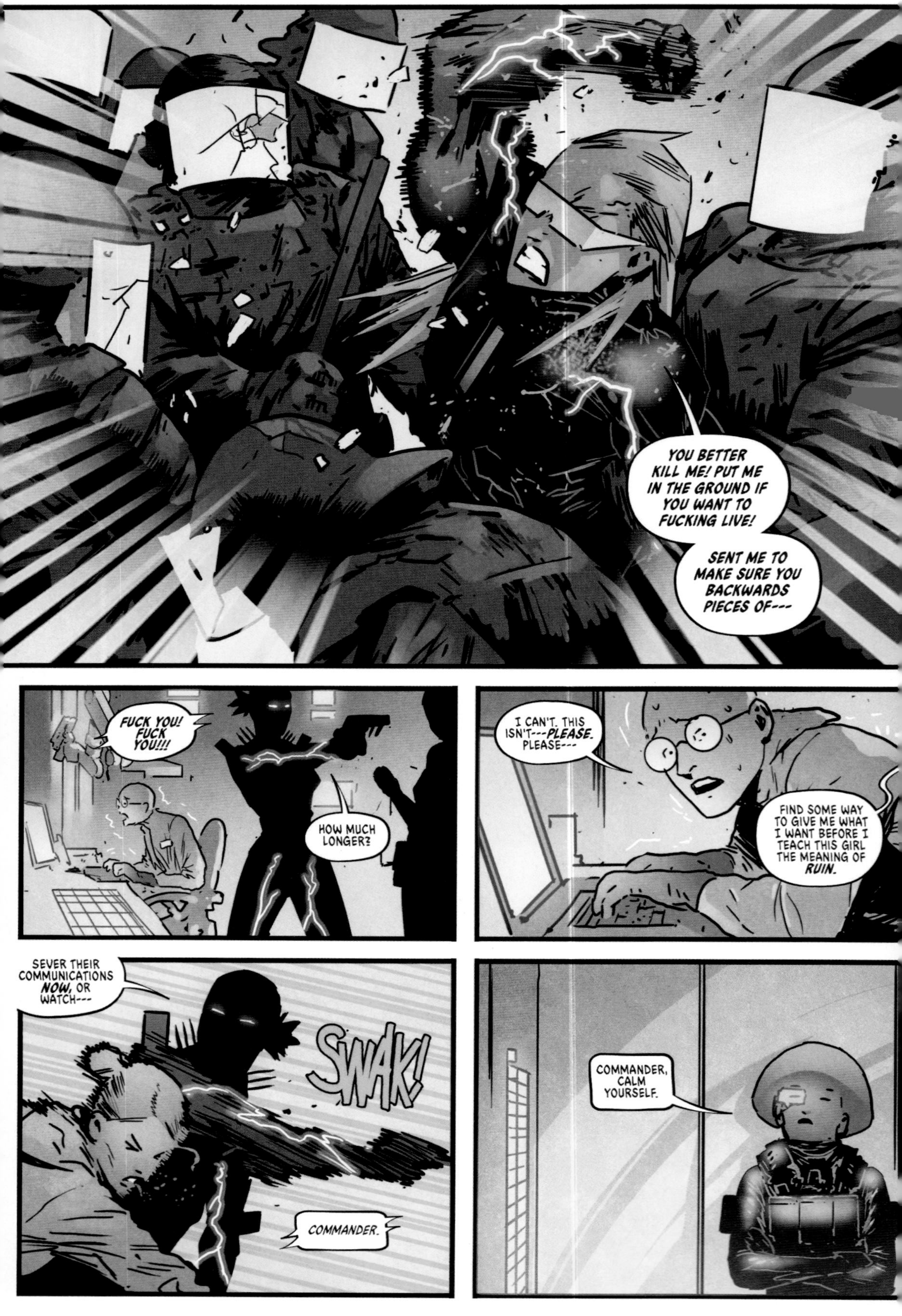
YOU BETTER KILL ME! PUT ME IN THE GROUND IF YOU WANT TO FUCKING LIVE!
SENT ME TO MAKE SURE YOU BACKWARDS PIECES OF---
FUCK YOU! FUCK YOU!!!
HOW MUCH LONGER?
I CAN'T. THIS ISN'T---PLEASE. PLEASE---
FIND SOME WAY TO GIVE ME WHAT I WANT BEFORE I TEACH THIS GIRL THE MEANING OF RUIN.
SEVER THEIR COMMUNICATIONS NOW, OR WATCH---
SWAK!
COMMANDER.
COMMANDER, CALM YOURSELF.

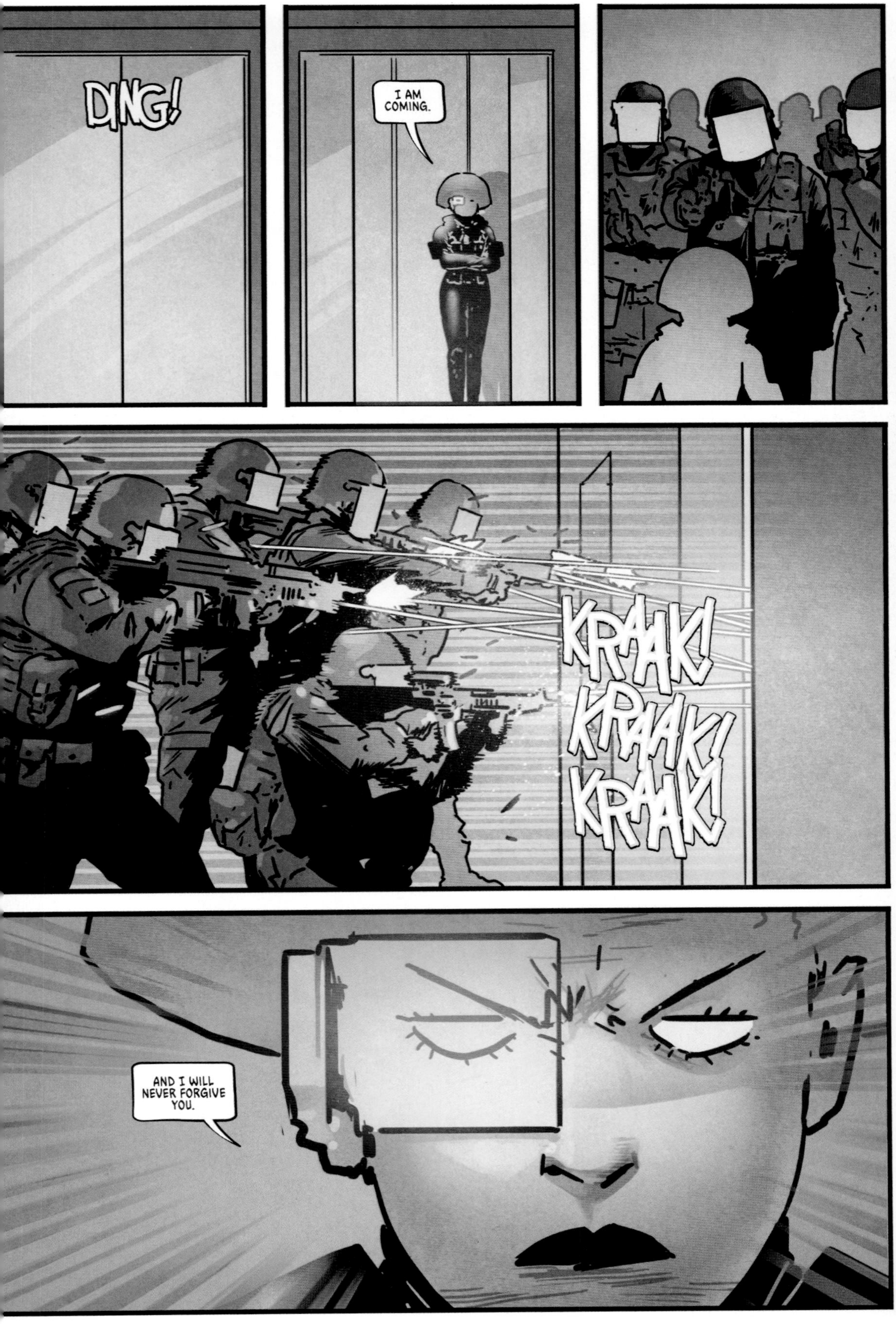
DING!
I AM COMING.
KRAAK! KRAAK! KRAAK!
AND I WILL NEVER FORGIVE YOU.

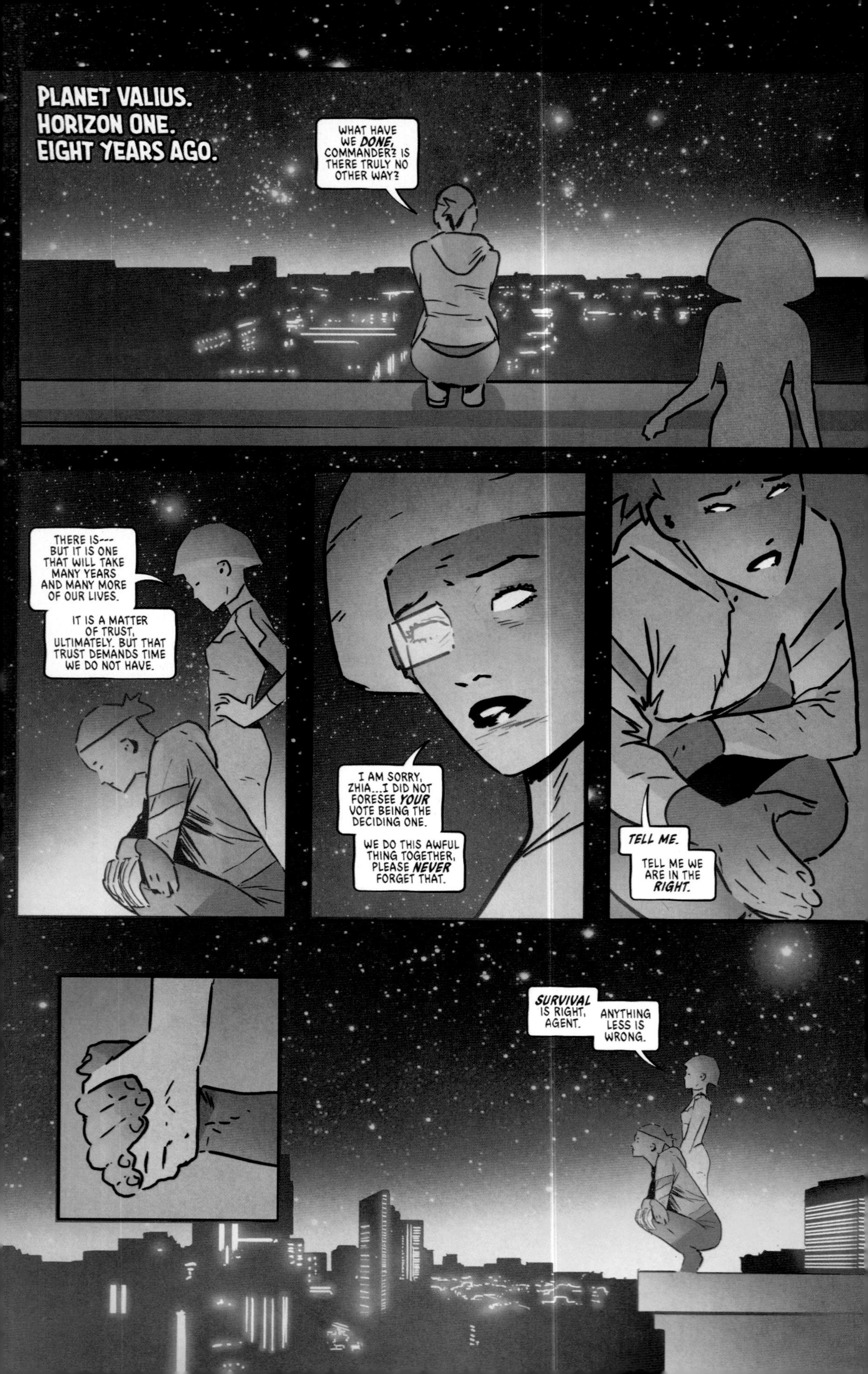
PLANET VALIUS.
HORIZON ONE.
EIGHT YEARS AGO.
WHAT HAVE WE DONE, COMMANDER? IS THERE TRULY NO OTHER WAY?
THERE IS--- BUT IT IS ONE THAT WILL TAKE MANY YEARS AND MANY MORE OF OUR LIVES.
IT IS A MATTER OF TRUST, ULTIMATELY. BUT THAT TRUST DEMANDS TIME WE DO NOT HAVE.
I AM SORRY, ZHIA...I DID NOT FORESEE YOUR VOTE BEING THE DECIDING ONE.
WE DO THIS AWFUL THING TOGETHER, PLEASE NEVER FORGET THAT.
TELL ME.
TELL ME WE ARE IN THE RIGHT.
SURVIVAL IS RIGHT, AGENT.
ANYTHING LESS IS WRONG.

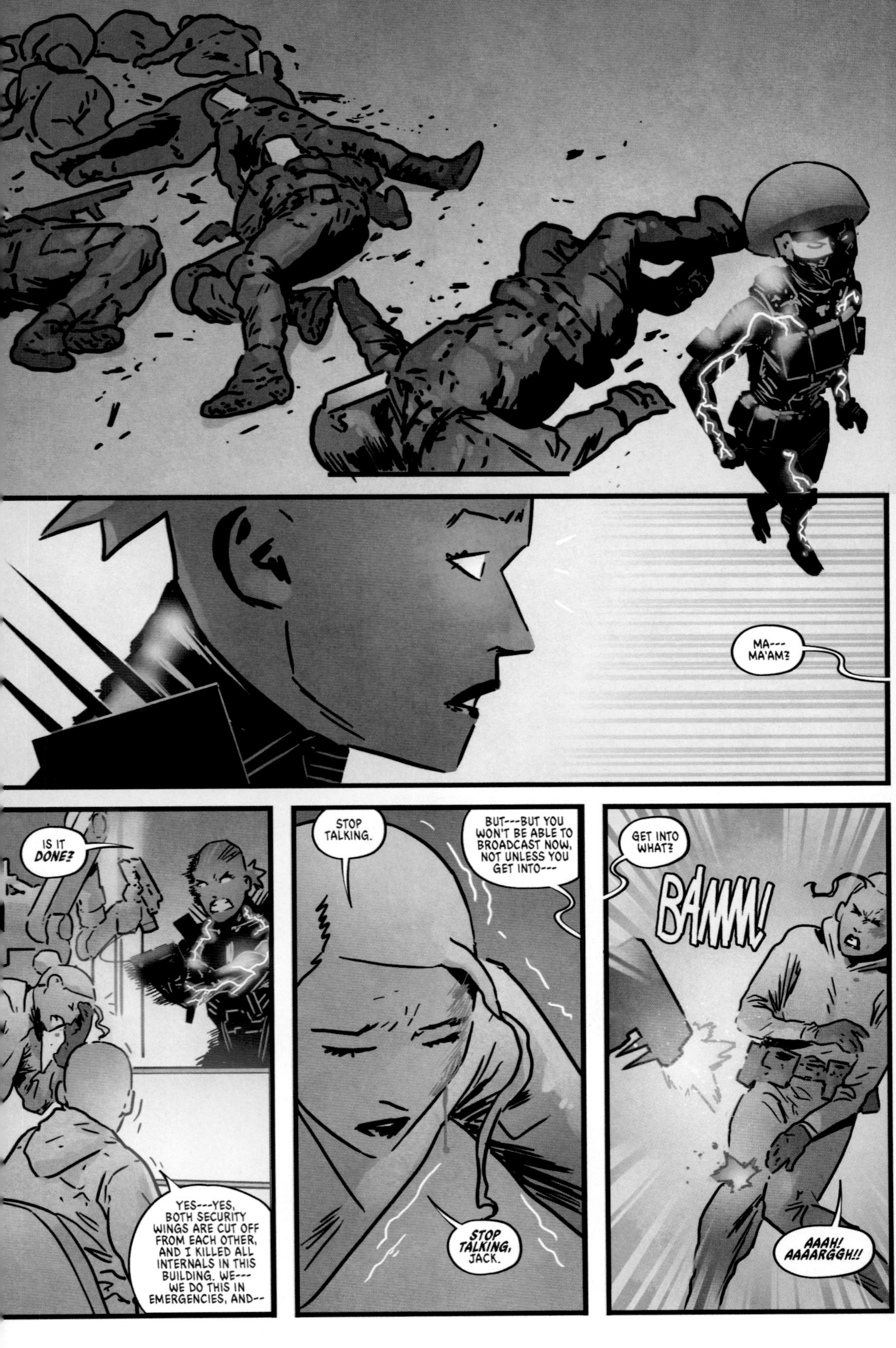

MA---
MA'AM?
IS IT DONE?
YES---YES, BOTH SECURITY WINGS ARE CUT OFF FROM EACH OTHER, AND I KILLED ALL INTERNALS IN THIS BUILDING. WE--- WE DO THIS IN EMERGENCIES, AND--
STOP TALKING.
BUT---BUT YOU WON'T BE ABLE TO BROADCAST NOW, NOT UNLESS YOU GET INTO---
STOP TALKING, JACK.
GET INTO WHAT?
BAMM!
AAAH! AAAARGGH!!

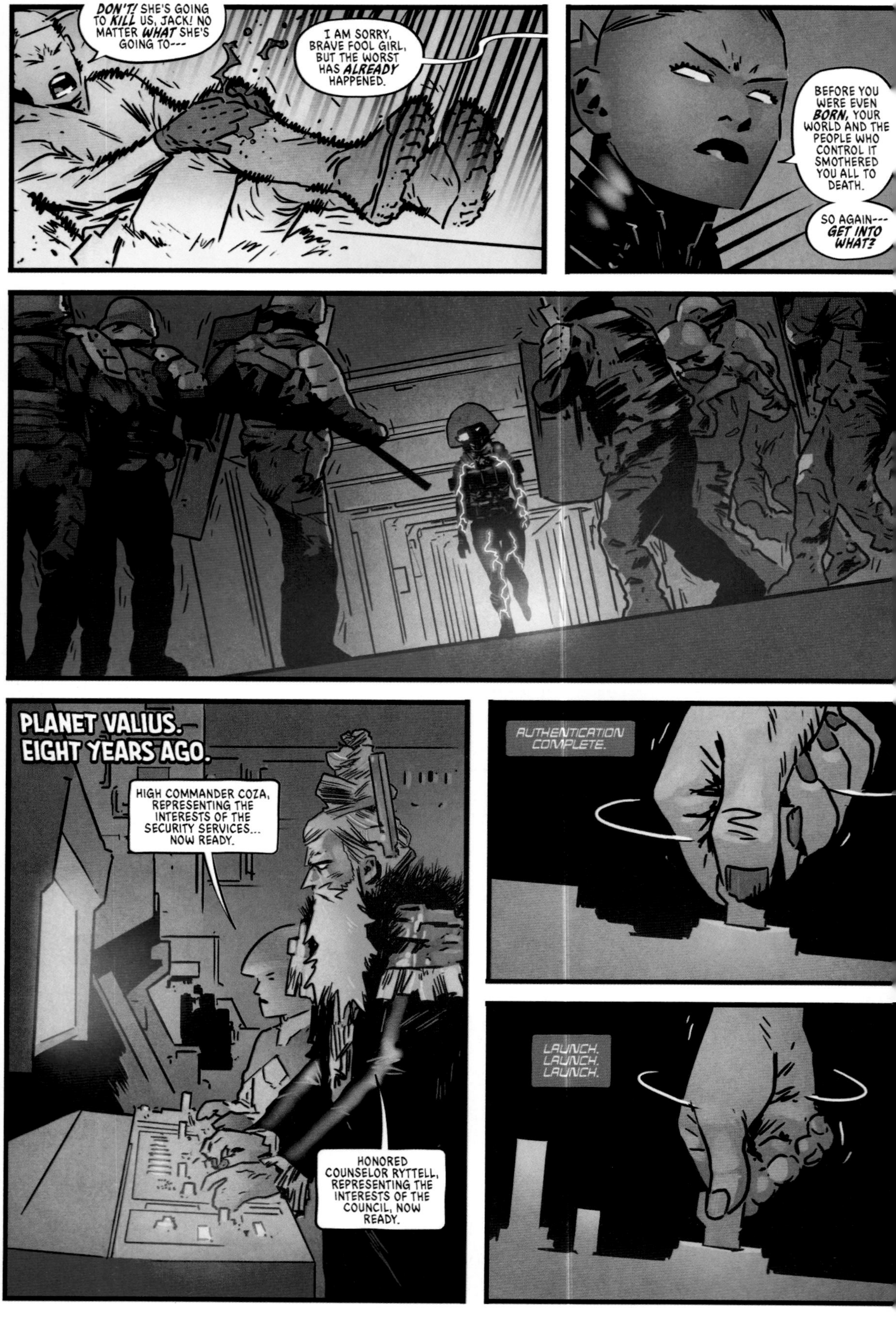
DON'T! SHE'S GOING TO KILL US, JACK! NO MATTER WHAT SHE'S GOING TO---
I AM SORRY, BRAVE FOOL GIRL, BUT THE WORST HAS ALREADY HAPPENED.
BEFORE YOU WERE EVEN BORN, YOUR WORLD AND THE PEOPLE WHO CONTROL IT SMOTHERED YOU ALL TO DEATH.
SO AGAIN--- GET INTO WHAT?
PLANET VALIUS. EIGHT YEARS AGO.
HIGH COMMANDER COZA, REPRESENTING THE INTERESTS OF THE SECURITY SERVICES... NOW READY.
HONORED COUNSELOR RYTTELL, REPRESENTING THE INTERESTS OF THE COUNCIL, NOW READY.
AUTHENTICATION COMPLETE.
LAUNCH. LAUNCH. LAUNCH.

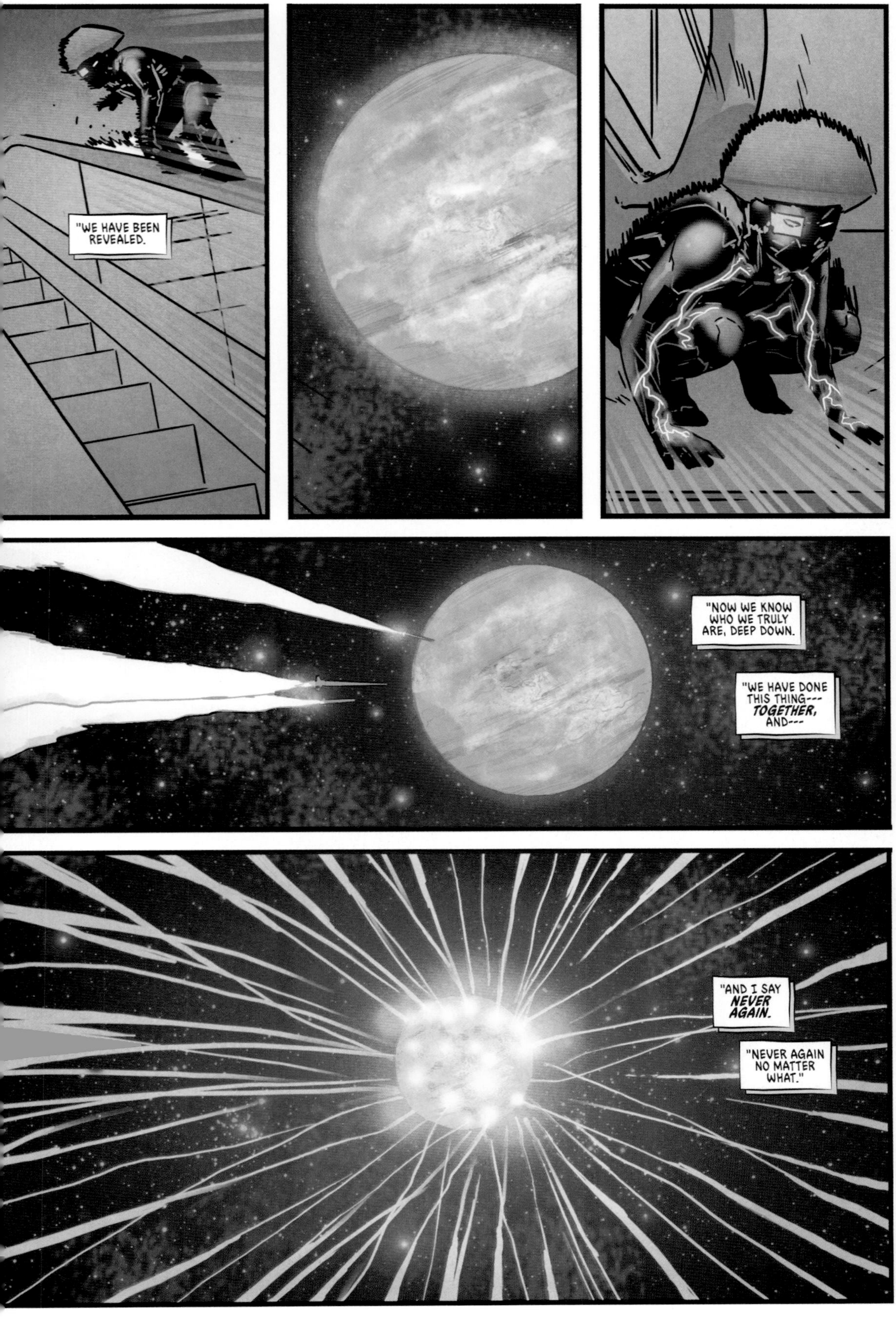
"WE HAVE BEEN REVEALED.
"NOW WE KNOW WHO WE TRULY ARE, DEEP DOWN.
"WE HAVE DONE THIS THING--- *TOGETHER,* AND---
"AND I SAY ***NEVER AGAIN.***
"NEVER AGAIN NO MATTER WHAT."

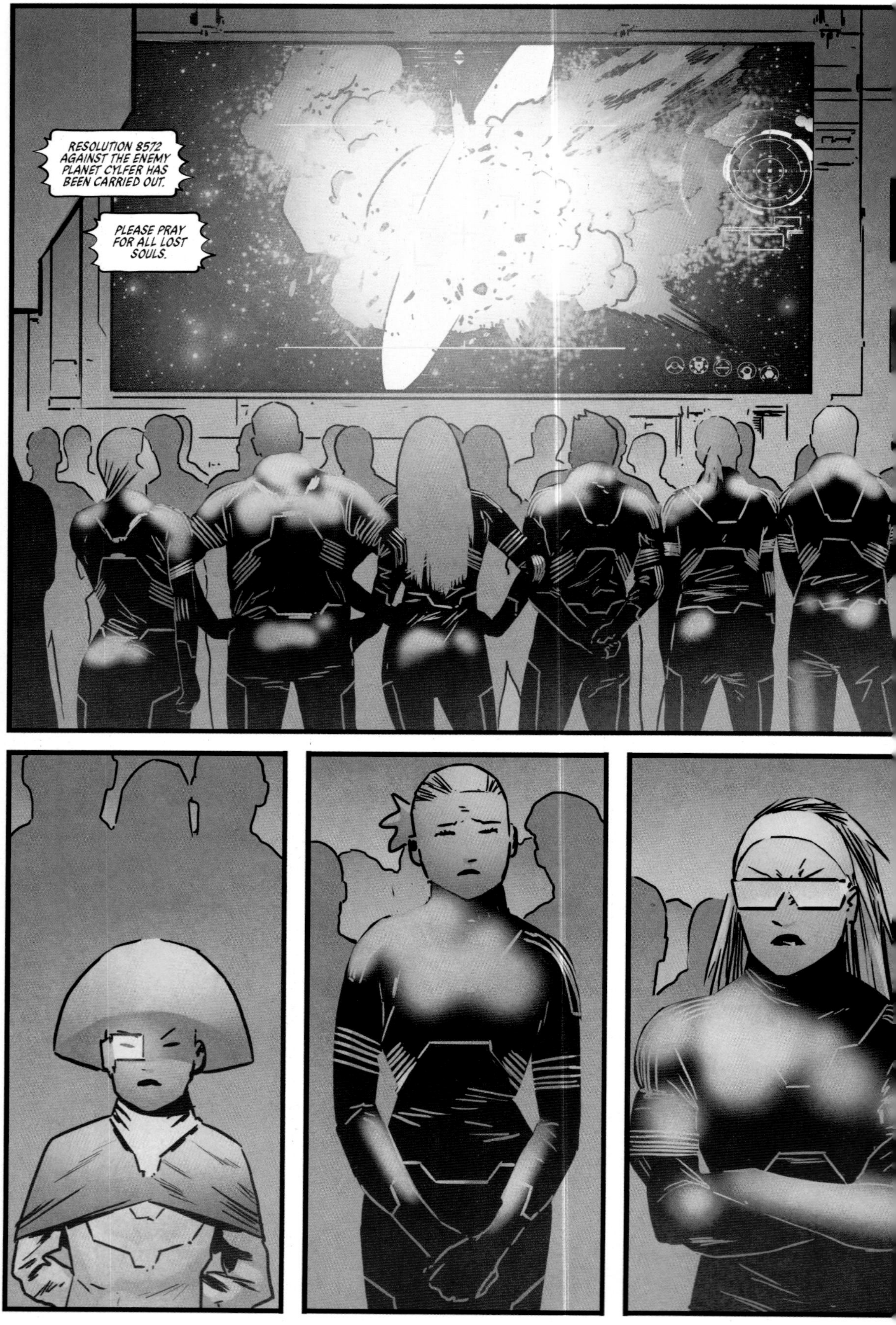
RESOLUTION 8572 AGAINST THE ENEMY PLANET CYLFER HAS BEEN CARRIED OUT.
PLEASE PRAY FOR ALL LOST SOULS.

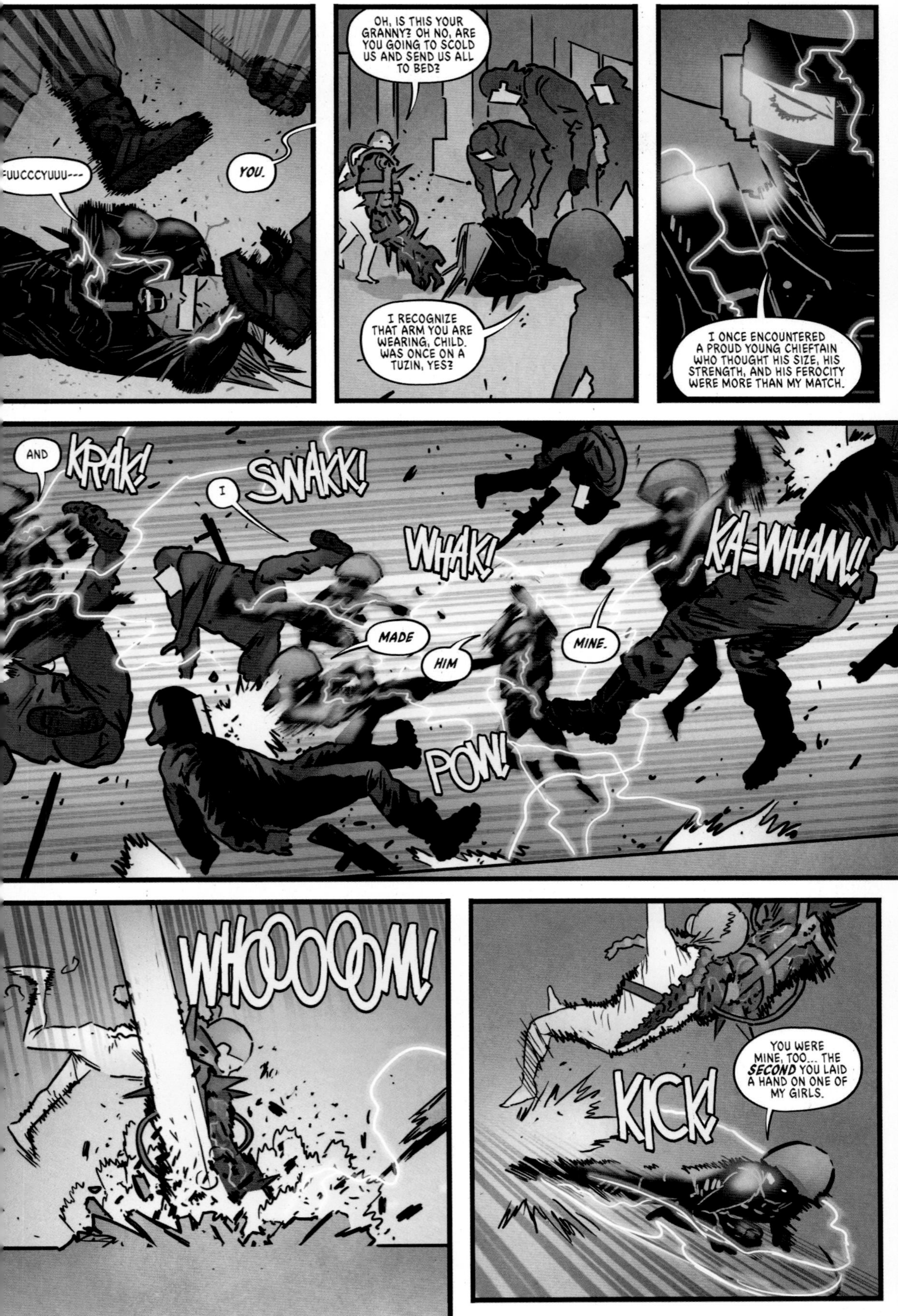
FUUCCCYUUU---
YOU.
OH, IS THIS YOUR GRANNY? OH NO, ARE YOU GOING TO SCOLD US AND SEND US ALL TO BED?
I RECOGNIZE THAT ARM YOU ARE WEARING, CHILD. WAS ONCE ON A TUZIN, YES?
I ONCE ENCOUNTERED A PROUD YOUNG CHIEFTAIN WHO THOUGHT HIS SIZE, HIS STRENGTH, AND HIS FEROCITY WERE MORE THAN MY MATCH.
AND
KRAK!
I
SWAKK!
WHAK!
MADE
HIM
MINE.
KA-WHAM!!
POW!
WHOOOOOM!
KICK!
YOU WERE MINE, TOO... THE SECOND YOU LAID A HAND ON ONE OF MY GIRLS.

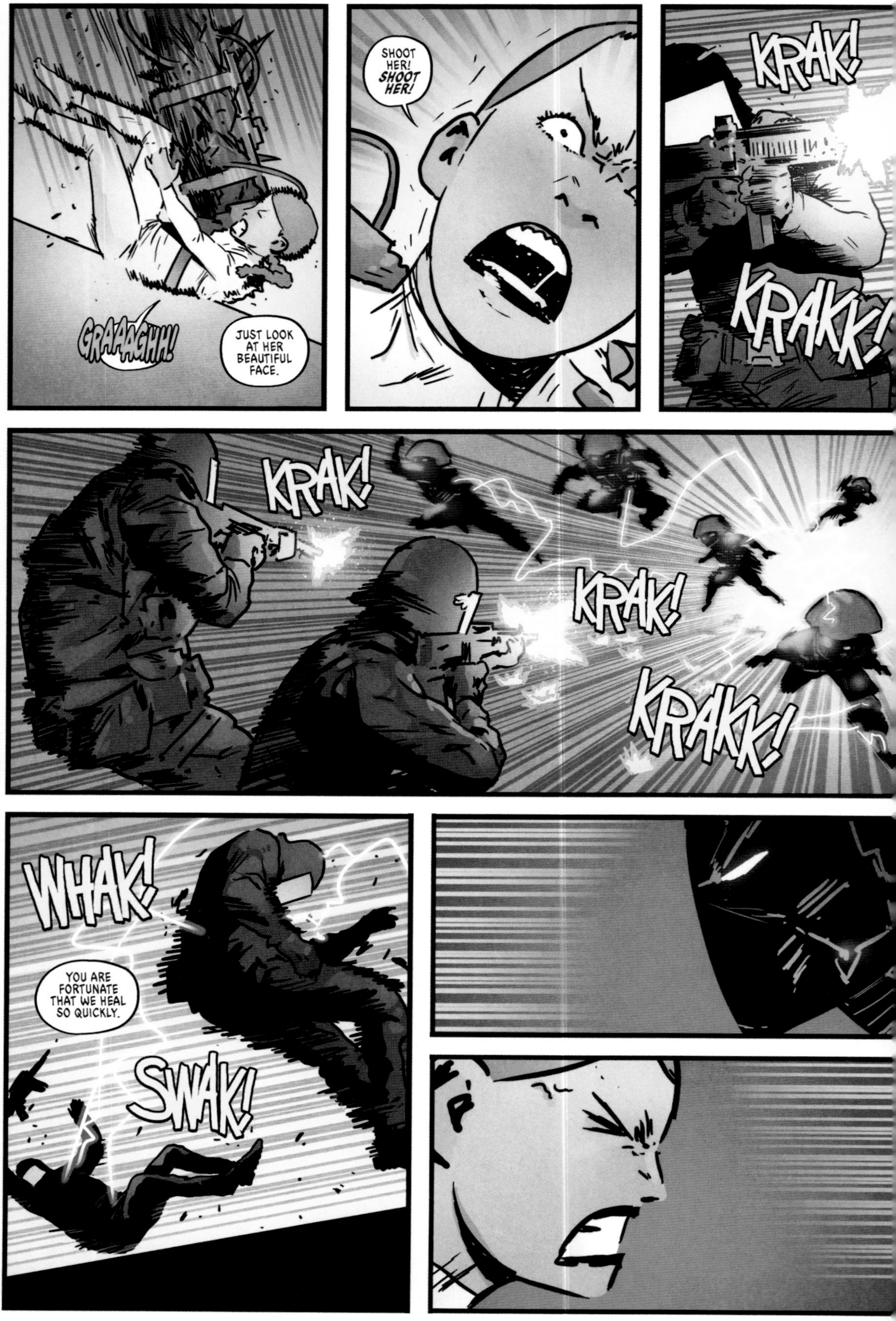
GRAAAGHH!
JUST LOOK AT HER BEAUTIFUL FACE.
SHOOT HER! SHOOT HER!
KRAK!
KRAKK!
KRAK!
KRAK!
KRAKK!
WHAK!
YOU ARE FORTUNATE THAT WE HEAL SO QUICKLY.
SWAK!

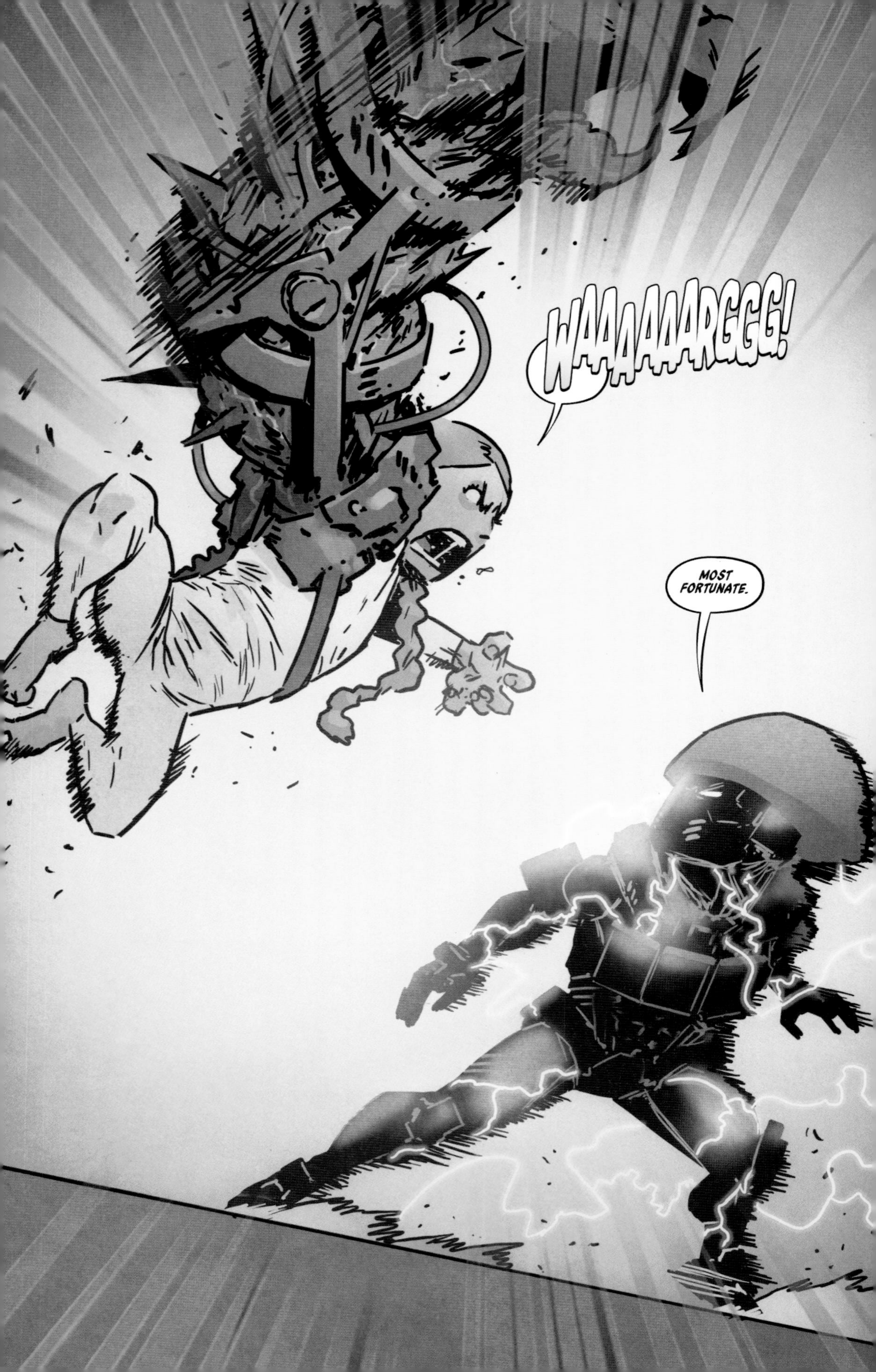
WAAAAAARGGG!
MOST FORTUNATE.

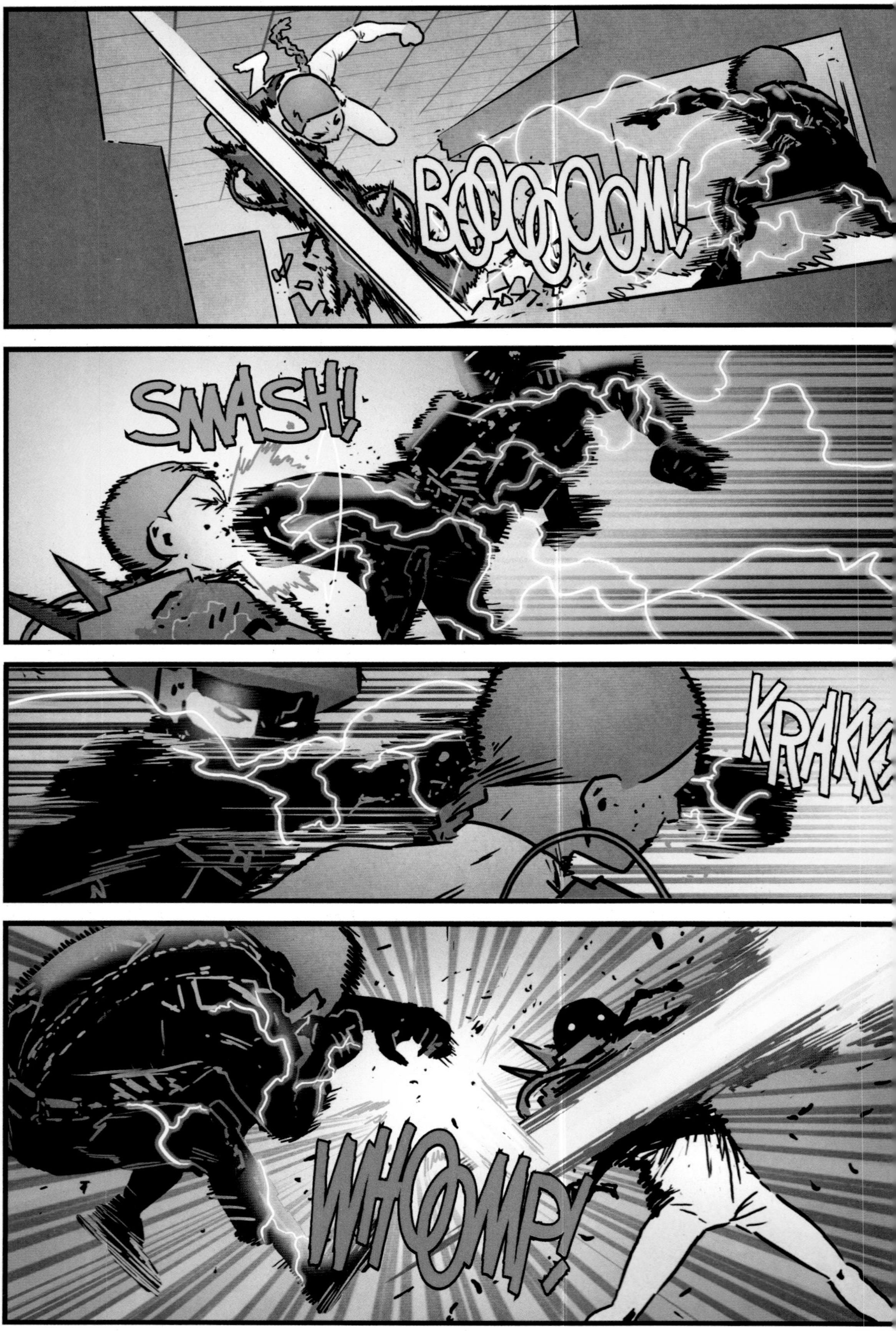
BOOOOOOM!
SMASH!
KRAKK
WHOMP!

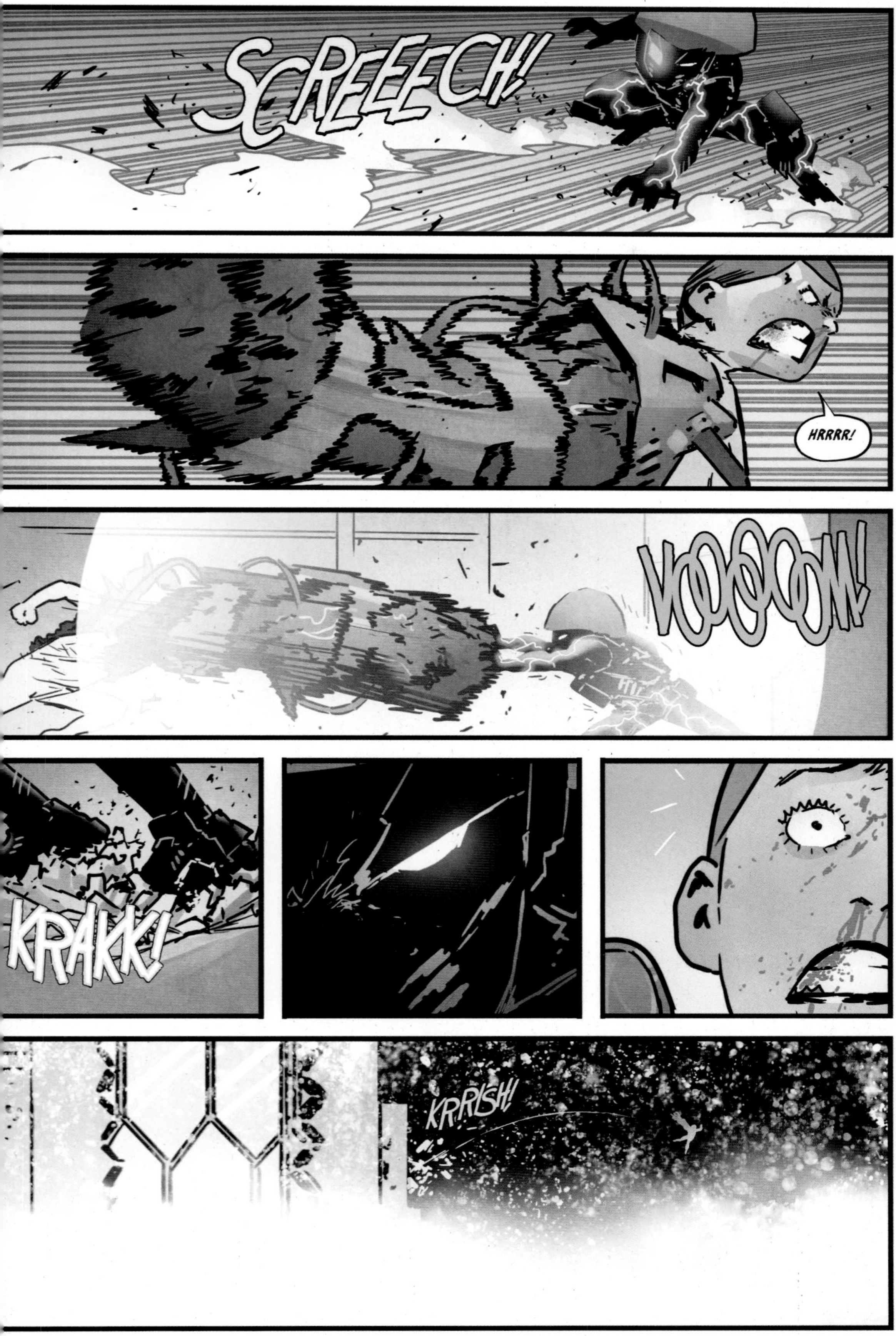
SCREEECH!
HRRRR!
VOOOOOM!
KRAKK!
KR.R.RISH!

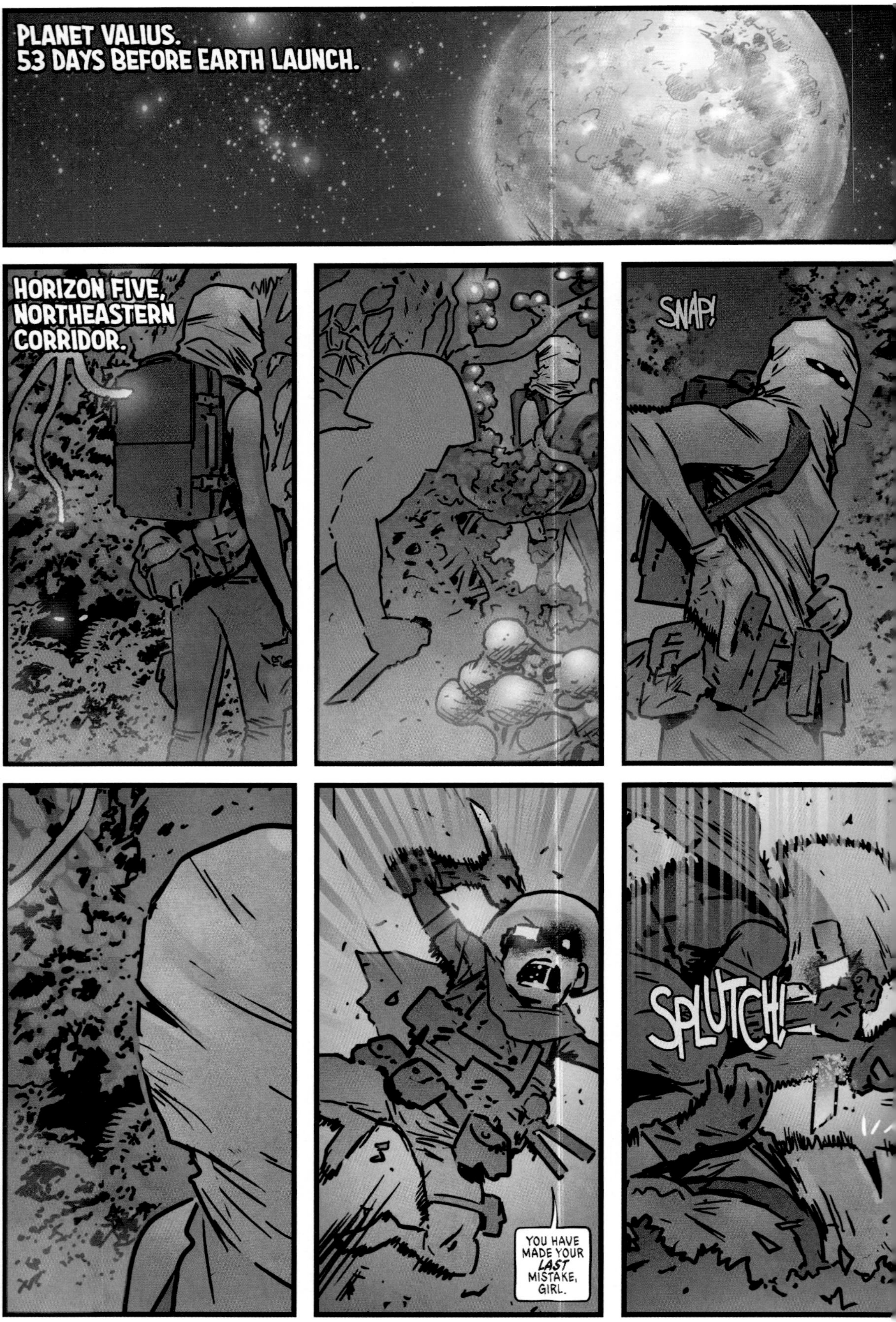
PLANET VALIUS.
53 DAYS BEFORE EARTH LAUNCH.
HORIZON FIVE, NORTHEASTERN CORRIDOR.
SNAP!
SPLUTCH!
YOU HAVE MADE YOUR LAST MISTAKE, GIRL.

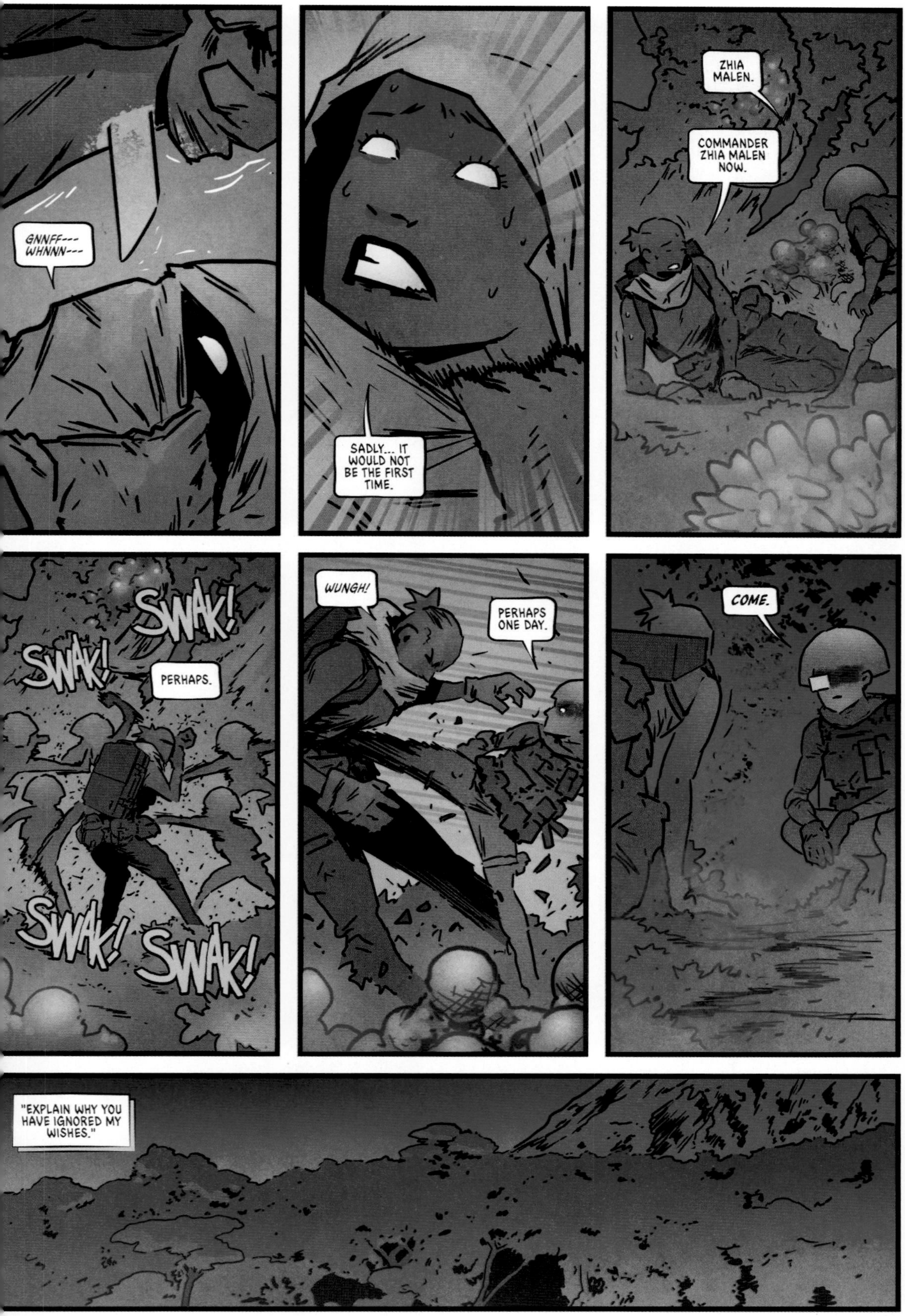
GNNFF---
WHNNN---
SADLY... IT WOULD NOT BE THE FIRST TIME.
ZHIA MALEN.
COMMANDER ZHIA MALEN NOW.
SWAK!
SWAK!
PERHAPS.
SWAK!
SWAK!
WUNGH!
PERHAPS ONE DAY.
COME.
"EXPLAIN WHY YOU HAVE IGNORED MY WISHES."

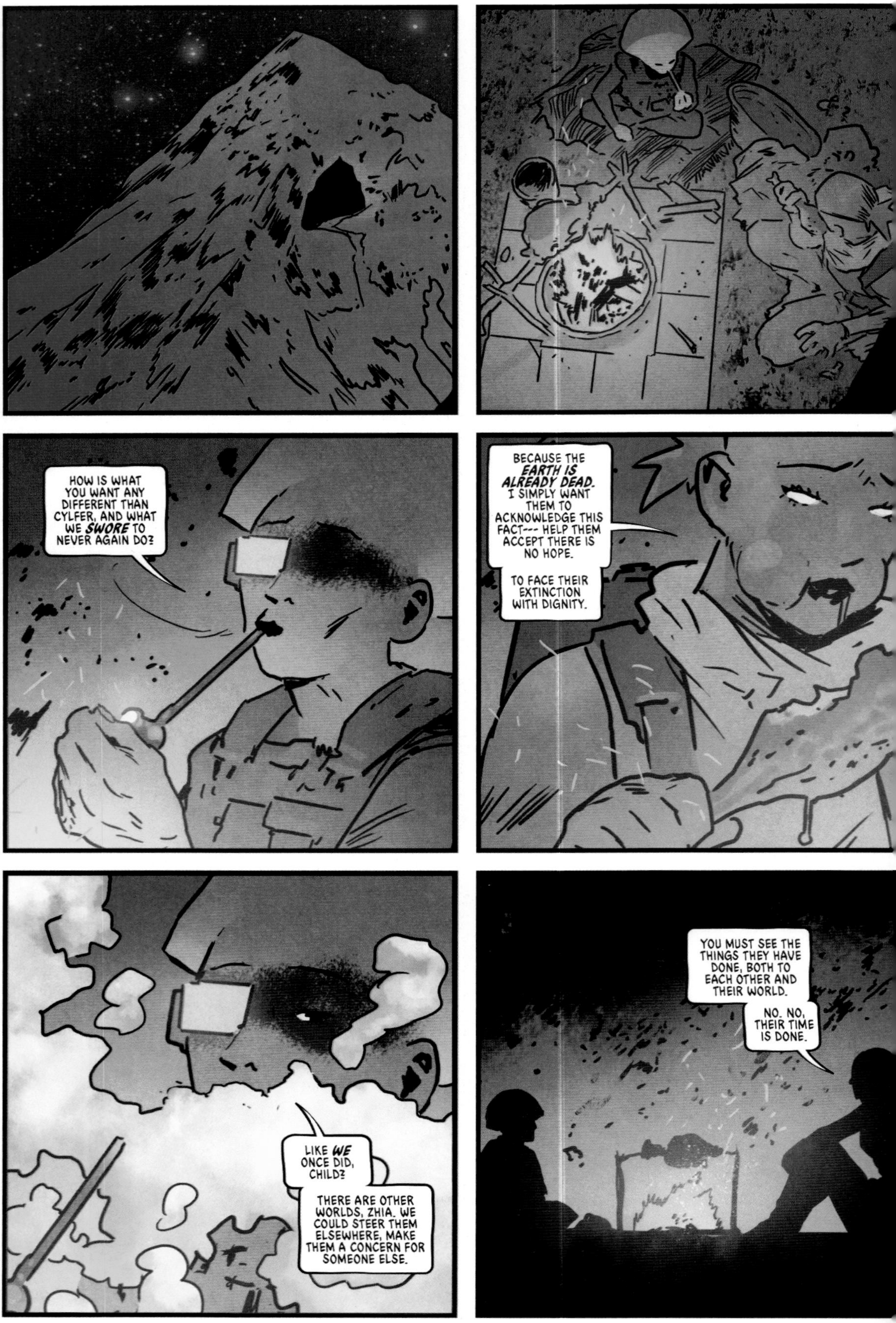

HOW IS WHAT YOU WANT ANY DIFFERENT THAN CYLFER, AND WHAT WE *SWORE* TO NEVER AGAIN DO?
BECAUSE THE ***EARTH IS ALREADY DEAD.*** I SIMPLY WANT THEM TO ACKNOWLEDGE THIS FACT--- HELP THEM ACCEPT THERE IS NO HOPE.
TO FACE THEIR EXTINCTION WITH DIGNITY.
LIKE *WE* ONCE DID, CHILD?
THERE ARE OTHER WORLDS, ZHIA. WE COULD STEER THEM ELSEWHERE, MAKE THEM A CONCERN FOR SOMEONE ELSE.
YOU MUST SEE THE THINGS THEY HAVE DONE, BOTH TO EACH OTHER AND THEIR WORLD.
NO. NO, THEIR TIME IS DONE.

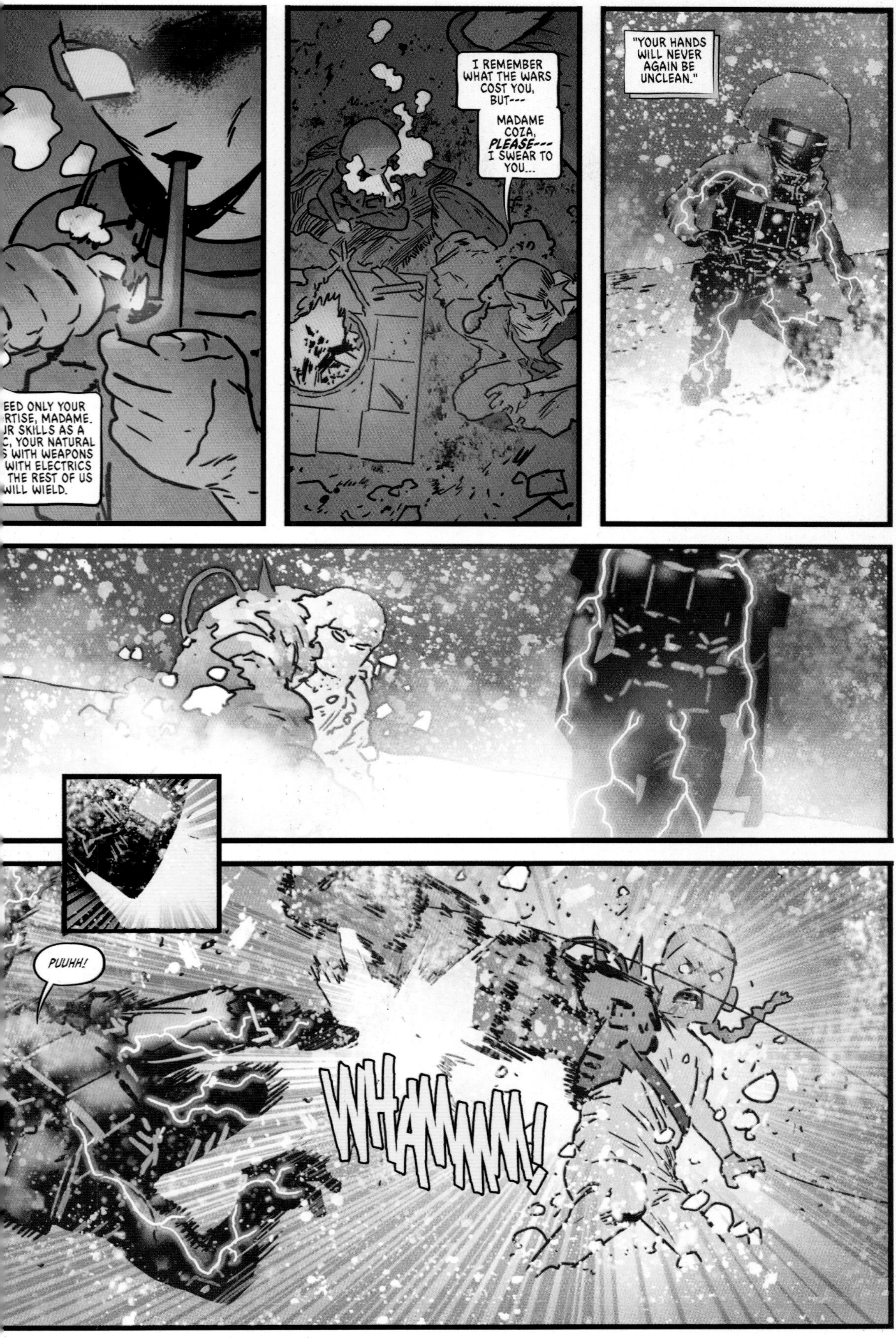

EED ONLY YOUR
RTISE, MADAME.
UR SKILLS AS A
C, YOUR NATURAL
S WITH WEAPONS
WITH ELECTRICS
THE REST OF US
WILL WIELD.
I REMEMBER WHAT THE WARS COST YOU, BUT---
MADAME COZA, *PLEASE*--- I SWEAR TO YOU...
"YOUR HANDS WILL NEVER AGAIN BE UNCLEAN."
PUUHH!
WHAMMM!

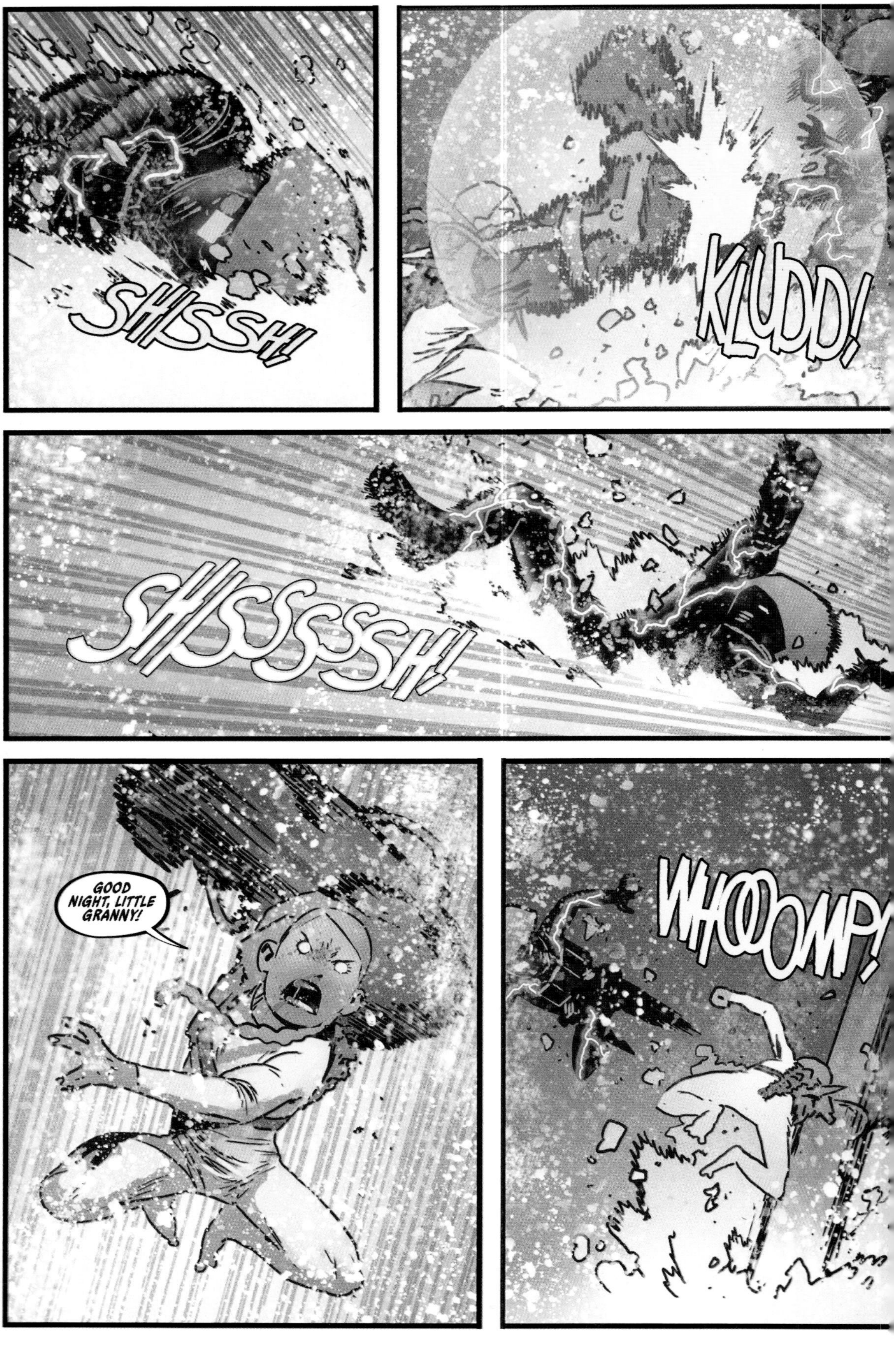
SHSSH!
KLUDD!
SHSSSSSH!
GOOD NIGHT, LITTLE GRANNY!
WHOOOMP!

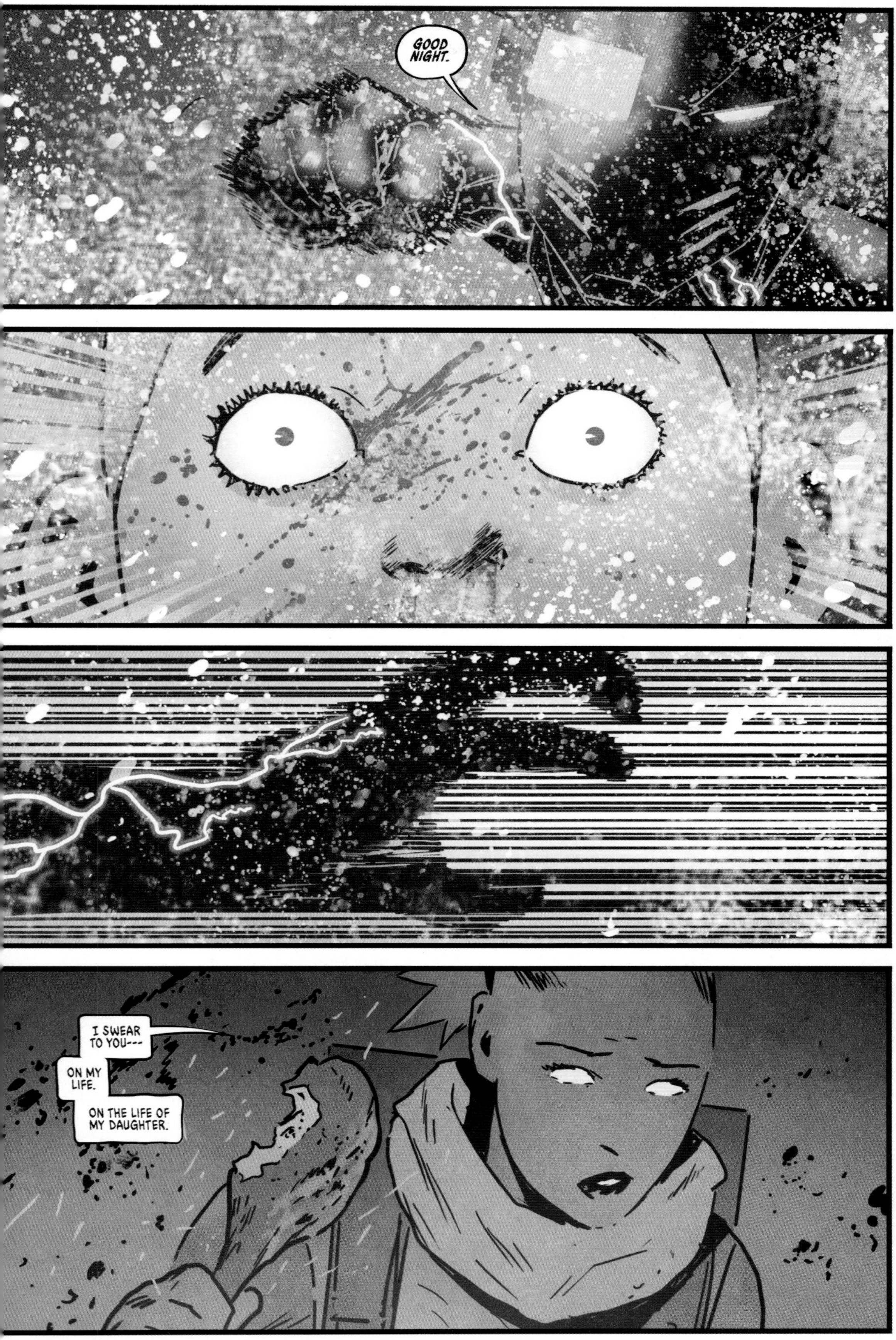
GOOD NIGHT.
I SWEAR TO YOU---
ON MY LIFE.
ON THE LIFE OF MY DAUGHTER.

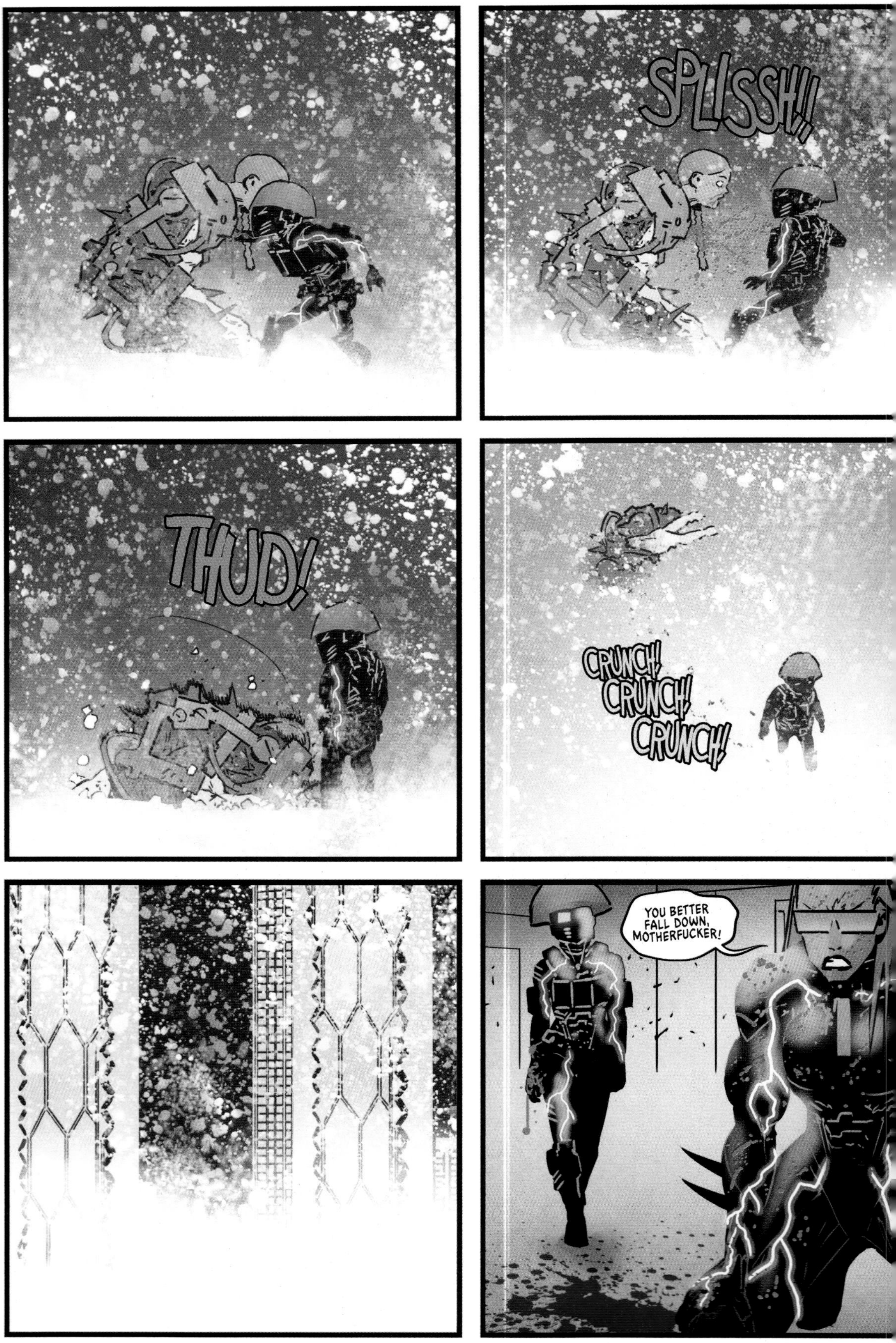
SPLISSH!!
THUD!
CRUNCH!
CRUNCH!
CRUNCH!
YOU BETTER FALL DOWN, MOTHERFUCKER!

WOOO!! WHY IS IT SO *HARD* TO KILL US? HOOO!

DID THE LITTLE JERK GET THE MESSAGE, MARIOL?

....

OH NO---

OH, MARIOL, NO.

MARIOL, I AM *SO SORRY.* I HOPED THAT---

PERHAPS *YOU* DID, BUT SHE *ALWAYS* KNEW IT WOULD COME TO THIS.

GIVEN ENOUGH TIME, I WOULD HAVE TO DECIDE---AND SHE *KNEW* WHAT THAT CHOICE WOULD ALWAYS BE.

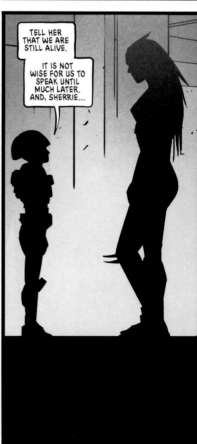

TELL HER THAT WE ARE STILL ALIVE.

IT IS NOT WISE FOR US TO SPEAK UNTIL MUCH LATER. AND, SHERRIE...

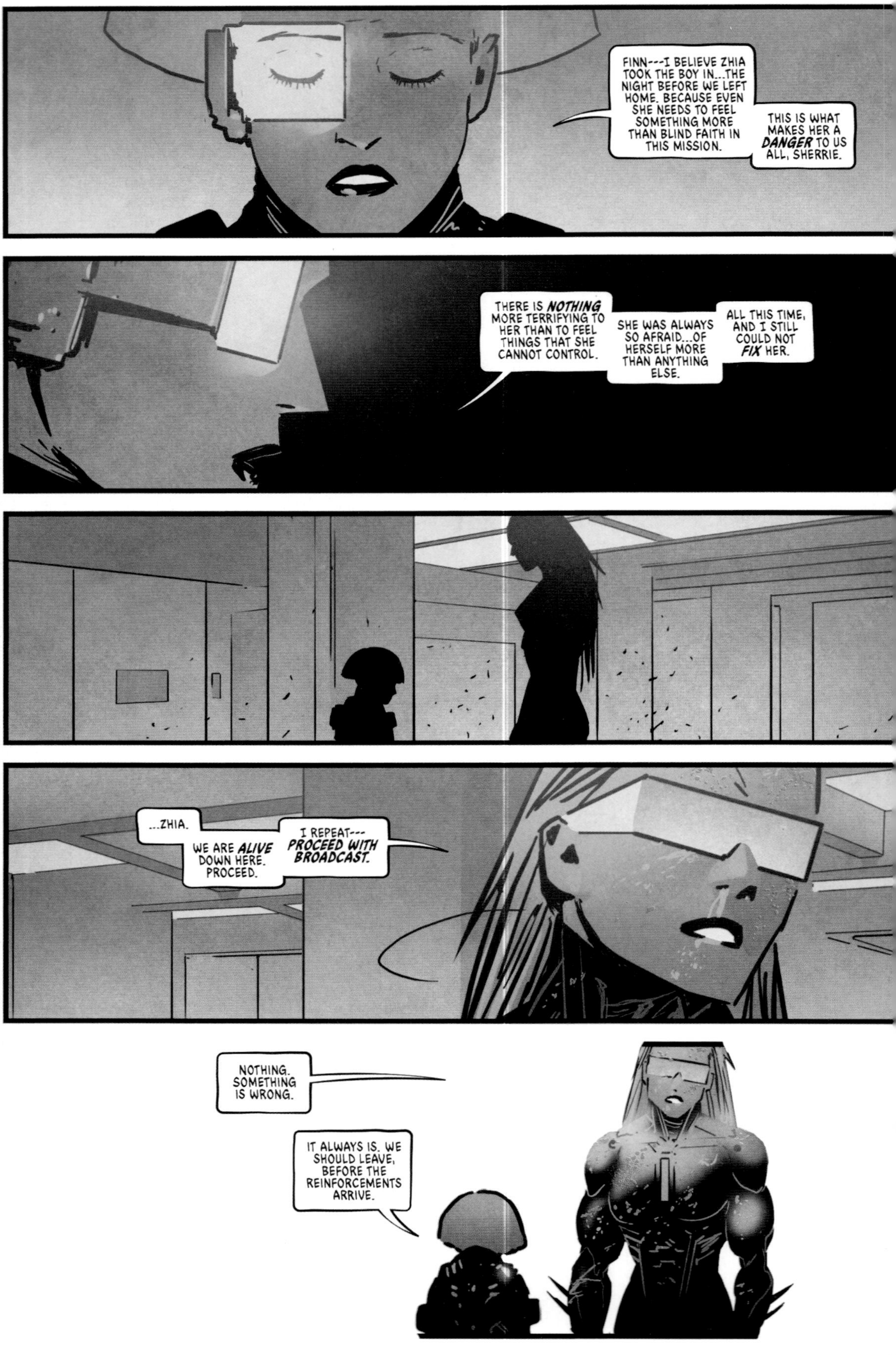
FINN---I BELIEVE ZHIA TOOK THE BOY IN...THE NIGHT BEFORE WE LEFT HOME. BECAUSE EVEN SHE NEEDS TO FEEL SOMETHING MORE THAN BLIND FAITH IN THIS MISSION.
THIS IS WHAT MAKES HER A DANGER TO US ALL, SHERRIE.
THERE IS NOTHING MORE TERRIFYING TO HER THAN TO FEEL THINGS THAT SHE CANNOT CONTROL.
SHE WAS ALWAYS SO AFRAID...OF HERSELF MORE THAN ANYTHING ELSE.
ALL THIS TIME, AND I STILL COULD NOT FIX HER.
...ZHIA.
WE ARE ALIVE DOWN HERE. PROCEED.
I REPEAT--- PROCEED WITH BROADCAST.
NOTHING. SOMETHING IS WRONG.
IT ALWAYS IS. WE SHOULD LEAVE, BEFORE THE REINFORCEMENTS ARRIVE.

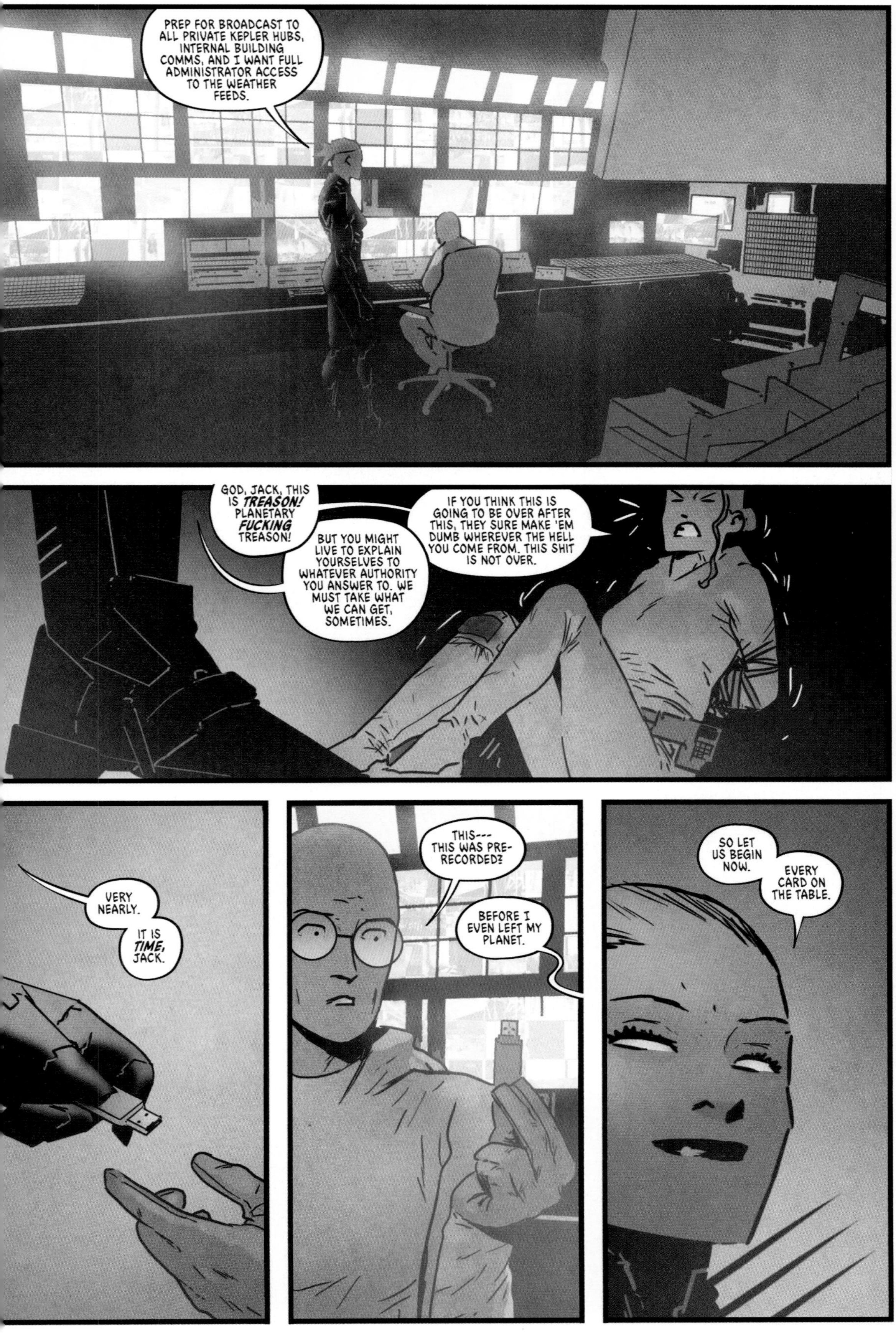
PREP FOR BROADCAST TO ALL PRIVATE KEPLER HUBS, INTERNAL BUILDING COMMS, AND I WANT FULL ADMINISTRATOR ACCESS TO THE WEATHER FEEDS.
GOD, JACK, THIS IS TREASON! PLANETARY FUCKING TREASON!
BUT YOU MIGHT LIVE TO EXPLAIN YOURSELVES TO WHATEVER AUTHORITY YOU ANSWER TO. WE MUST TAKE WHAT WE CAN GET, SOMETIMES.
IF YOU THINK THIS IS GOING TO BE OVER AFTER THIS, THEY SURE MAKE 'EM DUMB WHEREVER THE HELL YOU COME FROM. THIS SHIT IS NOT OVER.
VERY NEARLY.
IT IS TIME, JACK.
THIS--- THIS WAS PRE-RECORDED?
BEFORE I EVEN LEFT MY PLANET.
SO LET US BEGIN NOW.
EVERY CARD ON THE TABLE.

---WEATHER ALERT RE---KSSSSH---PEOPLE OF EASSSHHH---PEOPLE OF EARTH---
DO NOT EVER FORGET...WE WARNED YOU. WE TOLD YOU WHAT WOULD HAPPEN IF YOU DID NOT TAKE RESPONSIBILITY FOR THE THINGS YOU HAVE DONE, AND ADMIT HUMANITY IS NOW LOST.
THIS IS JACELL DAVIX OF THE PLANET VALIUS, AND IF YOU ARE WITHIN THE SOUND OF MY VOICE, THEN YOU ARE DEAD.
YOU HAVE ALREADY DIED, AND NO ONE CARED ENOUGH TO INFORM YOU...

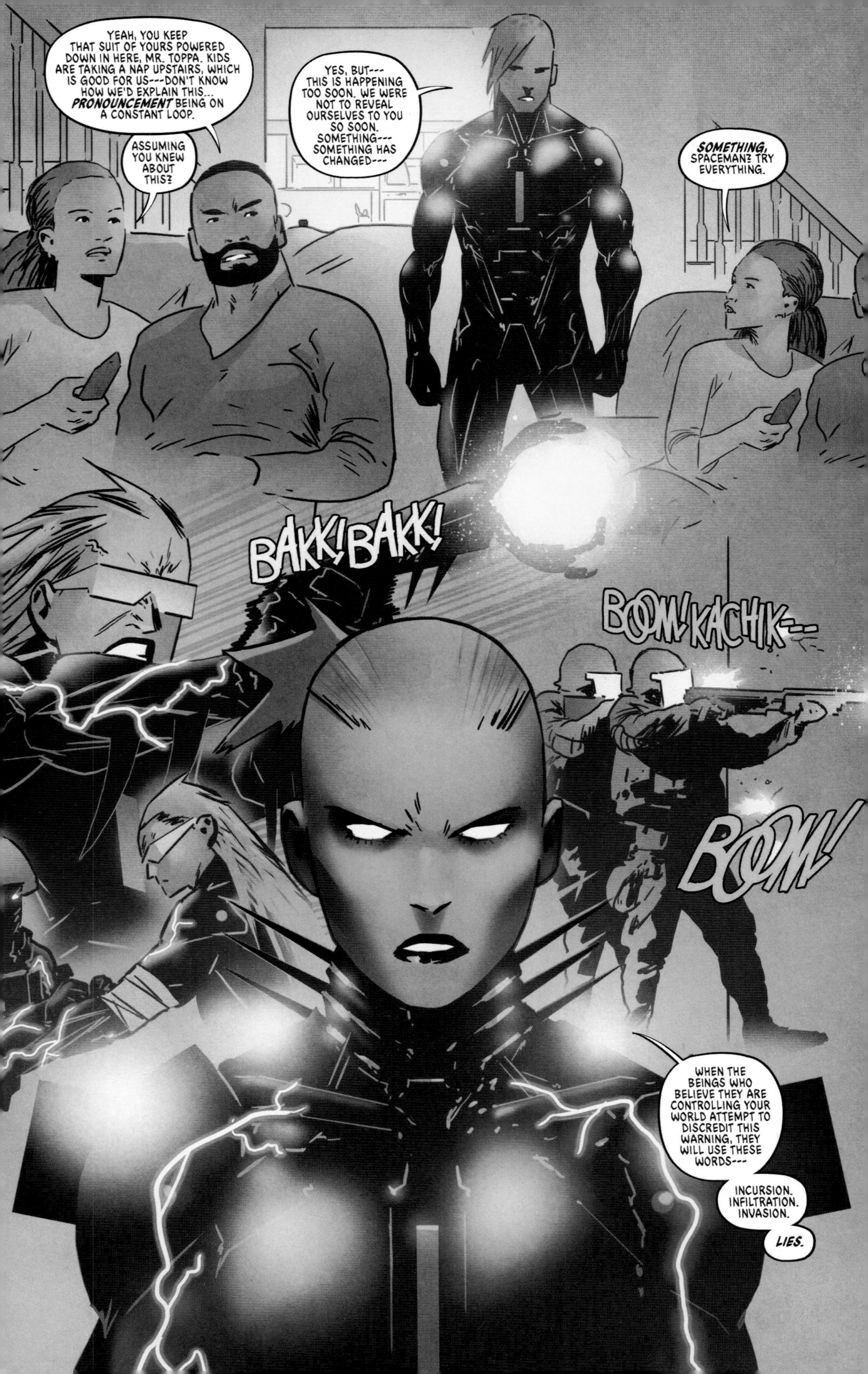
YEAH, YOU KEEP THAT SUIT OF YOURS POWERED DOWN IN HERE, MR. TOPPA. KIDS ARE TAKING A NAP UPSTAIRS, WHICH IS GOOD FOR US---DON'T KNOW HOW WE'D EXPLAIN THIS... PRONOUNCEMENT BEING ON A CONSTANT LOOP.
ASSUMING YOU KNEW ABOUT THIS?
YES, BUT--- THIS IS HAPPENING TOO SOON. WE WERE NOT TO REVEAL OURSELVES TO YOU SO SOON. SOMETHING--- SOMETHING HAS CHANGED---
SOMETHING, SPACEMAN? TRY EVERYTHING.
BAKK! BAKK!
BOOM! KACHIK---
BOOM!
WHEN THE BEINGS WHO BELIEVE THEY ARE CONTROLLING YOUR WORLD ATTEMPT TO DISCREDIT THIS WARNING, THEY WILL USE THESE WORDS---
INCURSION. INFILTRATION. INVASION.
LIES.

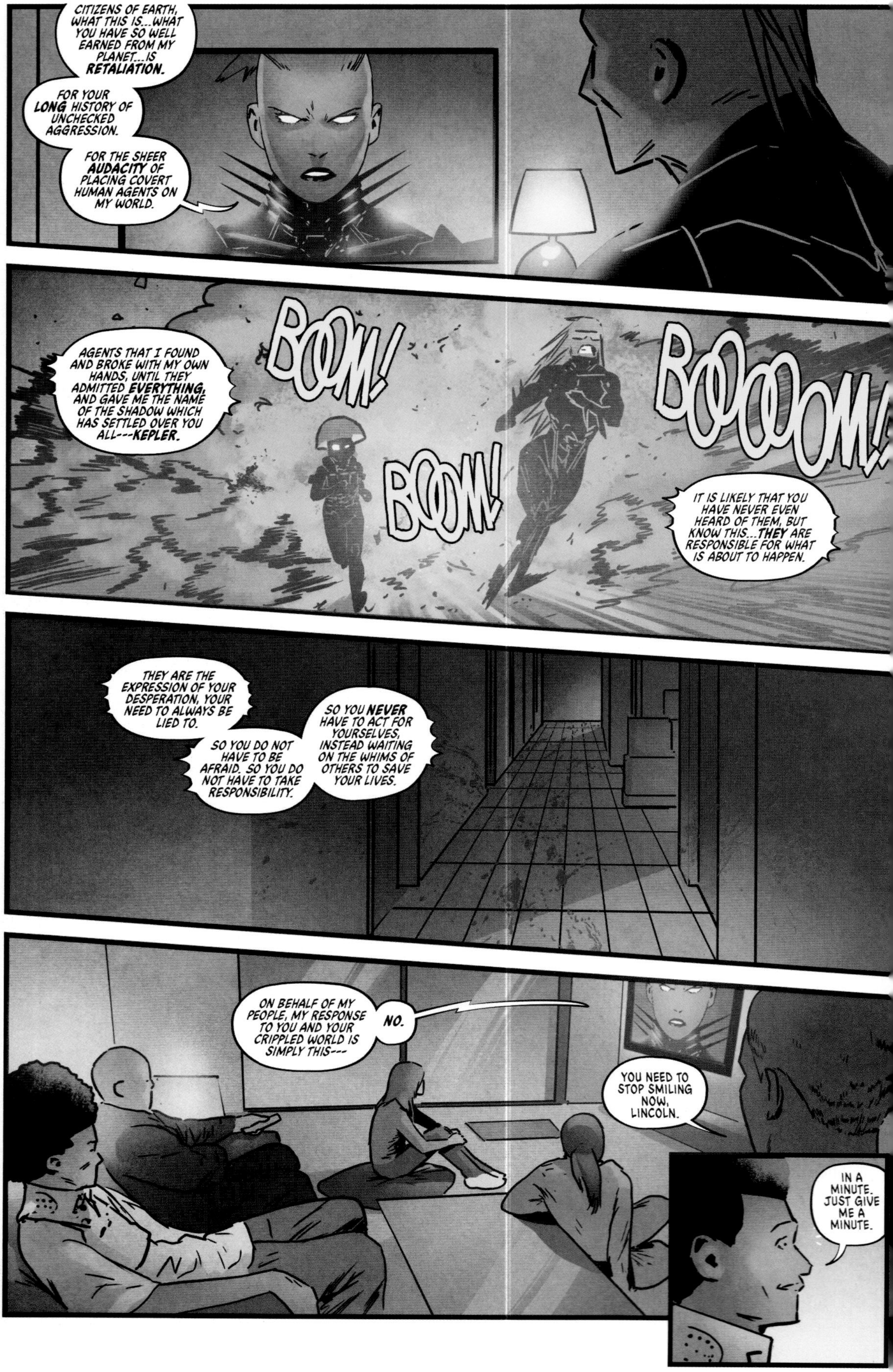

CITIZENS OF EARTH, WHAT THIS IS...WHAT YOU HAVE SO WELL EARNED FROM MY PLANET...IS RETALIATION.
FOR YOUR LONG HISTORY OF UNCHECKED AGGRESSION.
FOR THE SHEER AUDACITY OF PLACING COVERT HUMAN AGENTS ON MY WORLD.
AGENTS THAT I FOUND AND BROKE WITH MY OWN HANDS, UNTIL THEY ADMITTED EVERYTHING, AND GAVE ME THE NAME OF THE SHADOW WHICH HAS SETTLED OVER YOU ALL---KEPLER.
BOOM!
BOOM!
BOOOOOM!
IT IS LIKELY THAT YOU HAVE NEVER EVEN HEARD OF THEM, BUT KNOW THIS...THEY ARE RESPONSIBLE FOR WHAT IS ABOUT TO HAPPEN.
THEY ARE THE EXPRESSION OF YOUR DESPERATION, YOUR NEED TO ALWAYS BE LIED TO.
SO YOU DO NOT HAVE TO BE AFRAID. SO YOU DO NOT HAVE TO TAKE RESPONSIBILITY.
SO YOU NEVER HAVE TO ACT FOR YOURSELVES, INSTEAD WAITING ON THE WHIMS OF OTHERS TO SAVE YOUR LIVES.
ON BEHALF OF MY PEOPLE, MY RESPONSE TO YOU AND YOUR CRIPPLED WORLD IS SIMPLY THIS---
NO.
YOU NEED TO STOP SMILING NOW, LINCOLN.
IN A MINUTE. JUST GIVE ME A MINUTE.

NO, YOU **CANNOT** HAVE MY PLANET.

NO, YOU WILL **NOT** BRING YOUR BRAND OF WANTON DESTRUCTION AND CHILDISH DISREGARD TO SOME OTHER UNSUSPECTING WORLD.

NO, YOU CANNOT HAVE **ANOTHER** IN AN ENDLESS LINE OF SECOND CHANCES.

BECAUSE I DO NOT BELIEVE YOU HAVE ACTUALLY LEARNED YOUR LESSON.

AND THERE IS NOT ENOUGH TIME FOR YOU TO DO SO. NOT ANY LONGER.

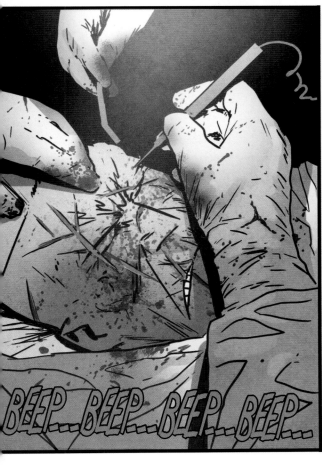

BEEP...BEEP...BEEP...BEEP...

AND YES, WE ARE FULLY PREPARED TO MEET OUR END RIGHT ALONGSIDE YOU, IF **THAT** IS REQUIRED OF US.

YOU CANNOT STOP US BECAUSE YOU CANNOT EVEN TELL YOURSELVES THE TRUTH.

YOU NEEDED ME TO TRAVEL HERE FROM WORLDS AWAY...SO THAT YOU COULD KNOW WHAT YOU HAVE LONG FELT INSIDE OF YOU WAS TRUE.

THEY ALMOST HAVE THE SOURCE, MADAME PRESIDENT...ANY SECOND NOW...

THERE IS NO HOPE. NO ESCAPE.

SO, CONGRATULATIONS.

MIGHT BE A WEIRD QUESTION, CONSIDERING---

NOW... NOW, YOU ARE FREE.

YOU GUYS HAVE A COMPUTER I CAN BORROW FOR A FEW MINUTES?

YOU HAVE SO LITTLE TIME LEFT---

---LET ME SHOW YOU.

THEY'RE GOING TO FIND US, AND THERE'S NO WAY YOU'RE GETTING OUT OF HERE!

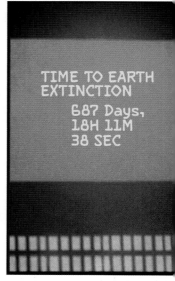

TIME TO EARTH EXTINCTION

687 Days, 18H 11M 38 SEC

THIS IS ALL THE TIME LEFT IN YOUR WORLD. NOT EVEN 700 OF YOUR DAYS REMAIN.

NO. NO, THAT CAN'T BE RIGHT. THEY SAID WE HAD---

THEY LIED, GIRL.

IT IS NEARLY OVER, AND WE WILL NEVER BE SORRY.

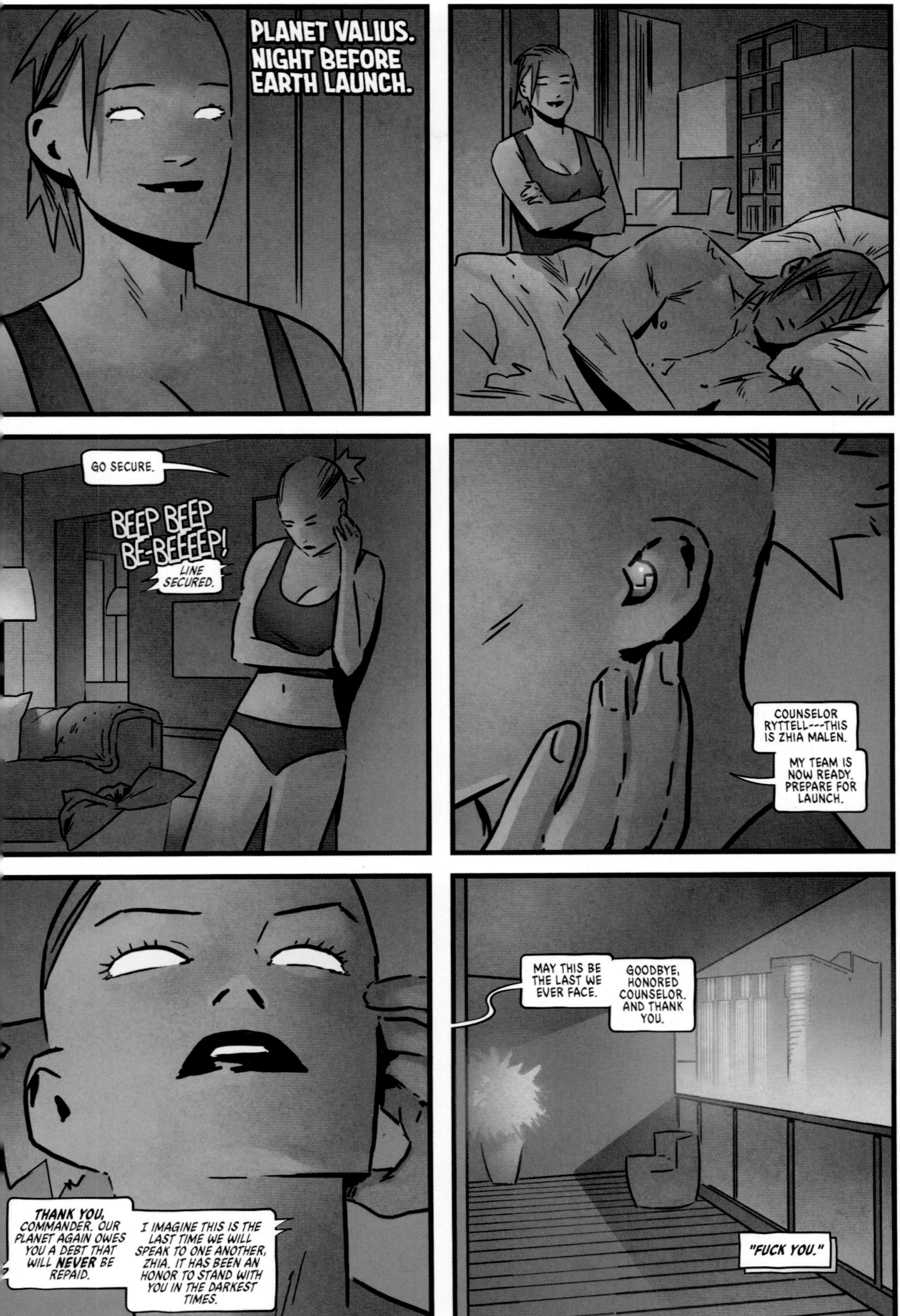
PLANET VALIUS. NIGHT BEFORE EARTH LAUNCH.
GO SECURE.
BEEP BEEP BE-BEEEEP!
LINE SECURED.
COUNSELOR RYTTELL---THIS IS ZHIA MALEN.
MY TEAM IS NOW READY. PREPARE FOR LAUNCH.
THANK YOU, COMMANDER. OUR PLANET AGAIN OWES YOU A DEBT THAT WILL NEVER BE REPAID.
I IMAGINE THIS IS THE LAST TIME WE WILL SPEAK TO ONE ANOTHER, ZHIA. IT HAS BEEN AN HONOR TO STAND WITH YOU IN THE DARKEST TIMES.
MAY THIS BE THE LAST WE EVER FACE.
GOODBYE, HONORED COUNSELOR. AND THANK YOU.
"FUCK YOU."

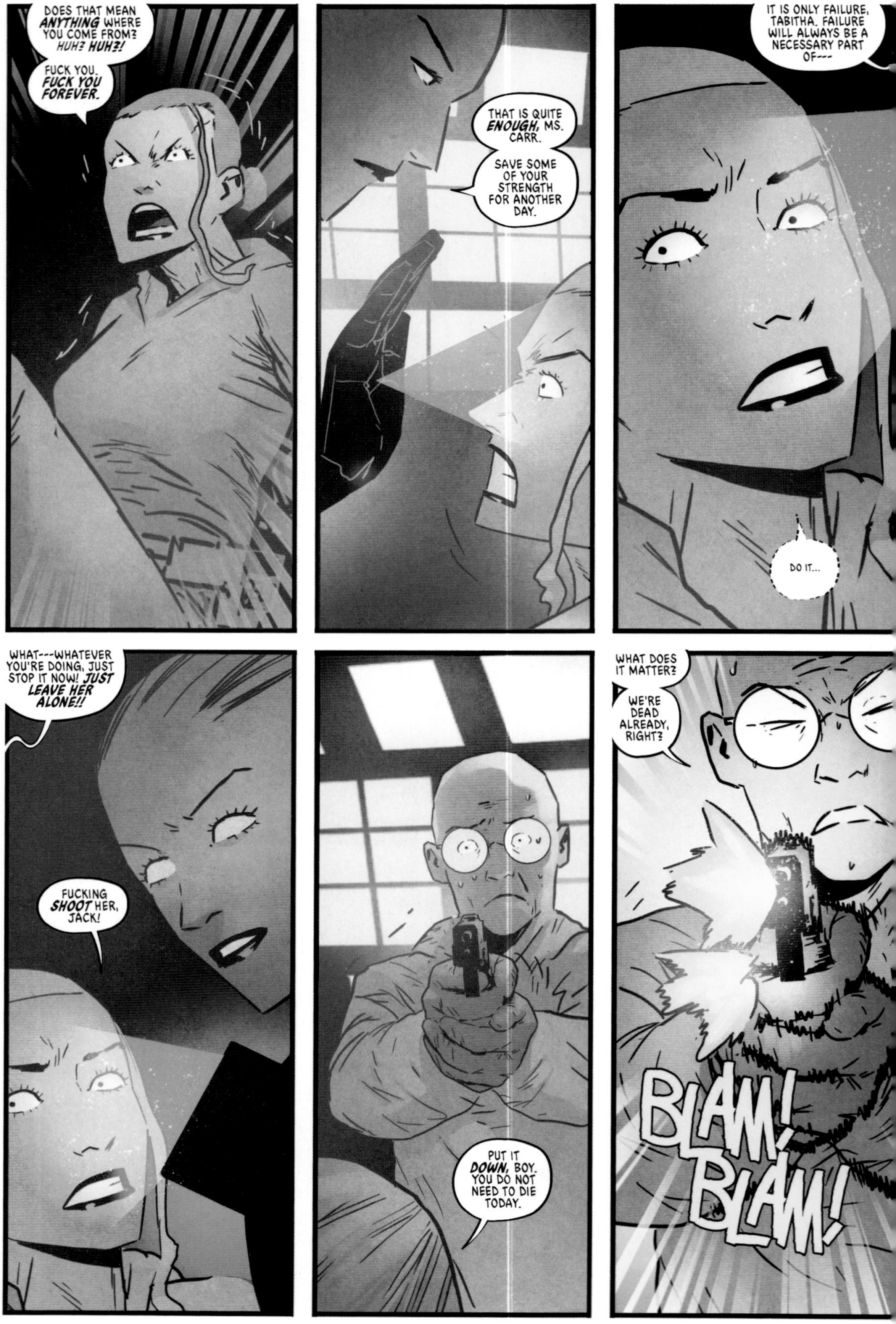
DOES THAT MEAN ANYTHING WHERE YOU COME FROM? HUH? HUH?!
FUCK YOU. FUCK YOU FOREVER.
THAT IS QUITE ENOUGH, MS. CARR.
SAVE SOME OF YOUR STRENGTH FOR ANOTHER DAY.
IT IS ONLY FAILURE, TABITHA. FAILURE WILL ALWAYS BE A NECESSARY PART OF---
DO IT...
WHAT---WHATEVER YOU'RE DOING, JUST STOP IT NOW! JUST LEAVE HER ALONE!!
FUCKING SHOOT HER, JACK!
PUT IT DOWN, BOY. YOU DO NOT NEED TO DIE TODAY.
WHAT DOES IT MATTER?
WE'RE DEAD ALREADY, RIGHT?
BLAM! BLAM!

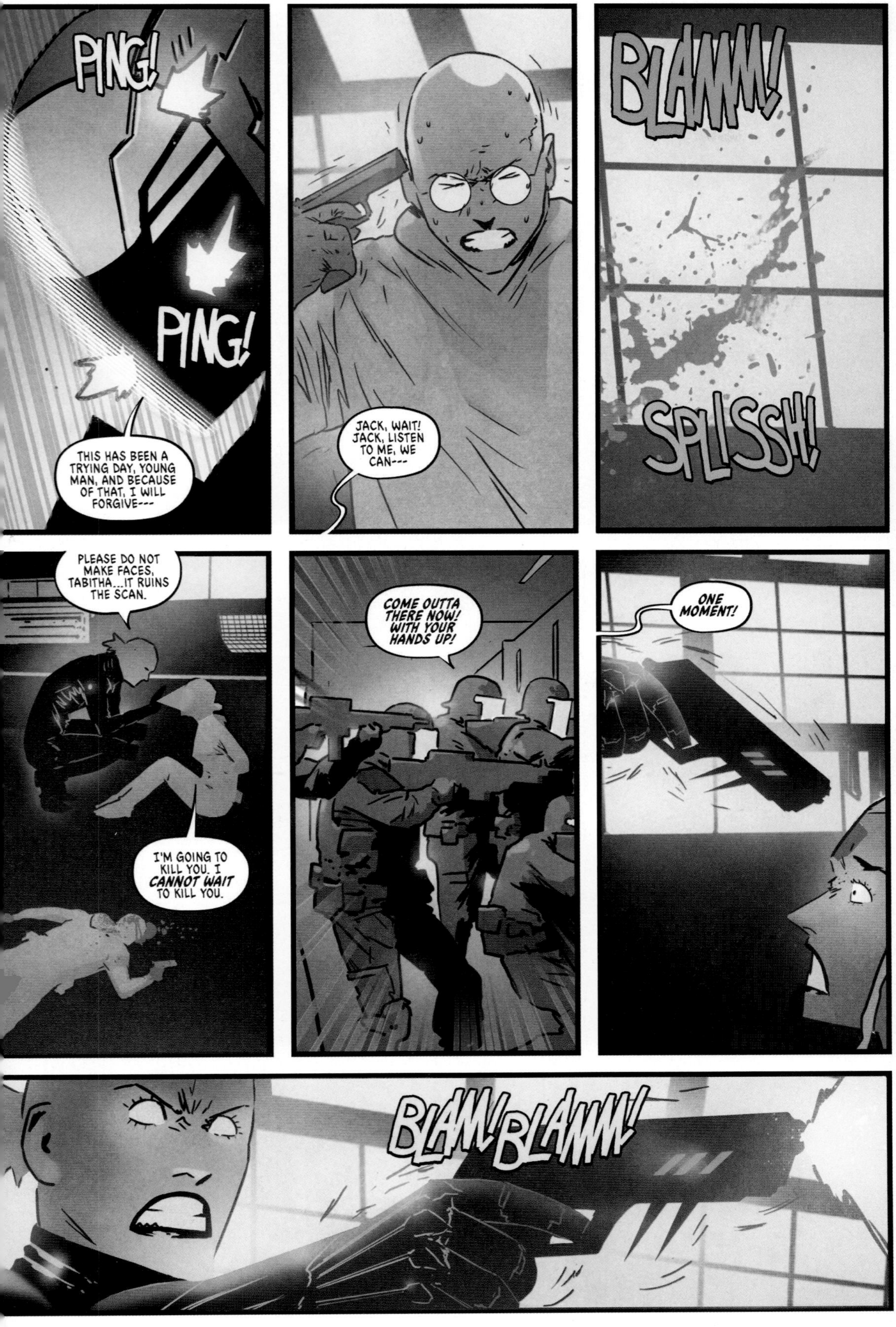
PING!
PING!
THIS HAS BEEN A TRYING DAY, YOUNG MAN, AND BECAUSE OF THAT, I WILL FORGIVE---
JACK, WAIT! JACK, LISTEN TO ME, WE CAN---
BLAMM!
SPLISSH!
PLEASE DO NOT MAKE FACES, TABITHA...IT RUINS THE SCAN.
I'M GOING TO KILL YOU. I CANNOT WAIT TO KILL YOU.
COME OUTTA THERE NOW! WITH YOUR HANDS UP!
ONE MOMENT!
BLAM! BLAMM!

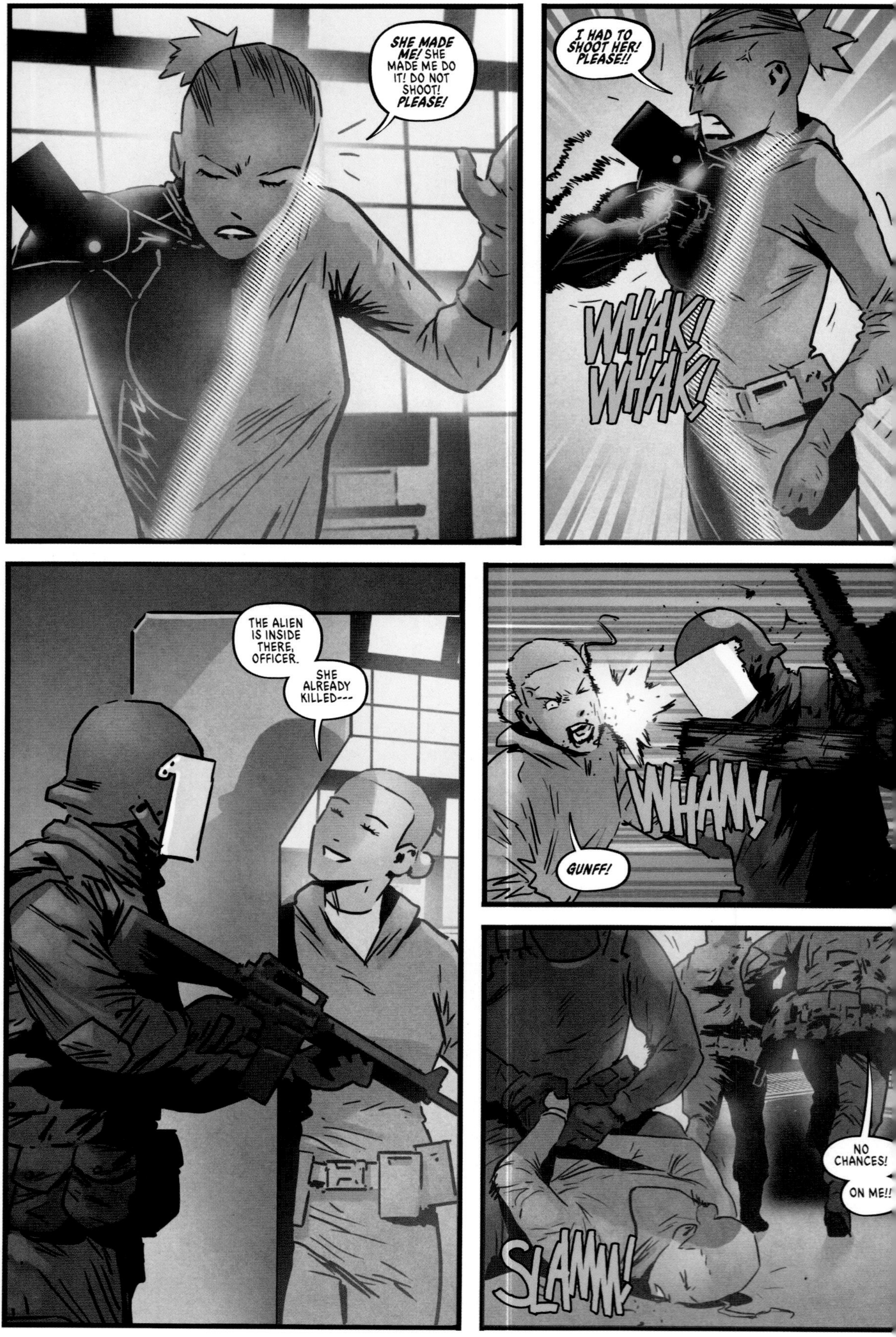
SHE MADE ME! SHE MADE ME DO IT! DO NOT SHOOT! PLEASE!
I HAD TO SHOOT HER! PLEASE!!
WHAK! WHAK!
THE ALIEN IS INSIDE THERE, OFFICER.
SHE ALREADY KILLED---
WHAM!
GUNFF!
NO CHANCES!
ON ME!!
SLAMM!

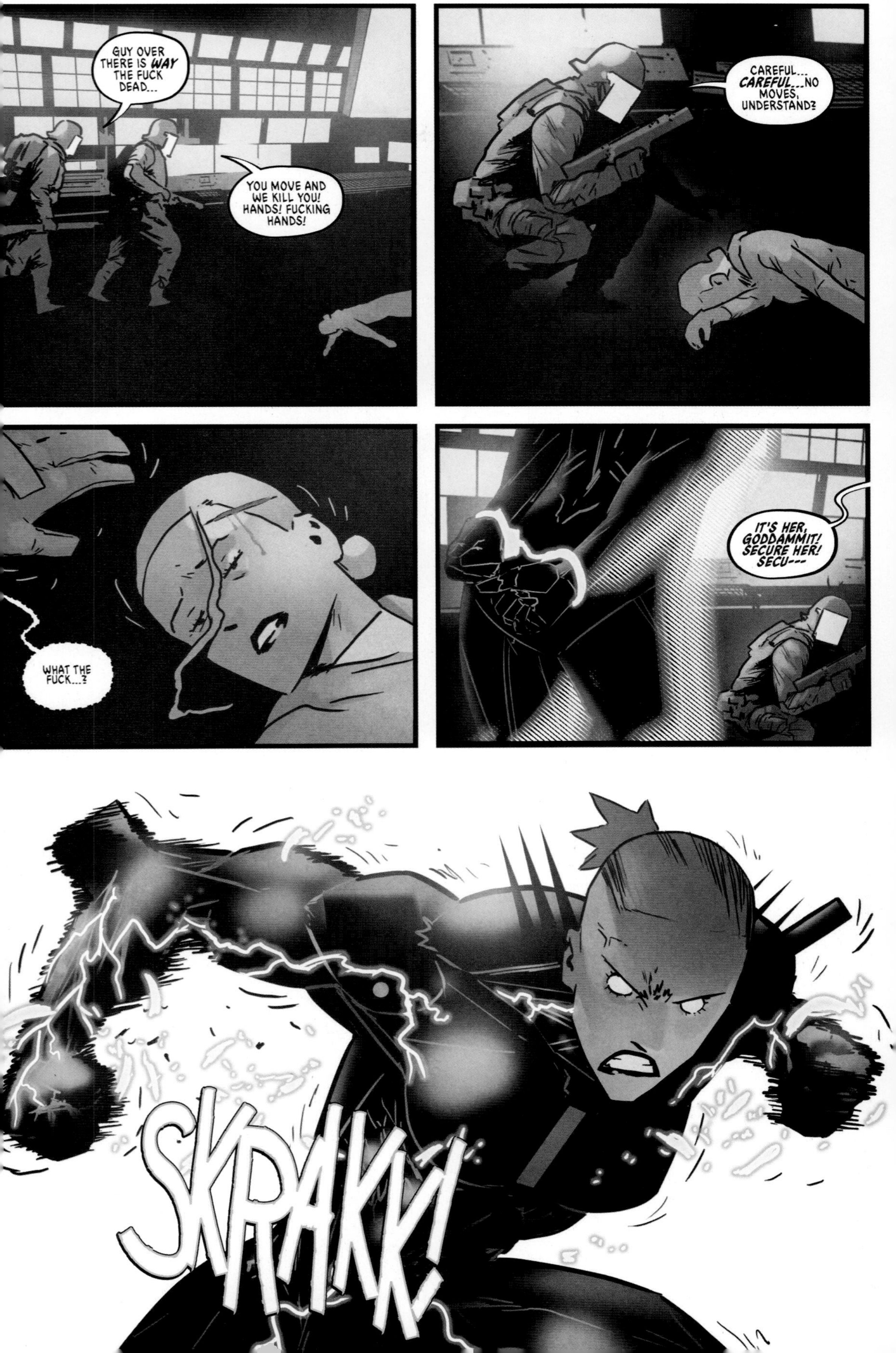
GUY OVER THERE IS WAY THE FUCK DEAD...
YOU MOVE AND WE KILL YOU! HANDS! FUCKING HANDS!
CAREFUL... CAREFUL...NO MOVES, UNDERSTAND?
WHAT THE FUCK...?
IT'S HER, GODDAMMIT! SECURE HER! SECU---
SKRAKK!

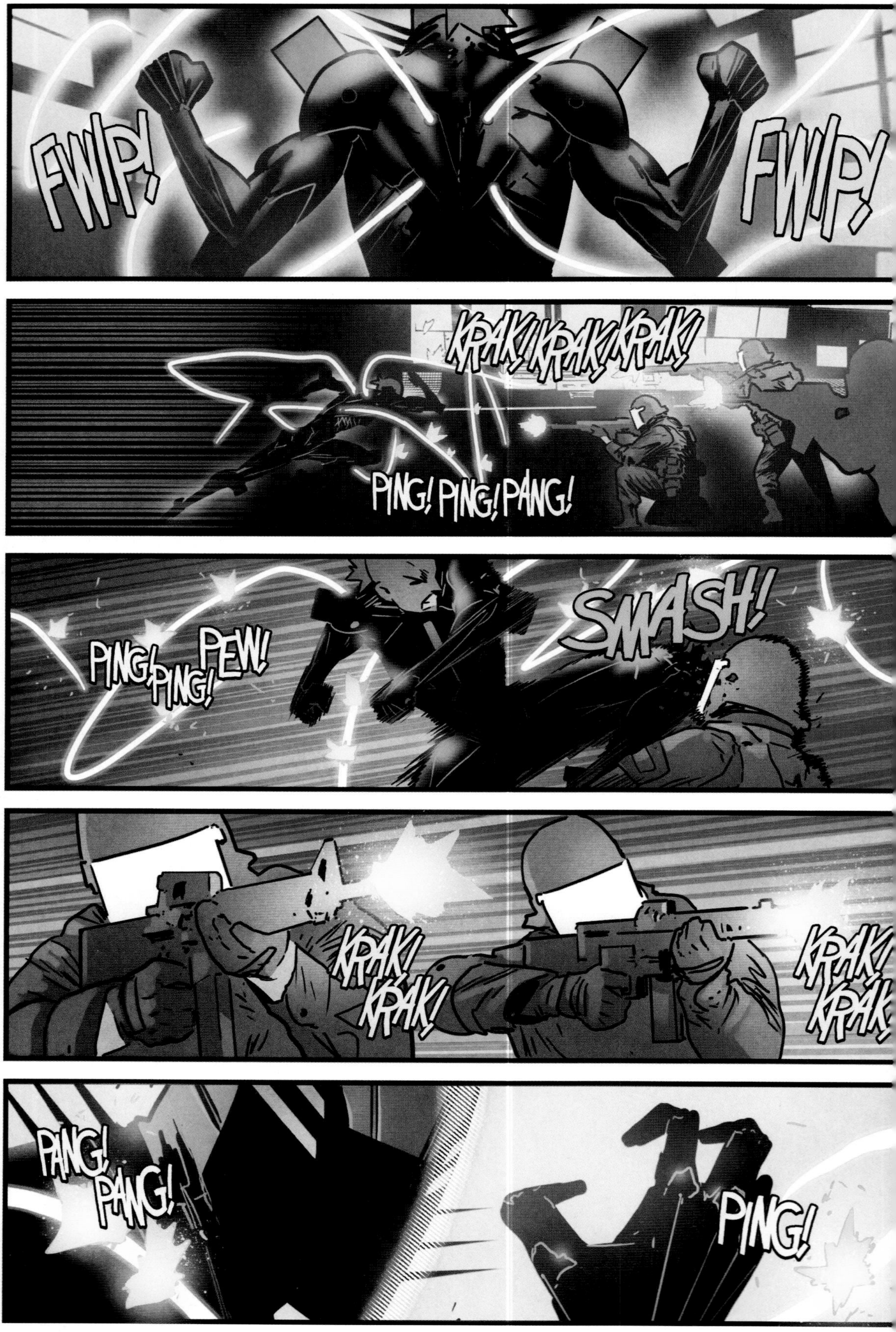

FWIP!
FWIP!
KRAK! KRAK! KRAK!
PING! PING! PANG!
PING! PING! PEW!
SMASH!
KRAK! KRAK!
KRAK! KRAK!
PANG! PANG!
PING!

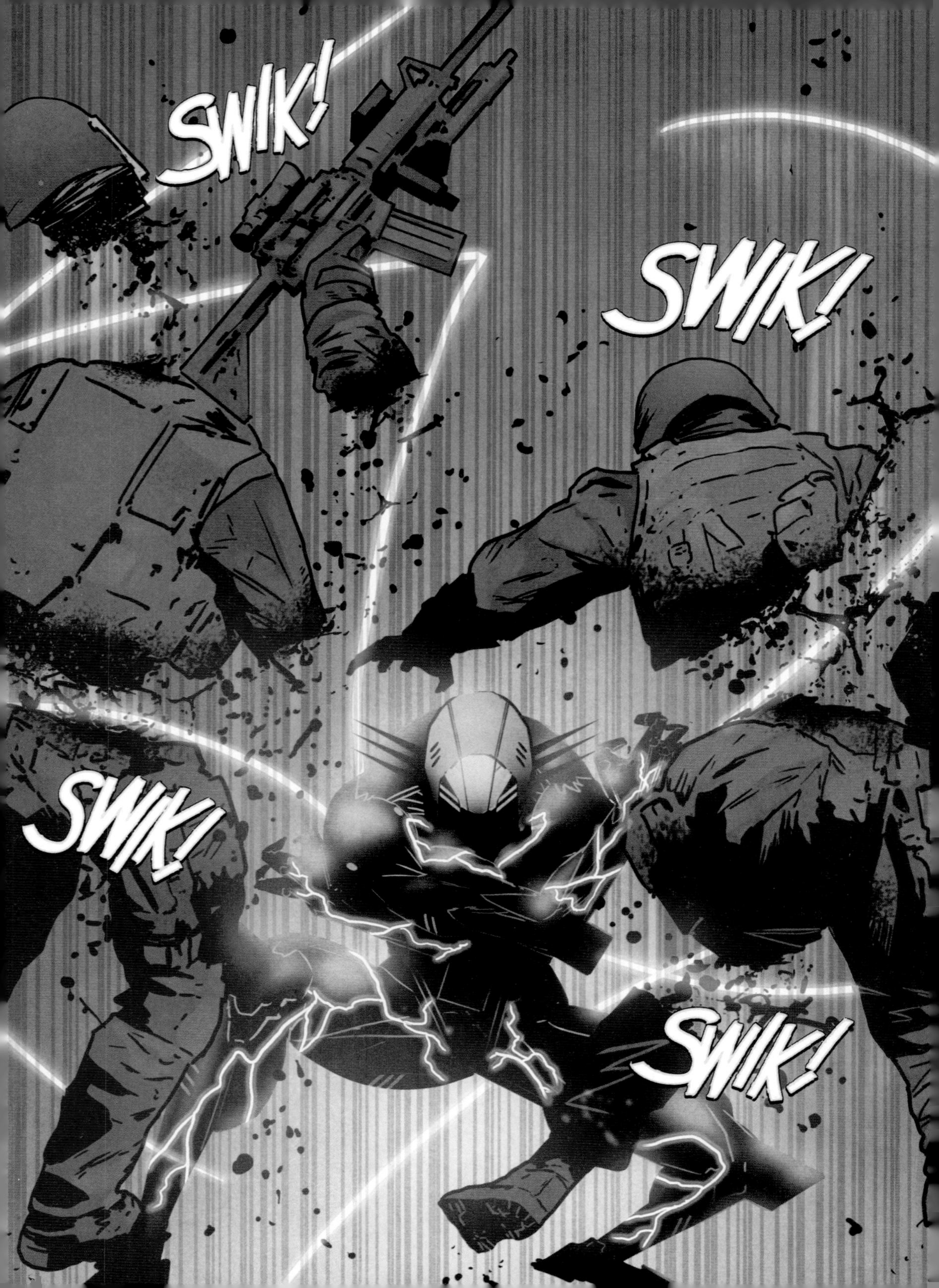
SWIK!
SWIK!
SWIK!
SWIK!

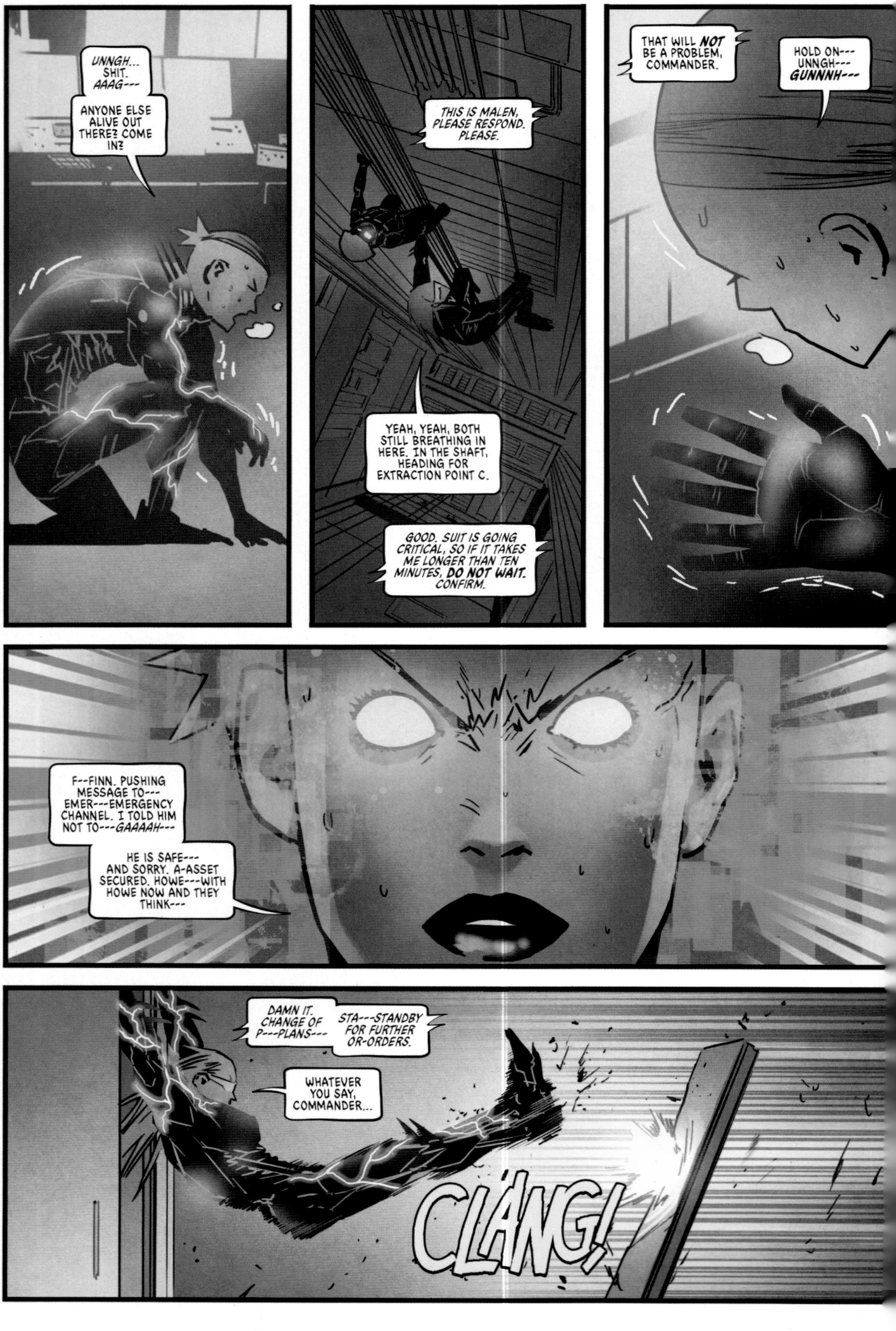
UNNGH... SHIT. AAAG---
ANYONE ELSE ALIVE OUT THERE? COME IN?
THIS IS MALEN, PLEASE RESPOND. PLEASE.
YEAH, YEAH, BOTH STILL BREATHING IN HERE. IN THE SHAFT, HEADING FOR EXTRACTION POINT C.
GOOD. SUIT IS GOING CRITICAL, SO IF IT TAKES ME LONGER THAN TEN MINUTES, DO NOT WAIT. CONFIRM.
THAT WILL NOT BE A PROBLEM, COMMANDER.
HOLD ON--- UNNGH--- GUNNNH---
F--FINN. PUSHING MESSAGE TO--- EMER---EMERGENCY CHANNEL. I TOLD HIM NOT TO---GAAAAH---
HE IS SAFE--- AND SORRY. A-ASSET SECURED. HOWE---WITH HOWE NOW AND THEY THINK---
DAMN IT. CHANGE OF P---PLANS---
STA---STANDBY FOR FURTHER OR-ORDERS.
WHATEVER YOU SAY, COMMANDER...
CLANG!

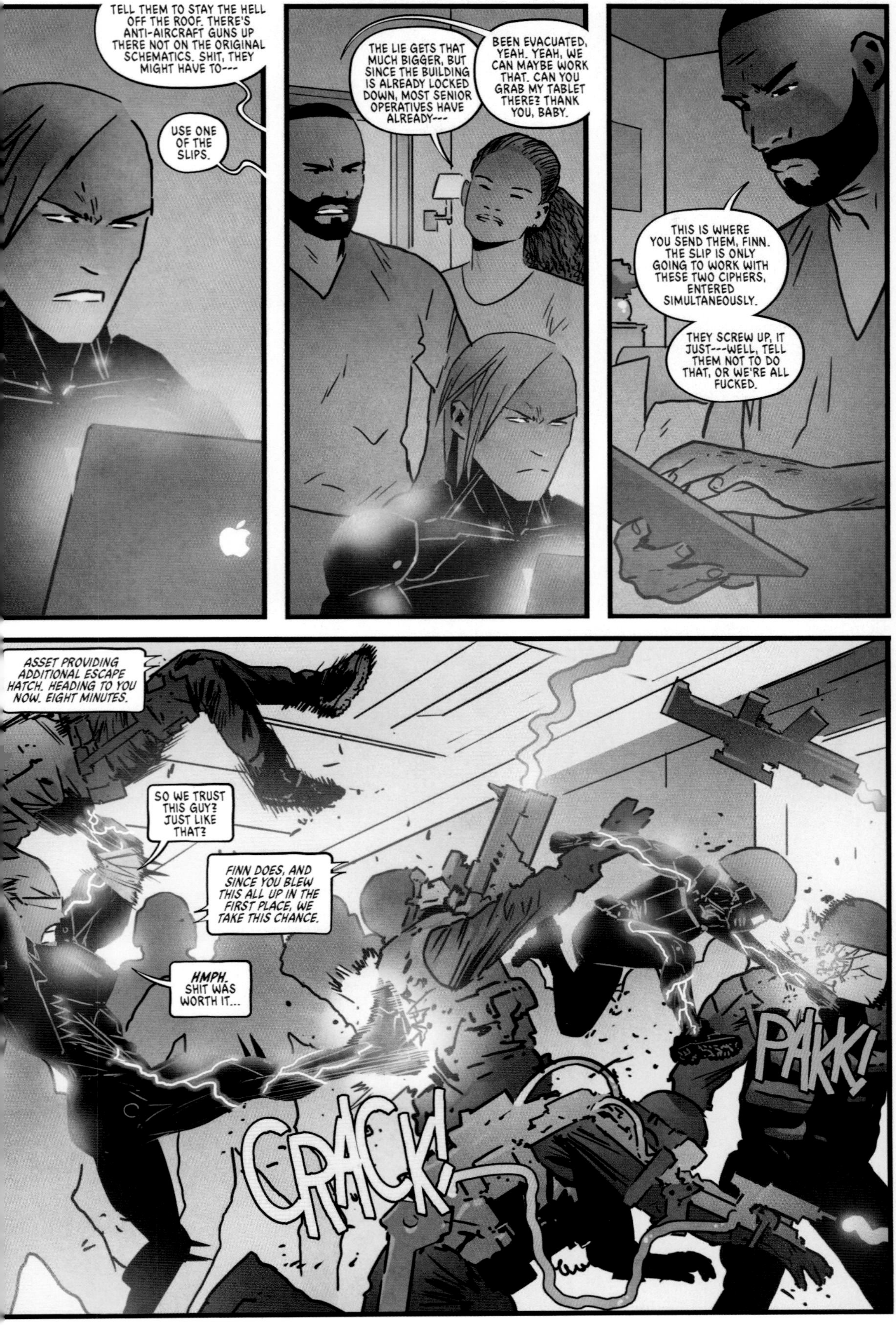
TELL THEM TO STAY THE HELL OFF THE ROOF. THERE'S ANTI-AIRCRAFT GUNS UP THERE NOT ON THE ORIGINAL SCHEMATICS. SHIT, THEY MIGHT HAVE TO---
USE ONE OF THE SLIPS.
THE LIE GETS THAT MUCH BIGGER, BUT SINCE THE BUILDING IS ALREADY LOCKED DOWN, MOST SENIOR OPERATIVES HAVE ALREADY---
BEEN EVACUATED, YEAH. YEAH, WE CAN MAYBE WORK THAT. CAN YOU GRAB MY TABLET THERE? THANK YOU, BABY.
THIS IS WHERE YOU SEND THEM, FINN. THE SLIP IS ONLY GOING TO WORK WITH THESE TWO CIPHERS, ENTERED SIMULTANEOUSLY.
THEY SCREW UP, IT JUST---WELL, TELL THEM NOT TO DO THAT, OR WE'RE ALL FUCKED.
ASSET PROVIDING ADDITIONAL ESCAPE HATCH. HEADING TO YOU NOW. EIGHT MINUTES.
SO WE TRUST THIS GUY? JUST LIKE THAT?
FINN DOES, AND SINCE YOU BLEW THIS ALL UP IN THE FIRST PLACE, WE TAKE THIS CHANCE.
HMPH. SHIT WAS WORTH IT...
PAKK!
CRACK!

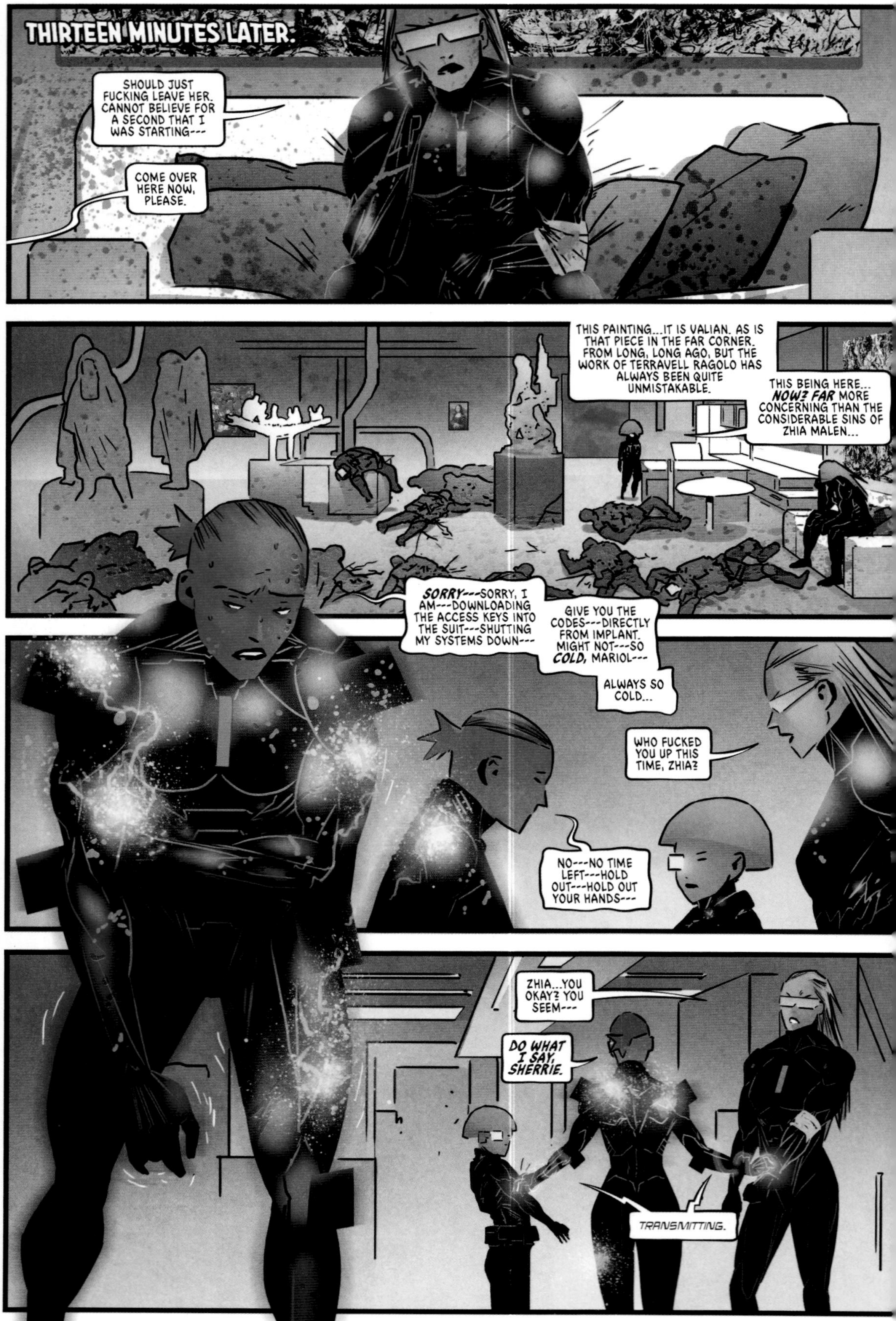
THIRTEEN MINUTES LATER:
SHOULD JUST FUCKING LEAVE HER. CANNOT BELIEVE FOR A SECOND THAT I WAS STARTING---
COME OVER HERE NOW, PLEASE.
THIS PAINTING...IT IS VALIAN. AS IS THAT PIECE IN THE FAR CORNER. FROM LONG, LONG AGO, BUT THE WORK OF TERRAVELL RAGOLO HAS ALWAYS BEEN QUITE UNMISTAKABLE.
THIS BEING HERE... NOW? FAR MORE CONCERNING THAN THE CONSIDERABLE SINS OF ZHIA MALEN...
SORRY---SORRY, I AM---DOWNLOADING THE ACCESS KEYS INTO THE SUIT---SHUTTING MY SYSTEMS DOWN---
GIVE YOU THE CODES---DIRECTLY FROM IMPLANT. MIGHT NOT---SO COLD, MARIOL---
ALWAYS SO COLD...
WHO FUCKED YOU UP THIS TIME, ZHIA?
NO---NO TIME LEFT---HOLD OUT---HOLD OUT YOUR HANDS---
ZHIA...YOU OKAY? YOU SEEM---
DO WHAT I SAY, SHERRIE.
TRANSMITTING.

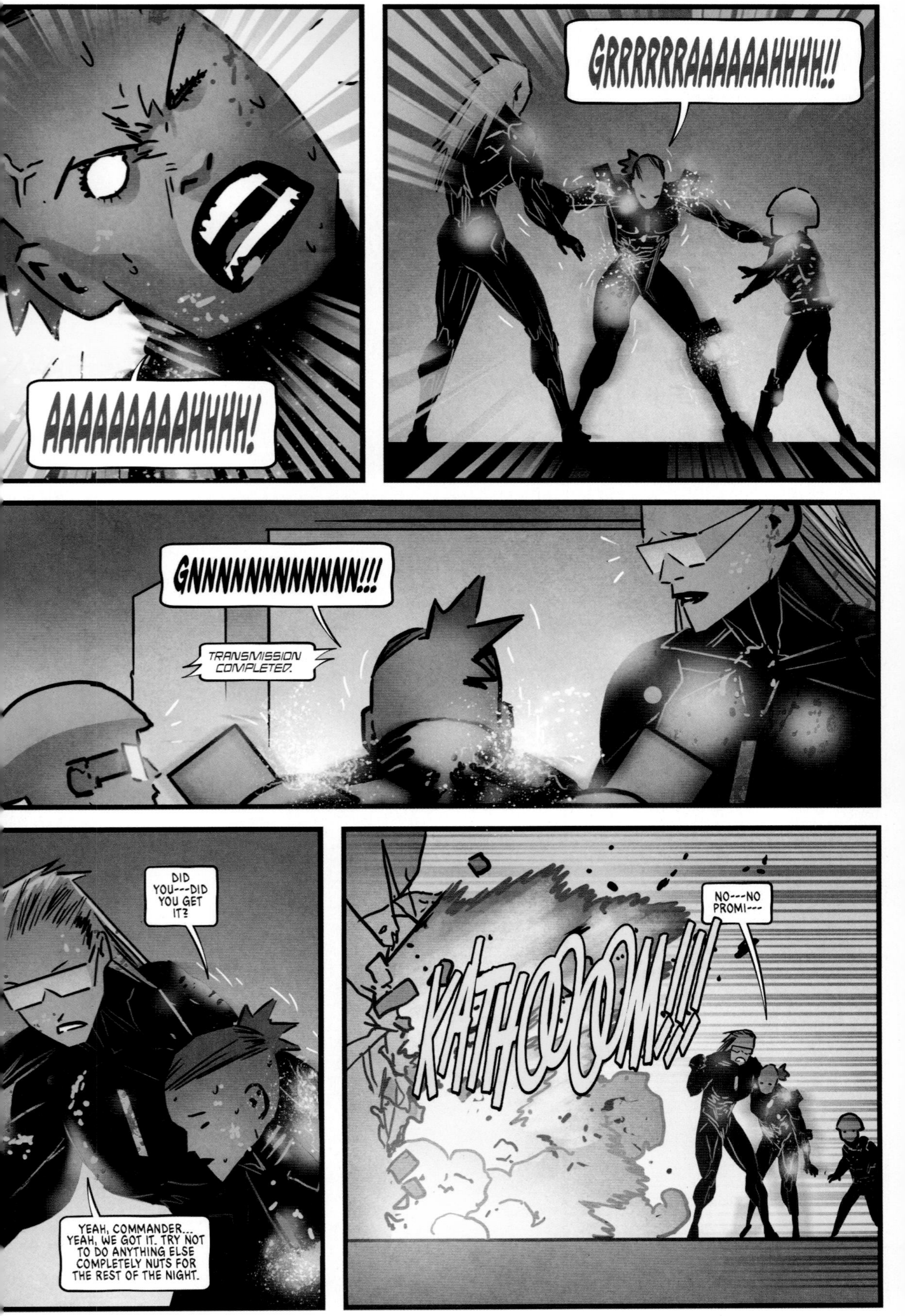
AAAAAAAAAHHHH!
GRRRRRAAAAAAHHHH!!
GNNNNNNNNNNN!!!
TRANSMISSION COMPLETED.
DID YOU---DID YOU GET IT?
YEAH, COMMANDER... YEAH, WE GOT IT. TRY NOT TO DO ANYTHING ELSE COMPLETELY NUTS FOR THE REST OF THE NIGHT.
NO---NO PROMI---
KATHOOOM!!!

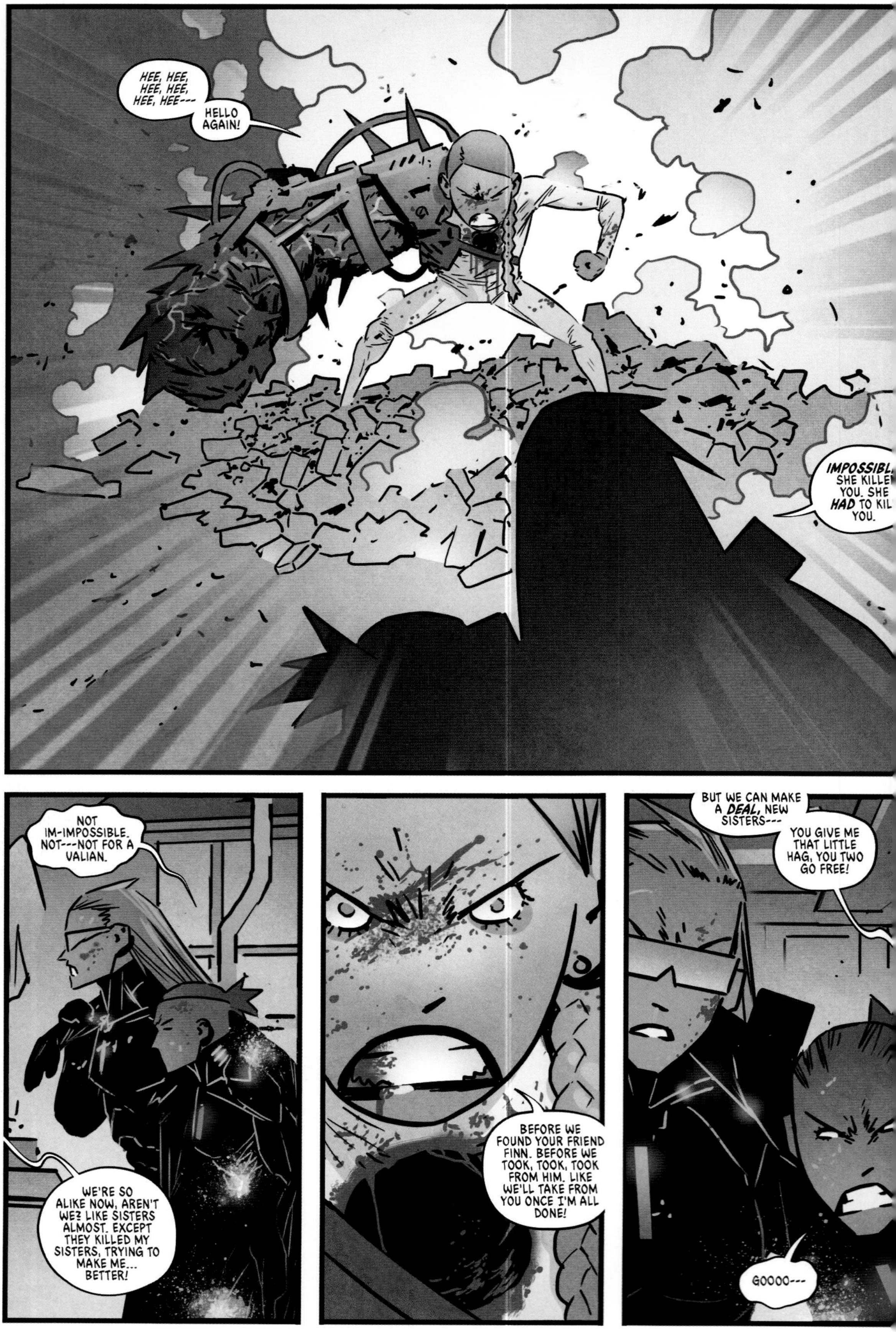
HEE, HEE, HEE, HEE, HEE, HEE---
HELLO AGAIN!
IMPOSSIBL SHE KILLE YOU. SHE HAD TO KIL YOU.
NOT IM-IMPOSSIBLE. NOT---NOT FOR A VALIAN.
WE'RE SO ALIKE NOW, AREN'T WE? LIKE SISTERS ALMOST. EXCEPT THEY KILLED MY SISTERS, TRYING TO MAKE ME... BETTER!
BEFORE WE FOUND YOUR FRIEND FINN. BEFORE WE TOOK, TOOK, TOOK FROM HIM. LIKE WE'LL TAKE FROM YOU ONCE I'M ALL DONE!
BUT WE CAN MAKE A DEAL, NEW SISTERS---
YOU GIVE ME THAT LITTLE HAG, YOU TWO GO FREE!
GOOOO---

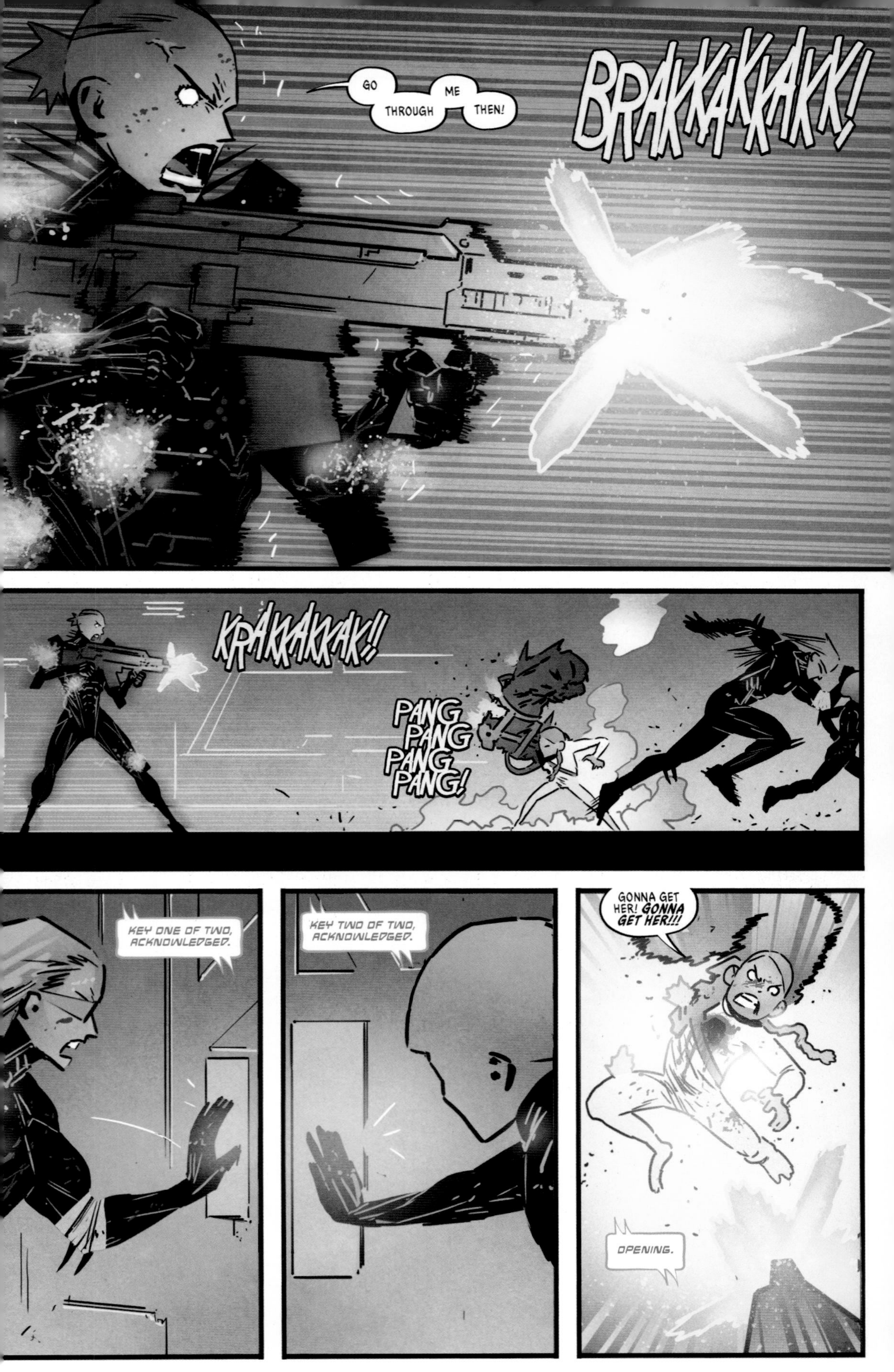

GO THROUGH ME THEN!
BRAKKAKKAKK!
KRAKKAKKAK!!
PANG PANG PANG PANG!
KEY ONE OF TWO, ACKNOWLEDGED.
KEY TWO OF TWO, ACKNOWLEDGED.
GONNA GET HER! GONNA GET HER!!!
OPENING.

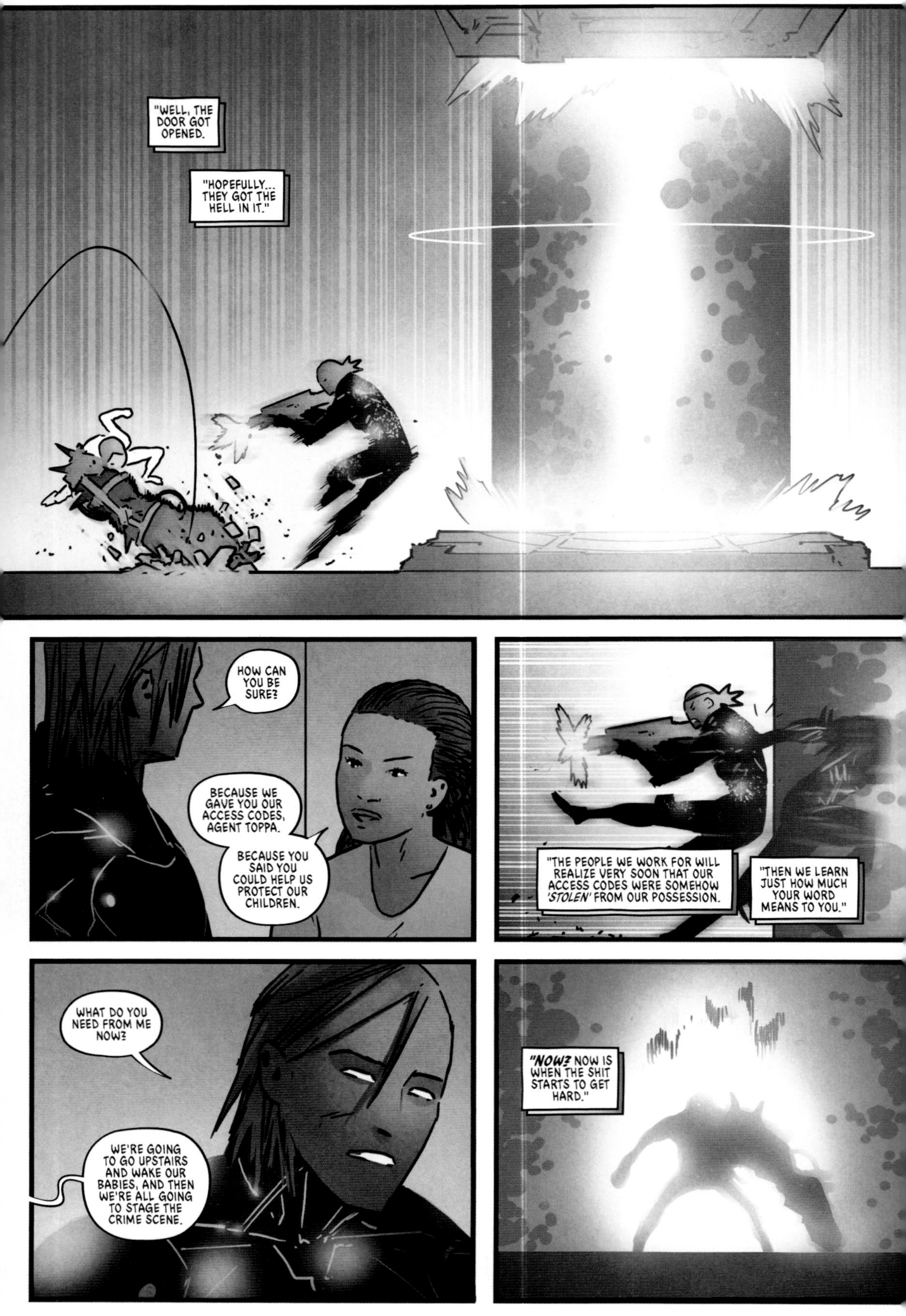
"WELL, THE DOOR GOT OPENED.
"HOPEFULLY... THEY GOT THE HELL IN IT."
HOW CAN YOU BE SURE?
BECAUSE WE GAVE YOU OUR ACCESS CODES, AGENT TOPPA.
BECAUSE YOU SAID YOU COULD HELP US PROTECT OUR CHILDREN.
"THE PEOPLE WE WORK FOR WILL REALIZE VERY SOON THAT OUR ACCESS CODES WERE SOMEHOW 'STOLEN' FROM OUR POSSESSION.
"THEN WE LEARN JUST HOW MUCH YOUR WORD MEANS TO YOU."
WHAT DO YOU NEED FROM ME NOW?
WE'RE GOING TO GO UPSTAIRS AND WAKE OUR BABIES, AND THEN WE'RE ALL GOING TO STAGE THE CRIME SCENE.
"NOW? NOW IS WHEN THE SHIT STARTS TO GET HARD."

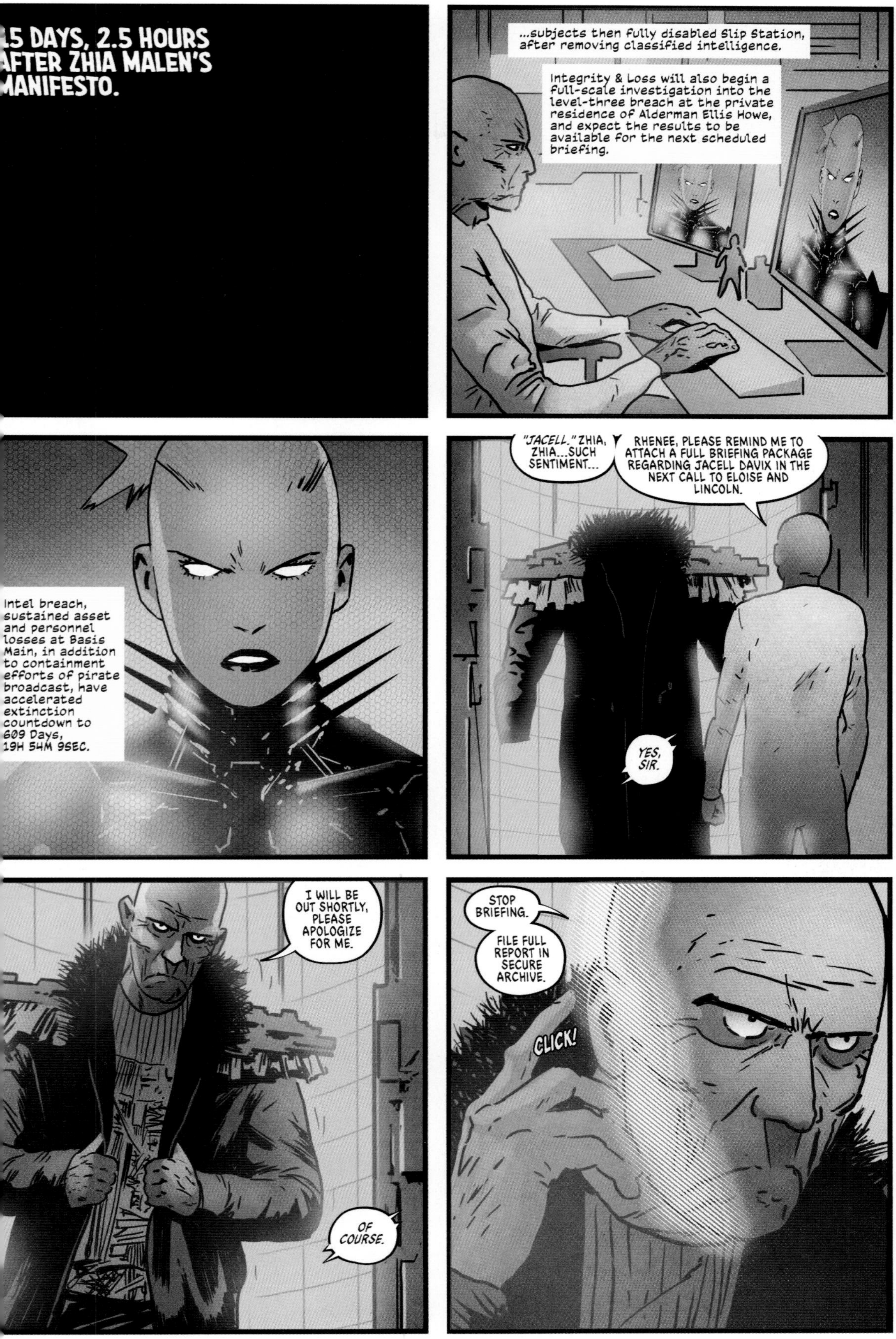
15 DAYS, 2.5 HOURS AFTER ZHIA MALEN'S MANIFESTO.
...subjects then fully disabled Slip Station, after removing classified intelligence.
Integrity & Loss will also begin a full-scale investigation into the level-three breach at the private residence of Alderman Ellis Howe, and expect the results to be available for the next scheduled briefing.
Intel breach, sustained asset and personnel losses at Basis Main, in addition to containment efforts of pirate broadcast, have accelerated extinction countdown to 609 Days, 19H 54M 9SEC.
"JACELL." ZHIA, ZHIA...SUCH SENTIMENT...
RHENEE, PLEASE REMIND ME TO ATTACH A FULL BRIEFING PACKAGE REGARDING JACELL DAVIX IN THE NEXT CALL TO ELOISE AND LINCOLN.
YES, SIR.
I WILL BE OUT SHORTLY, PLEASE APOLOGIZE FOR ME.
OF COURSE.
STOP BRIEFING.
FILE FULL REPORT IN SECURE ARCHIVE.
CLICK!

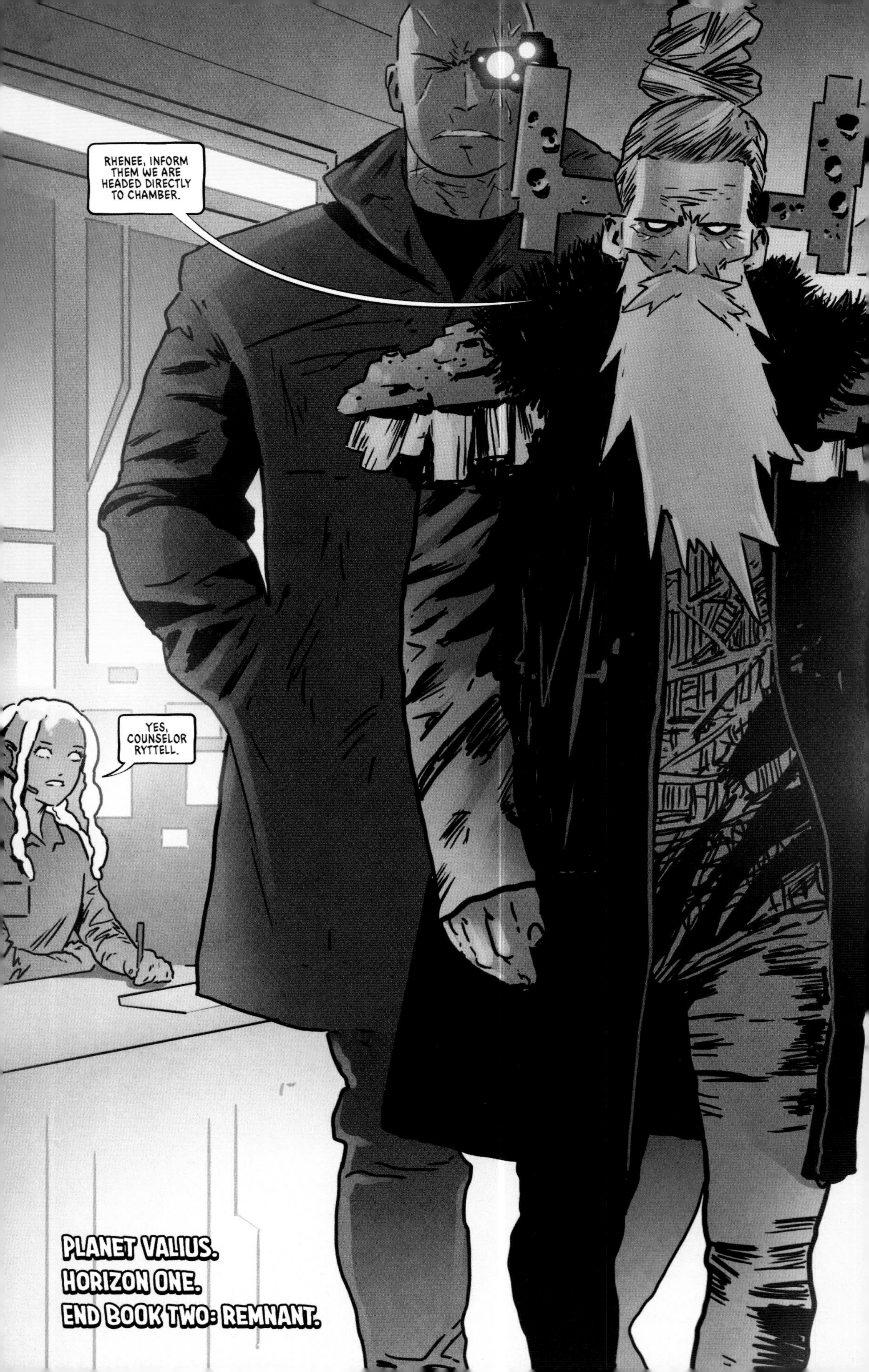
RHENEE, INFORM THEM WE ARE HEADED DIRECTLY TO CHAMBER.
YES, COUNSELOR RYTTELL.
PLANET VALIUS.
HORIZON ONE.
END BOOK TWO: REMNANT.

TO BE CONTINUED...

BECAUSE

THE EARTH IS

ALREADY DEAD.

I SIMPLY WANT

THEM TO

ACKNOWLEDGE

THIS FACT...

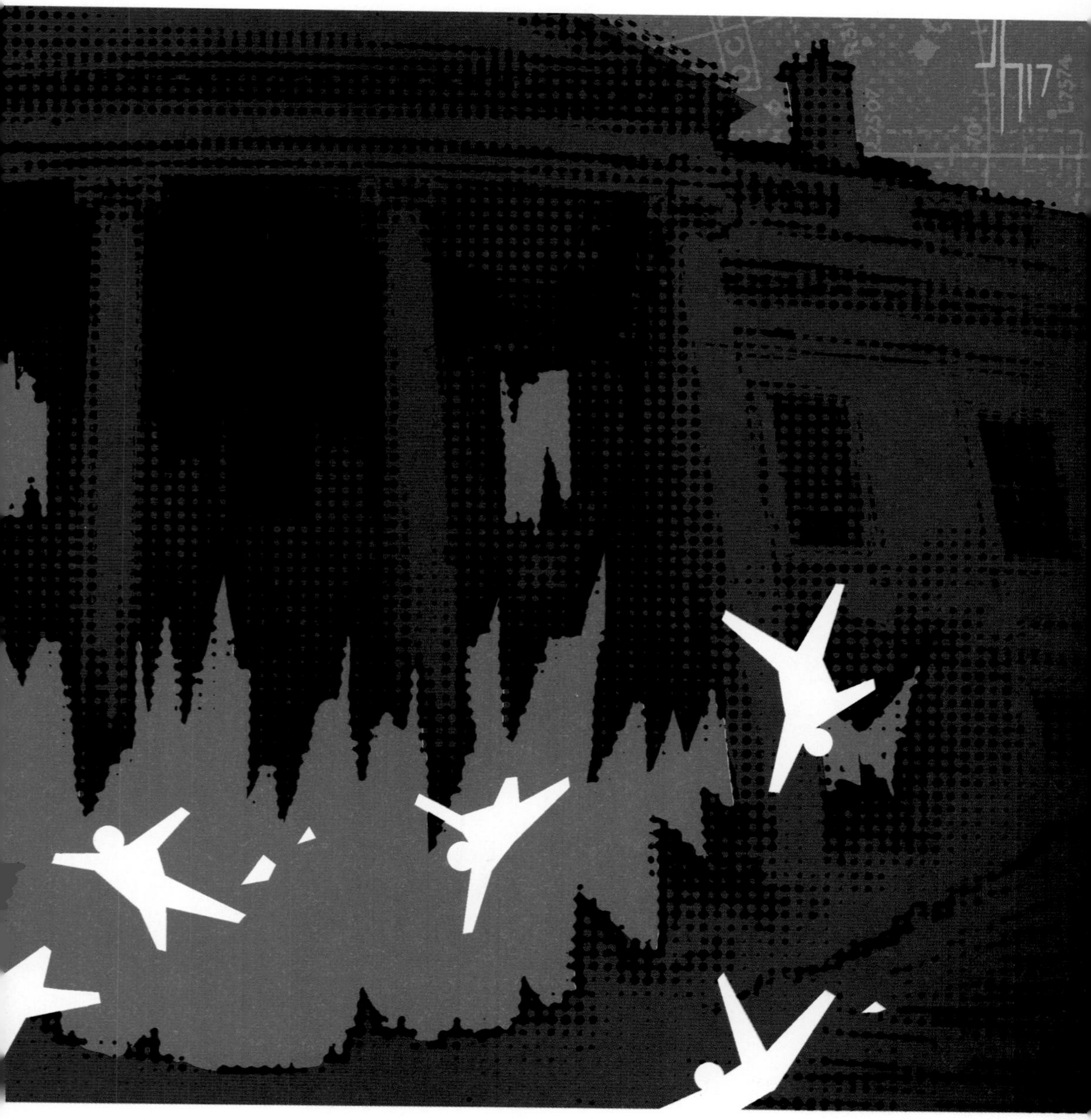

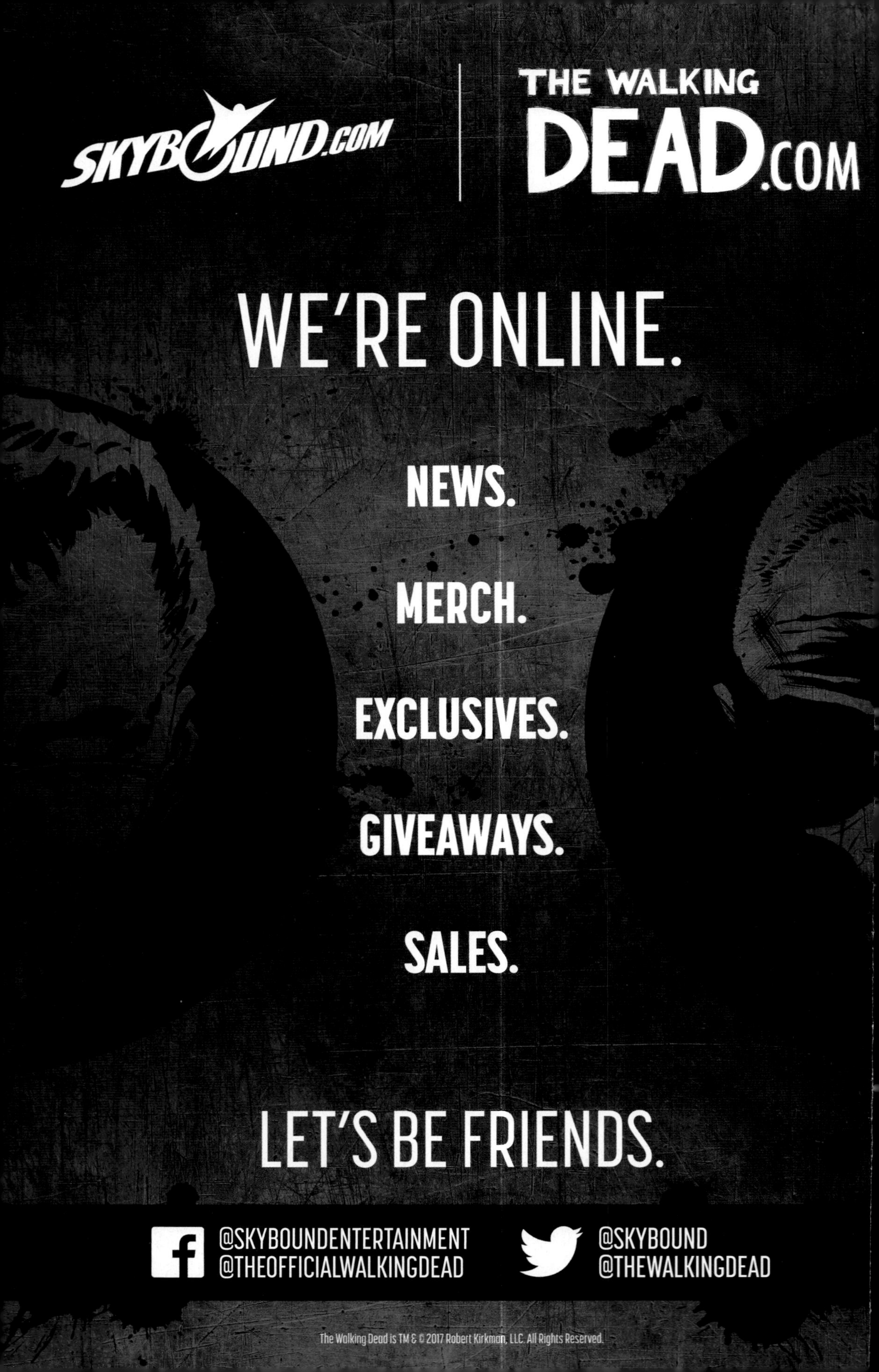
SKYBOUND.COM
THE WALKING DEAD.COM
WE'RE ONLINE.
NEWS.
MERCH.
EXCLUSIVES.
GIVEAWAYS.
SALES.
LET'S BE FRIENDS.
@SKYBOUNDENTERTAINMENT
@THEOFFICIALWALKINGDEAD
@SKYBOUND
@THEWALKINGDEAD
The Walking Dead is TM & © 2017 Robert Kirkman, LLC. All Rights Reserved.

FOR MORE OF THE WALKING DEAD

TRADEPAPERBACKS

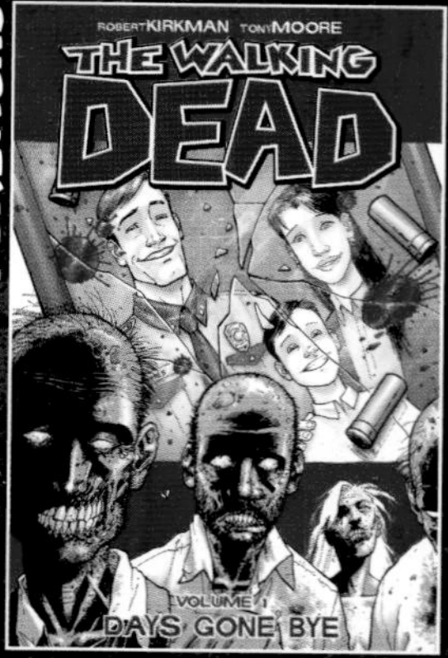

ROBERT KIRKMAN TONY MOORE
THE WALKING DEAD
VOLUME 1
DAYS GONE BYE

VOL. 1: DAYS GONE BYE TP
ISBN: 978-1-58240-672-5
$14.99
VOL. 2: MILES BEHIND US TP
ISBN: 978-1-58240-775-3
$14.99
VOL. 3: SAFETY BEHIND BARS TP
ISBN: 978-1-58240-805-7
$14.99
VOL. 4: THE HEART'S DESIRE TP
ISBN: 978-1-58240-530-8
$14.99
VOL. 5: THE BEST DEFENSE TP
ISBN: 978-1-58240-612-1
$14.99
VOL. 6: THIS SORROWFUL LIFE TP
ISBN: 978-1-58240-684-8
$14.99
VOL. 7: THE CALM BEFORE TP
ISBN: 978-1-58240-828-6
$14.99
VOL. 8: MADE TO SUFFER TP
ISBN: 978-1-58240-883-5
$14.99
VOL. 9: HERE WE REMAIN TP
ISBN: 978-1-60706-022-2
$14.99
VOL. 10: WHAT WE BECOME TP
ISBN: 978-1-60706-075-8
$14.99
VOL. 11: FEAR THE HUNTERS TP
ISBN: 978-1-60706-181-6
$14.99
VOL. 12: LIFE AMONG THEM TP
ISBN: 978-1-60706-254-7
$14.99
VOL. 13: TOO FAR GONE TP
ISBN: 978-1-60706-329-2
$14.99
VOL. 14: NO WAY OUT TP
ISBN: 978-1-60706-392-6
$14.99
VOL. 15: WE FIND OURSELVES TP
ISBN: 978-1-60706-440-4
$14.99
VOL. 16: A LARGER WORLD TP
ISBN: 978-1-60706-559-3
$14.99
VOL. 17: SOMETHING TO FEAR TP
ISBN: 978-1-60706-615-6
$14.99
VOL. 18: WHAT COMES AFTER TP
ISBN: 978-1-60706-687-3
$14.99
VOL. 19: MARCH TO WAR TP
ISBN: 978-1-60706-818-1
$14.99
VOL. 20: ALL OUT WAR PART ONE TP
ISBN: 978-1-60706-882-2
$14.99
VOL. 21: ALL OUT WAR PART TWO TP
ISBN: 978-1-63215-030-1
$14.99
VOL. 22: A NEW BEGINNING TP
ISBN: 978-1-63215-041-7
$14.99
VOL. 23: WHISPERS INTO SCREAMS TP
ISBN: 978-1-63215-258-9
$14.99
VOL. 24: LIFE AND DEATH TP
ISBN: 978-1-63215-402-6
$14.99
VOL. 25: NO TURNING BACK TP
ISBN: 978-1-63215-612-9
$14.99
VOL. 26: CALL TO ARMS TP
ISBN: 978-1-63215-917-5
$14.99
VOL. 27: THE WHISPERER WAR TP
ISBN: 978-1-5343-0052-1
$14.99
VOL. 1: SPANISH EDITION TP
ISBN: 978-1-60706-797-9
$14.99
VOL. 2: SPANISH EDITION TP
ISBN: 978-1-60706-845-7
$14.99
VOL. 3: SPANISH EDITION TP
ISBN: 978-1-60706-883-9
$14.99
VOL. 4: SPANISH EDITION TP
ISBN: 978-1-63215-035-6
$14.99

HARDCOVERS

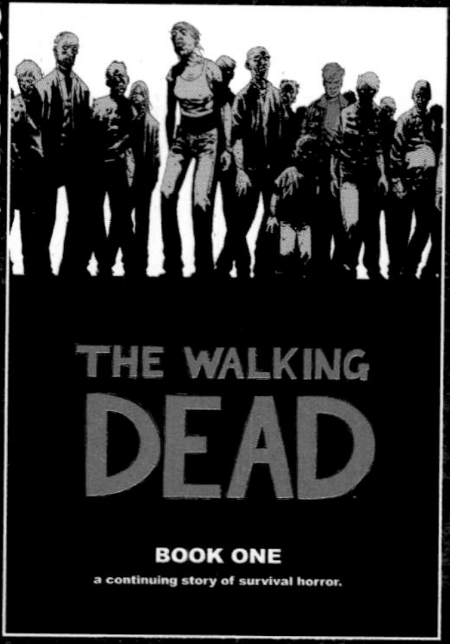

THE WALKING DEAD
BOOK ONE
a continuing story of survival horror.

BOOK ONE HC
ISBN: 978-1-58240-619-0
$34.99
BOOK TWO HC
ISBN: 978-1-58240-698-5
$34.99
BOOK THREE HC
ISBN: 978-1-58240-825-5
$34.99
BOOK FOUR HC
ISBN: 978-1-60706-000-0
$34.99
BOOK FIVE HC
ISBN: 978-1-60706-171-7
$34.99
BOOK SIX HC
ISBN: 978-1-60706-327-8
$34.99
BOOK SEVEN HC
ISBN: 978-1-60706-439-8
$34.99
BOOK EIGHT HC
ISBN: 978-1-60706-593-7
$34.99
BOOK NINE HC
ISBN: 978-1-60706-798-6
$34.99
BOOK TEN HC
ISBN: 978-1-63215-034-9
$34.99
BOOK ELEVEN HC
ISBN: 978-1-63215-271-8
$34.99
BOOK TWELVE HC
ISBN: 978-1-63215-451-4
$34.99
BOOK THIRTEEN HC
ISBN: 978-1-63215-916-8
$34.99

COMPENDIUMS

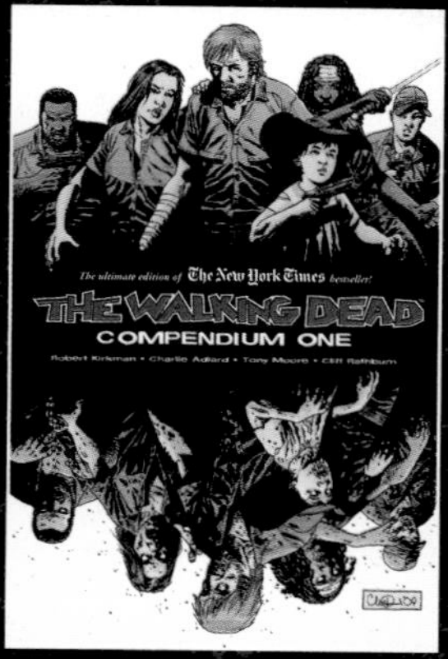

The ultimate edition of The New York Times bestseller!
THE WALKING DEAD
COMPENDIUM ONE
Robert Kirkman • Charlie Adlard • Tony Moore • Cliff Rathburn

COMPENDIUM TP, VOL. 1
ISBN: 978-1-60706-076-5
$59.99
COMPENDIUM TP, VOL. 2
ISBN: 978-1-60706-596-8
$59.99
COMPENDIUM TP, VOL. 3
ISBN: 978-1-63215-456-9
$59.99

SPECIALTY BOOKS

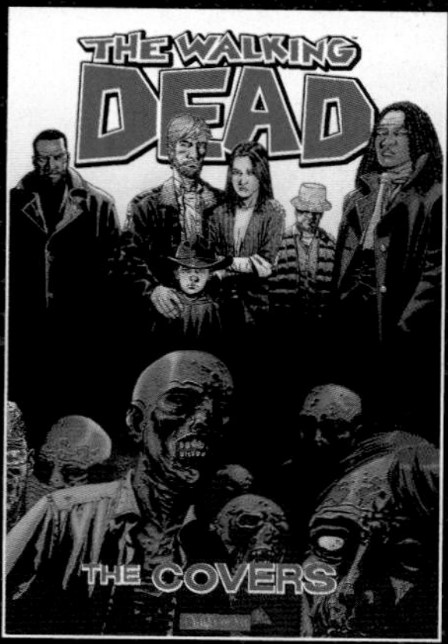

THE WALKING DEAD
THE COVERS

THE WALKING DEAD: THE COVERS, VOL. 1 HC
ISBN: 978-1-60706-002-4
$24.99
THE WALKING DEAD: ALL OUT WAR HC
ISBN: 978-1-63215-038-7
$34.99
THE WALKING DEAD COLORING BOOK
ISBN: 978-1-63215-774-4
$14.99
THE WALKING DEAD RICK GRIMES COLORING BOOK
ISBN: 978-1-5343-0003-3
$14.99

OMNIBUS

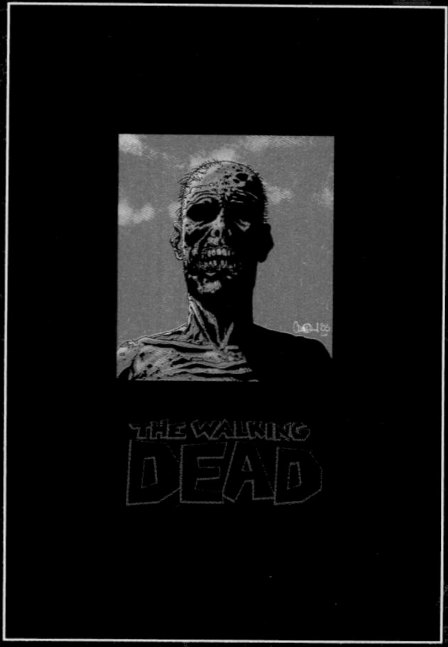

THE WALKING DEAD

OMNIBUS, VOL. 1
ISBN: 978-1-60706-503-6
$100.00
OMNIBUS, VOL. 2
ISBN: 978-1-60706-515-9
$100.00
OMNIBUS, VOL. 3
ISBN: 978-1-60706-330-8
$100.00
OMNIBUS, VOL. 4
ISBN: 978-1-60706-616-3
$100.00
OMNIBUS, VOL. 5
ISBN: 978-1-63215-042-4
$100.00
OMNIBUS, VOL. 6
ISBN: 978-1-63215-521-4
$100.00

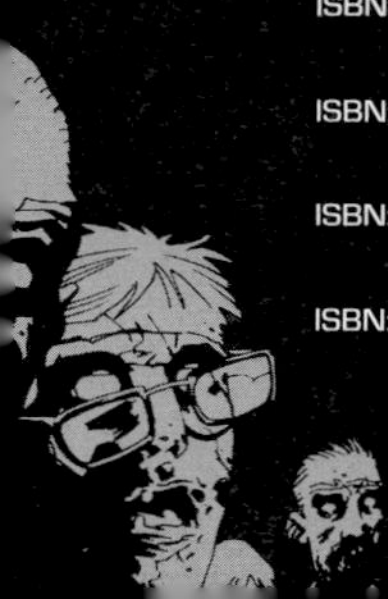

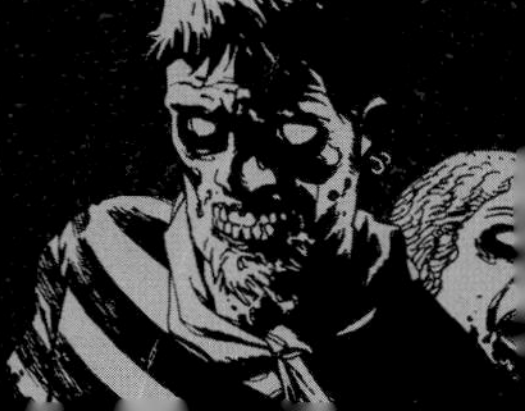

FOR MORE TALES FROM ROBERT KIRKMAN AND SKYBOUND

VOLUME 4 UNDER DEVIL'S WING
OUTCAST
BY KIRKMAN & AZACETA

VOL. 1: A DARKNESS SURROUNDS HIM TP
ISBN: 978-1-63215-053-0
$9.99

VOL. 2: A VAST AND UNENDING RUIN TP
ISBN: 978-1-63215-448-4
$14.99

VOL. 3: THIS LITTLE LIGHT TP
ISBN: 978-1-63215-693-8
$14.99

VOL. 4: UNDER DEVIL'S WING TP
ISBN: 978-1-5343-0050-7
$14.99

BIRTHRIGHT
WILLIAMSON
BRESSAN
LUCAS
VOLUME FIVE
BELLY OF THE BEAST

VOL. 1: HOMECOMING TP
ISBN: 978-1-63215-231-2
$9.99

VOL. 2: CALL TO ADVENTURE TP
ISBN: 978-1-63215-446-0
$12.99

VOL. 3: ALLIES AND ENEMIES TP
ISBN: 978-1-63215-683-9
$12.99

VOL. 4: FAMILY HISTORY TP
ISBN: 978-1-63215-871-0
$12.99

VOL. 5: BELLY OF THE BEAST TP
ISBN: 978-1-5343-0218-1
$12.99

CLONE
VOLUME 4
FOURTH GENERATION

VOL. 1: FIRST GENERATION TP
ISBN: 978-1-60706-683-5
$12.99

VOL. 2: SECOND GENERATION TP
ISBN: 978-1-60706-830-3
$12.99

VOL. 3: THIRD GENERATION TP
ISBN: 978-1-60706-939-3
$12.99

VOL. 4: FOURTH GENERATION TP
ISBN: 978-1-63215-036-3
$12.99

WILLIAMSON
LACI
RYP
GHOSTED
VOLUME FOUR · GHOST TOWN

VOL. 1: HAUNTED HEIST TP
ISBN: 978-1-60706-836-5
$9.99

VOL. 2: BOOKS OF THE DEAD TP
ISBN: 978-1-63215-046-2
$12.99

VOL. 3: DEATH WISH TP
ISBN: 978-1-63215-051-6
$12.99

VOL. 4: GHOST TOWN TP
ISBN: 978-1-63215-317-3
$12.99

CHRIS DINGESS
MATTHEW ROBERTS
OWEN GIENI
MANIFEST DESTINY
VOLUME 4 SASQUATCH

VOL. 1: FLORA & FAUNA TP
ISBN: 978-1-60706-982-9
$9.99

VOL. 2: AMPHIBIA & INSECTA TP
ISBN: 978-1-63215-052-3
$14.99

VOL. 3: CHIROPTERA & CARNIFORMAVES TP
ISBN: 978-1-63215-397-5
$14.99

VOL. 4: SASQUATCH TP
ISBN: 978-1-63215-890-1
$14.99

THIEF OF THIEVES
VOLUME 6
"GOLD RUSH."

VOL. 1: "I QUIT."
ISBN: 978-1-60706-592-0
$14.99

VOL. 2: "HELP ME."
ISBN: 978-1-60706-676-7
$14.99

VOL. 3: "VENICE."
ISBN: 978-1-60706-844-0
$14.99

VOL. 4: "THE HIT LIST."
ISBN: 978-1-63215-037-0
$14.99

VOL. 5: "TAKE ME."
ISBN: 978-1-63215-401-9
$14.99

VOL. 6: "GOLD RUSH."
ISBN: 978-1-53430-037-8
$14.99

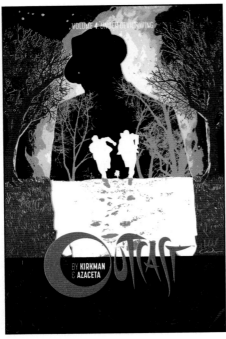

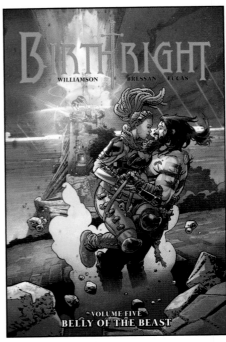

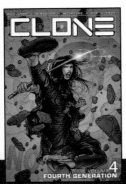

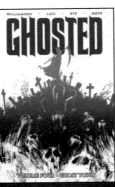

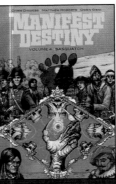

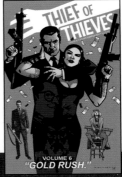